Idi Han whirled around, bracing for Topan's attack. She cursed herself instantly as she saw her sire had disappeared, long since fleeing the battle. But now, of course, she had her back to her adversary. He punched through her back, his fist passing through her ribcage both in the back and in the front, and plucking her heart from out of her chest. He held it out, unbeating, before her, as he lifted her off her feet, impaled on his forearm.

"Now, there's a stroke of luck," he said, pointing at a sledgehammer which a construction worker had left on the catwalk. "If I had my other arm I'd just rip your head off. But now we've got to do it the hard way. Shh, shh. Relax, darling. Sometimes the hard way is more fun."

She struggled, kicking, trying to extricate herself from the arm penetrating her, but there was little she could do. The sledgehammer lay on the floor, heavy enough not to be blown away by even the strongest wind.

"Oof. That handle looks a little dull. Not much of a stake, is it? Well, we'll make it work. Enough force and you can push a square peg through a round hole. That's pretty much what you've been trying to do your whole life anyway, isn't it?"

She relaxed and let Signari take her away. There wasn't really any pain anyway, just a weird feeling of fullness and violation. He stepped on the head of the sledgehammer, turning the head and bringing the wooden handle up into the air. He pressed her expurgated heart to the top of the wooden handle.

HUNTER OF THE DEAD

BY STEPHEN KOZENIEWSKI

Macabre Ink

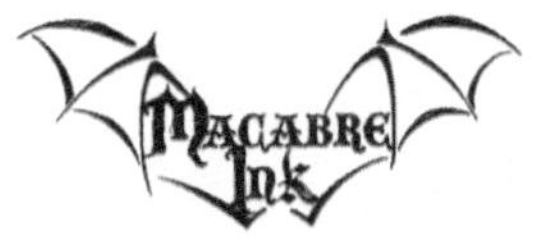

This novel is dedicated to John Waxler, without whom Cicatrice, Idi Han, and crew would still be consigned to their crypts.

THEY COME AND THEY GO

AN INTRODUCTION TO STEPHEN KOZENIEWSKI'S HUNTER OF THE DEAD

by Jonathan Janz

In my favorite baseball movie THE NATURAL, sportswriter Max Mercy (played by Robert Duvall) says to Roy Hobbs (Robert Redford), "They come and they go, Hobbs. They come and they go." Mercy's point, in the context of the film, is that he'll be writing columns far longer than Roy Hobbs will be playing baseball.

So actually the quote doesn't apply to this situation at all.

Okay, it might not apply directly, but it reminds me of the point I'll be making after this interminable lead-in.

My first paperback was published in March of 2012. I was around the genre for a while before that—mostly gazing longingly at book covers and wishing my name was on them—but I didn't become part of the publishing apparatus until that March.

Between 2012 and early 2019 (it's February of 2019 as I compose this introduction) a stunning number of new horror writers have appeared. Some receive serious fanfare—flashy blurbs, lucrative publishing contracts, major awards buzz; others become known gradually, appearing like the first subtle glow of a sunrise before...

Ah, hell. You get the point.

What astonishes me is even though I've only been at this game a relatively short period of time, many of the names that have appeared since 2012 have already faded into obscurity.

On a monthly basis there are new horror writers popping up, many of which—I'm frequently told—are the Next Big Thing, the successor to King. The real deal.

And within the year, poof! They're gone. I could fill a book (or at least a robust novella) with names that have blazed up and winked out since 2012.

"They come and they go, Hobbs. They come and they go."

When I first heard of Stephen Kozeniewski, it was from the genre's biggest champion of new voices, Mr. Brian Keene. For that reason, I made sure to store the name away since Brian's accuracy rate in identifying new talent is far greater than just about anyone else's. Brian fell for Stephen's work in a big way, so I figured I'd give one of his books a try too.

That book was HUNTER OF THE DEAD.

Friends, I want to tell you, the story you now hold in your hands is wild, unpredictable, and audacious.

It's also outstandingly written. For example…

Miranda blinked and strained her neck to see the rest of the dark figure. The horse was black on black, with black eyes that didn't even seem to reflect the moonlight. The man astride the charger was sealed in a wall of black plate armor, festooned with spikes and barbs. No mortal could have carried such armor; it must have weighed two tons. Like the horse's hair, the man's armor dripped with the dark, syrupy substance.

The devil here, as always, is in the details. Anyone with a junior high education can string a few sentences together. But what Kozeniewski does is create music. Note the balance of the first sentence. The striking detail in the second half of the second sentence ("black eyes that didn't even seem to reflect the moonlight"). The word choice in the third: "sealed in black armor," not "wearing black armor" or even "clothed in black armor." In the fourth line he breaks out a compound sentence featuring two independent clauses welded together by a semi-colon (forgive the English teacher/grammar nerd a moment, but most horror writers don't attempt to use semi-colons, and the ones who do rarely deploy them so effectively as Stephen does here). And after all that vivid imagery and nimble wordsmithing, Stephen ends the paragraph with another beautifully balanced sentence that's as rhythmic as a Fred Astaire tap dance.

If the above passage didn't do it for you, try this one on for size:

Nico's eyes darted around the room. Something about the funeral seemed off. A few family members were holding court at the front of the room, and a woman was kneeling at the coffin, apparently weeping. The pews were mostly full with darkly clad mourners. Externally it seemed like any other funeral Nico had ever been to.

But who holds a funeral in the middle of the night?

Why, you might ask, did I choose this passage to illustrate what I appreciate in Stephen's writing? The language is straightforward, the sentences short and mostly declarative. It's a well-written section, but it's not noteworthy, is it?

Oh, my friends.

Here Stephen uses a timeworn technique called interior monologue (the italicized sentence). Nothing earthshattering about that. A great many writers use it. But what sets this instance apart from the majority of writers is its impact, its wry undercurrent of humor, and its subtle tang of foreboding. The longer paragraph, it turns out, was just a set-up, a sleight of hand to get us looking in one direction while Stephen balled his other fist and prepared to coldcock us when we least expected it.

But who holds a funeral in the middle of the night?

Yeah, we answer, swallowing and smiling uneasily. Just who the hell does hold a funeral in the middle of the night?

The tools of the trade are essentially the same in all writers. We all use description, we all use dialogue. Most of us use interior monologue. But Stephen uses them far better than most. That's why "They come and they go" doesn't apply to Stephen Kozeniewski. It takes real skill to stick around, and Stephen has real skill.

And if you're still not convinced, how about takin' this little number for a spin?

"Why did you ask to look in that woman's mirror? Does your reflection go away eventually?"

She shook her head.

"I don't think so. I think that's more of a metaphor than anything else."

"How do you mean?"

"Well, you know, a lot of serial killers refuse to look in the mirror. The police go in to raid their lairs and they find all the mirrors smashed, all the pictures ruined. Like they can't bear to look at themselves, or something."

In this passage, of course, it's the dialogue that takes center stage, and as he did in the first two passages, Stephen shows off his writing chops in the manner he allows this section to develop. Like in the last passage, Stephen saves the clincher for the final line. But what a clincher it is!

By keeping the language relatively simple in the first part of the exchange, Stephen's readers let their guards down. When the notion of a metaphor is first mentioned, we're not expecting profundity. After all, most metaphors are either obvious or strained. But when we get to the payoff, we realize why the mirror is important, and what's even more interesting—to me, at least—is that by including the bit about smashed mirrors, Stephen is saying something about guilt, about that one atom of humanity drowning in a sea of soulless violence.

And this, my friends, is something else I appreciate about Stephen's writing. He allows the reader the elbow room to peer into the darkness and draw his own conclusions. Like the best writers, Stephen's books are about something, but he trusts the reader to make those connections rather than spoonfeeding everything to them, the way too many writers do.

If you haven't figured it out by now, I'm a Stephen Kozeniewski fan. He's a great guy, but that's beside the point. What matters today is that he's a great writer.

And having said that, I'll shut up now and allow you to see why.

PROLOGUE

Miranda ran her hand over the creature's bald, scaling head to calm it. In response, it moaned in hunger through its muzzle.

"Shh shh," she whispered gently, almost as though comforting one of her own children, "soon enough."

The sounds of gruesome dismemberment and ravenous gorging drifted under the massive oaken doors to Inessa's chamber. As usual, the master's favorite was taking her time devouring some morsel while Miranda was stuck waiting on her to be finished so she could clean up. The midden-beast stirred again.

"There, there," she whispered gently, scratching it under the ears.

Miranda knew each of the midden-beasts by sight. Secretly, she had a name for each, and though she had never been explicitly forbidden to name them, she had a strong suspicion the master would've punished her terribly if he'd caught wind of her naming the dumb brutes. The one she held on a leash now she thought of as Snuggles.

Snuggles was a gangly, hunched-over creature with only the barest scraps of sackcloth and burlap clinging to its thighs hiding its disgusting manhood. Its skin was dun, approaching gray, and its limbs were long and gaunt, almost skeletally thin. Its face was barely human, actually more mashed in like a pig's or an owl's, and only the barest hint of human awareness flickered in its sallow yellow eyes.

Each of the midden creatures looked somewhat similar to Snuggles, though none were identical. All were hideously misshapen in their own way, some sporting deformities and tumors, others scaling almost like fish or reptiles.

The sound of smacking lips and crunching bone from within the chamber abruptly ceased. Miranda straightened her back and tugged on Snuggles's leash to keep him from bolting when permission to open the door came. A man on the other side of the door suddenly spoke out in a recognizably Scottish brogue.

"Oy! Who's that, then?"

"M...M..."

She took a deep breath and composed herself. She wasn't that stuttering child anymore.

"Miranda. Uh...sir."

The door opened, startling her. Since being chosen by the master to receive The Long Gift, Inessa had grown noticeably surly and lazy. As a result, she hardly ever opened the door herself. A man emerged from Inessa's chambers, something that was not only strictly forbidden but was completely impossible. Grown men (except the master, obviously) were not allowed on the compound.

Wearing a ripped, sleeveless denim vest and sporting a bleached-white Mohawk, the man seemed like a reject from an '80s band. Though he didn't seem like the type to join the military (far from it, in fact) there was something martial about him, from the combat boots he wore to the pins and medals that festooned his vest. Like an extension of his Mohawk, a stripe of white paint bisected his face.

Miranda cast her eyes down. One of the rules of the compound was not to look at men. That had only ever meant the master before, but...

The Mohawk man grabbed her chin, nearly shattering her jaw with the strongest grip she had ever felt, and forced her eyes to come level with his own. Her long auburn hair hung over her face. She hoped it would hide the salty wetness of her eyes from his view, but a moment later he gently tucked her locks behind her ears and laid bare her weeping face. He seemed to stare straight through her, as though searching for something at the bottom of her eye sockets. His nostrils flared like a bloodhound's and she realized he wasn't concentrating on what he was seeing at all.

"You've eaten garlic today," he stated with just the barest hint of a Continental accent. "It's on your clothes as well."

"Yes," she agreed.

The sister wives who had not yet been granted the Long Gift had prepared spaghetti for supper and Miranda, like all the others, had done her part in the kitchen.

"She's mortal," he finally decided.

"Yes," she squeaked through pinched fish-lips, as though he had asked a question.

He let go of her as abruptly as he had grabbed her. Then his whole expression changed. A smile spiderwebbed across his face and he clapped his hands together.

"Italo Scavatelli," he said, bowing and doffing an imaginary cap, "at your service. Oh, and who's this little fellow?"

Scavatelli dropped to his knees and scratched Snuggles under the ears.

"Scav!" the Scotsman within shouted sharply, "Who's there?"

"Oh, it's just one of Cashley's disciples. With a ghoul."

Snuggles strained at its collar, eager to get into Inessa's room. It obviously smelled something inside. Miranda had never heard the strange creatures be called "ghouls" before but it seemed oddly fitting.

"A ghoul? Bring it in here."

Scav sent the immensely heavy door flying open with a single tap from his pinky fingernail and gestured for Miranda to enter. She obliged and immediately gasped. The walls were painted with blood and a barely living person shivered on the banquet table set up in front of Inessa's tub, most of the flesh picked from his (or her) bones. Shock or pain kept the nearly skeletal being conscious.

All that was perfectly ordinary, though. Miranda had gasped because the Scot was holding Inessa's jaggedly severed head by the spinal column, which dangled from her neck like soap on a rope. A few vertebrae still clung to the spinal cord, but most had apparently popped off in the process of what appeared to have been a hasty decapitation.

Snuggles must have felt the leash slacken and took advantage of her surprise, darting towards the half-dead person and snuffling at his exposed intestines. The thing that had once been a man looked down, eyes still moving in his faceless skull. Tongueless, an abortive moan rose from his gullet, as Snuggles disturbed what had formerly been his insides.

"Snuggles!" Miranda cried out sharply, before covering her mouth in embarrassment and worry.

The ghoul retired in frustration, unable to get any tasty viscera through its muzzle into its mouth.

"Snuggles. That's a hell of a name," the Scot said, and both of the intruders laughed.

Miranda sheepishly took the ghoul's leash and presented herself to the two men like a schoolgirl ready to receive her punishment. She tried not to look up, but it was hard to avoid staring at them. Standing side by side they seemed a greatly mismatched pair. Scav dwarfed his partner by a wide margin.

As though he had stepped out of a photograph, the Scot wore a military uniform she would've guessed originated from some time closer to World War I than World War II. He wore a nameplate which read "MacVicar." Like Scav, MacVicar also wore facepaint. A white stripe stretched from his forehead to the bottom of his neck where his throat disappeared into his blouse.

"Name," MacVicar said.

"Miranda."

MacVicar shook the spinal cord in his hand, sending vertebrae flying and inspiring Snuggles to pounce on top of one that landed nearby.

"Not your name. Hers."

"Inessa."

Scav knelt down and grabbed Inessa's head, turning it so it faced him. Her dead eyes were frozen, aghast with terror.

"Inessa," Scav whispered, "What a gorgeous name. And you are a thing of beauty."

Scav kissed the corpse's upside-down lips. Rankled, MacVicar shook the spinal cord to ward him off, and very nearly kicked him away like a dog.

"Oy! If you want to screw around with her the rest of her

body's there." MacVicar pointed at the ivory tub.

Inessa's arms and legs hung splayed out of the tub, striking an oddly seductive pose despite what had been an obvious struggle. Scav shrugged and walked over. Dragging what was left of her out of the water, he took the body by the hand and the waist, and began to waltz, humming the tune to "I Could've Danced All Night." There wasn't a drop of blood in the water or, it seemed, left in Inessa's corpse, judging by how pallid the jagged seam of her neck was. Scav leaned down as though to dip her, and caught Miranda's panicky eyes as he did so.

MacVicar turned back to Miranda. "What was your friend's surname?"

"She wasn't my friend." It was clear from his look that he wasn't interested in extraneous information. "I...I mean, we don't use last names around the compound. We're all the master's children."

MacVicar folded his arms in front of him, the dangling head still caught in his grasp.

"'The master,' eh? That'll be Cashley, then."

Miranda swallowed a lump in her throat, not sure how to respond. She nearly jumped as she felt a tongue tickle her earlobe and Scav's sonorous voice filled her ear.

"Care to cut in?"

"N...n....no," she said, shaking her head sharply.

"Then I suggest you be more forthcoming."

As the pseudo-punk waltzed away with his gruesome dance partner, Miranda could tell that MacVicar was losing patience. Suddenly, the half-devoured man on Inessa's dining board, with a feat of near superhuman strength, raised his head partway up and rasped out a few words. Their exact provenance was unknowable, but the look in his lidless eyes was clear: he was asking for help.

"Oy! Will you let that thing off its leash?"

She looked down, having totally forgotten about Snuggles, though the "ghoul" as Scav had called it, was whimpering and staring longingly at the mostly-dead man. Miranda reached into her pocket, but when she brought out the key to Snuggles's muzzle, her hands were shaking so badly she dropped it.

"Jesus suffering fuck," MacVicar muttered, walking over and easily wrenching the wrought-iron muzzle off Snuggles's face with his bare hands.

MacVicar smacked the ghoul on the ass as it leapt up, but it hardly needed any encouragement. With a mighty leap it landed amongst the agonized man's clump of intestines and began to greedily devour them, shit squirting out like filling out of an overstuffed éclair, as it fed.

"Now then," MacVicar said, digging into Inessa's throat and brains like a kid searching for a prize in a cereal box, "you're telling me Cashley's calling himself the master. Does he ever call you lot his 'House?'"

Miranda pursed her lips, pondering what the "right" response was. Scav was still off in his own little world, making a mockery of what was left of Inessa's corpse. MacVicar pulled a raggedy chunk of brain from Inessa's head, and tossed it to Snuggles, who abandoned his still-struggling meal to catch it in midair.

"Yes," Miranda said, "he speaks often of us as his House."

"Ooh," Scav said, as though smarting, as he twirled Inessa's lifeless body in a surprisingly elegant pose, "this might be worse than we thought, Connor."

"Well," MacVicar said, continuing to feed the eager ghoul, "the lepress thought Cashley was bringing immortals across without permission. This Inessa here is proof positive of that. You there, lassie. How many other immortals has master brought across?"

"You mean how many others has he granted The Long Gift?"

MacVicar scowled, apparently not liking the fact she knew that term.

"Aye, The Long Gift."

"Six. That I know of."

"Fuck me in the arse."

MacVicar turned and tossed Inessa's head through the window with a smash. Scav dropped Inessa's corpse to the ground and Snuggles descended on it, ripping apart tendon, muscle, and sinew. There wasn't a drop of blood in her whole body. Scav walked over and placed a hand on MacVicar's shoulder.

"This is bad," Scav whispered, though since Miranda could still hear him he probably wasn't trying very hard to hide his thoughts, "I always knew Cashley was loony tunes, but to form his own splinter House? With six other immortals? Maybe we should call for backup."

"Backup? No, I amnae letting anyone else share in this bounty. This one was still eating flesh. For all we know the other six are newborns, too. You there, Miranda?"

Miranda felt her heart race and the blood swished into her ear.

"Yes?"

"Those other immortals. Did they eat meat the way Inessa did or did they drink blood?"

Would lying help? She couldn't say for sure.

"They still eat...living people...the way Inessa did."

MacVicar thumped Scav on his chest.

"There, you see? He's gone mad and gone on a siring spree, but only just recently. Six newborns. We can take them, and Cashley, too. You finish this with me, my young get, and I'll give you my blessing. That's a promise."

Scav placed a hand on MacVicar's cheek.

"You're too good to me, Connor."

"Right. Well, let's kill this mortal and go hunt down the others."

"Wait! I can take you to the master!"

MacVicar smiled and snapped his fingers.

"Clever girl. Right-o, lead the way, then."

Scav gave Miranda what was probably supposed to be a playful shove, but turned out to be so hard her shoulder nearly popped out of its socket. Rubbing her shoulder, she led the way out of Inessa's private chambers, only risking a single glance back to see how Snuggles was doing. The ghoul was busy tearing into its double-sized meal for the evening. In a way, she mourned, knowing she'd never see Snuggles again whatever tonight's outcome, but in another way she knew the dumb brute would never miss her so it hardly mattered.

They stepped out into the chilly Nevada night. The moon was full and she felt terribly exposed as she pattered across the compound. She knew every inch of it by heart, but was terrified that one of her sister wives in the guard towers would spot her. If they guessed her intentions, and the intentions of the men trailing her, would they hesitate to shoot her? She suspected not.

Each step roiled her churning stomach, but much to her relief they finally reached the small, unobtrusive chapel where the master spent his days and most nights. Scav gave her a not-very-gentle shove toward the entrance. Taking a deep breath, she raised her hand and rapped on the door.

"I'm fine, thank you," the master's voice intoned from within.

She looked back at the two men. MacVicar nodded to her.

"Master," she whispered hoarsely, then cleared her throat and repeated it, "master, it's Miranda."

There was a prolonged pause. Miranda was terrified of what would happen next, but then realized she had no idea what it might be. When next the master spoke, it sounded like he was closer to the door.

"You know you're not to be here, child. Anything you need to say you should report to Inessa, and she will decide whether to inform me or not."

Miranda paused and straightened out her grubby gray jumpsuit.

"Th…th…" she bit her lip and forced herself not to stutter, "that's why I'm here, master. It's about I…Inessa."

That was certain to get his attention.

"Go back to your bunk," the master said sharply. "I'll check on my beloved. And consider an appropriate punishment for you."

Miranda turned to look at her captors, her jaws wordlessly opening and clenching. Scav gently pushed Miranda aside while, much to her surprise, MacVicar began singing. At first he sang at a light, almost conspiratorial volume, but by the final word he was belting it out.

"'The sergeant, when he enlisted me, winked his eye and

then says he, 'A man like you so stout and tall, can ne'er be killed by a cannonball!'"

There was a pause.

"MacVicar?" the master asked.

MacVicar put his boot to the entrance. The doors to the temple exploded inward right off their hinges, creating an unholy noise and knocking the master flat on his back. Though Miranda hung back, she had still never been this close to the master before, and in a way the chance to see him up close—even laid low and humbled—was too much to pass up.

Scav quickly passed through the archway and stuck a boot on the master's chest. The master smiled, displaying two deadly fangs. His teeth were still sticky with plasma, and the vital fluid dribbled out of his mouth, leaving a mark around his lips and chin like a clown's goatee of circus makeup. He wore a jumpsuit identical to Miranda's, though his was red instead of gray, not to mention clean and freshly ironed. Square plastic sunglasses obscured almost the entire top half of his face, leaving him unreadable despite his rictus grin. His skin sparkled in the low neon lights overhead. It made Miranda want to reach out and touch him.

"Well, well, well," Scav said, "if it isn't the Profane Prophet of Provo. How's tricks, Cashley?"

Miranda looked to the master for some clue what was going on or what to do. His nostrils were flaring, but otherwise he made no move.

"I'm afraid I haven't any change for you, Scavatelli. My House makes do without the pettiness of money."

"You hear that, Connor? 'My House' he says. You're House Signari, shit-eater," Scavatelli gestured at the white stripe down his face, "at least, you were until the lepress declared you *persona non grata.*"

MacVicar reached behind a pew and pulled one of the sacred texts out of the slot. Miranda lowered her eyes at the sight of the familiar black book, with its depiction of two arms coming together to hold a red apple. MacVicar tossed the book carelessly and it landed on the ground by the master's head. Miranda stifled a gasp at the display of blasphemy. MacVicar bent over and ran a pair of fingers across the master's skin. He rubbed the two fingers across his thumb and held it up for Scav to see.

"Glitter," Scav said with a laugh.

MacVicar stuck his hand into the master's mouth, and though he instantly bit down, severing several of MacVicar's fingers, MacVicar struggled with him until finally wrenching his fangs out of his face and revealing them to be prosthetics.

"Fake teeth. Fake blood. All this shit is a whole lot of smoke and mirrors for the mortals. I always knew you were into some funny business with your circle, Cashley, but I never thought you'd take it to the level of treason."

"I have every right to establish my own House. I have been in the American West since before Brigham Young…"

MacVicar stamped down on the master's face, squishing his head like a soggy pumpkin. Miranda gasped, but then watched in wonder as the shattered chunks of skull and pulverized brain knitted themselves back together and his entire head reformed, like a balloon reinflating. Only his thick plastic goggles didn't mend. The pallid, white, pupilless orbs housed in his eye sockets and the wretched landscape of scars connecting them told the tale of why he always kept that half of his face hidden.

"Pull the other one," MacVicar spat at him.

"Please, Mac, Scav," the master whimpered, finally sounding as though he understood how precarious his position was, "you don't understand the danger. There's something hunting our kind."

"Oh, yes, I've heard this fairy tale. There's a," Scav made quotation marks with his fingers, "'serial killer' taking out immortals."

"Aye, I heard about that, too," MacVicar agreed, "Probably just some Inquisitors getting too big for their britches."

The master shook his head wildly.

"No. You don't understand. It's far worse than you can possibly imagine. I need other immortals to help protect me, and Father Otto won't grant me permission to turn even a single get."

"Knowing you, Cash," MacVicar said, "I wouldnae either."

Suddenly the brass bell at the lone entrance to the compound began ringing. Miranda looked up to one of the guard towers. A spotlight shone on Inessa's chambers, illuminating the carnage within. An instant later the spotlight turned its attention to Miranda.

Dodging two poorly aimed rounds, she scurried into the chapel.

"Well, that'll be the alarm," MacVicar said, "I'd been hoping we might get a decent scrap out of this shit job."

The master took advantage of the distraction to reach up and twist Scav's leg, yanking it and wrenching it from its socket. Scav tumbled to the ground and the master popped up to his feet with a single flex of his back muscles. He stood now in the center of the aisle, backing away from the intruders and towards the altar, brandishing Scav's severed leg like a cudgel to ward them off.

Scrabbling to grab hold of a pew, Scav pulled himself upright, balancing on his remaining foot. Miranda stared at Scav's stump, wondering briefly if his leg would regenerate like a lizard's, but it didn't. It seemed that immortals were capable of healing almost any damaged flesh, but could not regrow lost parts. No wonder, then, that their clashes descended into bouts of dismemberment.

"Toss me the lad's leg, Cashley," MacVicar growled.

"You have no idea what's coming, fixer. You're going to wish you'd listened to me. I've seen things. Dreadful things hiding in the shadows. Otto Signari won't be able to stand against him. Not even Cicatrice will be able to stand against him."

Suddenly a hole exploded in the wall behind the altar. Perhaps sensing his distress, the master's six remaining immortal brides had eschewed the door entirely and simply punched their way in. The chosen few wore scintillating white jumpsuits to signal their elevated status in the compound.

"Ah," the master said with a grin, "the cavalry's arrived. Seems I have a leg up at last."

He tossed the full-grown man's leg as effortlessly as if he were passing a Frisbee. Scav snatched it out of the air.

"Newborns, Cashley?" MacVicar said with a snort. "Have

you even weaned them off flesh yet?"

"All that should matter to you, fixer, is how hard they'll fight for me. I don't intend to go gentle into the abyss."

MacVicar clapped his hands together.

"I do so love my job. Nothing like putting down a traitor as well as his Houseless bastards. How you feeling, Scav?"

Scav had reattached his leg to his stump, but the area where it had been torn away still seemed soft and scabrous. Suddenly his eyes alighted on Miranda, and flashed with a bestial hunger.

"Actually, I'm feeling a bit peckish. Maybe I'll have a quick bite before this imbroglio."

The pseudo-punk, with half his pantleg pooled around his ankle, lunged at Miranda.

"Wait!" Miranda shouted, pulling down her right sleeve and showing her wrist.

Scav paused, his head bobbing in the air like a bird's. "What's that?"

"Just a bit of cosmetics," she said.

She pulled her wrist across her jumpsuit, rubbing away the foundation. Underneath the makeup was a tattoo of a green double cross, with an olive branch to the left of it and a sword to the right of it.

"Inquisitor!" Scavatelli hissed.

"That's right. I spent the last three weeks infiltrating this cult for a shot at that sorry son of a bitch." Her finger shot out in Cashley's direction. "After all the shit I've had to take from him and Inessa, there's no way I'm letting two low-rent fixers eat my lunch."

She plunged her hand into her front cargo pocket, slipping her fingers between the pages of her hollowed-out copy of "the sacred text," and pulled out the Colt .45 hand cannon she kept hidden there. With her other hand she ripped open the seam of her pantleg and pulled a long, wicked blade from the scabbard that ran practically the whole length of her thigh. Thank God for Cashley's modesty rules. She'd managed to keep it taped there for her whole tenure in the compound.

Scav roared and charged at the vampire hunter, even as she filled the air with bullets. Their stopping power wouldn't do much to harm a vampire, but if she was lucky and destroyed his eyes it would buy her the precious seconds she needed to sever his head.

She managed to catch one eye, but not the other, and then when she took her stroke it went astray. It was enough to move him out of her guard, but the vital moment of surprise was lost. Now she would need all of her skill—and luck—to survive.

"Bury that glog quick, Scav," MacVicar shouted, bracing himself for the onslaught of Cashley and his six brides, "We've got bigger fish to fry."

Scav hissed and leapt at her. As though she had been struck by a bolt of lightning, she was suddenly on her back, both hands pinned to the floor and her weapons clattering away out of reach. The blow had knocked the wind out of her and as she fought the panic of being unable to draw in oxygen, she struggled, but she wasn't even a rag doll in his grasp. She was like a butterfly, already pinned to a board.

Then, like a tiny miracle, oxygen flooded into her lungs and she took a deep gasp. It had seemed an eternity, though she knew it had really only been a few seconds, and her wits finally returned to her. Looking up she wondered why the killing blow hadn't come. But Scav wasn't even paying attention to her.

The vampire was staring at the door. She glanced back down the aisle and saw MacVicar, Cashley, and the six newborns all staring at the doorway, too, paused in mid-movement like a VHS tape. That, more than anything, brought a sinking feeling to Miranda's stomach.

The sound of a horse snuffling cut through Miranda's torso like a knife. Defying all the boogeymen in her intestines screaming at her not to look, she turned her head toward the entranceway and caught sight first of the black hooves dripping a substance so dark it must have been tar, but she feared it was not.

Over her head, in a child's voice, Scav whispered, "*Il cacciatore del morto.*"

Miranda blinked and strained her neck to see the rest of the dark figure. The horse was black on black, with black eyes that didn't even seem to reflect the moonlight. The man astride the charger was sealed in a wall of black plate armor, festooned with spikes and barbs. No mortal could have carried such armor; it must have weighed two tons. Like the horse's hair, the man's armor dripped with the dark, syrupy substance.

The high helmet he wore had two long, curved horns, but otherwise it was nearly impossible to pick out any part of him. He had all the appearance of a blob of fresh black ink that had somehow been smeared on the landscape. He held a bastard sword in one hand, and in the other, seemingly defying the laws of physics; he held a long, pointed lance weighed down with what had to be a dozen corpses. From the hilt to the tip, stacked one on top of each other, each of Cashley's remaining wives and concubines, at least fifteen of them or so, had been pierced directly through the heart. Blood soaked their grey jumpsuits.

Their feud forgotten, Miranda and Scav rose to their feet. The horse slowly cantered into the temple. As it did, the knight merely shifted his lance, lifting it up into the air at a downward sloping angle. Alice's body toppled from the lance first. Peggy's followed.

And with barely a shake, the bodies of a dozen or more of Cashley's followers fell from the mounted figure's lance and formed a trail behind him, like Hansel and Gretel's breadcrumbs.

Cashley was the first to regain his senses. He cowered, pushing his brides into a semi-circular shield wall in front of him.

"I warned you. I warned you, MacVicar. Everyone's scared of a serial killer but now you see what's really happening."

The knight raised his lance in MacVicar's direction, as though lining up a gigantic pool cue for a difficult shot. Scav seemed to realize what was about to happen.

"No!"

"Scav, don't!"

Scav flew through the air like a bird of prey dropping onto an unsuspecting rodent, but his trajectory was immediately arrested. Without looking in his direction, the knight lashed out with his blade, and sliced cleanly through Scav's neck with a single stroke. His head came to a rest, balanced on the outstretched blade, while his torso crumpled to the floor.

"You motherfucker!" MacVicar roared, dropping to his knees. "You cocksucking bastard!"

His face remained dry, but Miranda could have sworn he was weeping. He was unable to produce tears. One of the many, dark in-betweens of being a vampire.

The horse reared back on its hind legs. Like a wave, the great darkling mass poured down the aisle. Even with the preternatural speed of his kind, MacVicar couldn't get out of the way before the figure was upon him.

The black knight's lance struck true, and the force of the blow impaled MacVicar practically up to the hilt. Miranda had never seen a vampire actually killed with a stake to the heart. It was nearly impossible—a joke. Practically every vampire wore a piece of armor across their chest, and judging by the glint of metal around the hole in MacVicar's body, the Signari fixer had been no exception. Miranda's mouth hung open as it occurred to her that the mysterious knight had pierced through an inch of plate metal and Kevlar, not to mention a man's ribcage, with a single stroke.

There was no way. Was it possible? Was this really the semi-mythic Hunter of the Dead?

The knight sat there astride his horse, holding up Scav's sire bodily, not half a meter from his featureless mask. He seemed to be examining MacVicar like a diner looking at a hair in his soup. Then he lifted his lance over his head and snapped it forward like a bullwhip. The crumpled mass that had been MacVicar flew off and smashed into the rear wall of the chapel, a few feet above Cashley's head.

"Protect me!" Cashley shrieked, ducking down so that his brides formed a barrier in front of him, and stumbling off toward the hole they had punched through the back wall.

The bastard sword cut an arc through the air and bifurcated one of the brides through her waist, sending her torso toppling forward before the blade passed through the back of the crouching Cashley's head. Cashley's corpse crumpled into a heap, his hasty retreat ended before it had even begun.

The five brides whose legs remained attached to their bodies tripped over one another trying to flee through the hole in the back wall. But that, too, was no avail. The knight was upon them in an instant, skewering hearts and ripping heads from their bodies with only his gauntleted hands. When those five were dealt with, he turned to look for the top half of the bride who had been split in two.

She was scrabbling away on her palms. The knight raised his lance.

"No, no, no, no!" the bride began muttering.

With a furious slam he brought the lance down through the middle of her chest, snapping the tip of the weapon with the force of the blow and sending it hurtling away to embed itself in one of the walls. The lance was so heavy that when he let it go it toppled to the ground and raised the halved vampire off the floor. She strained and struggled to pull herself free of the impaling lance, but her efforts were either in vain or too slow. The knight dismounted, retrieved his bastard sword from Cashley's severed head, and lopped through her brainpan at nose level.

Then, as if some eldritch and terrible god had cast its eye upon her, Miranda saw the horns of the knight's helmet turning in her direction. In that instant, she became certain that this was the legendary Hunter of the Dead.

Even weighed down with so much armor, The Hunter was upon her in a split second, and pressed his dripping sword to Miranda's breast.

"I...I'm on your side," she said, holding up her wrist to display her tattoo, "I'm an Inquisitor. We hunt..."

The blade drove into Miranda's sternum and exited just as quickly, drawing a trail of crimson through the air like an exploding firework.

NIGHT ONE

ONE

A few days before…

The young girl sat on the roof watching the sun set. Autumnal violets and crimsons devoured the fields and paddies of her homestead, and receded into the night.

She felt him before she saw him, like an arctic breeze raising goosepimples on her neck.

"I didn't think to wait for you so long," she whispered.

"My dear, I am but an ignoble caliban for making you wait," Topan replied. His Cantonese was flawless, as always. "I had to deal with your parents."

Her eyes opened wide and she turned to look at him. He was smiling; that flawless, charming smile that set everyone at ease, even her father who mistrusted everyone and everything. There was no guile in Topan's eyes, just delight.

She ran her hands through her hair, which was still messy from the day's work, and felt embarrassed suddenly. She was no one, a no-account night soil farmer from a no-account village in an underdeveloped section of Guangdong province. What would they say about her clothes and her hair and her fingernails in Beijing? Or, for that matter, in Guangzhou?

A hick, a rube, a nobody. They'd laugh at her. And yet…

And yet here was Topan, a wealthy foreigner, and he had eyes seemingly only for her. She couldn't believe it was her appearance. There were prettier girls in the village. It certainly wasn't her family's relative wealth. Though he had never explicitly said so, she believed he could buy their entire village many times over.

So why her? She shook her head, letting her messy brown hair fall *over her face. Best not to question such fortune.*

"And they're all right? I mean, they'll let me go away with you?"

He took her hand and kissed it.

"They won't be a problem anymore. I promise you."

"And we can leave? Go to Beijing or Hong Kong?"

He laughed.

"If you like. We can go anywhere you desire. First, though, I need to take you to meet my father."

"In Malaysia?"

"No. I didn't mean my biological father. He's long dead. I meant… well, you'll find out. My real father. In America."

"America?"

He nodded.

"How's your English?"

She paused before answering in that language, "Quite fine, thank you very much."

"Oh, you'll do magnificently in America."

She laughed and pressed her free hand over her face to hide the tears. He shook his head and parted her hair carefully before smoothing it over her ears and then gently forcing her hand away from her face.

"You shouldn't cover up so much. You're beautiful."

"I'm not, though. Not really."

"I told my father about you. I told him you were Iði's shining talk."

She stared at him and shook her head slowly.

"I don't understand."

He pursed his lips.

"In Norse myth Iði was a giant, one of three brothers. Their father was immensely wealthy and when he died the brothers, being giants and thus not famous for their accounting skills, had to invent a method for dividing the inheritance. So, each one took a mouthful of treasure at a time until they had three equal piles. And so today we have the saying for a treasure beyond reckoning, 'Iði's mouthful' or 'Iði's shining words.'"

The cicadas were roaring and she felt her heart pounding in her chest. She feared her face was as red as a cherry.

"I can't really be so precious to you."

"You have no idea of your own worth. I've searched for you all my life."

He wrapped his fingers around the back of her neck and placed his thumb on her cheek, stroking it.

"Topan..."

"Let me take you."

She froze, as if suddenly aware for the first time of the strange man's immense physical power. She felt certain if he squeezed, her neck would shatter, and if she tried to run, he could snatch her before she made it two steps.

"Topan, I don't know if..."

"My dear, all the preparations have been seen to. Now is the time. I'm afraid this is going to hurt. Quite a bit."

She tried to wriggle out of his grasp, but as she had suspected, his muscles were like iron. She slapped, punched, kicked, even delivered a devastating blow to his groin but he seemed to pay her no more heed than a mayfly buzzing about his ear.

"Topan!" she cried out, "Let go! You're hurting me!"

"Oh, I wish I could spare you this, my love. I remember the pain well. But you'll thank me for the Long Gift. In time."

With a single motion he ripped away nearly a quarter of her cheongsam, exposing her right breast fully. She struggled to keep herself covered, but he paid her little mind.

"I'm sorry about this, my dear, but it must be done and it must be done beforehand."

He sliced through the bare flesh of her bosom with the fingernail of his pinky as easily as if it had been a razor. She shrieked, partially at the pain, but more at the violation, and with the hand he still kept on her throat, he throttled her until she quieted, and tears flowed from her eyes.

When he was done carving her skin she looked down to see an oval—an eye, perhaps—split in two by a straight line with hatchmarks like a scar. He had marked her. Like a cow.

"Why?" she tried to whisper, but instantly she felt something cold driving deep into her neck, as though she were being stabbed with an icicle. It was not the usual chill of his icy grip. It was as though he were pouring coldness into her.

She gasped. No, it wasn't cold. It was blankness. An inky white touch. Death. She tried one last time to yank herself free of his grasp, but Topan was as impassive as stone.

The young girl coughed. She gasped when she saw the spatter of blood she had hacked up on Topan's face and shirt, like a tuberculosis patient. He made no move to wipe the splatter away.

Her limbs turned to ice. She nearly crumpled, but he held her aloft with his single arm alone. He wouldn't let her fall, wouldn't let her tumble. He pulled her close to himself, wrapped her in a cold but loving embrace.

"Please stop," she whispered, "Please let me go. I don't want this."

"It doesn't matter what you want."

She opened her mouth to speak again and realized she couldn't. Her mouth was full of blood. The blood was funneling up and out of her. Alarmed, she tried to pull away again, but he held her close, stronger than a team of oxen.

She felt her vagina open up, gushing with blood. Not like her menses. The warm red liquid poured out of her, hemorrhaging from her every orifice. She felt it fill her nose, trickle out both of her ears, even explode out her rectum like painful diarrhea.

She tried to speak, to scream, to make her wishes known, but everywhere was choked with redness. At last her eyes seemed to burst, and she felt the blood begin to trickle out of the corners of her eyelids.

That, it seemed, was the last of it. Her limbs and torso were emptied. What little blood remained in her brain was leaking out of her eyes now. The flow began to ebb, and she almost felt like she could move her tongue again without it being pushed to the floor of her mouth by an unholy stream of effluvia.

"What...?"

Then lightheadedness gave way to darkness. She fell, unconscious or dead, and collapsed to the roof. The last thing she felt was Topan finally releasing his grip on her.

The young girl awakened without opening her eyes. She was unclothed, but enveloped by earth and so didn't feel naked. She lifted her hands through the soil and pressed against the wooden top of the coffin until it popped open effortlessly. She sat up and pulled her knees into an embrace, as though she were sitting in the tub at home and not halfway around the world in a box full of Guangdong province dirt.

It was either thirty seconds or thirty thousand years before she finally rose, standing up in the box so that only her feet were still covered in soil. The dirt streamed down from her crevices and back into the box. Then she slowly stepped down from the dais to the ground. Her first night here two mortals had been present to greet her with warm water, rags, and towels. Embarrassed by her nudity and by the idea of having servants, she had asked them to leave and not return.

Apparently her orders only carried so much weight in her patriarch's manse, because someone had been by to draw a bath, and quite recently too, judging by the steam still rising from the water's surface. She stepped into the tub and watched as the dirt fled her body and sank to the bottom of the tub. A warm bath had been a once-weekly luxury back home. Now she could have one any time she liked, for only the price of asking.

A blank envelope sat in the soapdish, propped up in such a manner that she had to take the envelope before the soap, or risk it tumbling into the water. She ripped it open.

Join me in the dining room when you're ready.

There was no signature, but she recognized the sigil: a scar through a ruined eye. Her hand went to her heart, which now bore the same mark. Topan's doing. But the message was not from Topan.

She pressed her hand flat against her breast. How strange it was to feel the absence of something that had been so steady and unchanging all her life. Perhaps it was like going blind. Then again, perhaps it was like being blind all of one's life and one day being able to see. And, then being asked to explain blue. How is it possible to explain blue? Even moreso, how was it possible to describe not feeling her lungs drawing breath, her heart not beating, the blood not flowing through her veins?

She rose from the tub and stood silently on the cold tile, letting the water drip from her naked frame, her hair hung over her face like a veil. Not a shiver or a shudder crossed her shoulders, not a spot of flesh marbled with goosebumps. She could tell, distantly, intellectually almost, that she had left a warm bath for an icy tile floor, but it didn't bother her. It was like eating spicy food with a cold; it barely registered.

She selected a green *cheongsam* with yellow trim from the wardrobe, knotted her hair, and walked down the hall to the gargantuan oaken doors of the dining hall. She pressed lightly on the crack with her middle finger and each of the half-ton doors practically flew off their hinges opening inward. As the patriarch had taught her, she slammed the doors closed behind her and barred them.

As soon as she had finished barring the doors the dull, gray fog which had had seemed to settle permanently over her senses cleared, and she was struck as though by a razor through her belly. The smell of warm, palpitating mortal flesh struck her nose first, lighting a fire deep in the pit of her stomach. Even though the dining hall was cloaked in absolute darkness it took her only a fraction of a second to spot the source of her burning desire.

Set out on the table like a feast was a boy of no more than five or six. He lay on his belly trussed up like a pig. His mouth was sutured shut and his hands and feet were bound with razor wire. As he struggled in his panic, the wire sliced deep into his wrists and ankles, filling the air with the heavenly scent of young blood.

I can almost…

As soon as she pressed the tip of her tongue to his arm he shuddered and fell still. She licked a rivulet of blood away from the child's arm, tracing the flow up to his bonds and slicing her tongue deeply on one of the blades. As her tongue instantly repaired itself, she shook her head. The blood had tasted like milk gone sour, as though there was no longer any sustenance to be had from it once it had left his beating artery. No, the flesh had to be still living, the blood still internal to serve as sustenance.

Suddenly a queer thought struck her, a premonition, or perhaps the tickle of a sixth sense. She glanced around the room, her nose flaring as she tried to scent whether anyone else was present. There were no other mortals—she would have scented them immediately. But neither did she catch the whiff of another immortal. The patriarch, it seemed, has left this meal for her alone.

A low whimper emerged from the boy's nose. The sound was long and continuous, as though he was trying to cry but with his mouth sealed couldn't make it happen.

"Shh, shh, little one," she whispered, running her hand through his mop of sandy hair.

With some difficulty (and not without cutting some huge gashes in his arms and legs), she leaned him back on his knees so that his hands and feet were still behind his back, but he was upright. One hand steady on his shoulder to keep him upright, she used her fingernail to rip open the stitches over his mouth.

"I hurt," he whispered.

She wrapped her arms around him, not caring as she got entangled in the wire and her own clothes and hands were torn to shreds.

"Yes, I know."

"I want my mommy."

"She's not here, I'm afraid. You must get used to that idea."

"Will you be my new mommy?"

"I'm sorry, little one," she said, placing a finger on his lips, "but you must be brave. Give me a kiss now."

She pressed her lips to the child's mouth. A loud, sickening crunch resounded through the air and she tore her head back from his face, moaning orgiastically as she chewed the child's tongue. Part of his essence, his energy drained into her, and she felt it powering her, like turning over a motor, even as it cooled the burning hot ember of desire in her belly.

The child was trying to cry again but she bit down around his nose, chewing deep through the nasal cavity and lapping at the blood as it pooled. At that point the boy was hemorrhaging blood. She cursed herself. The patriarch had taught her to start with the extremities, but, of course, in the heat of her lust, she had forgotten and gone straight for the head.

She hoped the boy would not bleed out and turned to begin to suckle the flesh from his fingers, leaving cleaned bone and tendon jutting from his still unruined hands. Like a bowl of rice congealing and growing cold, she could taste the boy's flesh growing more and more unappetizing as his blood pressure dropped and his heartbeat fluttered on the edge of stopping.

Frantically she gobbled down great gulps of his arms and legs, and even snatched a handful of offal, but by the time she shoved it in her mouth the child had died. She spat the intestines and liver matter back out. Even still warm, it was no good to her with the boy dead. It was the life, the life itself that sustained her.

"There was a time," a voice dripping like molasses with pure malevolence intoned, "when our kind was not relegated to the shadows."

Her eyes turned upward and flitted around the ceiling. She staggered backwards, shocked to see her patriarch standing with his feet flat on the ceiling.

"How long have you been there, Father Cicatrice?" she asked.

"And there will be again."

In a smooth motion, Cicatrice fell, his feet tumbling over his head as he dropped, and he landed flat on the hard, oaken surface with an impact that would have shattered a mere mortal's legs. He reached down and picked up the dripping ruin of the five-year-old's corpse. To the young girl's nose, it already stank of uselessness and decay. He tossed the carcass into a corner and gestured for her to stand and ring a large bronze bell which hung on the wall.

She rang the bell and a small doorway to the kitchen and servants' quarters opened. A grotesque, dun-skinned creature emerged. Cicatrice called such things "ghouls" and though she had not learned their full background, she understood that they were failed immortals. She shuddered at the thought that had Topan been less skilled, or she less strong, she might have ended up one of those degenerate things, useful only as a mobile midden heap.

The ghoul delighted in its task, devouring the already dead flesh of the child, cracking bones and sucking the marrow from them, and noisily devouring every scrap. It howled over the razor wire, struggling to untangle its meal. It seemed the easy healing which was part of the Long Gift was not imparted to such base creatures.

"Who was he?" she whispered.

"The child of a deadbeat. His mother, I think, has not yet suspected he's missing. But his father will know when the cock crows, why his young Francis never returned. And perhaps he will pay back his gambling debt to me. Perhaps he will not."

The patriarch had an imposing figure and a terrifying visage. He wore a *tangzhuang*, every centimeter of it white like bleached bone, except for a red hourglass embroidered on the back. It looked expensive beyond all reason and might have been silk. He could have been an undertaker.

His face was hewn from marble, expressionless, and he had one ruined eye. A scar stretched from his forehead to next to his nose, and the eye which had suffered the scratch was red throughout and useless.

His good eye, though, was the more terrifying of the two. It bore witness to the coldness of nearly a thousand winters. His bad eye suggested he had been wrong once. His remaining orb suggested it would never happen again.

Across his chest he wore a string of garlic cloves like a bandolier. He took it off and dangled it in front of her face.

"The reason you couldn't smell me," he explained. "Put it on."

His Cantonese was, if anything, even better than Topan's. She put the string around her neck like a necklace. The herb didn't smell. Certainly it didn't smell potently the way she remembered it smelling in life. It was almost like an anti-scent, a no-zone where she could detect nothing.

"So I'm invisible to you now?" she asked.

"Not invisible. But I can barely sense you. And I am far more powerful than any immortal you will ever encounter again."

She moved to doff the necklace, but he held up his hand to stop her. He stepped down from the table onto a chair and then the floor.

"Leave it on for just a moment. You're troubled."

She tucked a strand of hair behind her ear.

"Am I so easy to read?"

"No," he replied, "In fact I find you extraordinarily difficult to read. Nevertheless."

She nodded.

"Should I feel ashamed that I felt nothing for that child?"

Cicatrice seemed to ponder for a moment. His face was glacial. She had yet to see his expression betray any of his secrets.

"It would not be unusual for an immortal as young as you to retain some…vestigial mortal emotions. But I have found your development to be precocious, so it does not surprise me that you don't."

She nodded.

"What did you feel, devouring him?"

"Just the pleasure of feeding."

"You're lying. Holding back. An admirable trait and it will serve you well. With others. But never with me."

Her eyes fell to the floor.

"I felt something new."

"Tell me about it."

She paused and closed her eyes, trying to bring the moment back. Everything now was so slow, like swimming through a morass. Time stretched out before her like an infinite plane. Any given moment lost all its power.

"As I tasted his blood, I could almost…sense it pumping through him. As though I could take the life directly from his veins."

Cicatrice's stare bore down on her. As always, his face was impassive, like a statue's, but she sensed something else almost there on the periphery.

"This is the most dangerous time of your new life. This is the time when you'll leave behind bodies and the mortals can track you if they know what they're looking for. Sometimes the mortal authorities never catch on; other times they suspect a newborn is a serial killer. Either way in a few years the problem always resolves itself. You've been with me for three days. You've been one of us for five. I have never seen an immortal capable of sensing the life in the blood in less than a year. For you to sense it in less than a week is beyond extraordinary."

"Then this is a good thing?"

"It might be."

She ran a hand through her hair and realized a small piece

of the boy's nose was stuck behind her ear. She fished it out and tossed it to the ghoul, who by now was messily lapping up the last bloodstains from its meal.

"If you're not lying to me, tomorrow I'll teach you how to drain the life from the blood."

"I'm not."

"Have you given any more thought to your new name?"

She narrowed her eyes.

"It mustn't be anything to do with my…old life?"

"That's correct."

"And all immortals must do this? Give up their birth name?"

Cicatrice shook his head.

"No. Some Houses do. Some Houses don't. The Signaris have no set rule. But all members of my House must abandon all mortal weakness. We are not Signaris."

She sucked her lower lip into her mouth.

"I've been thinking about a story. One that your…get told me."

Cicatrice wrapped his hands behind his back. If he was upset by her mentioning Topan, he didn't show it. She admired his unflappability. She wished she could replicate it one day, but feared she would always wear her heart on her sleeve.

"Which story?"

"The tale of Iði and his brothers. Of how they divided their wealth. Do you know it?"

Cicatrice nodded.

"When Topan told me that he implied that I was the treasure. 'Iði's shining mouthful.'"

"He's not wrong," Cicatrice said. "You are unique. And precious."

"Perhaps. But I don't wish to be told I'm any man's treasure. Instead, I'd rather be the giant, gobbling up the world by the mouthful. Claiming what is mine."

"So you're Iði himself."

"Yes. But I'm not Norse. I'm Han."

"Idi Han, then."

A knock echoed through the room. Idi Han turned to look, worried that perhaps she had forgotten to bar the doors when she came in. She had remembered. A massive board that would've taken five mortals to lift sealed the doors shut. The knock sounded once again, more urgent this time.

"A friend of yours?" Cicatrice asked drily.

She turned to look at him. Everyone she knew was ten thousand kilometers away.

"Father, I don't...I haven't..."

"Relax. A joke."

"Then you know who it is?"

"Not for certain, though I have a suspicion. Certainly no one I've invited."

The knocking turned into a pounding. The pounding turned to a thunderous flurry of blows and Idi Han gasped as the massive plank shuddered, and then finally cracked, sending the half-ton doors flying open.

TWO

All eyes in Phillip's Fill-Up were locked on the owner of the Saab that had just pulled up. Nico Salazar, who at twenty seemed way too young to already be a shift manager, stood behind the cash register grinding his teeth. Carter Price, who at fifty-something, seemed way too old to not at least be a manager, stood behind the deli case polishing his hands with a dirty rag.

"You think he's coming in?" Nico asked.

"I don't care what this guy does," Price replied, continuing to punish his knuckles with the rag. "At midnight I turn into a pumpkin."

Nico bit his upper lip. Saab guy was rich. Well, maybe not "rich.

Rich enough" seemed like a more adequate description. He was dressed to impress…well, someone, but obviously not a convenience store shift manager. Right now he was alternating between fiddling with the gas pump and glancing up at the store entrance, possibly making sure the lights were still on. Whether he decided to come in or not still seemed to be a coin toss.

"Your shift's not over 'til the last customer leaves."

Price grunted in disgust and tossed his rag off somewhere.

"That asshole is not going to want a sandwich."

"He might," Nico replied, dragging the second word out into a lengthy sing-song, "and you can't clean up until all the customers are gone."

"The hell I can't."

Price began disassembling the deli slicer. For an old dude, Price was pretty strong. He had a rough look to him: cut, like maybe he worked out, but more like prison lifting than to keep himself pretty. Prison was where he had no doubt learned to lift, after all.

Nico could hardly picture Price shaving, but he always seemed to have just a day or two of stubble, so he must shave sometimes. His hair was clipped close enough to bald that Nico could never quite identify the color.

Strangest of all, Price's right wrist had been bandaged for a while. Considering the nature of *that* sort of wound, Nico had never pried into it. But now that they'd been working together a while, he was starting to wonder if the bandages weren't an affectation. If he had been suicidal once, it should have long since healed by now. Of course, he might have been a cutter. Price seemed too old to be a cutter, but either way it was simply yet another conversation Nico never ever wanted to have with an employee.

"Don't do it. You'll curse us. Now he really will want a sandwich."

Price groaned and threw his arms up in the air before finally settling into his customary slouch against the sink to wait it out. "The Ballad of Whether We Can Close Up or Not" was one that seemed to play every night at about this time.

As Saab guy began to pump, the bell indicating the back door opening rang. Nico glanced up at the security monitor. Jackie, the delivery lady from the bakery, waved at the camera as she wheeled the next day's donuts in.

"Still warm," Jackie announced when she hit the floor, "You boys want one?"

Price licked his chops and held out his hands in a clamshell.

"Toss me a Boston Cream, Jax."

"Yeah, whatever," she replied, as she began stacking the donuts into their case for the fast-approaching morning shift. "Come get it yourself."

"Maybe I will come and get it," Price replied, and strutted toward the donut case.

Flirting again.

Jackie was a real nice lady. She was a tad overweight, but who could blame someone who carried pastries everywhere they went for a living? It wasn't like she was pumpkin-shaped, either, she just had a little more junk in the trunk than Nico preferred. Otherwise she was blonde, pretty, and about Price's age.

The two flirted shamelessly with each other every night. It had gotten to the point where Nico had been forced to check whether she wore a ring. (Price decidedly did not.) Now he was just wondering when Price would decide it was time to shit or get off the pot. He could do worse than to date Jackie, and Price had never given a hint that he had a girlfriend or much of a social life at all. Nico idly wanted that for the two of them, but had no real desire to intervene in the lives of two grown-ass adults. He had enough trouble dealing with his own (lack of) love life.

"Nothing for you, Nico?"

Nico shook his head. Jackie left her cart by the donut case and sidled up to lean against the counter opposite Nico.

"What are you two watching?"

Price returned from the donut case to behind the deli counter and began stuffing his face with cream and chocolate.

"We're trying to decide whether Picky Sandwich here is going to want mustard, mayo, or truffles."

"Oh, hell no!" Price shouted, rising to his feet, "That's not a picky sandwich eater. I'll tell you who that is. That's a Cigarette Dick. He wants some Benson and Hedges Slim Ultra-Lights or some shit."

Jackie clucked her tongue and went back to going about her business.

"You two are crazy."

Nico's eyes fluttered over to the wall clock, set perpetually slow by the owner, though the employees always ignored it and went by their phones anyway. Even the clock was quickly closing on midnight.

With a single ding of the front door, Nico's hopes of getting out on time were dashed. When the Saab owner juked toward the cash register instead of the deli, he tried to ignore Price's childish celebratory dance.

"Parliament Light 100s," Cigarette Dick announced, without so much as glancing in Nico's direction.

Nico looked up at his row upon row of assembled brands. Notably absent was the obscure(ish) brand in question.

God damn it.

"I'm sorry, sir, we seem to be out. Would Parliament Lights be all right? Or Parliament Regular 100s?"

Cigarette Dick finally deigned to look Nico in the face.

"Parliament. Light. 100s. Shall I repeat in *Espanol, amigo? Parliamento Light-o. Uno hundred-o.*"

Nico kept his face a mask of professionalism. He knew the score with people like Cigarette Dick. Scowl, and they'd yell at you for having a bad attitude. Smile, and they'd yell at you for being a smartass.

"Again, sir," he said, forcing his voice to remain as static as his face, "We are out."

"Why don't you go check? Don't you know how to do your job?"

Nico reached up and lowered the plastic scaffolding where they normally kept the Parliament Light 100s. Never before had he wished so much that a lone pack had gotten stuck up in the apparatus somewhere. But for the second time he saw that there were none.

"Okay, I just checked again, sir. We are out." Somehow he refrained from adding "still."

Cigarette Dick folded his arms and tapped his shoe.

"Why don't you go check in the back? Like I asked you to, twice? Like it's your job to do?"

Nico decided to swallow his explanation about how they didn't keep any secret stores of cigarettes in the back, when they arrived they filled them up at the cash register, and on a Sunday night, right before the next shipment arrived on Monday morning, sometimes they'd be out.

"Of course, sir," Nico said, "I'll go see if a pack fell out or something. Excuse me."

Nico locked the register and walked briskly to the back of the store. Just because he so badly wanted there to be a mislaid pack somewhere, he checked the empty, collapsed boxes of cigarette cartons. Of course, as he had already known, there were no cigarettes which had gone astray. He glanced up at the security camera and made sure that Cigarette Dick didn't attempt to go over the counter or anything. Nico would've been severely shocked if Carter would've made any attempt to stop even a blatant robbery.

Nico checked the time on his phone. Customers like Cigarette Dick considered taking the appropriate amount of time to do anything as a personal affront. It had to be long enough to seem thorough, but not long enough to seem like their time was being wasted.

Three minutes.

Nico sighed and glanced at the staff television. Black and white. Nothing good was on. Of course not. Mr. al-Azif, the owner of the gas station (whose first name was rather emphatically not Phillip) refused to pay for cable, so all they got was the God channel and a channel that played reruns from the "best" of the '70s and '80s. Sometimes Price got really into the Golden Oldie channel, but for the most part the employees just ignored the pointless old box.

He checked his phone again.

It's been long enough, I suppose.

Shaking his head in defeat, Nico exited the back room and lifted the leaf to enter the register area. He straightened his bright green polo shirt out and gazed into Cigarette Dick's eyes. He shook his head in false commiseration.

"So sorry, sir. None in the back either."

Like I already fucking said.

"You know what, kid? I want to talk to your manager." Cigarette Dick jabbed a finger at Price. "Hey, you!"

Price pointed his own thumb at himself by way of response, his mouth too full of chocolate and donut filling to say anything.

"Yeah, you, shitbird. I want to report this kid."

Price swallowed his ill-gotten pastry.

"Yeah, that's what I thought you said. Hey, Nico, this guy wants to report you. So write yourself up or something."

"Please finish cleaning up, Carter."

Price pretended to salute with two fingers, but busied himself at the sink. Cigarette Dick raised an eyebrow. He looked Nico up and down.

"You're the manager?"

"Shift manager, yes."

"And this fifty-year-old guy works for you? Hey, shitbird, what are you, an ex-con or something?"

Nico was mortified to see Price pull a sudsy paring knife out of the sink. Water and bubbles from the knife dripped to the deli floor.

"Yeah, actually, I am. You want to make something of it, you…"

Jackie stepped away from her cart and positioned herself surreptitiously in between Price and the customer. Her hand was on her hip, where Nico knew she kept a stun gun. She did late-night deliveries and didn't take chances with being mugged or raped.

"Carter!" Nico had no idea what Price had gone up the river for, but he didn't want to witness a repeat if it was a violent offense. "Sir, I'm happy to take your complaint, but I won't have you abusing me or my staff."

Cigarette Dick paused long enough to form a nasty expression on his lips when the front doorbell dinged.

"I'm sorry, I know the lights are on, but we're closed. What the fuck is that?"

Nico's expression must have turned to sheer horror because even Cigarette Dick turned around to look at the newcomer. Nico had no idea what he was looking at. The thing that stood on their plastic mat was a hulk of a creature. Even slouched over with its knuckles on the floor it was taller than Cigarette Dick's easy six feet.

Its skin was solid gray and its body was hairless. It could've been a man once, but its entire lower jaw was missing, its ears were long and flappy like batwings, and its eyes were solid yellow.

"What are you supposed to be?" Cigarette Dick asked, "Is there a comic book convention in town or something?"

Nico's heart stopped fluttering as he realized the man was probably right. It was just a costume. But in the store's bright lights it seemed so real.

With two steps the thing was on top of Cigarette Dick. It

reached out and with the ease of a delinquent child pulling the wings off a fly, ripped off both of Cigarette Dick's arms in one smooth motion.

"Holy fuck!"

Nico jumped back, away from the grisly display. With the monstrosity closer to him than before, he could see its tongue lolling out of its bottomless mouth. The teeth it retained in its upper jaw were sharp like knives. The customer had fallen silent, his mouth open in a soundless scream.

Jackie leaped forward and fired her stun gun at the creature. Two tiny chunks of metal flew out of the gun and 50,000 volts shot through it. Unfazed, it turned and buried its face into hers.

Unsure what to do, Nico slapped the silent alarm. He'd never had to use it before and didn't know how quickly the cops would show up. Suddenly a piercing whistle cut through the air and Nico and the creature both looked up to see Price standing on top of the deli display, a half-assembled meat slicer in his hands whirring away.

"Hey, asshole," Price said loudly, "why don't you try tangling with me?"

The creature hissed and let Jackie's lifeless body drop to the floor. Nico noticed with alarm that her face had been half chewed away while in the thing's godless embrace. With a single bound it leapt into the air at Price, though he had to be eight feet higher than it, positioned as he was on top of the deli display.

With a perfection that beggared belief, Price swung the meat slicer and caught the monster full in its neck. Nico watched in horror as Price held the meat slicer steady and the thing's jump halted. It seemed to be standing in mid-air as the slicer spun, making a hash of its face and neck but surprisingly casting off no blood, ichor, or other bodily fluids.

The thing dropped to the ground and Price flung the heavy meat slicer after it. He caught Nico's eyes.

"Are the gas pumps on?"

Nico's mouth worked, but he found he couldn't bring any words forth.

"Nico!"

"What?"

"Turn on the fucking gas pumps!"

Price leapt from the deli case and crouched as he landed in front of the register. He grabbed a roll of duct tape from a shelf of overpriced office supplies and began ripping the packaging off. Nico stumbled to his feet and flicked the buttons for the fuel. Price held out his hand.

"Come on, come on!"

The thing began to rise from its position, and Nico watched in horror as its mangled face began to reassemble itself mere seconds after being torn to shreds. When all the pumps were on he took Price's hand and felt the older man pull him over the counter. Together they hurried out into the parking lot.

The Saab stood at its fueling spot, the only car in the customer lot. Price grabbed the hose out of one of the pumps, depressed the handle, secured it with a few layers of duct tape, then dropped it to the ground so it began spraying a puddle of gasoline. He repeated the process at the next hose, and gestured to Nico to do the same.

"Is your car here?"

"Um, no," Nico said, shaking his head, "I take the bus."

"Shit."

Price dug into his pocket and tossed Nico a set of keys which he nearly fumbled, but caught before they splashed into the ever-widening pool of gasoline.

"Go and pull my car around. You know how to drive stick?"

"What about Jackie and that guy?"

"They're dead, kid! Go and get my car!"

Nico nodded and stumbled, knocking his knee badly against one of the pumps before getting a handle on his feet and pounding off towards the back lot where the employees parked. Even if it hadn't been the only car in the lot, Price's mint green 1963 Cadillac convertible would've been impossible to miss.

He stumbled, his messed-up knee hurting a lot worse than he had expected, and fumbled through Price's keychain before finding the right one. The car door was heavy and hard to open, and Nico had only ever driven standard once before, but somehow he managed to get the prehistoric behemoth moving and pulled it back around to the front.

The creature had emerged from the Fill-Up, and to Nico's horror it looked exactly as it had the moment it had walked in—not healthy, exactly, but utterly unharmed despite getting a faceful of deli slicer. It hissed at Price, who was backing away from the entrance to the store, and subtly motioning for Nico to keep his distance. Price's green Fill-Up polo was off, his rock-hard abs on display.

Not bad for an old guy.

Price had wrapped his shirt around one of the window squeegees that was stationed at every fuel pump.

"Yeah, I recognize you, motherfucker," Price said loudly. "You're supposed to be one of The Damned, right?"

The creature—the "Damned," Price had named it—its ears rose, pointing nearly straight up. So it was intelligent, if horrifying. Its tongue fluttered, as though it were trying to speak with its chapless mouth. It stepped towards him, more cautiously than it had been acting up until now.

Is that monstrosity really afraid of Carter Price?

"What does it mean that you're loose? All bets are off now? Cicatrice is gunning for us?"

Then, in a night full of awful noises, Nico heard the most heart-rapingly awful sound of his entire life. A noise came from The Damned's throat that it took him a moment to identify as a gruesome chuckle. It shook its head from side to side.

Price began to back up, surreptitiously moving closer to the car. The Damned slowly followed after him, and Nico watched with mounting anxiety as it stepped into the slowly broadening puddle of gasoline.

"So you don't know me, huh? This is just a co-inky-dink?"

The Damned nodded; its soulless eyes almost mirthful. Price nodded right back.

"Yeah, well, you might be king shit of the vampires—or that's what they say anyway—but I know one thing that kills every vampire dead. Even king shits."

The Damned paused and glanced skyward, furrowing its brow and squinching its eyes tight as though looking for something. Then its gaze returned to Price and it made a circular motion with its arm.

The sun's not rising anytime soon, it seemed to be saying.

"No, not that," Price said, opening his Zippo and sparking it alight with a single flip of his wrist, "this."

Price lit the makeshift torch he had fabricated out of his shirt and the squeegee. From the speed that the whole mess burst into flames, Nico realized he must have dipped it into the pool of gasoline.

"Oh, fuck," he whispered under his breath.

Price flung the torch in a spinning arc through the air and turned to run toward the car faster than any man his age should have been able. Nico's knuckles turned white gripping the wheel, and he was certain his heart stopped for the entire duration of the torch's arc through the air.

The Damned took just a second too long to realize what was happening. If it was a vampire as Price had claimed—and at this point, Nico found the assertion difficult to dispute—perhaps it came from a time when gas stations didn't exist. All the same, it seemed to realize its danger and turned to flee, but not before the torch struck the ground and a conflagration erupted through the night.

Nico felt himself being shoved aside as Carter hopped into the car and slammed on the gas. The Caddie practically burned rubber as it peeled out, and Nico looked over his shoulder to see a literal mushroom cloud engulf the Fill-Up as the underground gas reservoirs caught fire.

"Oh, shit!" Nico cried out.

"What is it?" Price panted, throwing his head over his shoulder to see what Nico was oh-shitting about.

A flaming silhouette was soaring into the night sky over the devastated convenience store.

"V…vampires can fly, can't they?" Nico whispered.

Price slammed on the brakes and as he nearly smashed his head into the dash Nico wished he had buckled up. The fiery figure traced a parabola through the night sky, in the opposite direction of where they were driving. It disappeared noiselessly, and Nico realized it had splashed into the nearby Cheyenne

Peaking Basin. The lake was black and invisible in the night.

"No," Price said, "But they can sure jump."

THREE

A few days before…

Rivulets of blood dripped from every corner of the violet-tinged world. Great cigarette burns appeared and disappeared all across her field of vision, blossoming and fading with the regularity of the tides, but in no discernible pattern.

And the soundtrack of the stereoscopic kaleidoscope from Hell was the beating of the awful drums. Louder and deeper and faster than even a jackhammer on the streets of Guangzhou, the sound seemed to emanate from between her ears.

Layered over it all was the incapacitating, overwhelming, gnawing hunger. She felt as though her stomach was trying to claw its way out of her torso. She was scarcely aware of her own body.

She was only vaguely aware of the voice and occasional face of Topan entering and leaving her vision, and pressing hard on her hand, and sometimes slapping her cheeks but doing little to rouse her from the deep reverie of agony.

Then one word, repeated over and over, gradually worming its way into her consciousness.

"Eat…eat…"

Topan's visage filled the full field of her vision.

"Eat!"

Some thick lump of flesh was under her nose. Unthinking, she bit into it, crunching through gristle, bone, and sinew with ease. She greedily gobbled down the first mouthful of meat, barely stopping to chew, then took another bite, and another.

The throbbing subsided. The drums receded. The purplish tinge to the world around her began to fade. And she found herself sitting in a chair in her sitting room, holding a severed human forearm in her hand.

Startled, she dropped it. The mangled mess of an arm clattered to the table and rolled once before settling against the centerpiece. Before she had gnawed through it in her blood-drunk rage, it had belonged to the person whose sprawled out body was arranged on the table like a feast. Bound and subdued, he was now scarcely even breathing, as the life leaked out of him from the arteries of his severed arm.

Her father.

She only became aware of the pained moaning as the horrible drumming faded from her ears. Her father's mouth was stuffed with cloth, tears flowing freely from his eyes.

Topan sat across the table from her, studying her with something in-between fascination and disdain. She dabbed her bloodied lips with a napkin.

"Not shocked to find yourself a cannibal?"

She shook her head demurely. His right eyebrow crawled up his face.

"No? How can that be?"

"Because you wish me to be shocked."

Laughing, Topan pounded the table.

"Cussedness! I admire it. I admire it more than almost anything else about you. And trust me, there's a lot to admire."

"I see you've lied to me. About a great deal."

Her father's breathing was becoming slower, strained. He was no longer conscious. She felt strangely disconnected from the whole scene, as though she were watching it from somewhere distant.

"Not so much as you might think. Most of what I said was true. I just held back the secret of what makes you so appealing."

"And what's that?"

"A potential beyond all reason. There is within you a potential to become the greatest of our kind, perhaps even to eclipse my own sire, Cicatrice. You'll meet him in time. He'll be very excited to meet you. And that's no small thing. Cicatrice doesn't let a whole lot of emotion cloud his day."

He sniffed at the air.

"And now that I've turned you, I see that I was right all along."

She felt her hands beginning to shake. The hunger which had abated was washing back in. The purple mist pushing in on the edges of her eyes told her that though her reason was regained, her hunger was far from sated. She saw herself devouring the old man by inches, from the toes up as he still breathed (even if just barely), and consuming every inch of his freshly flayed flesh before feeling full.

Unable to control herself she leaned forward and began to gobble away at the ragged flesh of her father's ruined shoulder.

"Yes, eat, eat. This first day you'll experience hunger like you've never known before."

She blinked, regaining her composure.

"But aren't you eating, Topan?"

"Not on fare such as this. Besides, this is all for you. Aren't you famished?"

"I am but this food tastes..."

"Ashen?"

Yes. Bitter. Worse than turned. Burnt.

She leaned in and to her surprise her tongue darted out and touched a pool of congealing blood. It tasted...off, though. Topan was on his feet as she closed her eyes. She could almost smell something, something that seemed bright like a light in her nose. Her nostrils flared and she tried to follow the source of the light.

Her eyes opened and her lips were pressed to the severed arteries of her father's missing arm. She felt Topan's heavy hand on her shoulder.

"What is it? What do you sense?"

"A power...a source...a..."

She suckled at the blood still dribbling from the dying man's arm. It tasted like warm maotai, *and the warmth spread through her almost instantly. Her eyes closed and she entered a state entirely unlike dreaming.*

It wasn't until Topan began shaking her that her eyes fluttered open. She finally felt full, but she looked down and saw that aside from those first few bites through his elbow, the father who had been her first meal was largely unmolested.

"I'm sorry, Topan, I lost track of time and..."

"Never be sorry for who you are, little one. I would say that even if you were no one of particular import. But would you believe me if I told you that in all my years of life I've never seen an immortal discover the power in the blood in her first night?"

The young girl rose and stroked the hair of the man who had raised her and who had filled her up so. He seemed so pathetic now, like a crumpled rag.

"At first I wanted to just eat him up. Strip the flesh from his bones and gobble it all down. But then I felt something. Like a light behind my eyes but I could smell it like an odor."

"It normally takes months, even a few years, for our kind to transition from feasting on flesh directly to drinking blood. You've nearly done so in a night."

"You've made me eat my father," she whispered.

He laughed.

"Would you have preferred your mother?"

He walked over to the broom closet and opened it, pulling her beloved mama, also tied up tightly and gagged. Mama dropped to her knees upon seeing Papa on the table, the tears flowing like the Zhu Jiang.

"I didn't know who you loved more. Girls tend to love their father. Mother-daughter relationships are...more fraught."

"Are you going to let her live?" she asked, the words already hollow before they left her mouth.

That shit-eating, snake charmer's grin which she had fallen for so many times before crossed his mouth.

"Of course not," he said, "I told you I would see to your parents. You can't leave loose ends like this behind. The memory of you alone, that's dangerous enough. But family? Searching for you? That's something we can't have. Besides, I haven't feasted yet tonight either."

Topan let his hand settle on Mama's mop of brown hair like a spider. Unbidden, a gasp came to her lips. The world was like moving through molasses, and only in spare moments did clarity abide.

"You're going to drink her blood?"

"Oh, no," Topan replied, his eyes shining in the moonlight, "In a century or so, when you're at the height of your power, that energy, that essence that you sensed in dear Papa here's blood? You'll be able to tap into it directly."

Topan's hand tightened on Mama's scalp. Mama began to roar, such as she could, behind her gag. Topan laughed, and though it seemed like nothing was happening, Topan's skin began to grow robust, his eyes began to glimmer, and he began to bear the look of satisfaction.

Mama, conversely, began to lose her sheen, the laugh lines under her eyes deepening into sharp wrinkles, her hair turning gray before the young girl's very eyes.

It was as though Topan was sucking the very life from her.

A moment later, reduced to a shriveled mummy, Mama's body stopped giving up its vital essence. Topan let go of her head and she tumbled forward, crumbling to dust upon impact with the floor.

"Now let's clean up this mess and get you home to America."

"You can't have her! You can't have her! She's mine, Cicatrice, mine, mine, mine, mine!"

"The giant of his own story," Cicatrice whispered in her ear.

Topan stood in the doorway, his fists raised in fury. He made quite a contrast to Cicatrice in his red, Western-style suit. Around his neck he wore a noose like a necktie. His face was distended with rage and he had the look of a man who hadn't slept in days. Cicatrice took a step forward, surreptitiously placing himself between Topan and Idi Han. He folded his hands behind his back.

"Hello, Topan," Cicatrice said, his voice utterly deadpan, "so nice to have you home after all this time."

Topan strode forward but stopped just short of laying hands on his patriarch.

"That's my get. I sired her. She is my gift to the ages."

"I am neither yours nor anyone's property," Idi Han said.

"Quiet, little one, or this will not go well for you after you're back in my hands."

"Do not call me that."

She glowered at him. He wheeled back, taking another look at her.

"You think you're someone special? Stop hiding behind your nursemaid's coattails, then, little one."

"I told you not to call me that anymore."

"Yes, she's chosen a name for herself," Cicatrice said, "One you taught her, in fact, Topan."

Topan's eyes narrowed. Cicatrice put his hand on Idi Han's shoulders and brought her around in front of him.

"Tell him," he said, tapping her shoulder.

"My name," she said, "is Idi Han."

"Idi…" Recognition dawned on his face. "The giant? From the story? I think you misunderstood the point."

"No. It's you who missed the point, Topan."

Topan looked from Cicatrice to Idi Han and back again. His anger either softened or he regretted threatening his sire. A voice which Idi Han did not recognize emerged from the smoke-filled doorway.

"Well, I'd say that's about enough primping and preening. I've little interest in internecine House Cicatrice politics."

Cicatrice, whom Idi Han had never seen so much as tremble, seemed to have developed a severe aneurysm at the sound of that voice. His grip tightened so much on her that he shattered both her shoulder blades. She gently tapped his hand and he relieved the pressure, her bones instantly knitting as he let go.

"Otto," Cicatrice said.

A man entered the room. He wore a sort of stylized armor, bronze but painted white in places, with a number of nasty barbs and hooks. His face was painted from the nape of his neck to his forehead with a broad white stripe, which continued, in a sense, onto his head in the form of a bleached white Mohawk. A wolf's pelt, complete with a wolfshead cowl, completed his rather eccentric ensemble.

By his side was a woman. She was clad in a labcoat and goggles and her face was speckled with oil, as though she had been pulled away from a workbench for this meeting. It took Idi Han a moment to realize that her hand was not flesh, but mechanical.

"Idi Han, this…*person*…is the patriarch of House Signari, Otto Signari."

Signari approached bullishly and grabbed Idi Han's hand. She almost wrenched away but he merely bowed and kissed the top of her hand delicately.

"Charmed," he said, with a wicked smile.

"And Sephera, an elder of the Teslans."

The woman nodded, adjusting the goggles on her head as though they were glasses and she was wearing them.

"Otto, Sephera, may I present my get, Idi Han?"

"Get?" Signari wore a contrived grin. "Well, now this *is* news."

"She's not yours!" Topan fairly shrieked.

Signari folded his arms.

"That's what your firstborn here keeps saying, anyway. That this delightful young member of our special fraternity of the night is rightfully his get. And that you stole her from him."

"I am no one's for the stealing," Idi Han said, taking a step forward.

Signari laughed, slapping his knee with the flat of his palm.

"I like her. She's a good one. Doesn't smell like much," Signari sniffed the air, and Idi Han surreptitiously stuffed the wreath of garlic she was still wearing into her *cheongsam*, "but then I guess you know these matters better than I do."

Topan sniffed the air, too, deliberately.

"Garlic. You're hiding her power. You don't want them to know how strong she really is."

He spotted the corner of the string around her neck and stepped toward her to grab it. As he reached out for her, Idi Han snatched his hand, twisting his wrist backwards, shattering every bone in his arm, and dropping him to his knees.

"Let's all keep our hands to ourselves," Cicatrice said, gently patting Idi Han's shoulder so that she released Topan and let him scuttle away as his wounds mended, "I must say, Otto, I'm used to Topan coming around, throwing tantrums, and usually demanding money. But what brings not only a House elder but a House patriarch to my doorstep on this of all nights?"

Topan's finger shot out, pointing in Cicatrice's direction.

"They're here to tell you that you have to give her back, Scar. Or it'll mean war."

Cicatrice snorted derisively.

"There hasn't been an open war between the Houses in three hundred years. You mean to tell me the Signaris would go to the mattresses over an internal House Cicatrice matter? I sincerely doubt that."

Signari rested his hand on the pommel of his sword, tapping it with each finger in turn.

"Right is right, Cicatrice. And it won't be just the Signaris."

Cicatrice turned a baleful eye to the one-handed woman, Sephera.

"You mean to tell me the Junkers are against me in this matter, too?"

Sephera cleared her throat; a gesture which it occurred to Idi Han was entirely vestigial.

"Well, you see, Father Cicatrice, with all due respect…"

"Oh, I see," Cicatrice said, cutting her off sharply but coldly, "It's not just two Houses. All twelve of you are arrayed against me."

Sephera nodded, seemingly genuinely chagrined.

"Then the council convened without my presence to deliberate?"

"This is a matter of some urgency, Father Cicatrice," Sephera said.

"Urgency? Decisions over siring and heirs in House Cicatrice? How could that possibly constitute an emergency?" Cicatrice eyed Topan. "What did he tell you?"

"Don't be obtuse, Father Cicatrice, please," Sephera mouthed, "It's unbecoming."

"This serial killer you're all so worried about?"

"Serial killer?" Idi Han asked, "An immortal serial killer?"

"Possibly," Sephera said.

"We don't know that," Signari stated flatly.

"More accurately I suppose I should say, a serial killer who preys upon immortals," Cicatrice corrected himself.

"It's no myth, Father Cicatrice. The data is as plain as the nose on my face."

"I can count as well as anyone, Sephera. I know there are more lives lost than can be accounted for by Inquisition activity or accidents or even by cold war. Yes, there is *something* preying upon our kind, whether you wish to call it a serial killer or something else."

"But what does that have to do with me?"

All eyes turned to Idi Han. Topan was the first to speak.

"You're my tonic, little one. You're my plan. My solution. The first rumors of the serial killer—or whatever you want to call it—started four years ago. I've been searching for someone worthy of siring for decades. Since the 1950s, wasn't it, *Father Cicatrice*? When we parted ways?"

"I seem to recall having to take you back under my wing since then."

"Yes, you're right. It's only in the last ten years that I really began to scour the Earth, obsessed with a single thought: somewhere, out there, was a human with the potential to become the most powerful immortal who ever lived. And he...*she*, rather... would root out the serial killer like a rat. It would be my contribution to history."

Cicatrice barked out a mirthless chuckle.

"And the council bought this load of horseshit? Without even seeking my presence to ask me if it were true?"

"Topan stood in your stead, old man," Signari said, "Your heir. Superior to all your elders. We thought it no great matter to have him stand in your stead. Especially when his grievance was the one before the council. Because of the conflict of interest, we thought it best to recuse you."

"Such a slight, Otto, I will never forget."

Sephera stamped her foot.

"Yes. It was a slight. A tiny cut to your honor. You lost face when your idiot crown prince appeared before the council behind your back. But this is such a small matter, Father Cicatrice. A matter of pride, really. Give the girl back to Topan. He's your heir, anyway. Perhaps finally having a get of his own to mentor will help domesticate him. Settle him down. Make him more like the get you always wanted."

Idi Han stepped forward. She realized what she had to do.

"Very well. I'll go with them."

"A selfless Cicatrice!" Signari sniggered, "Now I have seen everything."

Topan held his arms open; the smile on his lips suggesting all was forgiven. As if she had done anything wrong.

"Idi Han," Cicatrice said quietly.

She stopped mid-stride. She turned back to look at him.

"Where do you want to be?"

She pinched her eyes shut. Memories of the homestead came

back to her. Mama calling her in for supper. Papa keeping her up all night with ghost stories he shouldn't have been telling her (according to Mama.) The pigs, ducks, and goats. Even that damned good-for-nothing cat that had been too lazy to catch a rat in all its life.

"I want to be back home," she said, "In Guangdong."

In the uncomfortable silence that followed it seemed that each of the other four immortals had words, but none could give voice to them. She continued.

"But I understand that is not our way. An immortal must be guided, taught the code, taught how to stay safe, how to deal with all these new…conditions. So knowing that, if the choice was truly mine, I would stay with Father Cicatrice. But I am a small raft on a great ocean. I will not be responsible for a war among our kind. Not now. Not ever. So I'll go with Topan."

"You will not," Cicatrice said, "This is my manse and my House. The three of you have your answer. You can leave."

Sephera stamped her foot.

"Listen to reason, won't you, Father Cicatrice? A war? You'd have a war? Over what? How many in my House will have to die? How many in your House will have to die? Yes, Topan is acting like an infant. But give the baby his bottle and know that you're better than him."

"Go to Hell, Junker," Topan growled.

"Grow a spine and fight your own battles, coward," she rejoined.

Cicatrice slowly pulled a chair out from the table, turned it around to face his "guests" and seated himself before tenting his fingers.

"Sephera," he said, "I understand why you're here. There's never been any conflict between our houses. Of all the Great Houses, my interactions with yours could be called the most… congenial. So they sent you as the good cop. Knowing that to have twelve elders show up on my doorstep would raise my ire to such a state I would burn the world of immortals to the ground before giving way.

"And Otto is the bad cop. Delighting in the role, no doubt, from a grudge that dates back to a time before any other living immortal was sired. A time when we were not so wise, and more prone, perhaps, to childish displays of peacock plumage."

"You really should give up old vendettas, Cicatrice. It's unbecoming of a man your age."

"I'll settle accounts with you yet, Otto. That's a promise I've long stood by. But for the good of our kind, which must always be my paramount concern, I have long put off the revenge for our mutual sire."

"Oh, don't become all high and mighty on me…"

Cicatrice held up a hand to ask for silence, and even the overbold Otto Signari granted it to him.

"But this? This I cannot abide. A matter within my own House. Within my own lineage. A matter between my get and I. This is a matter that concerns no one not named Topan, Idi Han, or Cicatrice. But I know why the council is involved. My idiot former heir…" he looked at Topan. "Yes, if you hadn't guessed, you've been passed over in favor of your own get."

"You have no right…" Topan started to say.

Cicatrice stood. Without raising his voice, he continued.

"I have every right. I have the only right. I am patriarch of this House. The most powerful living immortal. None can challenge me. All my enemies exist at my pleasure. For the good of our kind. So that someday we will no longer need to be relegated to the shadows.

"But make no mistake of my consideration for weakness. The council would stand puffed up like a rooster on one matter so small they think I'll back down. But you know something? I'm not scared to take on twelve Houses. Twelve Houses are shitting their pants terrified to take on me. Not my House. Just me.

"You're children. Pants-wetting children. The only person here with anything approaching a backbone is my new get. And yes, she is my get. And my heir. And nothing can change that. You think you can push me down on this issue. And once I've set a precedent of giving an inch, you'll take ten thousand miles. You'll flay me hair by hair out of existence.

"Well, guess what? You want war over a tiny matter, a small matter, a matter so insignificant I couldn't possibly fail to back down? You have it. War it is, on behalf of my get. I would wipe every immortal from the planet and start fresh before I would give in to you and your joke of a council. Now leave my manse. Send your attackers if you really have the backbone to go through with it. But I know, as always, you won't.

"You are all dismissed from my presence."

Sephera seemed flustered. She nodded, and strode out the door. Signari, as always, was smiling.

"I've waited a long time for this, Scar."

"Enjoy the anticipation of our first battle, Otto. It's the only joy you'll get out of this."

Signari bowed elaborately and put his hand on Topan's shoulder.

"Come on, boy. A kingdom of ashes. That's what you'll inherit. But you can rebuild."

"Cicatrice," Topan growled.

"Topan," Cicatrice said, "I want to be clear on this matter. When this little mutiny of yours is finished and you come crawling back to me for the thousandth time to test my infinite mercy, be clear. Be one hundred per cent clear. There will be no mercy for you this time."

FOUR

Price's pants were already around his ankles. He fiddled with the key in the trunk lock like a cat burglar finessing a deadbolt.

"Come on, baby, come on…got it!"

The trunk popped open. Price kicked off his shoes and stepped out of his trousers. Nico hazarded a glance into the Caddie's massive trunk.

"Holy shit, Carter!"

Price's trunk looked like the storage closet of a museum—or a movie studio. Guns of every description sat alongside axes, crowbars, swords, and knives. More mundane supplies like bottled water, beef jerky, dehydrated meals, and candles filled up one corner. He was already pulling on jeans and knocking on the soles of a pair of heavy-duty steel-toed boots.

"You ever wonder why I drive a '63 Caddie, kid?"

Nico shook his head. Price couldn't hold back the shit-eating grin.

"Most trunk space of any car ever made."

Price dropped the boots on the ground and unrolled a black T-shirt.

"Somehow I doubt that," Nico replied.

Price shrugged.

"Well, that and a little thing called style."

Price slung a bandolier of shotgun shells over a shoulder and a bandolier of what appeared to be wooden stakes over the other. He slipped a sheathed machete onto his belt and buckled it, then started strapping a sawed-off shotgun to his other leg.

"So you're some kind of secret vampire hunter?"

Grunting, Price peeled back the bandage from his right wrist, allowing Nico to get a glimpse of a green double cross tattooed over his radial artery. It seemed spooky and ancient enough to be the sigil of an ancient secret society like the Illuminati. And the fact that Price had long kept it hidden seemed to suggest that as well.

"Inquisitor. But yeah, that's about the long and short of it, yeah."

"So what's the…plan?"

"The plan?"

Price reached into the trunk and with a reverence that belied his previous hurry, drew a tan leather or possibly deerskin jacket with tassels out of his collection of junk. He ran his hand along the painstakingly oiled surface of the jacket for just a moment before seeming to remember his earlier haste and threw it on. With the ensemble completed he looked like he could have stepped right off the stage of a '70s Dad Rock concert.

"The 'plan,' kid, is that you're going to get home. You said you came by bus?"

"What am I supposed to do, Carter? Wait by the crater that used to be the Fill-Up? How am I supposed to explain that?"

The faraway look in Price's eyes at that moment was something Nico had only ever seen on war veterans and in movies. "The Thousand Yard Stare" they called it sometimes. A symptom of deep, pervasive PTSD.

He sighed.

"You explain it, kid, by blaming it on that weird ex-con you worked with. 'He always was a firebug.' Some shit like that."

Price slammed the trunk shut loudly and walked back toward the driver's side. Nico felt liquid panic flood his heart and he hurried around the other way to block him.

"I'm not blaming this on you. What about that…that thing?"

"Kid, the longer you stand here in my way jawing about it, the closer that thing is to getting to civilization. If you really care—if you really give a shit—the best thing you can do is leave me to my job and make up the best cock-and-bull story you can to explain those bodies back there."

Nico's mind rushed. Jackie's family had a right to know

what happened. Didn't they? Even Cigarette Dick, well, sure, he had been a dick but no one deserved to die like that.

It was true there would be a lot of explaining to do. He'd have to make something up and quick, mostly involving how Carter had gone crazy, chopped off a guy's arms, tried to eat the donut lady's face, and then burned everything to cover it up. He'd say there'd been meth involved maybe...

But the truth is I can't unsee what I saw.

"You can't go after that thing alone, Carter. Either you take me with you or you have to kill me."

Price nodded.

"Option Three," he said.

With a speed and strength that belied his age, Price grabbed Nico by the scruff of his polo and tossed him out of the way. The last time Nico had slid across the macadam like that he had been seven years old, trying to pick a fight with Jorge Medrano, easily four years his senior and twice his size. On the playground he had been wearing shorts and both knees had been scraped to damn near the bone. This time his elbows were pretty fucked up, but at least he had been wearing slacks.

He rose to his knees, coughing; the old car's revving sound already filling the air. He looked up. Price had already turned the car around and was about to peel out down the highway in search of his quarry.

This is stupid. Really fucking stupid.

Nico stepped in front of the car and held out his hands, as though he was going to catch it by the headlights when it came. In the driver's seat, Price's eyes narrowed. He revved the engine once, twice. He didn't even bother saying anything. The message was clear: "Get out of the way, kid, or I'll run you over."

Nico shook his head.

"I'm coming with you," he shouted.

Price floored it. Nico gasped; his eyes wide as a deer's.

I should jump out of the way.

Instead, he braced himself, turning his head away from the onrushing vehicle and lifting his leg up into his chest like a flamingo. He waited a moment and didn't open his eyes again until he realized the hot yellow glow of the headlights in his face had disappeared. He turned.

Price had pulled up alongside him and was furiously unrolling the passenger's side window.

"You're a fucking idiot."

"I know."

"You barely even know me."

"Well, we've worked a few shifts together…"

"Why the fuck would you want to get involved in something like this?"

Good question.

"I've never been special. Never been privy to something special. I mean, vampires are real? How do you walk away from something like that?"

Price hung his head.

"I remember thinking the exact same thing when I was your age."

He turned off the car and stepped outside, reopening the trunk with just as much trouble as it had taken him last time. Nico joined him hesitantly.

"Can you shoot?"

"No."

"Know how to use a sword?"

"Hell no."

Price eyed him up and down. He suddenly felt naked in his dorky green embroidered polo, loser slacks, and unfitted ballcap with "Phillip's Fill-Up" embroidered on the front. He was a gas station clerk and had never been good enough to do anything else in his entire life.

Through clenched teeth Price asked, "Can you play baseball?"

"Well…yeah. Of course. Hell yeah, I can play baseball."

"Good enough."

Price reached into his voluminous trunk and pulled out a Louisville Slugger. Embedded deeply into the top half were long, razor-sharp steel blades. Nico took the bizarre weapon and traced an arc through the air with it. Used just like a bat, he could probably take someone's head off with one good swing.

Price tapped him on the chest.

"Remember: limbs, head. Everything else is crap. You slice a nightcrawler's belly open; he'll regenerate in no time flat. Now get in the fucking car, Mickey Mantle."

Nico nodded and hurried into the passenger's side, desperately trying to find a way to stash his implement of destruction so that it wouldn't gouge a hole in him if they hit an unexpected pothole. Price climbed in opposite and started the car.

"One last thing."

"Yeah?"

"Don't you fucking get me killed."

Nico shrugged.

"I'll do my best."

Burning rubber, they peeled off for the reservoir. Instantly, Nico had the feeling in the pit of his stomach that they were too late, like when he suddenly found himself alone in school after hours and all the lights turned off. Maybe it was his fault. Maybe if he had just listened and hadn't spent so long trying to be the hero…

And now look at me. I'm going to die. I can't fight that thing. It's going to rip my head off. And then my headless corpse will be a distraction and Price'll get killed, too. He'll be like, "Noooo!" but then The Damned will just…

He could've peed his pants just then. That felt a lot like being in school after hours, too.

Man up, Nico.

That was his dad. Back home in Puerto Rico. Back before…

"Stop daydreaming, kid. We're here."

Nico glanced along the edge of the lake. The car's headlights created a pool of visibility in the otherwise inky blackness of the night.

"There," Nico said, pointing.

Footprints led out of the water, as though the Creature from the Black Lagoon had emerged onto land. The prints were anthropomorphic, but inhuman. Almost like Bigfoot.

"Say, you don't think vampires are the source of…"

"Shut the fuck up, kid."

Nico swallowed his words. The prints led from the edge of the water to a small copse of trees. Price stepped out of the car and Nico did the same.

"All right, stay here. Stay in the headlights."

"Are the headlights UV or something?"

Price stared at him.

"No, kid. They're just lights. Unless you can see in the dark?"

"Are you pissed now because you wish you'd installed UV lights?"

Price shook his head.

"UV doesn't do anything to them. The sun is this whole other…thing. Look, just stay in the fucking light where I can see you. I'm going to go check out that grove. And if I don't come back, uh…"

Price thought for a moment, couldn't seem to come up with anything witty or useful, and simply shrugged. Machete in one hand, sawed-off in the other, he disappeared into the treeline.

Nick swallowed a lump in his throat. Suddenly, every scary movie and campfire story he had ever seen or heard came rushing back to him. And each and every one seemed to have a scene like this, where the heroes or the victims split up, and then one wasn't paying attention and…

"Get thee behind me, Satan!"

Nico turned and waved his bat towards the figure on top of the Caddie. Price came rushing back.

"What's wrong, kid?"

Of course, there was no figure on top of the car.

"Nothing, I just thought I…"

Price grabbed him by the scruff again, and as if to prove his above-average strength, pulled Nico up onto his tiptoes.

"Kid, I didn't think I needed to say anything…but shut the fuck up. That's all you have to do. You have one job. What's your job?"

"To shut the fuck up."

Price shook him.

"Try again. What's your job?"

"To…"

Nico pinched his lips closed. Price nodded.

"Okay."

Price stomped off into the woods again. Nico wiped a bead of sweat away from his forehead. This was not going well. This was not going well at all. One more shock to the system and he was going to unload his cheese and tuna sub into his work slacks. And he only had one other clean pair of pants...

Of course, none of that matters now.

"Kid! Come on up here!"

Nico glanced back at the Caddie.

"Should I bring the keys?"

"Eh...no, leave 'em. They'll be fine for a second. It looks like we've got nothing to worry about."

Nico stumbled up into the copse of trees and quickly found Price by the glow of a penlight. Price looked positively demonic in the low light.

"Take a look at this."

He pointed the penlight towards the ground. The Damned lay there. At least, what was left of it did. The thing's fur was still slightly charred from its earlier encounter with a fireball. But the thing had been hacked to pieces. Its severed head lay glaring limply; eyes open but dead, a few feet from the rest of its body. Arms and legs were strewn all akimbo, hacked off at elbows, knees and shoulders willy-nilly.

"Limbs and head," Nico said, "A friend of yours?"

Price bit his lower lip.

"I'll be honest kid: I don't see another Inquisitor doing this. I got lucky at the gas station but I was pretty sure there was no way I was walking away from this."

"You thought you were going to die and you brought me along?"

Price cocked his head and fixed Nico with a withering glare.

"Yeah. That's what I did. I forced you to come along. Twisted your fucking arm."

"All right, all right. So...is there like...something else that can do this? Are werewolves real? Frankensteins?"

Price tapped the penlight against his teeth.

"The nightcrawlers pretty much keep the riffraff out of

Vegas. This doesn't really look like a werewolf's work…I mean; this was done with a blade."

"So werewolves are real?"

"Just assume everything's real, kid. But what's really weird is take a look at that."

Price shone the penlight at the ground leading out of the copse in the opposite direction. A set of horse's hooves led out.

"Centaur…?"

"No such thing."

"Can we catch it?"

"We can try."

FIVE

Last night…

Benito whistled. He was a man who appreciated carnage and this…this was a metric fuckton of carnage.

"Place is a goddamned abattoir."

The little chapel was all but painted in blood. That meant humans had died here along with immortals. The trail of blood they had followed to this spot continued, in a sense, with a series of bodies in a row, connected by blood trails. Cashley's disciples, Benito guessed, kicking one onto her back. Every single one was a woman.

"Never been much for keeping a circle myself," Benito said, "But Cashley had a way of making it extra gross."

"They're just mortals, Benny," Hofstra said.

Benito turned to look at Hofstra's skinny, acne-riddled face and vulture-like nose. Whoever had granted him the Long Gift hadn't based it on his looks. With a single motion he reached out, cupped the back of Hofstra's skull, and slammed his head into the ground, smashing a tile. He waited until Hofstra had extricated his face from the ground, over-long proboscis gradually reforming itself to its original, ass-ugly design, before speaking.

"I know they're mortals, ass clown. I'm saying Cashley is a degenerate."

"Was a degenerate," Piker announced from the front of the temple.

Piker held up the top of Cashley's brainpan. Had he still been alive, Benito would've shuddered at the grotesque sight of Cashley's ruined eyes. So that was why he always wore those blocky sunglasses.

"This is weird, Benny," Hofstra said, apparently none the worse for wear, as he planted his fists on his hips, "No fixer would leave a job

in a state like this. What if someone found Cashley and planted him back in the dirt? He could regenerate."

"Maybe it wasn't fixers," Benito growled.

The rest of the gang was clattering around, looking for loot and, to a lesser extent, clues. Carson had picked up a big old sword from one of the corpses and was turning it back and forth in the waning starlight. Without a word, Benito took it from him and glanced up and down its length. It was the kind of blade an Inquisitor would use.

"Glog," Carson said, kicking the woman's arm so that her wrist turned upward. The telltale tattoo seemed to mock him.

"Shit," Benito grunted. "If this is one of these local, super in-step glogs..."

With the blade he cut the woman's jumpsuit from her breast, and then dug down into the flesh. Funny that she wore no bra. One of Cashley's weird proclivities, no doubt. Then the blade struck metal. He knelt down and pulled it out.

"What's that?" Hofstra asked, hanging over Benito's shoulder.

Just for good measure, he shattered the ugly fuck's nose again. The blinking device, attached to the dead woman's heart, should have been obvious enough for anyone, even a retard like Hofstra, to identify.

"A transponder. On a dead man's switch. This place'll be crawling with glogs any minute now. If it's not already."

He tossed the transponder down on Hofstra's prone form. He struggled to catch it, missed, and it clattered away elsewhere. He rose to go retrieve it, but Benito gave him a taste of boot.

"Leave it! Moron!" Benito whistled sharply, and waved his hand up in the air as though lassoing a bull. "Yo! Forget the spoils. Forget the bounty, too. We've got to get out of here. Bali bali!"

The gang of fixers groaned but obeyed, making their way back to the front of the temple and the still-running Hummer that waited outside.

"What's got you scared? They's just glogs, ain't they?" Carson grunted.

"You don't know these Las Vegas types. They're not the low-rent gypsies you're used to dealing with. They're militarized."

Piker was carrying Cashley's body in one hand and the skullcap someone had made of his head in the other.

"We should at least take Cashley's body. The lepress put a good bounty on him."

"Leave it," Benito said, "I don't want to get accused of bounty poaching. If another fixer doesn't claim it in a few days, then we'll claim it. But I don't want to show up at Damiana's manse with a body and find out someone else already took credit. I'd be a laughingstock and none of us would ever get work again."

"No one else is going to claim it."

Benito looked up. Sven had barely spoken since they'd arrived. In fact, he'd been standing in the same spot the whole time. Sven was Benito's trusted number two and had the best nose in the whole gang. He beckoned to Benito.

Benito approached. A severed head and a body lay crumpled at Sven's feet. Sven turned the face upwards so Benito could see it.

"MacVicar, too?"

Sven nodded and pointed toward a body crumpled in the aisle.

"Something went wrong here, boss. Real wrong."

Benito let his lower jaw jut out.

"Well, I guess we'll never know what. At least we can claim the bounty. Let's go."

"We can find out what happened. Boss, I know there's no love lost between you two..."

"You're right, there isn't. But I know what you're going to say. Don't let that affect my nose for business. I got a great big mound of Sicilian soil back home and I can easily afford to bury him. Then we can find out what's what and put him down again if need be. That what you were going to say?"

Sven shrugged, ever stoic.

"Fine. Grab him."

The Hummer punched a hole in the compound's back fence just as a caravan of Inquisition vehicles rolled in the front.

Scav shuddered with surprise as an angry, neck-shattering slap broke his repose.

"Wake up, you derelict."

Scav's eyes fluttered open just as a kick to the ribs caused his side to distend concavely inward. He spluttered and sat up sharply. Only a bare sheen of soil covered him, the sort of miserly amount that a child who refused to share his ball on the playground would've grudgingly given up. And true to that expectation, his brother Benito towered over him, a hulk of a man whose vacuous eyes shone in the moonlight, fluttering the burial shroud he had laid over his brother like a handkerchief in the wind. He was joined in a ring (well, hexagon, really) around Scav's supine body by five of the dirtiest, smelliest, angriest fixers who'd ever worked a job.

"Rise and shine, sleeping beauty," Benito said, driving the point home with another kick, You feeling better now that big brother took care of you?"

Scav's head was swimming. His hands went instinctively to his neck. There was something wrong. He hadn't felt pain like this…or much at all really…since MacVicar had granted him the Long Gift. Slowly, the bits and pieces of the last night began to reassemble in his mind like a jigsaw puzzle.

He'd been decapitated. After that, there was only blackness, emptiness. Not even the fitful dreams and vague awareness of his surroundings that usually marked his days asleep in his native soil. If that was death—true death—then Scav had to be at least partially grateful to his older brother for finding him.

"Benito!" Scav rasped, "It's so good to see you, brother!"

Scav struggled to rise but one of the goons grasped his shoulder with a hamhock of a hand and gently pressed him back down to a sitting position.

"If you're thinking to prey on my brotherly affections, you're barking up the wrong tree, Italo."

Benito spoke English for the benefit of his crew, but Scav was instantly transported back to his youth. Whenever he heard a sentence like that in their Sicilian dialect, he knew that it was about to be followed by being tossed off a roof, or having his pocket change stolen, or some other minor ignominy or pain.

"I would never dream of leaning on your 'brotherly affections.' I know what drives you, Benny. I haven't suddenly gone soft in the head, you know. I've scored a big payday. Big."

Benito looked around, making a big show of glancing from horizon to horizon, even raising his hand to his forehead to shield himself from an imaginary sun.

"And yet I don't see shit."

"I've got information you can't pass up, Benny. I mean it. It'll get you in good with Father Otto."

Benito growled.

"About Cashley? Father Otto doesn't give two shits about Cashley." Benito jammed his index finger into his brother's chest. "And I wouldn't try to claim that bounty on his head from the lepress, either. We already claimed it."

Scav shook his head.

"That's fine. I don't mind. But that's not what I mean. It's not about Cashley."

Benito raised his eyebrows. Scav could see he'd gotten his brother's attention at last.

"What then?"

The question barely needed to be asked.

"The Hunter of the Dead."

A snort erupted from his brother's stoic face. All six of the gangbangers practically fell over themselves laughing. When Benito finished, he effortlessly smashed Scav's nose up into his skull.

"Try selling a Cicatrice on a fairy tale. Father Otto hasn't got time for that bullshit."

"Let me ask you something. All of you." Scav glanced around at the six dull faces. "You know me. You knew MacVicar. You saw the carnage at Cashley's compound. Is that something he and I are capable of?"

"He is a weakling," one of Benito's deadbeat thugs, Carson, said, scratching at his long, greasy hair. "Both of them were."

"Killing Cashley's one thing," Piker added, "but there were six newborns there, too. That's a tricky fight for two fixers. Not to mention there was a glog at their back."

"You're all missing the point," Sven, who hardly ever broke his silence needlessly, said. "Everyone there was dead: fixer, target, glog, and bystander. Someone else swept in."

Benito fixed his gaze on Scav.

"And you mean me to believe it was some guy on a big black horse with a magic sword and the power to melt immortal brains with just a glare?"

Benito turned his back, but gave no other indication of

his thoughts. He took a few steps away from the ring, so Scav tentatively attempted to rise, but the pressure Sven applied to his temples would've been enough to kill a mortal so he remained seated. When Benito turned back around, he mysteriously had a mortar and a pestle in his hand.

"Oh, fuck me!" Scav shouted, attempting to scuttle backwards but immediately ramming up hard against Sven's legs, who immediately kicked him back into the center of the ring.

"You remember this?" Benito asked, raising the mortar and the pestle needlessly.

Of course.

The ceremonial objects were unmistakable. Relics of their childhood. Their real youth, back before Benito had been turned. In his hands, the silver ceremonial objects were just an ordinary bowl and stick. Even if there were holy water contained within, without a faithful hand present…

Oh, shit.

"Oh, shit, indeed."

Did I say that out loud?

"Yes, you did. I stole these from our childhood church. You remember? Mama used to take us to mass three times a week, sometimes every day. Until the cancer laid her low. I remember, when she first got laid up in the hospital my first thought was, 'Thank God. Now I can just lie about going to mass.'"

Hofstra, the omega of the group, sniggered like a schoolboy.

"Ice cold, Benny, ice cold."

Benito gave a look like he wanted to beat Hofstra with a 2x4 until he shut up, but perhaps in front of Scav he had to maintain solidarity.

"I remember no matter how hard she beat me, I never believed. But you, you loved all that God shit. You even took it with you to the other side. I thought there was something wrong with me when I brought you across. But now I know it was the poison you carried in your veins. Faith."

Faithless, the mortar and pestle were just objects to Benito. But as soon as the holy water struck Scav, it would instantly burn him with the force of his own faith. Benito had always been surprisingly enterprising in devising torture methods.

Benito raised the pestle high above his head and then brought it down like a butcher's knife. The liquid splattered all over Scav, who hissed and backed away from it. A drop got in his eye and he dug in to claw the offending orb out entirely. But when he stopped moving and held his regenerating eye in his hand, he realized he was in no pain at all.

"This isn't holy water."

Benito swung the pestle and the mortar in arcs around each other, as though he were a magician vamping in preparation for a trick.

"Its maaaagic, just like your God. Except instead of water into wine, Italo, I've turned water into…" Benito splashed what felt like half a liter directly into Scav's face. His remaining eye suddenly opened wide as he recognized the smell. "…kerosene."

"Oh, Lordy!" Benito cried out, turning and facing the ceiling as though he were truly moved, "It's a miracle! From useless holy water into goddamned lamp fuel!"

When Benito turned back, he gave up the game and simply splashed the whole pestle's payload onto Scav. He raised his foot for a kick and Scav held his arms up to fend off the blow that was coming next, but Benito was so tall it didn't matter. He lifted his jackbooted foot up into the air and brought it down squarely on his brother's windpipe, driving him backwards and onto his back.

Scav grunted under his brother's immense power. He had been strong in life, and was even moreso in death. Scav had noticed over his years that some immortals developed their powers in unusual ways. Some became gradually immune to the light; others could control their lifedraining with frightening exactitude. Some claimed to have powers of clairvoyance or transmogrification, but Scav had yet to see that actually demonstrated. Benito, being the typical thug that he was, had simply grown in raw, unchecked strength over the years.

Scav liked to think that his own power was survival, even in the harshest of conditions. He was like a cockroach. Let the nuclear rain come. He would survive. He had survived The

Hunter of the Dead after all. Just as he would survive this latest encounter with his sire and brother.

Scav didn't have to breathe, of course, but the real discomfort came from the feeling that with a twist of his shin, Benito could've popped Scav's head off his neck like a bottlecap. Benito leaned deliberately forward, shattering Scav's neck under the pressure. Benito's crew grunted peals of idiotic approving laughter.

"I always knew one day I'd have to take care of the mistake I made in siring you."

Scav pointed at his neck. Benito nodded and lifted his foot slightly, allowing the air back into Scav's dead lungs and his spine to begin to mend.

"You can't kill me," he wheezed, "It's the code."

"'Immortals shall not kill immortals?' Oh no no no, my dear brother, you are Houseless. MacVicar adopted you and became your sire, remember? Snatched you right out from my hands. And he never granted you his blessing. That means you have no sire, you have no House, you have no rights. I could kill you and no one would even bat an eye."

"MacVicar promised he would free me after we destroyed Cashley. You just have to let me talk to the lepress. Father Otto will grant an exception."

Benito put a cigarette in his mouth and Hofstra fell all over himself to strike a match and light it.

"Sounds like a lot of trouble. Plus it calls our bounty into question…"

"But what about The Hunter? People need to know about The Hunter."

Benito raised the lit cigarette over his brother, as though determined to drop it on his kerosene-soaked body.

"Why would I make it up?" Scav whimpered.

"You know, Benny, you kind of had a good idea earlier."

All eyes turned to Sven.

"What?" Benito asked, cocking his head.

"Why don't we send him to Father Cicatrice? This is his town."

Suddenly, Benito's eyes glittered with avarice.

"I'm picturing it now, boys. A pathetic, battered Signari fixer shows up on Cicatrice's doorstep. Houseless, he can't go home. But he thinks maybe he can trade information about Cicatrice's favorite boogey man for protection. Maybe cash. And then we have a mole in the organization, don't we?"

SIX

Price climbed up onto the hood of the Caddie. Sticking his hands behind his head, he sprawled out, lying back against the dashboard glass. Nico remained hunched up at the front of the hood, hugging his legs.

"How does a horse outrun a car?" Nico asked finally.

Without looking back to check, Nico guessed Price was shrugging.

"I don't know, kid."

"Maybe it was a vampire horse. Is there such a thing?"

Nico glanced back. Price shook his head.

"No. I mean, it's possible. Animals, I mean, they can be turned, but they don't last long. There's all these rules you have to follow. No sunlight and sleeping in the daytime and I don't know. We just got fucked, that's all. Happens all the time. Nothing prepares you for being an Inquisitor like constant disappointment."

Nico nodded.

Sounds like my whole life has been preparing me for this, then.

"So what do we do now?"

Price made a noise like an old-timey locomotive powered by mucus.

"Now we shake hands and wish each other the best of luck and…"

"Don't you pull that shit on me, Carter."

"Well, look who's getting so big for his britches. Sorry to clue you in on this, Nico, but the Fill-Up's gone and you're not my boss anymore."

Nico turned away. He hoped there weren't any tears running

down his face. He wasn't crying, but maybe there were stress tears. He couldn't really tell.

"So you be the boss, Carter. I don't have any ego in this game. I just want to help. But you can't tell me, 'Hey, Harry, there's a world full of wizards but you've got to go back and live on Privet Lane.'"

For a moment, Price was silent.

"Is that a…what is that, a movie or something?"

"Dammit, Price!"

Nico popped his ballcap off and ran his fingers through his sweat-drenched hair. He jumped off the hood of the car and started to walk away, changed his mind, and found himself beating a circuit into the dirt. Finally he looked up at Price when he was certain his face was dry.

"Where do we go? What do you do when you don't know what to do?"

Price took a deep breath.

"Kid, I'm really not the type of person you want to be following around. And I say that not because I really care about you. I've known you a little while, you're fine, but I don't really know you. I don't care what happens to you. You could get eaten by a vampire, and I'd shake it off the same way I've shaken off when lovers and family have been eaten in the past. But you're looking at me like I'm something special and I'm just not. I'm not even really a good Inquisitor. I'm kind of…a fuck-up."

"Well, who are the non-fuck-up Inquisitors? Take me to them. Maybe they'll give me some damn answers."

Price sat up. His face was suddenly alive, ideas rushing between his eyes.

"Actually…that's not a bad idea."

In his green polo and work pants, Nico felt instantly out of place in the funeral home. Thinking just a second too slowly, he snatched the ballcap from his head, but the jig was up. A very short woman in a demure black dress, arms jangling with brace-lets, stepped around from the podium and charged them as fast as her high-heeled pumps would allow. Nico wasn't certain, but he could've sworn her right eye was glass.

"Gentlemen, I'm afraid this is a closed…oh, Carter, it's you. You still have to leave."

"Bonaparte," Price said through clenched teeth, inclining his head toward the funeral director. "Little late for a funeral, isn't it?"

Nico's eyes darted around the room. Something about the funeral seemed off. A few family members were holding court at the front of the room, and a woman was kneeling at the coffin, apparently weeping. The pews were mostly full with darkly clad mourners. Externally it seemed like any other funeral Nico had ever been to.

But who holds a funeral in the middle of the night?

"This is a closed service, Carter," the woman, Bonaparte, said.

She put her hand on Price's shoulder and started to wheel him toward the door.

"At 3 am?" Nico asked.

With a visible effort, Price wrenched himself out of her grip.

"This is one of ours, isn't it? And you didn't even invite me. Spite is an unflattering trait."

It suddenly struck Nico what was off about the funeral. Machetes dangled at sides, every suit pocket seemed to bulge with a weapon, and wooden stakes seemed to make up disproportionate amounts of ensembles. The mourners were all loaded for bear, like Price. Even Bonaparte wore steel strapped to her side.

"Was it someone I knew?"

"Carter, you're making a scene. I know you don't have much dignity left, but…"

"Well, damn you, Bonaparte! At least tell me it was no one I knew."

A grim frown etched itself across Bonaparte's face. Price pushed her out of the way and stomped to the front of the mortuary chapel. Nico crushed his hat in his hands and tried to avoid Bonaparte's gaze. When he risked a glance he saw she was staring right at him, had been the whole time. Awkwardly, he cleared his throat.

"This is, um, a beautiful building you've got here."

"I wouldn't get involved with him, Nico. I know Carter Price seems like a pretty together guy. Cool, even. But you don't know him like I do."

"How…how did you know my name?"

Have these Inquisitors been watching me? Considering me for training? Maybe they put a camera in the Fill-Up to keep an eye on Price, and instead they saw me and thought I might be a good candidate and…

She tapped the plastic nametag affixed to his shirt.

"'Nico Salazar, Shift Manager.' Stick to shift managing, kid. Carter will lead you nowhere good."

Price's gait was grim and slow as he returned from the casket.

"Miranda."

Bonaparte nodded.

"She was a good…Inquisitor."

"One of the best."

"Bonaparte, I know there's a lot under the bridge between us, but I genuinely didn't come here to spar. And I'm sorry about Miranda. I know you two were close as well."

Sighing, Bonaparte seemed to relax.

"What do you want, Carter?"

"Can we talk for just a minute? Alone."

Bonaparte's lower jaw jutted out.

"I need the room!" she announced in a booming voice.

Like automatons the mourners rose and marched out of the chapel, streaming past Nico and Price. Most gave Price dirty looks, but a few pressed his shoulder. When the room was empty, Price unslung his stake bandolier and sent it crashing to the ground.

"God damn it, Bonaparte, why do you always have to make a big production number out of every little fucking thing?"

"You are grating on my last nerve, Carter. Normally I can stomach almost anything from you, but tonight…"

"All I meant is, couldn't you just have stepped around the corner?"

Nico could've sworn the woman was about to blush, but the

color never actually rose to her cheeks. She turned and walked slowly down the aisle towards the open casket.

"I guess that hadn't occurred to me."

"Why kick over a molehill when you can scale a mountain instead?"

"What do you want, Carter? I'm in no mood to discuss fighting philosophy. We've been over this ground a thousand times. And that's why we don't work together anymore."

Price nodded, seemingly acknowledging the détente.

"I came across something today I can't really explain."

"Well, you see, Carter, when a man and a woman love each other very much…"

"I saw one of The Damned."

Bonaparte crossed her arms.

"Of course you did."

"Ask the kid. He's a civilian."

The petite woman's eyes slid over Nico.

"One I'm sure you haven't coached."

Nico held up his hands as if warding off an attack.

"Hey, lady, I just found out vampires were real today. Nobody's coached me on shit."

Her eyes went first from Price then to Nico then back again.

"Describe the monster you saw today."

Nico took a deep breath.

"It was hairy and gray. Its jaw was missing. Like one of those creepy fish…I can't remember the name."

"A lamprey," Price said, his smirk obvious.

Nico snapped his fingers and pointed at Price.

"That's the one."

"All right," Bonaparte said, holding up a hand, "So you saw one of The Damned. What do you need? A legion of my best people to help you hunt it down?"

"That's just the thing, Bonaparte. That fucker's dead. That's what I need help with."

"Dead? How do you mean dead?"

"Uh, not living? It was an ex-vampire?"

"He's passed on," Nico said. "This vampire is no more. He has ceased to be. He's expired and gone to meet his maker."

Nico and Price grinned at each other, a rare moment of shared warmth.

"All right, all right! Sorry I asked. But dammit, Carter, how is that even possible? What could kill one of The Damned? It wasn't you, was it?"

Price shrugged.

"I'd love to take credit for it..."

"It was already dead when we found it," Nico chimed in.

Price nodded and jerked his thumb in Nico's direction.

"What the kid said."

Bonaparte rubbed her chin. She turned and faced Miranda's coffin, putting her hands behind her back.

"You've heard about this 'serial killer' the nightcrawlers are all on edge about?"

"Sure, I've heard rumors."

"I haven't," Nico said.

Bonaparte smiled.

"I like him."

"He's a pain in my ass."

"Same way you were a pain in mine?"

Price grunted and folded his arms. Bonaparte gestured for them to sit next to each other on a pair of folding chairs. The next row forward she sat side-saddle on a chair so she could turn around to face them.

"Here's the deal, kid," Bonaparte started to say.

"Don't you people ever get tired of calling me 'kid?'"

"'Tiger,' then. Here's an education for you. The first step to being an Inquisitor is knowing your enemy. Knowing how he thinks, knowing what he fears. If you want one of these one day..." She raised the stack of bracelets she wore on her right wrist. The jewelry had been cleverly hiding a tattoo: a green double cross with a tree branch and a sword, just like Price's. "...you'll pay attention to what Carter has to teach you. But remember you can always come back here and learn from the big boys."

"Whoa, whoa, whoa," Nico said, "I didn't sign up to join your crazy party. I just didn't want to be left behind."

"Yeah," Price agreed, unscrewing the top of his flask and

taking a sip of something putrid, "and I sure as shit didn't agree to train him."

"Sure," Bonaparte said, "That's not what's happening here. Well, I've got an army of mourners waiting outside for us to finish chatting, so you'll forgive me if I cut through the shit. I'm under no illusions about what an individual Inquisitor can accomplish. Carter's going to give you some cock and bull story about how staying independent is what keeps us strong or some shit, but the truth is that we've been doing that for over a hundred years and god damn it, it just doesn't work."

"A single Inquisitor working alone or with an apprentice doesn't endanger the whole organization when he's captured or killed," Price said, "Your little plan to unionize, organize, militarize? Put all of our eggs in one stupid basket? That's going to get us all wiped out at once, *Godfather*-style."

Price took a long swig from his flask and passed it to Nico. Nico stared at the inscription on the flask. It read, *Exurge domine et judica causum tuam.* Something about God judging something. He sniffed the liquid inside. It smelled like rocket fuel, or possibly some kind of bottom shelf bourbon. He pretended to take a drink and handed it back.

"So word slips out that more nightcrawlers are getting killed than the average. They all keep tallies, their little Houses. They always know how many there are, how many there are supposed to be."

"No nightcrawler is supposed to shit out another nightcrawler without his House patriarch's consent," Price added.

Bonaparte nodded.

"So now there's the legend of a serial killer. First thought is: an Inquisitor. They shook us down. They shook us down bad. But the truth is for all our tricks, for all our training, we're just not taking out enough of them to really make a difference to their numbers."

"Then why bother?" Nico asked, instantly regretting it.

"Because every one counts," Bonaparte and Price replied in near unison before exchanging a glance and then looking away in embarrassment.

"Anyway," the woman continued, "The next guess would

be an oldblood. An ancient, powerful vampire, gone off the reservation for some reason. It's as good a guess as any. But they can't find him. And their damn records are too good. No babies without permission, remember? The power differential is right, but it's highly unlikely there's an oldblood missing without anyone knowing."

"One of The Damned would be strong enough," Price said, "But from what you saw tonight, kid, do you see one of those monstrosities hanging back in the shadows and picking off nightcrawlers now and again?"

Nico shook his head. Bonaparte rose and began to strut down the aisle. Price and Nico followed her until they came to the altar at the head of the chapel.

"So you can see why we're so confused," Bonaparte said, "Nothing this powerful should be this patient. Nothing this patient should be this powerful. So we mostly chalked it up to a funny little mystery in the vampire community. Maybe one day it'll turn out there's an STD or something weird. No point obsessing over it the way they do, right? We've had people looking into it but not exactly clocking any overtime. That is, until today."

Bonaparte opened the tabernacle which sat on the altar. She reached in and drew out a tiny chunk of something black and globby, sealed in a Ziploc bag. Nico crossed himself.

"Those don't look like any communion wafers I've ever seen."

"Jesus Christ," Price whispered, about as irreverently as those words could be spoken.

He held out a hand.

"May I?"

Without saying a word, Bonaparte let him take the baggie from her and examined it from all angles. Nico wasn't looking as closely as Price was, but from what he could tell it looked like a shard of metal coated with some kind of black, oily substance.

"This can't be possible," Price breathed, "It's a children's story. A fairy tale nightcrawlers tell their kids to keep them in line."

"As someone who's witnessed about five different kinds of

fairy tales crawl out of the Grimm Brothers volume and try to eat me tonight," Nico said, "may I be the first to suggest that we dispense with all the 'gee whiz' bullshit and you just tell me what that is?"

"I really like him," Bonaparte repeated.

"That, kid," Price said, shaking the baggie as if by giving it a good shake it would cease to be and the world would begin to make sense again, "Would be the first proof (that I'm aware of) of the existence of The Hunter of the Dead."

SEVEN

The Dark Ages…

Brother Pablo swallowed the gasp which threatened to spring from his throat as they ripped the blindfold from his face. The woman who stood before him was entirely missing a solid quarter of her face. A line, more or less, drawn from the bottom of her right ear to the corner of her nose and everything below it was sheared down to the bone.

A ghastly smile began to take shape on the half of her mouth which retained lips. Pablo struggled to coax words from his suddenly desert-dry mouth in his finest liturgical Latin.

"In…in the name of His Holiness, I bring you a message from Rome, Lady Lilith."

She spoke, surprising him by falling into the vernacular of his Iberian home. "I am no lady. Not in any peerage which you and yours would recognize."

The two brutish men who stood on her right and left, but a few steps below her on the dais, began to chuckle. Pablo felt worms tighten around his belly and worried he might soil his travelling cloak. The half-faced woman was staring at him expectantly.

"How…how shall I address you, then?"

Her glacial mask softened and he knew that he had chosen the right words. For now at least.

"I am no more and no less than the mother of my household," she said, and placed a hand atop of the heads of each of her two factotums, "and all who dwell within."

A chain jangled off to Pablo's right side, and as hard as he tried to keep his eyes locked forward on her, he couldn't help but catch a glimpse out of the corner of his vision of the horrors of her throne room. The perimeter was littered with trophies from her favorite victims, in display cases like a museum's or a library's.

There was the lute of a famous minstrel, with his hands still attached, locked in place by rigor mortis. The walls were hung with the hides of men. Some were carved with ancient and arcane spells. Others had been inked and colored to form surprisingly complex tapestries. The centerpiece was the member of a famous lothario. She had ordered it dipped in wax while still engorged, then severed, so that it would remain erect for all time.

Chained at regular intervals between the displays were men and damsels—slaves, Pablo realized—kneeling, naked, and shivering.

"Mother Lilith, then," Pablo said, trying to keep his voice from faltering.

"Lilith sounds so formal. Stiff. My children call me Lily…like the lily of the fields."

Pablo pressed his lips together. The pope had warned him that the Luchesi woman was capricious—some said mad—and ran cold like Alpine snow one moment and hot like Vesuvius the next. There were rumors that the girl was Urban's own bastard daughter—but Pablo thought that madness. The pontiff had not spent nearly enough time in Rome for such dalliances. Then again, only a few moments would really have been required of him…

"Will…will you hear my message?"

Lily folded her arms. She stood upon the dais adorned in apparel unlike any he had ever seen before. Something about it screamed royalty, and yet it was impossible to deny the dark reversal of a papal gown as well. In all flowing crimson and violet, she seemed like far more than a mere human.

"Otto," she said, letting her hand fall on the brow of the man on her left, "My shield-bearer and protector. What say you?"

The man she had named Otto—Otto Signari, if the papal factotums had appraised him correctly—stepped forward, his blood-daubed ceremonial armor clanking as he stepped. He was a beast of a man, and his reputation both north and south of the Alps was such that Pablo found himself reciting the Ave Maria over and over in his head.

As though he were an animal tracking prey, Signari approached and sniffed at Pablo. It seemed as though Signari's lower right jaw, like that of his matriarch's, was missing, but when he spoke it became *obvious that his face had merely been painted with cosmetics to appear that way.*

"There can be no peace with men. Drain the life from his husk. Send his skull back to Rome. Let him serve the role of messenger that way."

As though with a will of their own, Pablo's hands reached up to fondle the crucifix around his neck. He took no other action, but merely closed his eyes waiting for the blow to fall. Instead, boots and gauntlets clanking, Signari returned to his spot on the dais beneath his matriarch. Lily's face was inscrutable. She gestured at the man on her right.

"Cicatrice, my most trusted and beloved counselor. What are your thoughts?"

Cicatrice was as famous for his guile as his counterpart Signari was for his swordarm. It was rumored that he had been responsible for the rise and fall of three Burgundian dukes before leaving France for greater opportunities.

His body was tightly wrapped in a linen shroud, with only minor modifications made for the fact that he moved, unlike the corpse such a garment was intended for. On his hip a handbell tinkled as he stepped down from the dais. It was a noise Pablo recognized well, for he had heard it many times. It was the type of bell used to call for Last Rites.

"May I?" Cicatrice asked, pointing at Pablo's chest.

Pablo found himself utterly unable to respond, transfixed by the other man's face. Like Signari, his jaw was painted like a skeleton's. But he also seemed to have a real deformity. His left eye was solidly red, and a vertical scar jutted from it, up into his forehead and down to the side of his nose.

Without waiting for a response, Cicatrice took hold of Pablo's crucifix and lifted it off his chest.

"Take hold of it, will you, Brother Pablo?"

"I…forgive me?"

Cicatrice tapped at the cross.

"Place your hand on your cross."

His hand shaking like a spastic's, Pablo slowly reached up and took hold of the bottom of his crucifix, while Cicatrice held the top. Instantly, the other man hissed in pain, and smoke began to billow from his fingers. With the ease of a child plucking a bloom of honeysuckle, Cicatrice snatched the crucifix from Pablo's neck, breaking the thick cord which held it there. As soon as Pablo's hand was off the icon, the smoke ceased.

Cicatrice held the icon aloft, as it seemed to pain him no more.

"There, you see. A man of true faith. His essence will be as foul to us as plague water."

"Cut off his head then," Signari growled. "We don't need to feed off of him."

"Quiet, my pet," Lily said, running her hand through Signari's hair. "You've had your chance. Let Cicatrice have his."

Signari scowled but said nothing. Grinning grotesquely, Cicatrice turned and tossed the crucifix back into Pablo's fumbling hands as though it were nothing.

"Do you have any idea how many men I've met who've tried to hurt me with that? Held it aloft like a totem? A good luck piece? And I ripped out each of their throats. Without the true faith in you that is poison to us, that is no more than two sticks of wood."

"I grow impatient, Cicatrice."

"My apologies, Matriarch," the charnel-clad man said, clasping his hands before him, "it's just that I feel a man of true faith is so rare in this world, that we could do better than to decapitate him."

"What do you have in mind?"

"A witness to...no, more than that. The instrument of your ascendancy."

Lily's eyes opened wide.

"My investor..." she whispered.

Cicatrice's head bobbed.

"Ever my font of wisdom," she marveled. "Go and fetch it."

"Matriarch," Cicatrice said, bowing and shuffling off.

Resplendent in her charnel gowns, Lily descended from the dais. Signari, Pablo noted, remained behind, a stormcloud brewing over him. She approached and placed an ice-cold hand on Pablo's cheek. He found himself unable to look away from her exposed mandible, where the workings of her very muscle and sinew were on display as she spoke.

"Oh, simple man of faith. Did you ever dream that you were born to such a destiny? To witness such events?"

"Begging your pardon, L...Mother Lily, but what of my message?"

A roar erupted as Signari strode across the room in what seemed like no more than three steps and drove his boot into the unprotected crotch of one of the naked slave boys. The slave collapsed like a dropped cloak.

"Idiot!" the savage warrior roared. "Imbecile! Do you think we don't know what you're here to tell us? That there's an army of Crusaders at our gates?"

Signari pointed to a wall, which Pablo noted for the first time had no window. It made sense that these creatures who eschew sunlight, who built their stronghold deep in the heart of a mountain, would have no use for windows, but it was still a most unusual sight.

Signari unbuckled his gauntlet and let it drop unceremoniously to the floor. With his ungloved hand he reached down and lifted the slave off the ground by the neck. Barely flexing his muscles, he yanked the iron chain straight out of the wall, ignoring the slave's obvious discomfort.

"Do you know what we'll do when your mighty defenders of Christendom cross our border? This."

The slave began to twitch and kick in Signari's grip, though the warrior neither tightened his grip nor moved at all. Pablo watched on in horror as the young boy aged a year, a decade, a whole lifetime in the space of a few heartbeats. His body began to shrivel and dry up, his skin furrowing, his hair turning gray. It was as though with the mere touch of his naked hand upon the slave's neck Signari was sucking the very life out of him.

After a moment the slave's body turned to brittle bones and dust, collapsing into a pile on the floor.

"How very histrionic, Otto," Cicatrice said, re-entering the room, "but for what it's worth, he speaks the truth. Your Crusader army bears us no threat."

Cicatrice carried with him a black velvet pillow. Upon the pillow sat a crown, though no ordinary crown. The bottom had been fashioned from the skull of a tall man, possibly a giant, with the mandible removed.

The craftsmanship was elegant, and simple. Each point of the crown was carved from bone: sturdy stuff, femurs perhaps. Quite how it all held together Pablo couldn't tell, but no doubt many mortal men like he had died to provide the raw material for many attempts to produce this perfect one. Part papal miter and part royal corona, probably one that would be used only once: at a coronation ceremony.

It dawned on Pablo then exactly what these fiends expected of him.

"I cannot commit this blasphemy."

"Good," Signari said, "then I was right all along."

"Brother," Cicatrice said, his voice all syrup and malevolence, "when you leave this place, you shall go unmolested. But we have been waiting for someone like you to tell the world that the Golden Age of the Immortal is now. If you can't meet this simple obligation, then you'll suffer for an eternity in our dungeons. It is a tough cross to bear, I know, but didn't Christ bear his oh so well?"

Pablo swallowed the speech he had been preparing. This was a madhouse, no simple den of vice nor court of ignominies. It would be better that he fled, and if conducting a fanciful imaginary ceremony made that happen faster, then so be it.

"Shall I say some words?" he whispered.

"Allow me," Cicatrice said. "Take the crown—with care, mind you, Brother—and step up on that dais."

Pablo did as he was told and Lily knelt before him, her gowns turning to a puddle of putrescence beneath her.

Cicatrice spoke, "My own sire, who granted me the Long Gift and taught me the ways of the world, I can think of no other immortal on earth worthy to bear this responsibility and this burden. May you lead long and wisely. It is therefore with whatever humble authority you have granted me, that I crown you the spiritual and temporal mistress of all our kind, Lily the Only."

His hands shaking, Pablo gently lowered the crown onto her brow. She rose, her gowns billowing beneath her. She grabbed Cicatrice's ear and cheek with one hand and planted a kiss on his face.

"My first act is to name you my chief vassal and head evangelist. Cicatrice, you are now patriarch of House Cicatrice. May you reign forever in the shadows."

She held out a scroll, sealed with wax and stuffed through a ring. The ring was carved from obsidian, and alive with graphic images of murder, torture, and rape. Cicatrice inclined his head.

"Your Worship."

Lily beckoned with a single ethereal finger to Signari.

"Otto Signari, I name you third most powerful amongst our kind. Warlord of my armies, trusted advisor, chief protector of the dark faith, and patriarch of House Signari."

She thrust another scroll towards him. Signari dropped to one knee, and reached up to accept the scroll and the ring. Cicatrice snorted loudly. Signari glared, but Lily only smiled. He immediately jammed the obsidian ring onto his finger and broke the wax seal of the scroll to read it over.

"And your first act as my chief protector," she said, "is to deliver these eleven other letters of patriarchy."

She gestured at a basket which had remained innocuously hidden on the dais throughout the ceremony. Pablo had not even noticed it before, but now that it was pointed out to him he recognized the protruding rounded sheets of parchment. Signari retrieved his gauntlet, tugged it back on, rose, and grabbed up the basket.

"I leave immediately, Your Worship."

He turned to eye Cicatrice.

"Father Cicatrice."

"Father Otto," Cicatrice muttered.

Signari disappeared with one last glance back from the darkness of the exterior hallway. Cicatrice turned to face the newly-crowned empress.

"Mat…I mean, Your Worship…what exactly…?"

"Not to fret, dear boy. I could tell you were having trouble deciding who to invite here. You forget how well I know you. Well, no more cause for regret. I made the decision for you. Eleven of the most important immortals, most with a number of important gets and vassals. They won't dare refuse to show now."

Unable to contain it, Pablo sneezed. Both of the fiends turned their gaze on him. Both stepped towards him. He held out his hands.

"You said I would return to my army unmolested!"

The new Empress of Immortals reached out and crushed his ear with her hand like a petulant boy crushing a daisy.

"And so you shall," Lily said, "Only older. And wiser."

With that, she drained fifty years from his life, and tossed him towards the exit.

"Is this story true?"

Cicatrice rose from his plush chair in the monstrous, labyrinthine library. After what felt like an eternity he returned with a book which seemed ancient beyond reason. He placed it on the table before her, open to a page.

The dust-covered manuscript was illuminated in glorious

lettering, and though she could sound out the words, she knew hardly any Latin. The book was illustrated, though, and despite having dulled with age it clearly depicted the Necropolis, Lily the Half-Faced, Otto Signari, and her own patriarch.

She reached out to touch the pages, but a hiss from Cicatrice suggested she not do so. It dawned on her that this book was so ancient, the oils of her fingers could ruin it irreparably. Instead, with great care, Idi Han slowly closed the ancient tome. She ran her fingers along the cover, which bore a massive dragon sigil and the words De Vermis Mysteriis.

"So the priest lived?"

"For another year or two. Historical records speak of the priest who turned from a youth to an old man in a single day. This book, though, is the only extant explanation of why. And copies exist only here and deep in the Vatican archives."

"Doesn't that concern you?"

"My enemies having information about me? No. The Inquisition concerns me minimally. They're boys playing with wooden swords and I treat them as such. Or perhaps more accurately they're Don Quixotes, tilting at windmills, all the time never guessing the windmills couldn't care less."

"Father Cicatrice, I appreciate you taking the time to confide…that is to say, to teach me about our ways, but is this really the right time?

"What other time would you suggest?"

"But Signari…the others…isn't the enemy at the gates?"

Cicatrice rose and beckoned her to follow him. He led her to a window, the first she had seen since being smuggled into Cicatrice's manse under cover of darkness, asleep, hidden in a crate of soil. The window was hidden behind a false compartment in the wall, perhaps to keep the ambience of near-absolute darkness. Cicatrice popped out the false back and opened wide the window.

A city of twinkling lights greeted her. She had rarely been to Guangzhou, and that had been nothing like this place. The decadence, the extravagance, the fountains and towers. This was a place where life began at sundown. The perfect home for an immortal.

"Las Vegas," Cicatrice said, "The Meadows. Sin City. My city. The seat of House Cicatrice. All the other Great Houses are located in ancient places of great renown: Tokyo, Rome, London. Do you know why I chose to place my seat here?"

"This is a place of night," she replied.

Cicatrice rarely if ever smiled, and never without purpose. He did not do so now, but if possible his face softened.

"You are wise. This is a place where living in darkness is no small thing. This is also a place where everyone comes at one point or another and makes…mistakes. I've been here since long before Bugsy Siegel first proposed turning a watering hole into a Mecca of vice. And I spent many years laying the groundwork for that moment. This is a new town, a town I built, a town built around me and my needs. Look out there."

Idi Han looked down at the streets of The Strip, packed with tourists and locals alike. Everyone seemed wealthy, drunk, and jaded. More importantly, they all seemed like ants from this vantage point.

"The mayor, the police, the city council, the judges, the politicians, the bureaucrats, they're all in my pocket. The business owners, too. I let them have their piddling profits as long as they know who is master here. Every immortal has a circle of mortal followers to service him. This entire city is mine. Every person in it, whether he knows it or not, belongs to me.

"But it's not just the powerful, Idi Han. They're just the most visible element of my hand. But you know what makes the human hand useful, what makes it the paragon of apes?"

"The thumb," she replied.

He nodded.

"The very smallest digit. It allows for manipulation beyond anything in the animal kingdom. And in this town my most valuable assets are the people on the streets. Valets. Prostitutes. Pit bosses. Dealers. Maitre Ds. Housekeepers. There's a camera in every room in this city, but more important: there are eyes on every street corner. And that's where I get my most valuable information.

"I have presidents and prime ministers all over the world under my sway. Kings and cardinals and everyone who visits here. Their affairs, their drugs, their foolish decisions. All put them in debt to me, and all strengthen my power. Now, knowing all this, Idi Han, how much do you think I fear Otto Signari and his idiot compatriots threatening me as I sit in the center of my own spiderweb?"

"It seems I've underestimated you, Patriarch. I apologize."

"No need. I feel no need for braggadocio, no need to prove myself. There's no reason you should've known any of this before I told you. But you understand why I'm not afraid to spend my time grooming my new heir rather than preparing for war. War has long since been prepared for. You still need to be groomed."

Idi Han looked back down at the De Vermis Mysteriis.

"What happened next?"

Cicatrice placed his hand on the book, but before he could continue, a knock came at the door. Idi Han looked to him.

"More interlopers?"

"I've never known Otto Signari to knock." Cicatrice replaced the grimoire. "Enter!"

A smartly-dressed Samoan woman entered. Her cheeks were sunken in and it seemed like she had two purple eyes from lack of sleep. Her arms and neck were covered with long-healed razor blade scars, and she still had patches over what looked like fresh wounds. She was as gaunt as a rail...barely there, really.

She dropped to one knee in front of Cicatrice's chair, refusing to look in his eye, and clutched her breast with her hand. Her stringy hair hung over her head, obscuring her face and eyes.

"Forgive the intrusion, Father Cicatrice," she said, her voice like a wisp on the breeze.

"Idi Han, this is Hedrox. She was head of my circle until your arrival. But tradition holds that a new get should oversee her sire's circle. Hedrox, Idi Han will be taking over for you."

"I am pleased to have another immortal to serve, Father Cicatrice," the woman whispered, "I do so miss Elder Topan's firm hand."

Idi Han scowled, wondering if she had caught a glimpse of mischief in the cultist's eye. Cicatrice, as usual, was unmoved.

"Topan's name is to be stricken from all records. He is excommunicated from my House."

"I shall make the necessary changes, Patriarch."

"Idi Han is my new heir. You will record that as well."

Hedrox paused, just a moment too long for Idi Han's tastes. Was Cicatrice really ignorant of his cultist's disgruntlement? If she had noticed it so soon, surely he had.

"I'm very pleased to hear that, Father Cicatrice."

"I sense that you're really not."

Cicatrice placed his fist under Hedrox's chin and gently raised her head so that the hair fell away and revealed the skeletal woman hidden beneath the mane.

"Do not question my memory, for it is long, and faithful service is always rewarded. When Idi Han is installed and comfortable with her new position, you will have that which you have so long coveted."

Hedrox's eyes shone with a joy that only a mortal could muster.

"The Long Gift?"

Cicatrice did not reply. He placed the tips of his fingers together.

"Hedrox, you used to tie the nooses Topan wore, didn't you?"

"I did, Father."

"Go fetch a few meters of rope and show me."

Hedrox bowed and disappeared.

"I thought you granted Topan your blessing in the 1950s."

"I did," Cicatrice said, "he showed such promise back then. But he went on to make many mistakes and many enemies. So many that it was only out of respect for me that they let me rein him back in twenty years ago rather than ask—and rightfully so—for his head. I put him back in charge of my circle and tried to set him straight but after another futile decade I just let him go again. I simply don't care what he does anymore. He thought finding you would bring him back into my good graces. Any other questions?"

She paused for a moment.

"Yes. Why do you make that mortal promises you will never keep?"

Cicatrice turned to look at her.

"I'm sorry. I've spoken out of turn."

Cicatrice shook his head.

"No. You are my heir. More importantly you are an immortal. And a member of my House. You have liberties I don't grant the brethren. To answer your question, I have become most adept at dangling the carrot."

"I sense the carrot is beginning to lose its sheen."

"You are right, of course. Topan's influence, no doubt. She'll have to be executed shortly. Perhaps I'll leave that task to you."

"Father Cicatrice…"

She trailed off.

"I told you, don't be afraid to speak your mind."

"How is it that you can trust a mortal with our secrets?"

Hedrox returned with a few lengths of rope in varying colors. Cicatrice switched over to Cantonese.

"Most of what I tell the brethren is lies. You must understand: in the daylight, they're the only thing between us and eager Inquisitors. So it is important to surround yourself with mortals, to protect yourself with them. Besides, I find it comforting that there are so many of them that are willing to serve us. It makes me less concerned about our numerical disadvantage. What is your favorite color? Respond in English."

Idi Han's mouth worked for a moment at the strange request.

"My favorite color?" she replied. "It's…red."

"That was Topan's favorite as well. It's a good color. The color of blood. The color of this House."

He pointed at Hedrox's right hand, which contained among many other coils of rope, a blood red one. Hedrox nodded, and with dazzling speed, began to make thirteen knots.

"Now, tell me, Hedrox, why did you knock on my door unbidden when I expressly said I was not to be disturbed until I said otherwise?"

Hedrox nodded, her eyes still not on Cicatrice. Her fingers played the rope like a violin. Idi Han had never been a stranger to knots, having yoked the oxen and tethered the barn, but she had never seen someone as adept as this mortal apparently was.

"Yes, Father Cicatrice, you did say that, but you also have a standing order. An order that supersedes all others."

Cicatrice was silent so long that Idi Han wondered if something was desperately wrong. He never showed emotion, but now he was silent and it was terrifying.

"The Hunter of the Dead has been sighted?"

Hedrox nodded as she completed the last loops of her noose.

"Allegedly. Patriarch. Shall I cut this to Idi Han's measurements?"

"Leave it. Who sighted The Hunter?"

"A very ill-reputed member of House Signari. A fixer, not even finished his apprenticeship. His name is Italo Scavatelli. Apparently Benito Scavatelli's brother in life and he brought him across."

"Yes. I'm familiar with them both."

"Signaris?" Idi Han said. "Then this is a ruse."

"An exceedingly strange one. The Signaris are gutter-dwellers and Italo Scavatelli is not even well-regarded amongst them. You don't send a peasant to treat with a king."

"But you might send a clown to fool one."

Hedrox proferred forth the noose.

"Your tie, Idi Han."

Cicatrice shook his head.

"No, you misunderstood, Hedrox. That's for you."

For the first time Hedrox looked up into her patriarch's face, perhaps to confirm a joke. She may as well have kept her head down for all the impassiveness of Cicatrice benefitted her. She slipped the noose around her neck, and fitted it under her collar as though it were a necktie, the same way Topan wore it. She tightened it up to her throat.

"Have the Signari sent in."

"Right away, Father."

Hedrox rose. She reached into her chest and drew out a razor blade she wore around her neck. She lifted the end of the noose and made ready to cut it at about waist length.

"I told you not to cut that."

Hedrox blinked, but after a moment nodded.

"Yes. Yes, of course, Patriarch."

She disappeared from the room, the endless string of rope

trailing behind her like a sad tail. A moment later she returned and gestured for a bedraggled punk to enter. The punk's hair was partially up in a deflated Mohawk and he wore a wretched denim vest and a Misfits T-shirt under it. Every bit of him looked as though it had been beaten, battered, and seen better days.

Hedrox attempted to slip out but Cicatrice held up a hand.

"Wait."

Hedrox nodded, folded her hands and dutifully waited in the doorway.

"Italo Scavatelli," Cicatrice said with a grunt, "my new heir, Idi Han."

The man looked at her, not really seeing her.

"No more Topan? I thought he…"

"We had a disagreement."

No more, it seemed, needed to be said.

"Idi Han, this is Italo Scavatelli, quite possibly the least impressive immortal on the planet. He and his adoptive sire Connor MacVicar have been bums for decades. And when I say bums I don't mean they were delightful roguish scamps who never caused anyone any harm and made their own way in a world they never chose. I mean they were indigent parasites, suckling at the teat of anyone who would bother to have them. The distance from he and I may seem to be only a few meters, but in reality it is as far as the sun is from the moon."

Scavatelli sucked in a wholly unnecessary breath to pump up his chest.

"Father Cicatrice," Scavatelli replied, "you know I wouldn't bother you. You know I wouldn't…"

"Then don't, Signari. Hedrox!"

Startled, the mortal hurried back inside.

"Yes, Father?"

"Your rope." He gestured at the noose around Hedrox's neck. "Toss it over that ceiling beam there."

Hedrox looked up at the ceiling. She swallowed a lump in her throat, but did as she was ordered. The rope was now split into two parallel lengths, one snaking up to the ceiling, the other dangling down.

"Hand that end to Scav here."

Hedrox turned and looked at the Signari. Scav shrugged, also apparently unclear what was going on. Hedrox handed him the length of rope.

"Now that you know precisely how I feel about this... individual standing before me, I want to make yet another point. This man is an immortal. He is one of my kind. As diminished as he is from me, that is nothing in comparison to how diminished any mortal is from one of our kind. Now, Scav, if you will favor me with a bit of your time, please, pull on the rope."

Scav looked from Cicatrice to Hedrox and back again.

"Hey, listen, Father Cicatrice, if this is some kind of a lesson, hey I know better than to touch that which is yours. This is your disciple and I..."

"Spare me the platitudes, Scav. You've come seeking my protection. You're beyond groveling and at this point you're fully within my power. This is not some trick to put you in an awkward position. This is me making a point to a very stubborn mortal."

Scav shrugged and despite Hedrox's wide-eyed stare he tugged on the rope until Hedrox's feet dangled off the ground and she choked, scrabbling at the noose she had so ably tied herself only moments before.

"Are you listening, Hedrox? Are you listening as this piece of shit chokes the life out of you? I don't care. I don't care about you. You're not one of my kind. You're nothing to me. Property. To be used, to be abused. I am no more upset watching this happen than I would be if my car had been broken into. You understand that?"

Whatever Hedrox understood or not, her choked cries did not especially illuminate.

"Now, this young woman? She is important to me. Not just to me, but to my kind. She is my heir. Whatever you thought you had coming to you, the Long Gift, whatever. Understand it's mine to give or to withhold as I see fit. I've seen fit to withhold it from you, and grant it to her. Your position in queue or however you want to look at it is meaningless to me. It is devotion I look for in choosing a new immortal. And you have shown by failing this test that you are still not worthy of it. If you had taken Idi Han's appearance with aplomb, you might have been next. Now I don't know. Let her go, Scav."

"What? Oh, sure. Sorry, Father Cicatrice."

Scav released the rope and Hedrox dropped to the floor. Her legs crumpled up beneath her and she lay on the ground, gulping for air like a fish out of water.

"I don't know. Maybe I made a mistake in choosing you for my circle in the first place."

"No!" a strangled cry came from Hedrox's throat.

"No what? No I shouldn't have chosen you? Then I release you. Go back to your kin, Vizriel. I'm sure they miss you."

Hedrox scrabbled, barely able to rise above a crouch. On her hands and knees she dragged herself before Cicatrice, hands raised in pleading as though clasped in prayer.

"Please! No! Patriarch! Please!"

"Please what?"

Hedrox's rasp took on something of a semblance of a human tone again.

"Please don't dismiss me."

Cicatrice shook his head.

"But how can I keep you if you are jealous of my heir? Who knows, if I died tomorrow, she would be your new matriarch. I'm not certain I can take that risk with you."

"Please, Idi Han, please, I would ever serve you. Please don't make me go."

Hedrox dropped her head to the ground and banged it against the tile, her hair flying back and forth in time.

"Well, it seems the choice is up to you, my beloved get. Shall we retain her?"

Idi Han looked from her emotionless patriarch to the wretch on the ground to the bemused punk. A few days ago such a scene would have been far beyond her imagination. Now she understood that she had been brought into a life where power dictated ancient codes of behavior and all sorts of people were beholden to one another. It was time to become mature.

"It seems you've mastered the carrot and the stick, Father Cicatrice," she said in Cantonese, then continued in English, "If she's served you well this long, Patriarch, then I think she's deserving of a second chance."

Cicatrice nodded.

"A wise decision. Every time your mouth opens I become ever more convinced I made the right choice anointing you my heir. Yes, Hedrox shall have a second chance. And know that among immortals, second chances are exceedingly rare. You owe your good fortune to your future matriarch, Hedrox. She is far more merciful than I have ever been faulted with being."

"Yes, yes!" Hedrox cried, "Thank you, Idi Han, thank you! I swear eternal fealty to you!"

"Get out."

Nodding, and bobbing up and down like a water-drinking bird toy, Hedrox disappeared out the door, her long tail of a noose trailing behind him. Cicatrice lit an unfiltered cigarette in a bone holder and turned on Scavatelli.

"Now then, Scav, pretend I haven't much time for you… in fact, I haven't any…and tell me what you know about The Hunter."

Scav bit his lower lip. He looked from Cicatrice to Idi Han. Idi Han gestured for him to sit, half expecting Cicatrice to belay her with a wave, but he did nothing. Tentatively, Scav pulled out a chair and seated himself across from them.

"Well, that's not the first thing I want to talk about, all due respect, Father Cicatrice."

As ever, Cicatrice's face remained impassive.

"Your position is tenuous. Is MacVicar dead?"

Seemingly unable to find words, Scav only nodded.

"Then you're not a real boy. Sireless. Houseless. By rights I should destroy you."

"But that's just it. My sire told me he'd release me tonight. And then he was killed."

"By The Hunter of the Dead?"

Scav nodded.

"Are you sure? Before you answer, understand that if you're lying to me or worse, if you're wasting my time, whatever you fear is going to happen to you if you turn yourself in to your own House will pale in comparison to what I will make you suffer. I don't make idle threats, you understand that?"

"I understand."

"Are you certain you saw The Hunter of the Dead?"

Scav looked from Cicatrice to Idi Han and back again. The look in his eyes was haunted.

"Yes."

Cicatrice glanced at her.

"Do you believe him?" he asked in Cantonese.

"I do."

"That's because he's telling the truth. And it vexes me deeply. Tell me everything you know, Scav, and you'll have my protection, such as it is."

With obvious relief, Scav began to recount meeting The Hunter, and how it had dispatched his travelling companion. She looked to Cicatrice for some sign of distress or even acknowledgement. He was as placid as though the man were recounting a series of bookkeeping statistics.

"And I thought I should come to you," he concluded.

That was the only part that seemed to be a lie, but something still bothered her about the story. He hadn't explained how he had escaped. No excuses, no explanation. He had simply left it out.

Cicatrice nodded. He rose and folded his arms behind his back, turning his back on the Signari.

"This was last night?"

Scav nodded.

"And you've spent the intervening time doing what? No, nevermind. I already know. You've spent it trying to get back into the good graces of the Signaris, isn't that right?"

"Yes."

"And so you come to me as a last resort at nearly dawn the day after the fact. The trail has gone cold. Many lives will be lost because of your dithering, I think."

Cicatrice walked to a shelf and pulled out an atlas. He opened it on the table to a map of Nevada. He pressed his finger to a spot west of the city.

"Cashley's compound is here if I'm not mistaken."

"That seems right."

"Then The Hunter could be anywhere by now."

"Perhaps he's headed to Los Angeles," Idi Han said.

"No, I don't think so," Cicatrice said, closing the atlas. "He is drawn to immortals like a moth to a candle. L.A. is very lightly populated by our kind. Strange, even with Cashley's excesses I can't imagine why The Hunter would awaken after all these years, and be drawn to Vegas, no less. There are only a few dozen of us here."

Scav snorted, a noise that was physiologically totally unnecessary. The smile that had started to play across his face withered under Cicatrice's oppressive gaze.

"Something amusing, Scavatelli?"

The Signari looked from Idi Han to Cicatrice like a drowning man looking for a lifesaver. Sadly, whatever the joke was, Idi Han hadn't been let in on it.

"Uh…" Scav said, choosing his words as though he were picking his way across a minefield, "I've never said this to a patriarch before, but you're wrong, Father Cicatrice. There are dozens of immortals in town. Hundreds, maybe."

EIGHT

Keys seemed to be a constant issue to Carter Price. He stood in front of his apartment door, purring and stroking the doorknob, trying to get it to accept his advances as though it were a woman or a particularly treacherous cat. Nico, for his part, couldn't take his eyes off the exposed pipe in the hallway of Price's building that was dripping water at a disturbingly steady clip. It had turned the floor below it into a mold civilization that threatened to collapse at any moment.

"There it is," Price cooed, as the door opened, revealing all its secrets.

The inside of his apartment was, somehow, even less impressive than the outside. Without even turning his head, Nico could see all there was to see in the studio. A naked mattress (thankfully stain-free, at least) was jammed in one corner. Price appeared to own precisely two chairs, which did not match and appeared to have been rescued from the curb. Kicking off his muddy shoes in whichever direction they cared to land, Price stomped into the closet-sized partition containing a stove and a fridge which could out of kindness be called a kitchen.

"You want something to drink?"

"Yeah, actually, that sounds great," Nico said, slowly closing the door. He hadn't realized how parched he was until Price asked.

"Well, I've got coffee and bourbon."

"Er...coffee, then."

The sounds of water splashing and a cheap coffeemaker percolating filled the apartment.

"How do you take it?"

"However you take yours is fine."

"I take mine with bourbon."

"Oh."

As good as that sounded after the night he'd had, he wasn't sure alcohol would put his senses in the best shape for vampire-hunting. In fact, he was pretty sure it wasn't helping Price any, but clearly he had not seen the things Price had, either.

"Lots of cream, lots of sugar, then."

Price ruffled through some cabinets and opened the fridge.

"I've got…black."

"I'll take black then."

Price emerged from the kitchen nook a moment later, steaming mugs in either hand. One had a crack and read "World's Worst Lover" and the other one had obviously been bought at the airport and depicted the iconic Las Vegas sign. Sinking into his camp chair, Price clinked glasses, and then, true to his word, filled out his half-empty mug from his flask. He sighed loudly.

"You can take the bed. I almost never make it over there, anyway."

"Thanks," Nico replied, eyeing the mattress warily.

"I know I'm not going to convince you to go home at this point, kid, but is there someone you want to call? Let them know you're okay?"

Nico shrugged.

"There is no one. Not really."

"Oh," Price said, taking a sip of his upper/downer mélange, "not even back in…where is it, again?"

"Puerto Rico."

"Ah," Price said, closing his eyes, *"La Borinqueña."*

That was surprising.

"You've been?"

Price nodded.

"Beautiful island. Knew a girl there once. Got hired for a couple jobs down there. Didn't pan out."

"Vampire hunting jobs?"

"Yeah. Believe it or not."

Nico leaned back in his folding chair as best he could.

"I guess I had the opposite problem. Couldn't find a job. Thought I'd make my fortune here and ended up at the Fill-Up instead. Beats the army, I guess."

"Joined the marines myself."

Only one decoration adorned Price's walls. It didn't look like something the military gave out. Nico halfway rose to get a better look at it, but realized how drowsy he was despite the coffee and sank back down.

"What's that?"

Price opened a single eye and glanced at the wall.

"That's my stake, you know."

He raised his right arm to display his Inquisition tattoo. Nico squinted to take a closer look at the stake on the wall. It was beautifully carved and engraved with Price's name. The end was hollowed out, as though it had been woven together from pieces of wicker, but really it had all been carved from a single piece of wood.

"So they give you a stake when you join the Inquisition?"

"Yeah. It's like the symbol of your completion of your…what do you call it?"

"Apprenticeship?"

"Yeah, that. It's not like I've used a wooden stake since my master handed me that one."

"No? Why not? Can't you kill a vampire with one?"

Price giggled, a distinctly un-Price-like noise that signaled how deep he was into his cups.

"Just to be clear, kid: there are only two ways to 'kill' a vampire: fire and sunlight. Oh and we don't say 'kill.' We say 'put down.'"

"Like a dog?"

"Yeah. Exactly like a dog. But since there's nothing more dangerous than strapping a flamethrower to your back, and you can't exactly command the sun to rise, your only real hope as an Inquisitor is to incapacitate him. And that means severing the head or staking the heart."

Despite his obvious drunkenness he rose from his chair and crossed the studio apartment to open a closet. He dragged out a dummy with comical facepaint meant to resemble Bela Lugosi. As the dummy came loose, a small canister rolled out of the closet and came to a rest at Nico's feet. He picked it up.

"What's this?"

Price grunted.

"Diffused garlic. Nightcrawlers rely on their...they call it their sense of smell but I've never been sure if that's a metaphor or not. A canister of garlic gas won't do anything to harm them, but it'll confuse them. Blind them, essentially."

Nico nodded and tucked the canister into his pocket. Price plucked a stake from his bandolier and tossed it to Nico, who fumbled before securing it. Then Price tossed the dummy at him and clicked the button on a stopwatch.

"Stake that nightcrawler!"

Startled, Nico flipped the dummy onto the ground and rose from the chair. Fatigue was pulling on all his muscles and his eyelids.

"What?"

"Go on, stake the son of a bitch!"

With a sigh, Nico got down and straddled the dummy. He raised the stake over his head and brought it down hard on the dummy's heart area, which was helpfully marked in red.

"There," Nico said, "Satisfied?"

"Are you kidding me?" Price said, "That thing's nothing but a sandbag and you've barely punctured the fabric."

Price tapped the stake lightly with his foot and it went clattering away.

"You didn't even pierce the ribcage, let alone the heart."

Nico rose, clapping the imaginary dust from his hands.

"All right, I get it, Carter. Leave off."

In a sudden explosion of emotion Price tossed his "World's Worst Lover" mug against the wall so violently that it shattered. He waved the stopwatch, still running, in Nico's face.

"Are you kidding me? Are you fucking kidding me? You expect to fight vampires...you expect me to teach you how to fight vampires...and this is your level of dedication? You can't even push a piece of wood through a burlap dummy?"

Nico opened his mouth to respond, but instead bit down on

his tongue to stop himself. The old man was right. He grabbed Bela Lugosi and dragged him over to where the stake had fallen. He grabbed the stake and drove it repeatedly into the heart area, but no matter how hard he pressed it, it seemed not to want to penetrate down to where the heart would've been in a person.

He held it in place and pounded on it with his fist, finding his hand soon bloodied.

"I need like...I need a hammer or something."

Nico looked around the room wildly. Price clicked the stopwatch loudly and held out his hand. Nico didn't take it, but rose. After a moment's thought, he handed the stake back to Price.

"Sorry, kid, but you're long dead. I figure you have maybe five seconds, tops, to put a stake through an unsuspecting vampire's heart. It's already been almost thirty. And the dummy wasn't fighting back."

Price sank back into his chair.

"So stakes work but...they don't work? Basically?"

"Yeah. That's a good way to put it. I've never seen it done successfully. An ordinary person doesn't really have the strength to put a piece of wood through a ribcage. As you noticed, you'd need a mallet. And hopefully while you're pounding on a stake with a mallet, you don't break the tip, or else you'll be trying to put a dull board through somebody. And all this is assuming your target isn't wearing a chestplate. And I've never met a vampire who didn't."

"Why do you carry them, then?"

Price reached up and rolled one of the stakes in his bandolier backward and forward.

"They're a bit like gang colors. I guess we're all prima donnas, us and the nightcrawlers both. The Signaris wear these white stripes down their faces when they're on the job and the Druids go naked and we...we wear these. To show off who we are. In the old days they used to say you could deputize somebody into the Inquisition by handing him a stake. In fact..."

Price handed the stake back to Nico. The sun was rising. Price leaned back in his chair.

"Better get some sleep. It's going to be a long night tomorrow."

Nico glanced down at the naked mattress. In his sleepdrunk state, it looked unnaturally appealing, and he flung himself into it without even putting away his drink or brushing his teeth. Price was already snoring loudly in his chair when Nico's eyes closed.

NIGHT TWO

NINE

The Eighties...

Scav wanted to weep but the tears wouldn't come to his eyes. He was drained, dead, empty. Neither blood nor bowel nor tear duct moved within him. He glanced over at the mittens that had been made of his hands, the molten steel still cooling. They didn't hurt—not in the way anything had hurt before Benito had turned him—but they were unpleasant. As the steel cooled he felt what little give there was fade until he could barely even flex his fingers.

Benito was kneeling next to him, similarly saddled with a still-cooling yoke and hands gloved in steel. Benito was still struggling against his bonds, unlike Scav, who had given up almost instantly. If these... he still hesitated to use the word "vampires" but it seemed increasingly impossible to call them anything else...wanted him bound, then bound he would stay. Surely they knew their business by now.

The vampire whose face and body had been deformed by a terrible case of leprosy in life kicked Benito. It was a half-hearted kick, as the woman seemed to have difficulty lifting her legs.

"Stop squirming."

"You think you can hold me, Damiana? I'm not beaten yet."

Benito's back and shoulders strained against the yoke, and for a second, Scav almost believed he would break it. The lepress—Damiana— knelt down with some difficulty and grabbed Benito by the chin. Her hands and face were pocked with pustules and marks, such that her eyes were barely visible and her mouth would barely open. As a result, her voice was a low rasp.

"If I want you to stay put, you'll stay put. I've dealt with hundreds

*of little shits like you for Father Otto, and I know your limitations."
She reached up and placed one deformed hand on Benito's yoke. "This
yoke is too much for any immortal short of an oldblood to break, even at
full strength. And when was the last time you fed? Now be silent until
Father Otto is ready for you."*

*A bell tinkled and the entire assembled crowd rose to their feet.
Scav struggled, wondering whether he should attempt to rise, but a
moment later he felt the pinch of the lepress's bloated hands grasp his
spine through his shirt and yank him to his feet. She had done the same
with Benito with her other hand.*

*Otto Signari came clattering down a spiral staircase into the make-
shift courtroom. He wore a full suit of armor, though it seemed not to
burden him at all, and a white stripe divided his head and neck, and
continued down his suit of steel.*

*"Sorry, sorry, everybody. I didn't mean to be late. Just got off the
horn with my 'old buddy' Cicatrice and you know how cranky talking
to him makes me…holy fuck. Who did this?"*

*Scav glanced back at the lepress. It was hard to tell, but her face
seemed to be distended in a grin. Scav turned back to the front of the
room. A woman—young, firm, nubile—lay strapped to a gurney. From
her head to her toes, she was lined with candles, tiny birthday candles.
There had to be hundreds, and for each a tiny hole had been drilled in
her skin or bone, and the candle placed inside. Either she was deeply,
deeply drugged, or so deep in shock that she didn't seem to be railing
against the pain anymore.*

"Is this for real? Wait a minute…what year is this?"

*"After Common Era nineteen hundred and eighty-seven, patri-
arch," Damiana answered as loudly as she could.*

*Signari glanced up. A broad smile crossed his face. He waggled his
gauntleted hand at the lepress.*

*"Damiana, you old trickster. The eight hundredth anniversary of
Mother Lily granting me the Long Gift. I had completely forgotten. Are
there really eight hundred candles?"*

*The wax that was dripping from dozens seared the young woman's
skin, to no visible effect. Scav would've believed there were, indeed,
nearly a thousand candles.*

*"It took some preparation, Father Otto. But this is as big a day for
the House as it is for yourself."*

"Come down here. Get down here, Damiana, you old monster."

Signari gestured for Damiana to join him and the lepress descended from the docket and allowed herself to be embraced in a glorious hug by her House patriarch. She never attempted to take the liberty of hugging back. Signari rubbed his hands together.

"Well, let's have a taste, shall we?"

Signari pressed his forehead to the top of the girl's head, the only part of her that wasn't buzzing with sizzling wax. Signari rose a moment later, his eyes wide and his mouth agape.

"My God, Damiana, she must be one in a million! What a flavor! Everybody, share, share, everybody have a taste. Even the blood-drinkers, yeah, you guys just go last. Be kind to the fellow after you: just a taste. Come on, everyone in good standing."

As the crowd flooded in to have a bite of Signari's "birthday cake" the patriarch himself walked Damiana back to the docket. He kept his arm around the lepress.

"You've always been my best elder, Dami. You know that, don't you?"

"It's never unpleasant to hear, Father Otto."

"Listen, I've been thinking about this for a while. I know it's not exactly a pleasant duty, but the rewards are...well, you can probably guess what the reward is. Will you represent my interests in Las Vegas with that reptile Cicatrice?"

"Of course, Patriarch. I shall miss Rome."

"Don't miss it too much. You'll be back here soon, if you know what I mean."

Signari patted Damiana hard on the cheek. Suddenly he noticed the Scavatelli brothers.

"Benito Scavatelli. And you I don't know."

"Italo Scavatelli, Patriarch," Damiana said.

"I see. How far back on the docket are they?"

"Fourth or fifth."

"Let's just deal with them now so you can get the first flight out of here. All right, everybody get a slice of cake? Okay, take your seats, take your seats."

The crowd receded as one of Signari's mortal disciples dragged the gurney out of the room. Now, in addition to being drilled full of holes, she was criss-crossed with the scars of the blood-drinkers' razor blades.

Signari didn't sit, but stood behind a podium. He didn't seem the type to get too comfortable with sitting.

Damiana grabbed Scav and his brother bodily and tossed them both to their knees at Signari's feet.

"Benny, Benny, Benny. You are just barely out of diapers. How long have you been draining force without drinking blood?"

Benito grimaced.

"A few days."

"What was that?"

"A few days, Father Otto."

"And when did your sire release you from your apprenticeship?"

Benito scowled. The lepress struck him, hard enough to shatter his jaw.

"The same, Father Otto."

Signari nodded knowingly.

"So Quentin, a longtime, well-trusted, well-known to me member of this House in excellent standing, did right by you. He trained you even to the point where you don't even drink blood anymore. That's dedication. That's righteousness. That's doing right by one's get. And you immediately turn around and do what?"

"I broke the code."

"Broke the code? You spat in Quentin's face. I ought to call him up here and let him decide what to do with you. What do you think about that?"

"Father Otto, if you understood the love I feel for my only brother, you would understand..."

Signari rolled his eyes.

"Shut him up."

Damiana smashed Benito's face again, shattering his jaw in multiple places and causing him to sever his own tongue. Suddenly, Signari's eyes alighted on Scav.

"You don't look like he loved you very much."

You're god-damned right he didn't.

"And you smell like..." Signari wrinkled his nose, "A churchyard. You still have faith, don't you?"

Scav opened his mouth, but no words would come.

"Oh, don't be shy. Nothing you say or do is going to affect my verdict one way or the other. I've already decided what to do with the

both of you. You may as well just get in the habit of answering your patriarch truthfully."

"I have faith."

"I knew it. You stink of it. I can't imagine how your brother could bear to drain you, let alone sire you. It's like getting a mouthful of poison. Well, your dumb ass is responsible for this, Benny, what do you think I should do with you?"

"Uh...let us go? Make my punishment to teach my little brother the code better than I learned it. Responsibility can go a long way toward stabilizing a person."

"Yeah, no. You two don't see each other anymore. Let's talk about all the ways you broke the code. First, you sired a get without your patriarch's permission. You think I let just any rabble into my House?"

"Well, I thought it was just a formality, Father Otto. A rubber stamp."

"A rubber stamp? Because I usually say yes? I usually say yes because my houselings usually don't come to me with half-cocked proposals. And I trust the people I sired to sire good people and so on, so that everybody in the House is more or less worthy of my trust. Now you go and you bring an immediate family member across? Oh, that's strike two, by the way. You know, if you were House Temuchin, they'd've made you slaughter your entire family the moment you were brought across. The code's strict about that, too. You leave your mortal kin behind along with all your mortal weaknesses. Clearly you haven't."

"I'm sorry, Father Otto."

"You are sorry. You're a sorry sack. And the worst thing you've done is to make your sire look like a fool. I had faith in him. Quentin was going to be an elder. Now?"

Signari gestured at someone behind Scav's back. He turned to look, but it was too late. A head came tumbling down at the floor before them. Scav didn't recognize the man, but gathered it was Quentin, Benito's sire. Benito seemed stunned.

"You can't...you can't punish him because of what I did!"

Signari chuckled.

"It's not wise to tell a House patriarch what he can and can't do. Especially in his own manse. No, Quentin suffered for your stupidity. Now as for you, you can pay me back with twenty-five years of service

as a fixer. Make it fifty. Damiana?"

The lepress reached down and strained the metal, as Benito did the same. Suddenly the yoke shattered. It would be some time before Benito would be able to weasel his way out of the rest of his bonds, but he was free to do so at his leisure now.

"Now, as for you, my boy. First of all, I like the hair. I'd like it better dyed white."

"Of course. Any...anything you say, F...F..."

"All right, all right. Now, officially you're an immortal without a House. That means you're nothing. You have no standing. Within a House, only a patriarch can order a death sentence, and then only as a last resort. Yeah, I see you looking down at Quentin's head. He hasn't had a decent get since I turned him five hundred years ago. He's been a complete and utter failure to me. If it wasn't your idiot brother, it would've been some other screw-up.

"But you? No House? Anybody can kill you. Cicatrice. Temuchin. Teslan. Druid. I don't care. Nobody cares. Now I do have the authority to grant you an adoption. Normally I wouldn't but men of faith are hard to turn. And therefore valuable. But you're also a goddamned abomination. An immediate blood relation of a houseling in poor standing."

Signari seemed to ruminate for a minute.

"Tell you what: we'll let fate decide. If there's someone in this room that's willing to adopt you, we'll go that way. If not, we'll go the other way."

Signari gestured at Quentin's head on the ground. Then he looked up at the audience.

"How about it? Any takers for a new get?"

The silence blared in Scav's ears for a moment. He nodded, accepting the judgment of the fates, and waited for the hammer to fall. Then, to his surprise, a Scottish brogue cut through the quiet.

"I'll take the boy. Just because I know it'll piss off Benito Scavatelli."

Father Otto tugged the heavy metal gauntlet off his hand and flexed his fingers. He leaned back in the chair at the head of Damiana's table. The chair was "his." Even as senior elder (and, it was assumed, Father Otto's expected heir) Damiana could not sit at the head of her own table without explicit instructions from Father Otto to do so and to make a proclamation in his stead.

Father Otto reached out and put his thumb to the forehead of the ginger young woman before him. She was snuffling (as they all did at this point) though her tears had long since gone dry and she was unable to make herself understood through the heavily-articulated harness gag she wore. Some Signaris preferred their meals screaming, or even kicking, but Damiana was a bit toned down and preferred to eat in relative silence, or at least in conversation with other immortals, not over the incoherent shrieks of their meals.

"How is she, Father Otto?"

Father Otto removed his thumb from the ginger's forehead and sucked it, making a sour face and shaking his head.

"Too bitter."

"Do you prefer a virgin meal, Father?"

Father Otto shrugged.

"Not necessarily. That one though…I think she had a rough life. I need a little less stress."

Damiana nodded and pressed the button down at the foot of the table where she was sitting. The table was actually rather ingeniously designed. The center held still but the outside was a conveyor belt of sorts. At each "setting" of the table was a small, seamless, locked box, which contained a kneeling mortal, restrained and gagged as Damiana preferred them. By pressing the button the conveyor belt activated and the settings moved down a place. Damiana activated the device three more times until a towheaded, ten-or-possibly-twelve (who really cared when it came to mortals?) year old boy hung before Father Otto, petrified and no longer even trying to scream in fear.

"Not much stress in a schoolchild's life. And a virgin, though you said that's not a necessity."

Father Otto shrugged and reached out to put his thumb against the child's cheek. He seemed to consider for a moment, then, like a connoisseur selecting a bottle of wine, nodded. Damiana leaned forward and prepared to devour the meal before her, a rather crusty old man who was giving her the stinkeye. Normally Damiana got the choice of meals, but, of course, when hosting her patriarch, the choice was his.

"Excuse me."

Father Otto and Damiana both looked up. Topan was glaring at them. It was hard for Damiana to get used to the idea of dining with a Cicatrice. Both she and Father Otto had long made it a policy not to do so, and the Cicatrice sitting there, red noose around his neck proclaiming his loyalty, was like having a splinter in her eye.

"Yes, Topan?" Father Otto asked, affecting an innocence in his voice that many recognized as false, though only a lieutenant as long-standing as Damiana recognized as hiding, deep, deep fury.

"If this is not good enough for Otto Signari, why is it good enough for me?"

He gestured at the ginger mortal, which in the process of Father Otto selecting his meal, had looped around to Topan's seat. Damiana rose before Father Otto could respond. In all things she deferred to her patriarch, but as host, this matter was hers to rectify. She walked to Topan's seat. The other immortals seated around the table were buzzing, whispering in one another's ears. Some were Signari, a few were from the other Houses, but none, as was customary, were of House Cicatrice save his heir alone.

"This mortal is not to your liking, Elder Topan?"

Topan folded his arms.

"That's not the point."

Damiana looked to Father Otto for some sign of what to do, but her patriarch was inscrutable, watching with a twisted smile on his face.

"Forgive me, elder, I miss the point entirely then."

Topan fixed her with a glare as though he were chastising a schoolchild or a mortal, not an elder of House Signari.

"The point, lepress, is the insult."

Damiana's face turned stony. She knew other immortals called her that. She wasn't so ignorant to think that others didn't make fun of her condition behind her back. But it had been a long time, long before she had become an elder of her House, even, since someone had called her a lepress to her face.

Topan continued.

"If it's not good enough for the patriarch of House Signari, what makes you think it should be good enough for the patriarch of House Cicatrice?"

Father Otto howled in laughter, pounding his thankfully ungauntleted fist on the table, but otherwise offered no hope and in fact waved off her pleading look as though to say, "No, no, don't let me interrupt you." Damiana was very old, and had long since learned the values of patience and abstinence. She didn't let any emotion cross her face.

"It is customary that the elder of this manse has her selection of the meat. Or, when he's present, the House Patriarch. Everyone else is fed randomly."

"Randomly?" Topan repeated, attempting to copy Damiana's inflections, "This is how seriously you take your hosting duties, Damiana? Just tossing random pieces of meat at people and hoping they're not offended, is that your methodology?"

"These are all top-tier specimens, carefully culled from my farm and the wild..."

"Push the button, you deformed freak, and let me have a finer cut."

In the silence that followed, a pair of flies fucking would've been a cacophony. After a moment, Damiana nodded.

"You don't care for this meal?"

"I do not care for anyone's sloppy seconds. If I am to be patriarch of the most powerful of the Great Houses, I demand the best."

Damiana reached out and grabbed the shrieking ginger around her throat. With a pinch she severed her spinal column and the girl fell dead.

"You don't want my hospitality, Cicatrice? Then starve."

Topan's chair flew out from behind him as he leapt to his feet. His hands were not clenched in fists, but curved into claws, his preferred fighting style. Damiana struggled to open her mouth and bare her teeth. Suddenly Damiana felt a great gauntleted hand drop down on her shoulder, rubbing bone against bone. Father Otto's other, ungloved hand, came down on Topan's shoulder.

"Come now, children, none of this," Father Otto said, "Are we all satisfied with our posturing? Everybody feel they've proven who's toughest?" Father Otto glanced from one face to the other. "'If that big meanie Otto Signari hadn't intervened, I would've taken him lickety split,' right?"

Topan cast his gaze down and while Damiana tried to keep Father Otto's eyes, she couldn't either. Father Otto clapped his hands down on both of their shoulders again, this time a paternal pat.

"Good. Topan, grab your seat. Literally. Damiana, you take yours. By that I mean just sit down."

Topan skulked off to retrieve his chair from where it had slammed to a halt against the wall. Spitefully, allowing it to screech across the floor like fingernails on a chalkboard, he dragged it back every centimeter.

Father Otto followed Damiana back to her position at the foot of the table and hovered over her as she sat. Once both of them had seated themselves, Father Otto reached out and pressed the red button. He pressed it again and again, inexpertly, until his own meal of tow-headed waif was before Topan.

Then he walked behind Topan and dropped his hands down on the Cicatrice's shoulders, massaging his neck and upper back.

"Topan is right. I mean, he's being a little bit of a jerk about it, but he's right. Soon he'll be patriarch of House Cicatrice. I forget sometimes; I'm used to all the deference, all the best things in life. Topan's been a black sheep for a little too long. Manners go the way of the dodo when you're out in the cold, I think. But let's not forget, any of us, that it was Cicatrice who put Topan out in the cold, Cicatrice who stole his get, Cicatrice who arranged a separate peace with the Inquisitors for his House. Cicatrice has taken every effort to stick his finger in each of our eyes. He has nothing but contempt for the other Great Houses, and he reserves the greatest contempt for mine especially, and for me personally. That's how Topan was raised: to be contemptuous. It's no surprise he at some point was going to turn his contempt on the wrong person. And that person was my very own heir, senior Elder Damiana here."

Father Otto ruffled Topan's hair. He gestured at the little boy.

"Go on, son. Finest cut of meat. It's all yours. I don't even want it. I want to eat like you today. You can eat like me."

Tentative, Topan reached out and pressed both hands to the sides of the boy's face. With a dreadful slowness that betrayed his relative youth and inexpertise, he slowly began to drain the boy's life essence. Father Otto returned to his position at the head of the table without sitting down.

"Eat, eat, please. Don't wait for me."

The others began to enjoy their meals. Sephera, the Teslan elder, had been left with the croaked ginger. She surreptitiously called to one of Damiana's mortal disciples to bring her something else, rather than make a scene as Topan had. Damiana admired her composure.

As if proving a point about his seniority, Father Otto reached out and barely brushed the tip of his index finger against the meal he had been provided. At the mere touch of his hand, the twentysomething man's hair turned grey, his skin sank into his bones, and his flesh turned to dust. All the other diners stopped eating to look at Father Otto. Father Otto was sucking his fingers.

"Deeeee-lish! You do put on a hell of a banquet, Damiana."

"Father Otto..." Damiana started to say.

But he held up his hand to silence his senior lieutenant. With that, Damiana realized Father Otto was posturing, but he wasn't going to be building to a reckoning. He was just making a point to Topan, in case he had missed it, about who the real superior was here. Topan seemed to sour on his meal and lowered his hands.

"I've got to say, this is a celebration I've long dreamt of. I was the cockroach under Cicatrice's heel before any of you were glimmers in your sires' eyes. But now, finally, after almost seventy years of him acting with complete impunity—by which I mean complete lack of respect—you've all come around to my way of thinking about him. He has bullied the other Houses. He has made light of us. Thrown us to the Inquisitors and never offered a hand when he's the damn reason why we have to suffer the brunt of their piffling wrath. And now, breaking the code, stealing Topan's get, he's finally gone too far. The man is not above the law, not above the law he himself espouses.

"For a long time now I've considered declaring war on

House Cicatrice. But I refused out of respect. I refused to go it alone. I thought to myself, 'Otto, you need to go along to get along.' But the truth is now all of you see. He has nothing but contempt for our code, contempt for our ways. He told us not earlier today, Sephera and I, that his will trumps the code.

"Well! Very well then! We'll put his will to the test. And now that even his own heir is against him and with us, all of us, a united front, I think the next incarnation of House Cicatrice is going to be much more cooperative. Much more beneficial, I should say, as a partner in the immortal community."

Father Otto tossed himself back into his chair. He rubbed his hands together vigorously, his gauntleted hand making a total scabrous mess of his unclad hand, but it instantly healed.

"Now then! To brass tacks. Damiana, will you show the fixers in?"

Damiana nodded, rose, and went to open the door. She avoided wrinkling her nose as the most odious filth of the immortal world filed into her dining hall. Dozens and dozens of fixers poured in. Most were Signaris, proudly displaying their stripes, but the other Houses were represented as well, including a few Teslans with shiny replacement parts and naked Druids. She'd have to remember to set the cultists loose with a few scrub brushes in here after the midden ghouls had dealt with the remains of their meals.

"Benito, my boy!" Father Otto said, rising and embracing one of the fixers with a look of near-unhinged glee on his face. Damiana was chagrined to recognize Benito Scavatelli. "How's my favorite fixer?"

"Always pleased to be in your service," Benito replied, bowing his head, but he could hardly hide his own smile.

"You haven't seen your brother lately, have you?"

Benito was a little too quick to shake his head.

"Oh, no, Father Otto. Not since you put us straight."

Father Otto seemed to consider for a moment.

"Well if you do happen to come across him, let me know. He was supposed to check in with Damiana about a matter. Haven't heard a peep from him, though."

"I'll let you know if I hear anything, Father Otto, but I try to walk the straight and narrow these days. You told me to leave the boy alone so I have."

Father Otto gave Benito a Roman kiss and then slapped him hard a few times on the cheek fraternally. He walked around the room, shaking hands and clasping shoulders with the scum-of-all-Houses fixers.

"Hi. How you doing? Good to meet you. We met in Paris, didn't we? No? I'm almost sure of it. I never forget a face. How are you?"

After finishing his circuit Father Otto didn't return to his seat, but instead draped his hands over the back of it. He gestured for Damiana and whispered in her ear.

"Is this all that came? I thought you put the word out weeks ago."

"There are many more, Father Otto. Almost five hundred, all told. These are just the ringleaders. It's all I can fit."

Father Otto nodded.

"Welcome, ladies, gentleman, children of all ages. I want one thing from you. Name your price."

The fixers exchanged glances. Silence reigned supreme for a moment.

"Our price for what?" one of the Teslans asked.

"Excellent question," Father Otto replied, affixing the asker with an imaginary beam from his finger. "What is your price for the sort of job that a House patriarch asks you to name any price for?"

Instead of silence, this time, it was as though a muted rumbling swept through the room. The fixers, many of whom were with partners, were debating back and forth what Father Otto was asking and what he might be getting at, or be up to, depending on how much they trusted him. Benito Scavatelli was the first to affix his balls to his crotch and step forward.

"I want to be patriarch of my own House."

"You don't lack for ambition, Benito," Father Otto replied with a contagious laugh. Even Benito laughed at the Patriarch's pleasure in his brassiness. Then, to Damiana's utter surprise he cut through the giggling din with a, "Done."

In that instant she could've heard a pin drop.

"I'm sorry...?" Benito murmured.

"I said 'done,' boy-o. Don't you know not to keep asking once you get the answer you were looking for? Any manjack here who delivers will be made my senior elder and heir apparent. Signed, sealed, delivered, in a contract carved in stone. When I die, House Signari is yours. Hell, I may even retire in my dotage, you never know."

Almost without even realizing it, Damiana was on her feet, her chair scraping the floor behind her. All eyes in the room turned on her.

"Father Otto..."

"No reflection on you, Damiana. You've served me loyally all these years. But the bounty's been set. You're welcome to claim it yourself, of course."

That started the fixers into such riotous laughing that Damiana would've probably blushed had she still had blood flowing through her veins. Damiana was an excellent bureaucrat, Father Otto's trusted confidante and *consiglieri*, a major-domo *par excellence*, but a street fighter and bounty hunter she was not. Like all Signaris, she loved a good scrap, but her preferred martial arts were fencing and falconry—dignified sports. No one would've ever mistaken her for a fixer. With what she could recover of her dignity, she seated herself.

"So what do you say, boy-os? Want a taste of *la dolce vita*? A shot at being boss of bosses? Then bring me back my mark, *tout suite.*"

"And who is your mark, Father Otto?" one of the fixers, a Teslan with a bionic eye, asked.

"Ah, yes, therein lies the rub. You don't get to be patriarch unless you bring down a patriarch. One of you fine young immortals in this room today is going to bring me the head of Cicatrice." Father Otto allowed the fixers to mutter to one another for just a second before continuing, "Oh, don't act silly. You're looking for sanctions, you're looking for proof above and beyond the fact I'm offering you a big fat plum as a reward? Elder Sephera?"

The Teslan coughed, obviously an affectation for an immortal, and rose to her feet.

"The council has met and discussed the matter. Father Cicatrice has gone too far around the bend this time. All the Great Houses are in agreement. It's war."

"Thank you, Sephera. It is war, boy-os. And the fastest way to end this war is to cut off the head of the snake. Look, let's face it. Immortals don't kill immortals. And killing humans, well, it gets boring. Like shooting fish in a barrel. You're all like me, you became fixers to get the thrill of a sanctioned fight with another immortal. You and I both know there's nothing like it. And you wouldn't be the best fixers in the world if you weren't constantly challenging yourselves. Well, you finally get it: the ultimate challenge. What do you say? Think you're up for it?"

Benito stepped forward.

"It'll be my pleasure to bring you the head of that Cicatrice scum, Father Otto."

Father Otto patted Benito's face a few times with his gauntleted hand.

"Attaboy."

"Wait!"

All eyes in the room turned to Topan, who looked like he was ready to rocket out of his chair. He pointed a finger around the room in every direction.

"All of you, all of you listen to me."

"Shut up, Cicatrice scum."

"Turncoat."

"Traitor."

"Shitbag."

Topan grabbed his chair and with a petulant flick of his wrist shattered it to pieces on the ground. He grabbed Benito, a man easily twice his size, by the neck, and lifted him off the ground, holding him parallel to the floor, his arm fully extended to do it. He jabbed the splintered end of the chair leg into Benito's chest. All he had to do was release his grip on Benito and the fixer would drop by gravity and impale himself. Benito struggled, but was obviously outclassed by the Cicatrice. Damiana's eyes widened. She had always assumed Topan was useless and weak.

"He's not yours to kill, Topan," Father Otto growled, "Not for an insult. He's a Signari."

"And I wouldn't harm a hair on his head, Otto. Just so long, that is, as he and everyone here, and oh yeah spread the word to all your scumbag friends on the streets, there's a little girl with Cicatrice. About eighteen years old. An immortal. Chinese. Beautiful beyond all reason. You can't miss her. And I'd better not miss her at the end of all this."

"All right!" Benito grunted between his thrashing, "Don't touch the Chinese girl. Spread the word. Got it."

Topan let Benito and the wooden stake drop at the same time, and they clattered into each other.

"Cicatrice losses are acceptable," Father Otto said, "Except for the girl named Idi Han. She's Topan's get. And Topan is the new patriarch of House Cicatrice. Even I can't protect you from his wrath if any harm comes to her. *Capisce*?"

"*Capisce*," Benito muttered, and led the exodus.

Father Otto waited until the door slammed. Languorously, he kicked the broken piece of chair up into his hand. Topan stared at him defiantly. It was a child's petulant stare. Father Otto jabbed the stick into Topan's neck.

"You've got a way of letting your emotions control you, my little tempest-in-a-teapot. That won't serve you when you're a House patriarch."

Topan grunted out a laugh.

"I used to think being a House patriarch meant something. Now it seems like you're just giving it out to every Tom, Dick, and Harry."

Father Otto glanced over at Damiana. He pointed the jagged stick in her direction.

"Damiana is my heir apparent. I haven't named her as such but she's my senior elder. I haven't had a get in almost five hundred years. Know what happened to that one?"

"No. I'd love for you to tell me, though."

Father Otto clapped his gauntleted hand down on Topan's head. He was so much taller than Topan, and his hand so massive, that he nearly palmed Topan's head. Judging by the pained look of defiance in Topan's eyes, Father Otto was squeezing his melon and all but trying to burst it.

"Cicatrice killed my last get. I haven't gotten over it, to be honest with you. Her name was Katarina. Not a good-looking girl. But then I don't fuck my gets like some immortals. But you wouldn't know anything about that, would you, Topan?"

There was a sickening crunch as part of Topan's skull disintegrated under Father Otto's gauntlet.

"That would be a violation of the code," Topan managed to huskily spit out.

"You're right! It would be! So would killing another immortal without cause." Father Otto snapped the fingers of his free hand. "Oh, but now that I think about, our Houses are at war. You're a perfectly legitimate Signari target. And did I mention that I really, really never got over Katarina's loss?"

"Go ahead, then," Topan growled, folding his arms defiantly, "Pop my head off. See what it benefits you."

"That's just it. Cicatrice doesn't give a shit about you. Killing you in exchange for my Katarina? It'd be like trading a hunting dog for a gnat. A wife for a dung beetle."

Father Otto relinquished his grip on Topan's head.

"You're useful to me, Topan. That's why I give you a lot of leeway." Father Otto held up his hands as though he were weighing two pieces of fruit. "Be cautious, though. Sometimes our leeway can outpace your usefulness. Damiana, if any of those fixers actually attempt to claim their prize…well, I'll just leave it to your ample devices to settle accounts with them, sound fair?"

"Most fair, Father Otto."

"Thank you. I'll be retiring to my chambers. Good evening, all."

A muted chorus of "good evenings" followed Father Otto out the door.

TEN

Nico yawned. Having worked second shift so long, he was having trouble getting used to Price's odd hours. They were walking down the hallways of one of the buildings of the University of Nevada. They'd gotten turned around on campus more than once already. It was hard to navigate in the burgeoning darkness.

"Doesn't it make more sense to go vampire hunting during the day?"

Price shook his head.

"You'd think so but not really. They get entrenched in a city like this and they burrow down and down like a tick you can never dislodge."

"But they've got to be vulnerable. They're just sitting in a coffin, right?"

"Sure, if you could get to the coffin it'd be great. But nightcrawlers always surround themselves with renfields. Cultists. People who guard their coffins and make useful bloodbags. Sometimes they manage the vampire's wealth and business. It's disgusting."

"So they hypnotize these people?"

Price shook his head.

"No, that's a myth. Nightcrawlers run their circles—that's what they call it, a 'circle'—like a cult. Some of the renfields are deceived, some are bribed, some even know what's really going on and they do it for the promise of eternal life. A promise that just never seems to come true."

"So anyone I meet could be a slave to a vampire?"

"A lot of people are. It's pretty scary because the only

advantage we've got on them is numbers. But as more and more people serve them…well, I guess it's just a matter of time before we're the ones who are outnumbered. Ah! Here we go."

Price stopped at the entrance to the professor's office. An embossed fake gold plate on the door read HOLLY ANN KASPRZAK, P.HD.

"So who is this lady again?"

Price took a swig from his flask.

"She's a professor."

"No shit. Teaching what? Vampire Studies?"

"History, I think. Something obscure. She's got tenure so it doesn't really matter."

"And she's really an Inquisitor?"

Price wiggled his hand in the air, a bit unsure.

"Eh."

"Eh? What does that mean?"

"She's not an Inquisitor exactly. But she's knowledgeable. I think she'd probably consider herself a neutral party in an age-old conflict. Like a reporter or…Switzerland."

"How do we know we can trust her, then?"

"Shut up, kid."

Price knocked on the door. He stared down the barrel of his flask.

"Empty," he muttered.

Silence reigned.

"You know, it's late. She's probably at home with her family."

Price shook his head.

"No family. She's here."

He pounded on the door again with the flat part of the bottom of his hand.

"Holly Ann! Are you in there? It's Carter Price!"

The door opened inward slightly.

"Uh…" Nico said, "Does that mean come in?"

"Grab him!" a voice called out from inside the office, "Gently, please!"

With a speed that betrayed its length, a thick brown snake shot out between the crack, tongue flicking in and out of its mouth. Brown with black and yellow spots, it slipped right between Price's legs. Price jumped out of the way.

"Jesus Christ!"

"Grab him, Carter!"

"You grab him!"

Shaking his head, Nico quickened his pace to a speedwalk to keep up with the snake and reached down to grab it. Holding it by both hands around the neck (torso?) he looked into the thing's dead, reptilian eyes and its tongue flicked out and tickled his nose. He nearly dropped it but held fast.

"You're strangling him!" Price said, approaching.

"No, I'm not, I'm…oh shit."

The snake was wrapping itself around his hips.

"Oh, nevermind. I guess he's strangling you instead."

A bespectacled woman with long, curly brown hair emerged from the office. She was wearing a pullover with the collar zipped up Mandarin-style.

"Carter Price, you old devil!"

She walked up to Price and embraced him in a big hug.

"Hey, there, Holly Ann. Who's your new boy toy?"

"Him?" she said, walking up and stroking the snake under its chin. "This is Brutus. He's a Sumatran blood python."

"Blood?" Nico squeaked, as Brutus's tail made its way around Nico's neck.

Professor Kasprzak reached out and gently encouraged Brutus to entwine himself around her shoulders instead.

"So-called because of their red colorings when they're full-grown. Of course, Brutus here is just a baby, aren't you, sweetheart? Which is why you like to run away. But you mustn't run away." Kasprzak nuzzled at her pet. "Who are you?"

"Nico Salazar, ma'am."

"Ah, yes. The famous shift manager."

Nico was taken aback.

"You've heard of me?"

"No," she said, tapping at his nameplate, "It's on your nametag. How green is your new apprentice, Carter?"

"Apprentice, I dunno…"

"That green, huh? Haven't even changed out of your work clothes yet, eh? Well, come on in, boys. As much fun as chasing down a naughty snake is, something tells me you're here for a different reason."

As a triptych, they entered Kasprzak's office. It was a lavish and richly decorated affair. There were terrariums with turtles, lizards, and snakes lined up along one wall, bird cages in each corner, and cages full of mice, rats, guinea pigs, and hamsters. She gently let Brutus out into a nicely-appointed terrarium which had been decorated with rocks and small plants.

The office was hot from all the heat lamps and little warm-blooded creatures. And it smelled halfway like a zoo. Nevertheless, mittens, scarves, knitted caps, and even full sweaters hung over every inch of furniture. Kasprzak dropped down into the chair behind her desk, which whirled her halfway around before she pushed herself back to face the two men. Grabbing a ball of yarn and a hook she resumed crocheting a winter sock.

She gestured for them to take seats in two plush chairs opposite her. Nico picked up a folded tablecloth from his seat, sat down, and set the tablecloth on his lap. Price just knocked a stack of doilies off his chair onto the floor.

"Do you teach biology?" Nico asked.

She chuckled.

"Nope. Information technology."

Nico glanced around but couldn't even spot a computer.

"Your office doesn't look like…"

"I'll bet when you get home at night you don't want to see another cup of coffee or newspaper."

"Or sandwich," Price muttered.

"That's true," Nico agreed.

"Anyhoo, what can I do you for?"

Price reached into his pocket and pulled out his phone. He handed it over to Kasprzak. She adjusted her glasses, looked at it, adjusted her glasses again, took her glasses off, cleaned them, then adjusted them again.

"Real?"

"As far as I can tell."

"Where is it?"

"Bonaparte has it."

"Will she let me take a look?"

Price shrugged. Kasprzak clucked her tongue and shook her head from side to side.

"When will you two just kiss and make up already?"

"When she admits she's wrong about everything and disbands her group."

"I suspect she'd say much the same about you. Nico, is it?"

"Yes, professor."

Kasprzak wore a delighted face and smiled at Price.

"Oh, he's very polite. You picked a good one, Carter."

"I didn't…nevermind."

"Nico, darling, will you grab that afghan?"

Nico rose and walked over to the wall Kasprzak was pointing at. The colorful result of some long crocheting labor of hers hung over what could have been more aquariums or terrariums or God only knew what all else. He grabbed the blanket.

"Yes, go ahead. Pull it down."

He yanked and stepped back, worried that he would open up a flow of junk that wouldn't stop. But behind the afghan was simply a bookshelf. He scanned the titles. Quite a few were utterly inscrutable to him, not even in the Latin alphabet. Amongst the ones he could read were *The Pnakotic Manuscripts, The Tome of Eternal Darkness, Unausprechlichen Kulten, The Malleus Maleficarium, De Vermis Mysteriis, The Book of Eibon, Cultes des Goules, Vlarney the Vampyr,* the collected works of Poe, Lovecraft, and Machen, and the *Naturom Demento.* Nico ran his fingers across the incredible collection.

"Not exactly *A++ for Beginners.*"

Kasprzak shook her head. Then she tapped her temple with her index finger.

"Nah. All that stuff's up here anyway. Is there one called… something…wormy wormy germy. Shit. I can't remember."

"Uh…*De Vermis Mysteriis*?"

Kasprzak snapped her fingers.

"That's the one."

Nico reached up to grab the correct tome and started to pull it out.

"Jesus, be careful, kid!" Price said, "That thing's eight hundred years old."

Nico whirled around, the book in his hand, and held it up. It had a glossy new cover and the pages were still white.

"No it's not. It says copyright 1998."

"Reprint, I'm afraid," Kasprzak said, "Still, pretty tough to find. A lot of private copies have gone mysteriously missing."

"Mysteriously missing in the sense that..." Nico prodded.

"In the sense that if the nightcrawlers get wind you have one, they'll take it. And probably kill you," Price growled.

"And they bought all the copies on eBay. Selfish pricks."

Nico put the book down on Kasprzak's desk. He and Price scooted their chairs forward to get a better look as she flicked through it.

"Too bad there's no index," she muttered, "Medieval monks weren't much on going back through their manuscripts after they illuminated them. I keep meaning to make an index one of these days, but I've got so much on my plate."

Nico glanced around the room at the chirping birds, lazing reptiles, and department store's worth of textiles.

"Ah ha!" she said. "Here it is."

She turned the book around so the other two could see it. In a distinctly medieval style, with no real sense of lines or dimensions, was something not too different from an ink blot test. The illustration was all in black.

"A Rorschach test?" Nico asked.

"This was made about 800 years before the term 'psychology' was coined, kid. Look, it's a man on a horse."

Price pointed out the different parts of the figure and suddenly Nico could see it. A man all in black holding a lance in one hand and a sword in the other, atop a horse, also all black. Blood or oil or something dripped from both, further obscuring the nature of what they were looking at. Nico flipped a through a few pages. All of the other illustrations, though bizarre, were outlined and colored in a more traditional style.

"Why did they do this one like an ink blot?"

"That's how the legend goes. He's like a blot of ink on the horizon, dripping with some kind of weird oily substance. I

     Stephen Kozeniewski

never got the full story on that," Kasprzak chimed in.

"Hey, wait a minute," Nico said, looking closer at the illustration, and running his finger along it, "This looks like a poster or something I've seen on dorm walls."

"You probably have," Kasprzak agreed.

She rose and walked over to an umbrella stand stuck in one corner of the room. Instead of umbrellas, rolled up tubes of paper occupied it. She ran the rubber band down on two or three to check their contents, before finally saying, "Ah!" and unrolling a poster fully.

The poster was "framed" with the stylistic inscription "Frank Frazetta" at the top and "Death Dealer—1973" in smaller letters at the bottom. Nico nodded. That was the image he had seen before. A knight, or an executioner, maybe, holding a bloody hybrid of axe and scythe, astride a black horse with what almost looked like a biohazard symbol on its harness. The knight held a shield with a black eagle inscription, but his face and body was obscured, as though in shadow…or as though it were shadow.

"That's the one," Nico whispered, "So this is the guy we're dealing with."

Kasprzak shrugged.

"This is an iconic illustration in, ah, the fantasy genre. I've heard stories that Frazetta based it on the actual Hunter of the Dead. Or, at least, this illustration from *De Vermis Mysteriis*. There's even a story that Cicatrice once visited him to make sure he hadn't seen the real Hunter. Any idea if it's true, Carter?"

Price shrugged.

"There are a million stories about Cicatrice and The Hunter. As far as I know, that's all they are. Stories. Fairy tales. Nursery rhymes."

"So, what's the…story?"

Kasprzak sat back down in her chair. She looked at Price.

"Wouldn't it be cool if I turned out the lights and put a flashlight under my chin?"

"The coolest, professor." He snapped his fingers. "Ah, but then, how would we see the illustrations?"

Kasprzak grimaced.

"You're right. Picture the scene. Eight centuries ago. The Dark Ages. Rome collapsed. The great empires of the colonial age had yet to rise. Really, there were few proper places you could call a state. Europe was a patchwork of feuding nobles. Peasants tilled the earth, living hand-to-mouth. What the nobles didn't take from them, the church did. And the church was rife with corruption."

Kasprzak opened *De Vermis Mysteriis* to an illustration of a great forest, fading to blackness on the outskirts, surrounding a simple rural village. The people were overworked like oxen, and fat lords and churchmen happily patted their bellies and whipped the peasants.

"Imagine not being able to walk to a neighboring village without fear of being torn apart by wolves or highwaymen or hell, just a noble who considers peasants good sport. It was a place and time where life was cheap and that's exactly the sort of place and time where vampires thrive. While humans were shivering in the cold and barely able to prop up what we call civilization, in the shadows a new society was taking form."

She flipped the page. A wolf bayed against the moon and dark figures emerged from trees.

"For the first time in a long time the vampires began talking to each other. Instead of preying upon villages and moving on, they were considering ways to extort for the blood, flesh, and lives that they need to survive. They even began to establish plantations where they farmed people like livestock. While mankind was rotting on the vine, the crop of vampires was growing strong."

She flipped to the next page, which was a work almost like something out of Gray's Anatomy, though obviously scrabbled together centuries before ideas like "humours" had fallen out of vogue. The monk who had scribbled it had taken great pains to differentiate the vampire from a man. It had horns, hooves, serrated teeth, hairy legs, and explanations in Latin of how all of its various (presumably imaginary) inner organs worked.

"Every man had a lord who ruled the day. But the vampires ruled the night. The people cowered behind the walls of their towns and prayed all night in their churches for God to deliver them. Faith was strong amongst the common folk, and faith is a poison to the dead, but the church had grown decadent and opulent, and clergymen were as apt to help the vampires as to shepherd their flocks. Some called it an Age of Faith. We who study the occult call it the Golden Age of the Vampire."

She flipped to an illustration of villagers praying in a church, while vampires plucked their babies out of the windows and messily devoured them.

"Death and blood bathed the land in opulent red. The vampires feasted each night in crazed Bacchanal. Any man foolish enough to be caught outside the city gates at night stood no chance of survival. The people fought back with weapons both spiritual and conventional. At the height of the Golden Age, each night became a monstrous battle for survival. And each night the numbers of men dwindled, and the numbers of vampires swelled like a bloated corpse. And then when day came again, the vampires retreated to their safe hiding places, and the good people could pretend they did not exist, so long as the sun was up."

The next illustration showed a line of vampires dancing together, seven in all, blood dripping from their mouths and bodies. They carried goblets of blood and naked women (witches?) kneeled and praised them in a circle.

"At the height of the Golden Age, a vampire of unusual clarity of vision and unholy power, sometimes called Lilith or Lily the Half-Face or in some texts, the Quarter-Face, founded the Necropolis, the City of the Dead. It was built into a volcanic mountain and is sometimes described as a gothic castle of towering obsidian spires. Humans were kept as livestock. The blood flowed, and no vampire ever went hungry. Vampires flocked there in numbers never before imagined. Lily the Half-Faced dreamt of an empire of the dead. The dead thought of it as their Camelot, their Rome, their 'glorious, bloodstained city' and homeland of all vampires."

She flipped to an unusually complex drawing of a black mountain, shown as though it had been split in half and its inner workings exposed. At the top was the vampire queen, quite literally missing half her face. She held a goblet carved from a skull, from which blood dripped freely. Beneath her was a banquet hall, gruesomely decorated with trophies, furniture carved from bone and human skins nailed to the wall. Vampires feasted, some drinking from golden goblets of blood and others laying their victims on the table to feast on them directly. Below, humans wailed as they were chained and fattened up for the slaughter.

"What happened?" Nico whispered, realized his mouth was dry as sandpaper.

ELEVEN

Earlier that night…

"Where are we going, Santa?"

Santa held his gigantic hand down to Alessia. She placed her own diminutive paw into his and he clasped her tightly, seeming to envelop her entire hand with his own.

"Hold on tightly, now, my dear. Have you read Through the Looking Glass?*"*

Alessia brightened up at the mere mention of her favorite book. Well, second favorite. She liked the first Alice book better.

"Oh, yes, sir."

"Well, then you'll be very pleased. That's where we're going."

She was so stunned for a moment she couldn't say anything and tripped over her own feet. She would have tumbled facefirst to the ground but Santa pulled her up to her feet. He was very strong.

"We're going to Wonderland?"

"We'll be there shortly. Just a trip down the rabbit hole and we'll be there."

She found herself flustered by excitement and could barely talk as they descended into a cave. It was cold and she began to shiver. As soon as she was shivering she realized how truly strange this place looked, how it was unlike anywhere she had ever been before. She tugged on Santa's shirt.

"Santa, I'm scared. Are you sure Mom said this was okay?"

Santa scooped her up into his arms as though she weighed nothing. She wrapped her arm around his neck and nuzzled his shoulder.

"She insisted. She said that you had been a good girl, Alessia, and

that I should give you a special treat. You have been a good girl, haven't you?"

Her mind flashed back to peeing her pants in the department store, scrawling in crayon on the wall, jumping on mom's bed when she wasn't home, and the dozens of other tiny transgressions which had filled her world and worried her no end.

"But it's so far from Christmas!"

"Well, I have to fill my time somehow, don't I? The elves spend all year making the toys. What else am I to do with my time but to visit my favorite children?"

She nodded. That made sense.

"What happened to your eye, Santa?"

"I had an accident. I got into a fight with the Easter Bunny."

"Is he all right?"

"He'll be fine. And look. You've been so brave and we're already here."

Alessia turned and looked but all she saw was a dead end to the cave. Santa put her back down on the ground and revealed a secret door. She clapped with wonder as he inserted a giant golden key and turned it. This was just like something out of The Polar Express *or some other magnificent storybook of discovery and wonder.*

"Here we are, Alessia. There's the rabbit hole."

She looked out over the wide expanse before her. The rabbit hole seemed to go on forever in every direction, just like the time they had visited San Diego and seen the Pacific Ocean. The rabbit hole was scarier than the ocean, though, because it was gloomy. She even felt a little thrill of terror looking at it.

"We're going down there?" she whispered.

"Yes," Santa replied, "But not just yet. First I have to put on my hat."

He picked her up and placed her on a tall stone table. Her legs dangled over the side and she kicked them.

"Your Santa hat?"

"Oh, no," he said, "This is a different hat. Don't you remember what I told you? How I'm going..."

He gestured for her, as he had earlier when teaching her the funny word. She racked her brain, and was just about to give up when it hit her.

"In gabino!"

"In cognito," *he said, smiling, "Exactly. No, I'll be wearing this hat."*

He lifted up a fancy hat that sort of reminded her of an Indian headdress, only not quite. It was lined with feathers and almost resembled a crown. When he placed it on his head she giggled.

"That's a silly hat, Santa."

"It is," *he agreed, "It's a very silly hat. But Wonderland is a very silly place. Now there's one last thing we have to do. I want you to look up at the ceiling."*

She looked upward. In a ring hanging like bats from the ceiling were pale-looking people. She gasped, but then remembered how strange Wonderland had seemed to Alice. This was just like meeting Tweedle-Dee or the Mock Turtle. She began to count, mouthing each number.

"Thirteen," *she concluded.*

"Yes, very good. My friends need some medicine."

"How are they going to get it, being way up there?"

"Well, you're going to give it to them."

She squealed in a combination of delight and terror, not sure if he was teasing, and slightly afraid he was.

"I'm going to go up there?"

"No, you're going to stay right here. Just keep looking up at them."

Santa placed his hand on her chest. She felt weak, light-headed, as though she had just spun around in circles for a little bit too long on the lawn.

"There, you see?"

Blinking, she refocused and was astonished to see little streams of light coming out of her fingers. They were like firefly freeways, and they stretched out like a rope up to the ceiling, and each stream of light ended at one of the thirteen sick people. They seemed to shiver and grunt in pleasure as her streams of light struck them.

"Santa, I'm glowing!"

"You sure are, Alessia. Now think about when you went to the doctor's and had to get a shot."

She pinched her eyes shut and shook her head.

"I don't like getting shots."

With her eyes closed, she heard Santa's voice whispering into her ear.

"Nobody likes getting shots. But just remember: a little pinch and then it's over. Are you ready? Little pinch."

She felt a horrible pain in her chest where Santa had placed his hand. This was worse than a little pinch. This was like being punched in the stomach. She opened her eyes and gawked at her own tiny heart, still attached to her by red strings, beating in Santa's palm.

"Now in ten seconds or so it'll be over. That's about the amount of time it takes your brain to realize you're already dead."

The heart stopped beating and she fell against the stone table, blackness swallowing her as her chin struck it hard.

The sun had only just set and wisps of deep violet still trailed through the night. Idi Han took a deep breath of the frigid night air, though she didn't have to. She wanted to see what it was like. Intellectually she knew it was cold, but the discomfort of coldness had all but fled her body. She realized that in her simple cheongsam she was barely dressed for a desert night, but hadn't even thought to ask for something heavier.

Scavatelli was walking briskly, not back towards the city, but outside its limits into the desert. Even as unfamiliar as Idi Han was with the local geography, she could tell by the stars that he was not going the right way.

"And just where do you think you're going?" Idi Han asked.

"I'm sorry, my young friend. I know promises have been made and I can't explain everything to you but my business in this city is concluded. You haven't seen The Hunter that I did. And I don't ever want to see him again. In fact, you can come with me if you like."

"You promised my sire, the most powerful living immortal and patriarch of the most powerful of the Great Houses..."

Scav stopped and held up his hand, a light, sneering expression on his face.

"Now let's get one thing straight. I may not look like much, I may not sound like much, but I'm not a complete fucking fool. Cicatrice is not your sire. Everyone knows the old Scar swore never to take on another get after the nightmare Topan turned out to be. So what's the real deal between you two? You got something to blackmail him with? Or is he just toying with you?"

Idi Han pursed her lips, unsure how to respond. Scavatelli held up his hands, as though in mock surrender.

"Whatever. Nevermind. I don't care. And I don't have time for it now. But look, you're a good kid. You're more powerful than I am, that's just natural power. I can smell it from here even through all that garlic you're wearing. We Signaris are a House of stray dogs, you know. I could get someone else to adopt you, maybe I could do it myself if Father Otto accepts me back into the fold. I happen to be in need of a new travelling companion. So, hey, what the fuck, come with me if you want. But if not, just leave me be. Please."

Idi Han stood waiting in the moonlight as Scav turned to go again, her breast roiling. A few days ago she had been back home in Guangdong. Now she was a million kilometers away, in a strange land she knew nothing about, and she had no idea whether she should even trust the man who had promised to look after her.

The last man who had promised to look after her had turned out to be a rapist, a lunatic, and a monster. Not just a human monster, but a monster of myth and legend, of seafoam and cloud. How was Cicatrice any different from Topan? Who knew if he was even worse?

Perhaps I should learn to look after myself.

"Father Cicatrice ordered you to take me to this encampment of yours."

Scav jammed his hands into his vest pockets and turned around.

"You don't want that. Just trust me. I don't want that. You don't want that. We could go on the open road, the way me and my sire did. Old Connor, he used to tell me he hopped train cars during the Depression. Made meals out of stewbums like they were candy. Now I wasn't sired until the '80s, but that was a hell of a time, too. We'll have to get you new clothes of course."

"What's wrong with my clothes?"

"What's right with them?"

If I mean to look after myself…this is my chance.

A smile split Scav's face in two. He was ready to run. Idi Han sighed and his smile melted away.

"Whatever he is to me…whatever he is to you…Cicatrice entrusted us with this task. He can't go among the fixers. He's too well known. And he's probably their target. Once you've shown me this place, I don't care what you do. But you will fulfill your promise at least."

Scavatelli reached up and gouged eight great furrows into his own face with his fingernails, laying bare muscle, sinew, and meat. Idi Han stepped back, tensing herself for battle, but when he began knocking at his own forehead she realized it was just a nervous tick. His horrible wounds were already healing over. The Long Gift of immortality in full effect.

"I warned you. I tried to warn you. Whenever you think of me, remember: I tried to warn you."

"I won't think of you."

Scav turned and headed back toward the city. He led her to an overpass. As the cars and trucks rolled by overhead, two concrete tunnels led down ominously into the depths below the neon city.

"Do you know where you are?" he asked.

She nodded. She had been paying attention to the street signs.

"Thank you. Good luck."

She grasped at the garland of garlic bulbs around her neck to make sure it was still there. Cicatrice had warned her not to remove it and not to show off her skills if it could be avoided. She had nearly laughed in his face then. Her skills mostly amounted to cooking rice and yoking oxen without getting kicked.

A hiss like a tea kettle sounded.

"Ah, hell," Scav said, "I can't let you go down there. But you owe me."

She cast him a sidelong glance as he re-appeared at her side.

"For remaining true to your word?"

"For hanging around The Hunter of the Dead's hunting grounds, how about that?"

They passed into the labyrinth. At first she wanted to look for light, but in a moment she remembered she didn't need any. Her eyes could pick out everything in the dark as well as in the light—even the colors of the graffiti.

A few mortals rose to stop them, but upon seeing Scav they returned to their business. Sections of the sewers and tunnels had been laid out like apartments. Each had a coffin, sometimes two, or else a platform of some type covered with dirt and a burial shroud. Mortals busied themselves cooking, cleaning, and looking after the effects of their immortal masters, but Idi Han could spot none of them.

"Where is everybody?"

"Out fixing. Or seeing the town. Or...just about anything but hanging out in a dank sewer. Come on, I'll take you to my encampment."

Probably looking for Cicatrice, in other words.

As they continued through the maze, Idi Han took care to note the twists and turns they took. She was supposed to be doing reconnaissance, after all. It quickly became apparent from the habitations that people had been living here for many, many years.

"How long ago did you say that you all descended on this place?"

"A few weeks. Maybe a month. The lepress—I mean, Damiana, she's the Signari elder here in Las Vegas—put out a call for fixers. As many fixers as could be found. She said there was work in Las Vegas for the next hundred years."

A few weeks? People have been living here for years.

She wondered briefly how many of the mortals living here had pledged their allegiance to the fixers when they arrived… and how many had been brought.

They soon reached Scav's encampment. It was separated from the rest of the habitations by a few shower curtains. Wooden pallets lined the ground, and Idi Han could tell by the water stains that they were necessary to avoid flooding.

She counted six sleeping areas. A mortal, her eyes sunken and her face pale and drawn—Hedrox's features, writ small— rose with some difficulty from a small cookpot over a camp stove.

"Welcome back, Master Italo," she practically whispered.

"Thanks," Scav replied, his eyes darting all over the place.

"Are you hungry, master?"

"Famished," Scav replied.

The disciple seemed to notice Idi Han for the first time. Her wits were slow, her senses dulled. The labyrinth of scars up and down her arms and neck suggested she had given a great deal of blood to her immortal masters.

"Oh, but you have a guest," the mortal said, "Guests should eat first. Mistress?"

The woman bowed deeply before Idi Han, and the razor blade that dangled on a piece of cord around her neck hung in the air, an offering. She glanced at Scav, who seemed visibly disappointed that the cultist had approached her first. She glanced at the woman.

She had rushed out of Cicatrice's manse without feeding. He had placed a great emphasis on not wasting another moment now that the plot against him was fully revealed. She could feel the hunger in the pit of her stomach, not as strong as the first night when she had mindlessly feasted on her father, but aching, nonetheless.

Now, though, there was something different about the mortal presenting itself to her like a trussed fowl. She could sense, like candles flickering in the night, points of great power in the woman—arteries, she realized, and the heart strongest of all. The power flowed through her like sap through a tree. It was so close when she closed her eyes she could practically see it.

"I'm sorry," Scav said, ripping her out of her reverie, "You're not still a newborn are you? Do you need me to show you how to..."

"No," Idi Han said, raising her hand, "I can handle it."

She realized with surprise that her hand was trembling as she took the razor. She cut her palm severely, and if blood had still flowed through her veins, she would have spilled a gallon on the palletized sewer floor.

She took more care as she nicked the neck of the woman prostrating herself before her. With her supernatural senses, she had struck true, and the blood that bubbled up from the cut was rich with the essence that the immortals sustained themselves with.

Idi Han pressed her lips to the woman's neck, as though kissing a lover, and almost instantly stopped. She didn't taste the energy the way she had tasted the flavors of food, but something about it seemed off. It "smelled" strange. Her eyes rolled open and she looked at Scav.

He was watching her.

She pretended to suckle at the woman's neck, corking the actual flow of liquid with the flat part of her tongue. As she pretended to drink and drink, Scav's smile gave the game away. Somehow the woman's essence had been poisoned or drugged, whether through conventional means or supernatural, Idi Han hadn't the breadth of knowledge to guess. Perhaps a human riddled by disease or addiction was not safe to drink from. Or perhaps, as garlic hampered the immortal "nose" other ordinary spices and tinctures had drugging effects.

She smacked her lips audibly, and wondered briefly if it was customary to thank the bloodbag for her contribution. Knowing how Cicatrice had treated Hedrox, she guessed not.

"Thank you, Scav," she said, "I was famished."

He nodded, and she watched carefully as he took his own pretend drink.

"You may leave us," Scav said, and the cultist nodded and disappeared.

"Well," Idi Han said, "I've got to get back and report what I know. And you've got to…anyway, thanks for the snack."

She started to walk past him, but he put an unwelcome hand on her chest.

"Hold on." Scav glanced off into the distance as though he saw something she could not. But nothing was there. Just expectation. "Let me show you something."

He reached into his pocket and drew out a beaded necklace with a Christian crucifix at the end. He didn't look at it, but pointed it towards her. Idi Han hissed in an unrecognized pain.

"You're hurting me," she said.

"Faith," he said, "That woman you drank from was clergy once. Her life energy will make you slow and weak for a time."

"You drugged me."

"In effect, yes. I'm still a believer myself. It's rare, almost unheard of amongst our kind. But I was raised Catholic and I can't shed myself of it. That's why I can make this work on you."

His own hand was sizzling where he grasped the beads of the necklace. As he moved towards her, Idi Han felt the pain rise in her gorge. So this was what Topan and Cicatrice had alluded to. The pain of encountering faith. Faith in a divine or greater power. Faith, the ultimate antidote to the desire to live forever as an immortal, channeled through a relic or totem. She backed away from him as the invisible black flames licked her body.

"I'm sorry, Idi Han. I tried to convince you to leave, remember?"

"Why are you doing this?"

He closed his eyes and bit his lip.

"My brother...he put me up to it. But now I'm starting to think there might be another way. A way out for me. Cicatrice's young, untempered heir is too great a prize to pass up. I've killed Cashley. Now I've captured you. Father Otto will have to take me seriously. Have to reward me. I'm sorry. I didn't want it to turn out this way. But now we've been seen here. My brother and his goons will be on their way."

Idi Han plunged her arm forward, as though dousing it in a bucket of ice. She grabbed his hand, snapped his wrist, and turned the idol back on him. He hissed in pain as her own fog of doubt lifted, and she clenched his hand tighter and tighter even as he tried to drop the holy symbol.

"I'm sorry you took me for a fool," she said, staring into his eyes as he bit back at his own supernatural bile, "But I've known you meant to betray me ever since we reached this place."

"You never drank..."

She shook her head mournfully from side to side.

Idi Han clenched her fist, and felt Scav's bones crunch to shards beneath her grip. He gasped, a gesture unusual at best for an immortal. She reached out with her other hand and gripped his shoulder blade, feeling the sting of the holy symbol as her arm passed the invisible wave of its path. She yanked, and with a single pull his arm came fully out of its socket, and she grasped his severed limb in her hand.

The holy icon was pulverized to plastic fiber. Its power to

harm vanished with the separation from the faith of its wielder. The meat of his severed limb was perversely, bleakly white, devoid of the blood which normally gave muscle its healthy red color.

Idi Han cracked Scavatelli across the face with his own severed bicep. He stumbled forward into the pallets, scattering coffins and spilling grave dirt, unable to brace himself without his missing limb. He rolled away from her, half covered in dirt now.

"Wait! Let me explain!"

She brought the arm down with such force over his crown that the forearm and the bicep split asunder. The shoulder haunch, or what was left of it, flew off into the sewers. The shattered ulna was now showing through what was left of his forearm. She drove the splintered bone down into his eye, lifted it out, checked to see if his lips were still moving, and then drove it in again and again until his mouth fell dumb. It was odd to cut so deep and draw no blood.

She rose to her feet, dropped the shattered chunk of Scav's arm by the rest of his body, and hurried back out into the bright blinking lights of Vegas.

TWELVE

"The Crusades began. History as we record it looks at the Crusades as an attempt to recapture the Holy Land. But at least some texts—which you'll find roundly mocked if acknowledged at all in conventional academia—speak of the attempt to bring low the Necropolis. The European kingdoms united, in a fashion, and sent an army of knights to march on the grand city of the vampires."

Kasprzak flipped a page. The picture was a familiar one, the medieval attempt to explain an army when the idea of numbers and units was a bit sketchy even in the mind of a fairly well-educated monk. Many banners, no doubt of great significance to a medieval audience, waved amongst the assembled forces, but all bore a red cross on their shields. At the head of the army was a clergyman in either transparent or white vestments holding aloft a silver cross. She tapped him.

"This happy customer here is, ah, unnamed in the texts, but we refer to him as the White Bishop. The Crusaders didn't know it, but the crosses painted on their shields, and silver crucifix the bishop carried were some of their most potent weapons. It's said that the horses refused to enter the shadow of the Necropolis, and the Crusade was almost turned back before it began. But the White Bishop plunged in, unafraid, and the assembled knights were so shamed by a simple clergyman's bravery, that they dismounted and followed."

The professor turned the page, which portrayed an army of vampires emerging from the Necropolis, headed by Lily the Half-Faced.

"The armies clashed. Neither side could seem to gain the advantage until Lily the Half-Faced met the White Bishop in single combat. Lily was a vampire far beyond anything the Bishop had ever encountered before. But Lily had also never encountered a man of such singular faith before. The two clashed for hours but neither could gain the advantage."

"An unstoppable force meeting an immovable object," Nico said.

Kasprzak looked up and smiled.

"Exactly. And then, as so often is the case, a quirk of fate turned the tide of history. A knight's sword was knocked out of his hands, flew through the air, and knocked the crucifix out of the White Bishop's hands. Lily was able to push through and drop the Bishop to his back. But the Bishop wore a scapular. Lily recoiled in horror from the holy object and the Bishop rose to deliver the *coup de grâce*. But a sword suddenly plunged through the Bishop's back and out his front."

Kasprzak turned the page. A vampire with one red eye was driving a sword through the Bishop's back. The other vampires surged forward, destroying the Crusaders.

"Cicatrice."

Kasprzak nodded.

"It was a hard-fought battle, but in the end, the vampires were victorious. And unlike a mortal army, whose numbers dwindle after combat, their ranks grew fat with the freshly dead. The vampires had not only defeated Christendom's mightiest warriors, they had converted many of them to their side. The sun was rising, so the vampires retreated to the Necropolis. And at the next sunset, Lily the Half-Faced declared a Crusade of her own—an unholy Crusade, to cast down the kingdoms of men and their church."

Kasprzak leaned back in her chair and put her fingertips together. Nico realized he was practically falling off his chair. He settled himself back.

"Then what happened?"

"See for yourself."

He turned the page. It was the strange inkblot figure.

"The Hunter of the Dead. So what happened?"

Kasprzak shrugged. Nico turned to look at Price. He rolled his eyes.

"The Necropolis was never heard from again."

"Nor has any archaeological evidence of it existing ever been found," Price muttered.

"Lily the Half-Face disappeared. An entire army of vampires and supposedly an entire city was completely wiped from the face of the earth."

"And there were no survivors?"

"Cicatrice. And supposedly Otto Signari had left earlier, at Lily's request. To this day Cicatrice blames Signari for not bringing back reinforcements."

"What did Signari say?"

"He said he delivered the messages as ordered and it wasn't his fault none of the patriarchs responded to her call."

"Huh," Nico said.

"The point of the story, kid, is that The Hunter isn't real. It's a boogeyman. Something vampire sires tell their get to keep them in line. 'Follow the code or The Hunter will come for you. Listen to me or The Hunter will take you.' Same as Santa or the Tooth Fairy."

"Carter, I've never seen a vampire scared of anything. But they *are* scared of this horseman." She tapped the illustration heavily. "Boogeyman or not, they believe in him and they are terrified of him."

"They're terrified of Cicatrice. Cicatrice is the one who spreads this legend. I don't believe it's real. I don't even believe the Necropolis was real."

"The proof that the Necropolis existed is the way they live. The code exists because they believe The Hunter was revenge for the hubris of gathering too many vampires in one place. That was when the code was established: no large gatherings, no public identities. They've lived in fear ever since that if they broke the code The Hunter would resurface."

"It's a myth, Professor. The time the code was founded was the same time the Inquisition started to really get going. People were actively hunting witches and vampires. The only way they could survive was by going underground."

Kasprzak picked up Price's phone and waved it in his face.

"So what do you make of this little piece of evidence?"

"That's what I'm here to ask you about. It's got to be somebody faking it, right?"

Kasprzak looked at the picture again. She shook her head.

"I can't be sure of anything without getting a look at this object. I guess at a minimum I could attempt to date it. If it's really medieval then…at least an argument could be made in favor of The Hunter resurfacing."

"What about that serial killer the vampires are all worried about?" Nico asked.

Price and Kasprzak both turned and stared him down. He felt like he could disappear up his own asshole and no one would notice.

"I'm sorry. I didn't mean to interrupt."

"No, no. Go on, my boy. What were you going to say?"

He coughed into his fist.

"Well, um, I heard Carter and that lady he calls Bonaparte talking about a serial killer that only kills vampires, that all the vampires are scared of lately. So, you know how there are copycat serial killers?"

Kasprzak slammed the butt of her hand down on her desk, over and over.

"That's the way to think! Whatever you're paying this boy, it's not enough, Carter!"

Price nodded.

"Actually, that's not bad thinking. Somebody's knocking off nightcrawlers in the shadows. He's not getting the reputation he wants. So he dresses up like The Hunter of the Dead. Suddenly everyone's paying attention."

"And this is the same guy who killed our Damned?" Nico asked.

Kasprzak snorted.

"Killed one of The Damned? The Damned can't be killed. Well, not easily, anyway."

Price gritted his teeth.

"We saw one that was."

Kasprzak's eyes went wide.

"My God, Carter. Tangling with The Damned...their reputation alone..."

"Yeah, I tangled with one, all right. Their reputation is... well deserved."

Kasprzak leaned back in her chair.

"Well, you may well be dealing with the actual Hunter of the Dead, then. I can't imagine anyone else who'd be capable of killing one of The Damned. Barring maybe Cicatrice."

"Yeah, I was afraid you'd say that."

Price sighed and crossed his arms. He tipped the plush chair back.

"Well, why don't we go talk to this Cicatrice?"

Price and Kasprzak turned to stare at Nico.

"What? I just said talk. I didn't say piss in his cornflakes. Blood flakes. Bloody cornflakes. Whatever."

Price looked at Kasprzak, and rubbed his chin.

"Actually...what do you think, Professor?"

"Well...there is something of a truce between House Cicatrice and the Inquisition."

"A truce?" Nico asked. "How the fuck did that happen?"

"It happened during the '50s. It was actually a rather complicated plan that his get, Topan, put into action..."

"Eh, with all due respect, Professor, let's hold off on a second round of story time. The important thing is there's a truce. At least, every Inquisitor I know of knows not to fuck with any Cicatrices. They flash the scar on their hearts and it's like a get-out-of-jail free card. The question is, does Cicatrice reciprocate it?"

"I don't think he's scared to kill Inquisitors. Although most vampires don't kill Inquisitors unless directly attacked. They usually prefer to turn them on their enemies."

"So there is actually a lot more crosstalk between vampires and vampire hunters than you've let on?" Nico asked.

Price shrugged.

"I don't like being played. But my opinion is a dead nightcrawler is a net positive. Whether I did it because it played into some other nightcrawler's political bullshit is beside the point."

"Everything I know about Cicatrice suggests he is fixated on The Hunter," Kasprzak said, "Perhaps he never really got over that early life trauma. If you go to him and suggest that The Hunter is back, he may just assist you."

"But what if my theory's true and he just made it up?"

"In my experience, people are even more proprietary about their lies than about their truths."

Price turned to Nico.

"Put on your big boy pants, kid. We're headed to the Aztec."

THIRTEEN

The Red Scare...

Maurice Valais ran his handcuffed hands through his sweaty, unkempt hair, trying to turn it into something akin to a decent man's cut.

"How long do you plan to keep me in here?" he shouted at the top of his lungs.

In disgust, he kicked the leg of the metal table in front of him, realizing from the sharp knock it gave him that it was nailed to the ground. He pushed the chair back, and it screeched loudly along the tile floor. He rose and began to pace. Those were the only two things he had to do in the tiny interrogation room: sit at the table or pace.

A huge mirror covered the top half of the entire back wall. Maurice had seen enough cop shows on the idiot lantern to know what that meant. The mirror was a ruse. The G-men were back there watching him, probably enjoying seeing him scurry around like a rat in a cage.

"Fuck you," he said, raising a middle finger in the rigid digit salute towards the mirror, "Fuck you and fuck your boss. Yeah, you can tell The Pepsi-Cola Kid I said that."

Maurice tried to kick over the chair but it was too heavy. Everything was metal and heavy and cold and inhuman. He slammed his back into a corner and sank to the ground, hanging his head in his hands.

"Mr. Valais?"

Maurice looked up. He blinked, realizing it seemed he had fallen asleep in the corner, though he had no idea whether for a few minutes or a few days. The door was a bright rectangle of light and a shadow figure stood ensconced within.

"Congress ready for me? I won't sign my own death warrant, I can tell you that."

"Actually, Mr. Valais, you might be happy to know that we've worked something out."

"What does that mean, 'worked something out?' Who are you?"

The figure stepped through the doorway, and as the bright light of the hallways receded behind him, he came into more contrast. Maurice rubbed his eyes.

"A Chinaman?"

The Oriental stranger's lips quirked. He was wearing a business suit just like a regular American, and he barely even had an accent at all. It was queer. Damned queer.

"Malay, to be technical, but no doubt you're not interested in technicalities at present. You can call me Topan."

The Chinaman extended a hand. Valais nodded.

"I see. I shake your hand, you have some hidden camera around here, and snap, suddenly you've got photographic evidence of me giving aid and comfort to the enemy. Well, nothin' doin', bub. I'm true blue, all-American. I was quarterback of my high school football team, and, yeah, I fucked the captain of the cheer squad on prom night. No matter what you or your boss McCarthy say, you can't take that away from me. Or all the slants like you I killed in Indochina, you can't take that away from me either. I'm true blue, true blue, it doesn't matter what you say."

The Chinaman retracted his hand, but the smile remained rigid on his face, as though in rictus.

"I suppose it's my own fault for trying to offer an idiot pleasantries," the Chinaman said. "I'm fairly certain that if there were a hidden camera here..."

"And you're going to pretend there's not?"

"I'm fairly certain that if there were, your hands being cuffed would say all that needs to be said. But not to worry, Mr. Valais, I don't work for Senator McCarthy. Why don't you have a seat so we can discuss it?"

Maurice licked his lips.

"Thanks, I'm good here, Fu Manchu."

The Chinaman nodded, the smile finally fading from his face.

"Perhaps you need some clarification about who I am," he said, grabbing Maurice by the shoulder and pulling him to his feet as though he were a ragdoll. "My name is Topan. And I'm Malaysian. Not

Korean. Not Japanese. Not Chinese. Malay."

Topan thrust Maurice at the table, which struck his jaw with a shudder that resounded through his whole body. He felt the hard chair strike his back, then his knees, and force him into a sitting position. Topan grabbed the other chair, the heavy metal nightmare, and dropped it on the other side of the table like it weighed nothing. He flopped down on it and stared deeply into Maurice's eyes.

"Are we clear?"

"Crystal," Maurice said, through the blood pooling in his mouth. He had nearly bitten through his tongue when Topan had tossed him against the table.

"Good," he said, nodding and placing a briefcase down on the table. "Now, as I said, I don't work for Senator McCarthy. In fact, I've been working rather diligently to get you out of this congressional hearing. Can I assume that we're at least both on the same side in not wanting you to go before McCarthy?"

Maurice sensed a trap, but wasn't entirely certain what it was yet. He simply nodded, and swallowed another mouthful of bloody saliva, wishing that his tongue would stop bleeding.

"Good. Progress. Now, my pa...my boss has called in several favors. Both Nevada senators, a whole bevy of congressmen, and G-men up and down the chain. There's a problem, though. You know what they all said?"

Maurice shook his head.

"'There's no crossing Joe McCarthy.' No one wants to be considered a Red. It's not the right climate for sticking your neck out like that. The best that all these supposedly powerful men could get me is this meeting with you right now. How do you like that? American democracy in action."

"Hey, if you don't like it, you can go back to..." Maurice paused as Topan stared him down, "Malaysia."

"It's nice to see that your faith is not misplaced. So seeing as this is the best we could arrange, here's what I'm going to do for you. I'm going to go over some of the questions that the Permanent Subcommitee on Investigations is going to ask you. Forewarned is forearmed or something like that, don't they say that?"

"I suppose."

Topan nodded.

"So what's going to happen is I'm going to ask you questions just like Senator McCarthy or his cronies would. And you're going to answer them. And you're going to do it calmly, and correctly, and you're not going to sweat and you're not going to sound nervous, because sweating and sounding nervous makes you look guilty. And then I'm going to redirect you, just like Senator McCarthy and his cronies would. And I'm going to try to make you sweat all over again, and you're going to not let me. Think of it like a game of chess. You like chess, don't you?"

"I fucking hate it."

Topan nodded.

"Good."

He turned his briefcase towards himself and opened it. Maurice tried to glance around to see what was inside, but Topan had already slammed it shut before he could catch a glimpse of anything. In his hands, Topan held a stack of white 3x5 cards. He shuffled through them as though they were a deck of cards before finally settling on one.

"Ah. Here's a good one. Maurice Valais, are you now or have you ever been a member..."

"...of the Communist Party?" Maurice completed. "No, asshole. I told you I'm true blue. You'll never pin a single un-American word coming out of my lips on me. Sure, I voted against Truman, but who wouldn't? That's not un-American, that's just...by God, that's more American...participating in the democratic..."

"Mr. Valais," Topan interrupted, "that wasn't the question I was going to ask you."

Topan held the 3x5 card between his index and middle finger and held it out towards Maurice. Maurice leaned back in his chair and folded his arms, deliberately refusing to take it. Topan's eyes narrowed and he simply placed the card down in full view. He sat back, waiting, knowing that Maurice's curiosity would get the better of him sooner or later.

And damned if it wasn't sooner. Maurice glanced down, just for a second, but then he read the index card, faster than he even meant to.

It read, "Maurice Valais, are you now or have you ever been a member of the secret Catholic organization known as the Inquisition?"

Maurice blanched.

"What are you...how are you...?"

"Well, what did you think you were here to answer questions about, Mr. Valais? Your communist affiliations? Joe McCarthy isn't an idiot. You don't even have a soft pink past. You don't even have a pro-union voting record. You were called here because in the course of all these wonderful diggings and investigations, the truth about vampires—well, not vampires because we're too careful—but the truth about you retarded vampire hunters finally came to light."

An icy fist grabbed Maurice's heart and refused to let go. He clutched at his chest, loosed his tie. Topan waited.

"Breathe, Mr. Valais, breathe. It's what you're good at after all."

"You're a...you're..."

"One of your long hated, long hunted enemies, yes. I don't know what it is that causes you people to keep bashing your collective head against the wall pursuing us, but now here we are. All the mysteries of a thousand-year-long secret war about to be laid bare because of one gloryhound politician and one vampire hunter who can't think to keep his tattoo hidden."

Topan opened his briefcase again, tossed a photograph from within onto the table next to the index card, and slammed it shut again. Maurice put his finger on the photograph. It showed him, sitting around a table with some of his Marine Corps buddies, easy, unforced smiles on all of their faces as they smoked cigars and tossed chips into a poker pot. And there, plain as day if you were looking for it, on Maurice's barely uncuffed sleeve, was the double cross.

"I don't...this isn't enough to hang me with. This is barely...this is nothing."

"Let's try another question shall we?" Topan said, tapping the assembled top of his packet of index cards. Topan took one of the cards, set it at the top of the pile, cleared his throat (a deliberate, obviously unnecessary gesture for a vampire) and read it aloud. "Mr. Valais, is it true that you kept a record of your misadventures in this so-called 'Inquisition?'"

Maurice ripped his tie off. Still, it felt like his throat was constricting, choking him. Topan waited a moment, before tossing the index card off into a corner of the interrogation room.

"No answer for that one? Let's try another. 'Isn't it true you kept this diary in a green stenograph pad? This green stenograph pad?'"

Topan opened his briefcase, tossed a steno pad on the table, and slammed it shut. His hand quivering, Maurice reached for the pad. In a moment of pique, he snatched it off the table, jumped up from his chair, ran to a corner of the room with his back to Topan and eagerly attempted to rip the book to shreds. He clenched his eyes shut and braced himself for the vampiric strength of the body slam which he knew was coming.

When it didn't come he slowly let his eyes open and turned back to look at Topan, who wasn't even looking at him, he was simply shuffling papers idly on the table. Maurice looked down at the shredded pages he had left on the floor like a hamster's nest. Blank. All of them blank.

Slowly, he retook his seat.

"Pleased with yourself?" Topan asked, still not looking at him.

"What was the point of that?" Maurice asked, his voice hollow in his throat.

With both hands, Topan tapped the stack of index cards together until they were all lined up perfectly.

"I got the book back," Topan said. "Obviously. I've already burnt it. That was the first thing I did and it cost me a great deal of money and effort and political capital. There is an innocent evidence clerk who will be in jail for the rest of his life because of you."

"Sacrifices have to be made," Maurice said.

"I'm glad you agree."

"In the struggle against your kind there will be sacrifices, yes. But if we don't struggle, all the innocents will suffer."

"You sound like maybe you're trying too hard to justify yourself. That's the sort of thing that will make McCarthy smell fear. And pounce."

Maurice slammed his manacled hands, now balled-up fists, down on the table.

"Why'd you tell me that story? That some man's going to jail because of me? You expect me to recant? You expect me to throw my hands up in the air and say, 'Oh, Lordy, I was wrong!'"

"I already told you, Mr. Valais. I'm trying to shake you up. With a fake diary. With a story about the consequences of your actions. And you are very easy to shake."

"Stop toying with me, bloodsucker. Just kill me. It's the only way your secrets stay buried."

Topan nodded. He leaned back, tipping his chair back, and crossed his legs up on the table.

"You know, that was my House patriarch's conclusion as well. First thing he said to me. 'Topan, silence that man. Do whatever you have to do, bribe whoever you have to bribe, get to him, and end him.' Normally an edict like that? No one would gainsay it. But I thought to myself that there might be another way. A better way. One that leads to a better ending for both your kind and mine."

Maurice snorted.

"You went to the mats against a patriarch for me?"

"No, not for you, Mr. Valais. Before I took on this task, I had no idea who you were. Not where you went to school, not where you were born, not your significance in the Inquisition hierarchy, not even your name. Of course I know all of that now. I know everything about you now. But the reason I went to the mats was for the opportunity you represent."

Topan opened his briefcase. For the first time, he left it open, though still facing away from Maurice. He reached inside and drew out two tiny objects, tossed them on the table.

"Recognize those?"

Maurice picked one of the pieces of metal up, examined it. Turned it over. Checked the inscription.

"My mother's wedding ring. And my father's, I suppose. You're threatening my parents if I talk?"

Topan remained eerily silent. Maurice tossed the two rings off into the corner where he had ripped up the steno pad. They clattered and clanged to a stop.

"You're an idiot, then. You said you knew everything about me and you don't even know I don't speak to my parents? Hurt them, kill them, I don't care. The old man never met a bottle that could keep him from tanning my ass. And the old lady touched me. They can both rot in Hell for all I care. Know everything about me. I'll bet you didn't know that."

Topan reached into the briefcase and pulled out another ring, held it up to the dim neon light before placing it down on the table.

"That's my high school class ring," Maurice said, rubbing an identical piece of jewelry on his own hand.

He picked it up. There were initials inscribed on the inside. N.H.

"Nikki Howard. My old high school sweetheart. You really are batting .0000, Mr. Topan. I'm an Inquisitor. We don't let family and

relationships hold us back. And a girl I haven't seen in twenty years? That's supposed to sway me?"

"You had a breakdown on the way here, didn't you?"

"Yeah, in Richmond."

Topan reached into the briefcase and drew out a wrench. He let it drop heavily to the table.

"Light Brothers," Valais read, "I think that was the name of the garage."

Topan nodded.

"It was. You remember your second grade teacher, Mrs. Kopas? Did you know she lost her husband in the war?"

"Yeah. Maybe I knew that. I remember she always wore a..."

Topan placed a yellow ribbon on the table.

"What the hell else have you got in there?"

Topan made a welcoming gesture.

"Have a look."

Maurice angrily grabbed the suitcase and turned it towards him. The case was brimming with bric-a-brac. Some of the souvenirs he instantly recognized. Others he didn't know at all. Most tickled something in the back of his mind, but didn't immediately remind him of anything.

"This pipe. That belonged to Tommy, my childhood friend. We used to smoke it behind the courthouse. And isn't that Old Man Keene's eyepatch? He was my neighbor when I lived in Cinci..."

Maurice rifled through the briefcase, taking great handfuls of all manner of bracelets, keys, wallets, and personal mementos.

"What are you trying to tell me? Are you threatening everyone I've ever known?"

"Please, Mr. Valais."

Topan loosened his tie, unbuttoned the top few buttons of his shirt, and revealed his breast. A mark like a tattoo marked him, but it was actually a scar depicting a bifurcated red eye.

"You recognize that, don't you?"

"House Cicatrice," Maurice whispered.

"You were particularly fond of harrowing my House. Tell me, in all your time focusing your energies on my people, have you ever known any Cicatrice to resort to petty threats?"

Maurice sank back in his chair, letting two handfuls of personal *effects scatter to the floor.*

"You've killed everyone I've ever met?"

"Yes."

"But there are...police. Family members. You can't just...kill all those people."

"It was time-consuming, yes. And costly. And Father Cicatrice was...ambivalent. But I convinced him to go through with my plan."

Maurice ran his hands through his hair.

"But...why? Just so you could let me know you did something... unimaginably cruel before you kill me?"

Topan laughed heartily. It was the sort of laugh only a vampire or a truly deranged murderer was capable of. The sort of laugh that seemed to delight in human suffering, even revel in it.

"I'm not going to kill you, Mr. Valais. What would be the point of that now? No, you live. You live and you stand as a shining example of what happens to anyone who ever crosses House Cicatrice again."

The door opened. The light that streamed in seemed to come less from the choirs of heavenly angels than from the screams of Memnoch's tortured souls. A soulless, bespectacled G-Man stood there, his dark glasses and gray suit and hands folded in his lap betraying what he wanted. He stated it anyway.

"Time with your lawyer is up, Mr. Valais. It's time to testify."

Maurice stared pleadingly into Topan's eyes.

"What do I tell them?"

"Frankly, Mr. Valais, I don't give a shit. You're a drifter with no past and no connections to any person living in this country. They might conclude you're a spy. They might conclude you're a madman. That doesn't matter to me. All that matters to me is that you understand this: you, Mr. Valais, are persona non grata. *As literally and liberally as that term can be used. You are an un-person, a non-person.*

"And from now on this is what happens to any Inquisitor who so much as lays a finger on a Cicatrice houseling. Anyone you meet after today, dies. Anyone you call on the telephone dies. Anyone you think about in passing and fills up your mind's eye dies. Your punishment is exile from the human race."

Scav's eyes fluttered open. Before he could even see what was going on around him, a brick of a fist smashed his stomach and intestines to jelly. He could feel his regenerative powers acting sluggish. He had still not yet fed today and he had already lost an arm and been beaten badly.

"I'm feeling stupid right now, Sven," Scav heard his brother's voice intone, "Did I miss something?"

"I couldn't say, boss," Sven replied.

His eyesight returned grudgingly to him. He was upright—not standing, but dangling from a drainage pipe which sprouted from his pelvis like an extended penis. No doubt Benito's goons had enjoyed that malicious little joke immensely. He must have started to topple upside-down at some point because a dagger shoved through his shoulder held him in place.

Their encampment was a mess. Several of the coffins had been toppled, and some of the goons were running their hands through muddy messes of gravedirt which had dropped to the ground. Things would be unpleasant for all of them tonight, but Scav most of all.

"Let's see," Benito said, ticking off on his fingers, "I saved my brother from certain death. My own kin. You would think I could trust my own kin."

"There's just no one to trust in this world, boss. Just you and me, and you less than me."

Hofstra, the omega, rose from the muddy mess of his sleeping area. Adding insult to injury, his funeral shroud had been torn. He practically charged at Scav's impaled form, but two of the other goons grabbed him and easily held him back.

"I'll kill him! Let me kill him, Benny."

"Shut the fuck up, Hofstra," Benito growled. He jabbed a finger into Scav's sternum. "I set a trap. A moron-proof trap. I provided a former pastor and cut her to pieces so she looked like a regular bloodbag. All you had to do was show up and drug an eighteen-year-old girl. If you could've kept her from running for half an hour we wouldn't be having this conversation. Instead, I come back to our whole place is smashed to shit and you…"

Benito held up Scav's missing forearm. Turning it horizontal he pressed it against Scav's windpipe.

"Give me one good reason," Benito said leaning deliberately forward and shattering Scav's neck under the pressure, "One reason not to be done with you once and for all."

Scav pointed at his neck. Benito nodded and relieved the pressure, allowing the air back into Scav's dead lungs and his spine to begin to mend.

"I can still help you catch Idi Han. There's still time."

"Oh? How's that?"

"Check my pocket. Inside my vest."

Benito jammed his hand into his brother's pocket, rifled around, and drew out a small remote-control device.

"A transponder," Benito said. "You planted a bug on her?"

Scav nodded.

"Right now she's on her own. Everyone has orders to leave her alone, right?"

"Yeah."

"If we can grab her before she gets back to the Aztec, we'll have a bargaining chip Cicatrice can't ignore. You'll be able to draw him out. I guarantee it."

"So it's true then, all this chatter about him jumping this newborn up to his heir? And he really cares about her?"

"From what I saw, yes."

"So Topan's out and Rahim and the other elders just don't give a shit?"

"Topan's out. That's for sure. As for the elders, when have you ever known Cicatrice to give a shit what anybody else thought? He introduced her to me as his new heir. And the way they interacted, yeah, he'll do anything for her. But time's a-wastin', Benny. We've got to snatch her up now."

Benito turned to Sven.

"What do you think?"

"A newborn who was eighteen when she turned? How hard could she be to bag? And even if this all is bullshit, there's still the original plan. Torture her until she tells us what she knows."

"Yeah, but you'd better bet every crew in this city is doing that to every Cicatrice houseling they can put their hands on. I'd sure hate to be a Cicatrice in Vegas tonight."

"She's not just any Cicatrice, Benny," Scav said, "Trust me. She's the real deal. I don't know how much she knows, but she's worth her weight in gold."

Benito glanced down at the transponder receiver. It was probably telling him exactly where Idi Han was right now. Scav pushed all thoughts of betraying the poor kid out of his mind. It was his life or hers. Besides, he had given her a chance.

"Don't I always come through for you?"

"Yeah. Maybe you do. All right, let's bag the girl."

"All right! The Scavatelli brothers back in the saddle again. Help me down."

"Nah, you stay here."

A splash of cold kerosene struck Scav in the face. Benito wasn't even the one to light the match. One of his idiot followers tossed the cigarette at his gesture. Scav felt the flames consuming his body. He made up his mind not to scream, but couldn't keep even that promise to himself.

FOURTEEN

The town was in an eerie state of soporific silence. Nico had never seen Sin City this quiet. A curfew had been placed in effect, which Nico and Price were effectively breaking. Police cars prowled every corner, and they had been forced to hide from several. The fountains at The Bellagio and the fire show at The Mirage had been halted. Black helicopters flew very low overhead, spotlights shining down on the city. One zoomed past. Price grabbed Nico and pulled him under an overhang.

"What is going on?"

"Take a look."

He pointed. The helicopter was loaded for bear with Gatling guns and hellfire missiles. A gunship.

"The casinos are practically on lockdown, the cops are on the rampage, and now the National Guard has been called in? Tell me this isn't related to our mysterious Hunter."

"I wish I could, kid. But there's only one person in this city with the clout to do all this."

"Cicatrice."

Price nodded.

They continued on. Nico clenched his Lousiville Slugger tightly so that his hands wouldn't shake. Price, rather boldly, walked with no weapon drawn. Though he had showered that morning at Price's, an altogether unappealing affair, he was still wearing his sweat-stiffened work uniform from the previous night.

"I wish I wasn't still wearing this stupid outfit," Nico grumbled.

Price shook his head.

"Kid, you go back to your apartment now and the cops are going to lock you up and throw away the key. 'Vampire' doesn't look like a real good cause for arson and murder on any blotter. And the LVMPD have a vested interest in pinning this sort of thing on anyone but a vampire."

Nico scowled. There were two dead at the Fill-Up and according to the internet he wasn't just a person of interest, he was the prime suspect. Swinging by his apartment for a change of clothes was not the smartest move right now.

"Is that what happened to you?"

"Something like that," Price replied through clenched teeth, and Nico realized he shouldn't have asked. "Besides, if it's really bothering you I said you could borrow something of mine."

"You're like 250 pounds. And you dress like Roger Daltrey."

"I'm surprised you know who Roger Daltrey is. Fucking kids these days. I don't even know how you can listen to…whoever."

"Yeah, we're supposed to know all your bands or Western civilization is ending. But God forbid a Baby Boomer would know an artist that's been popular in the last decade."

"Ah, it's all crap these days. Anyway, I don't mind the uniform. It's kind of dorky, but kind of confusing. Throws people off. Part of being an Inquisitor is stagecraft, kid. You think a nightcrawler sees me coming and goes, 'Oh, here comes this guy in the deerskin jacket; I'm sure no bullshit's about to go down?'"

"That might be the…"

Whatever it may or may not have been, Nico found himself caught short. They had reached The Aztec. The building was either an eyesore or an act of architectural genius. Nico had difficulty telling the difference in the middle of the Vegas Strip. What he did know was that, while gaudy, it closely resembled an angular Mesoamerican pyramid. Each letter in the word "Aztec" lit individually before dazzling together in a great display.

"The heart of darkness. Try not to shit yourself, kid."

"Try not to shit yourself…yourself. Old man."

They crossed the street and entered the sliding glass doors. Nico practically had to shade his eyes from all the glowing lights inside.

"Howdy, folks!" Price said, loudly doffing an imaginary cap at the two security guards who blocked the entrance, "I know you've got orders not to let me in, but I've got business with the man upstairs."

Nico noticed dozens of cameras installed along the ceiling, all swiveling to point at them. The guards seemed ready to eject them, but then they both received a message through the earpieces they wore like secret service agents. They stepped aside and made it a point to gesture welcomingly inside.

"Thanks."

Nico glanced around. The casino was oddly packed, considering the seeming state of emergency that had descended on Las Vegas like a shroud.

"It's a publicity stunt is what it is," he heard one of the players shouting loudly to his spouse, who wore hearing aids. "They just want to keep us in the casino and gambling is all!"

And, indeed, it seemed that the curfew had forced every tourist who might otherwise be at the Hoover Dam or taking a mule-guided tour of the Grand Canyon into packing the casino floor, bored out of their minds.

"So many bystanders," Nico said. "Should we be worried?"

Price shrugged.

"Nightcrawlers are usually pretty discreet. Don't live long in this game if you're not discreet."

"If we get into a fight with this Cicatrice, there's going to be a heck of a lot of witnesses."

"If we get into a fight with Cicatrice, we're both dead, so I wouldn't worry about it."

Nico rolled the bat, still slung over his shoulder, back and forth in his hands. Price seemed to know his way through the Aztec surprisingly well. It all seemed like a great maze to Nico, and he understood why. He had been in casinos in San Juan that had been the same way. Guests weren't supposed to be able to find their way out. They were supposed to stay where they were and play. That was why scantily-clad women wandered around with free drinks. That was why there were chairs everywhere and smoking was allowed.

Price, though, didn't get caught up in the labyrinth. He

made a beeline for a miniature version of the Aztec pyramid that the building was shaped like. This pyramid, of course, was made of plastic, or maybe Styrofoam, and had an artificial moat surrounding it, fed by artificial rivers running down the steps of the pyramid.

"How do you know the way?" Nico asked, "I thought you were blocked from being in here."

"I'll let you in on a secret, kid. I don't know what the fuck I'm doing or where I'm going. But I'm doing it confidently. And as long as you can do that, people will listen to you."

A skeletal, haunted-looking woman in a gray business suit with her neck all bandaged up emerged from an entrance that appeared midway up the mini-pyramid. She walked down to the only break in the velvet rope surrounding the plastic monstrosity.

"Mr. Price," the grey-suited woman rasped, inclining her head just enough to almost not quite count as acknowledgement, "I see you've made quite a show of bringing weapons into our casino. My name is Vizriel Hedrox. Mr. Cicatrice has asked me to meet with you. If you'll step this way…"

Hedrox gestured towards one of the casino restaurants. Nico furrowed his brow, but perhaps the woman had a private table or even a private room in the back.

"Ah…Hydrox, was it?"

"If you please."

"Yeah, I know a flunky when I see one. You're not even an immortal. You're one of these shitbrick renfields that don't even know how fucked they are. You know he's never going to turn you, right?"

Hedrox's face turned stony.

"I'm afraid I don't follow. But I've been asked to meet with you, and, of course, if you're hungry…"

Price dug his finger into Hedrox's chest.

"And I just told you, I've got an appointment with your lord and master."

A smile cracked Hedrox's stony face. She reached out and with a strength and speed that belied her unhealthy appearance, nearly snapped Price's finger as she wrenched it away from her chest. Twisting his fist, she drove him to his knees.

"As a matter of fact, Mr. Cicatrice just told me not to let you in to see him under any circumstances. So you don't. Really."

The woman released Price's hand and he staggered back, surprised at the ferocity of the maneuver. Nico took a step or two back. He had mistaken Hedrox for easy prey, but now the woman seemed like a brick wall. Still, he had seen Price face down a vampiric monstrosity only the night before. A businesswoman who knew kung fu or whatever couldn't be an insurmountable barrier.

Instead of charging the woman like a rhinoceros, Price just gestured at Nico.

"Have you met my new partner, Nico Salazar?"

Hedrox turned and pretended to size up Nico without even really setting eyes on him.

"Charmed, I'm sure."

"Have you heard of the ancient discipline of ho tan fow?"

"Mr. Price, if you…"

"Just humor me. Have you heard of it?"

Hedrox pinched the inside of her lower lip between her teeth.

"I have not."

"My partner is a master. Some say he's *the* master. Like what the Gracies were to jiujitsu, Nico here is to ho tan fow."

"That is impressive."

"He's been all over. Trained everywhere. Dojos in Bangkok. Gyms in Rio. Almost got into the Yankees. You know the Yankees?"

Hedrox pinched her nose.

"Mr. Price, I'm happy to…"

"Do. You. Know. The Yankees?"

Hedrox sighed.

"Yes, of course."

"Okay, good. So believe me when I say we're not talking about some two-pump chump here. Would you like a demonstration?"

"Yes, very much so."

Price gestured at Nico.

"Go ahead, son. Don't be afraid."

Hedrox turned to look at Nico expectantly. Nico turned back to Price.

"What do you want me to…?"

"Just swing away, Nicky baby. Show her you got that ho fan tow."

"I thought it was ho tan fow."

"That, too. Go ahead, Nico."

Nico shrugged and steadied his bat. He turned it sideways so that the blunt bat and not the razor blades would strike. He slammed it into Hedrox's ear, with enough follow through that Price had to jump out of the way of the bat's arc. The renfield crumpled to the floor.

Nico turned to look at his mentor.

"Is that all you wanted me to do?"

Price grinned and stuck both hands in his pockets.

"Yup."

"Then what was all that other shit about?"

Price raised a finger in the air.

"It's fun to punch somebody. But to get somebody to say, 'Punch me' first…that's a beautiful thing. Come on."

Price began to climb the papier-mâché pyramid. Nico glanced back at Hedrox's ruined form.

Well, you lay down with dogs, I guess…

Price was taking the pyramid steps two at a time. Nico had to scrabble to keep pace with him.

"Does this really strike you as a good idea?"

"You know how to scare off a shark, kid?"

"Aren't you supposed to punch him in the nose?"

"And you know how to scare off a bear?"

"I didn't think you could scare off a bear."

"A bear only attacks you because he's bigger than you. That's why they rear up on their hind paws when they attack. If you can make yourself bigger than a bear, they don't attack."

"So we're making ourselves bigger than Cicatrice?"

"In a manner of speaking."

"You know, John Lennon thought he was bigger than Jesus once."

"Yeah, I think I heard that."

"You know how that worked out for him?"

Price stopped just a step from the entrance to the pyramid. "Nah, how'd that work out for him, kid?"

Nico shrugged.

"Who knows? He's dead now."

"Fuckin' kids. Come on."

Two cameras disguised as torches followed Nico and Price as they plunged inside. The hokey plastic pyramid hid a high-tech warren, populated by pencil-pushers and computer operators, all seemingly wearing headsets. It didn't take Nico long to see what the hive was buzzing with. Everyone was monitoring cameras, some were seemingly talking with the National Guard and the police and just generally organizing the lockdown that had recently gone into effect.

SWAT teams were prowling the streets, obviously on a mission. Searching for this (so-called) Hunter of the Dead, perhaps. When Nico caught up with his mentor he was standing outside a doorway. A red-haired renfield barred the way, but she didn't matter nearly as much as the solid steel doors. Like everywhere in the Aztec (and, it seemed, Vegas) a camera eye greeted them.

"What are you expecting to happen here, Mr. Price?" the woman asked.

Suddenly the doors, hydraulically powered, slid open. If this had been a horror movie, Nico would have sworn fog would have come billowing out, but, of course, it did not.

"That," Price said, cheerfully manhandling the renfield out of the way with just a little pressure on her shoulder.

Together they entered the *sancta sanctorum* of the most powerful immortal alive. The room was a conference room, rather than a private office, and seated at the far end was a blond man with one cold eye, one missing eye, and skin as pale as ivory. Behind him a wall of video monitors showed everything that was going on in the casino, if not the city.

"The legendary Inquisitor Carter Price," the man said, his words like ice water.

"The legendary douchebag Cicatrice."

Nico had to stifle a laugh, but it still came out as a snort. He instantly regretted it, as Cicatrice turned his icy glare on him.

"And you must be the famous shift manager, Nico Salazar."

Nico's eyes nearly boggled out of his head. How did Cicatrice know who he was? Then, his face reddened as he remembered he was still wearing his nametag.

"Yeah. Kid's my boss."

Cicatrice laughed, deliberately, mirthlessly, as though he were unable to find things amusing any more but wished to make a show of his disrespect.

"Seems appropriate, you taking orders from a fifteen-year-old."

"I'm twenty." Nico suddenly realized how childish that sounded. He wouldn't be welcome at the big boy's table sounding like an elementary school student. "And…and I'm his apprentice."

"Oh, so you've taken an apprentice, Price? Tell me, boy, has he taught you anything you couldn't have learned from the back of a cereal box?"

The roof of Nico's mouth tasted like sandpaper as he attempted to come up with an answer.

"He…we practiced staking a dummy."

Cicatrice leaned back in his chair, tenting his fingers together. He didn't smile, or laugh again, but his shit-eating pleasure was clear nonetheless.

"Staking practice," Cicatrice repeated. "As long as you're infantilizing the boy, you may as well take him to Circus Circus, Price. I could probably get you a free pass. I know you can't afford it."

"Fuck you, Scar. It's his second night on the job and he already took out one of your elite renfield guards."

Cicatrice turned and made the "come hither" gesture to Nico.

"Come here, boy."

Nico felt Price's fist clamp down on his shoulder.

"Don't," Price whispered.

Cicatrice shook his head and rose from his chair.

"So mistrustful, Price. All I wanted was to get a better look at the boy."

Nico felt another hand drop down over top of Price's. He turned to look and saw that Cicatrice was already behind him. He had crossed the long conference room in the blink of an eye—less than that really.

The blood flooded Nico's head and he felt the ground tumble away from his feet. When he managed to reorient himself, he realized that he was standing, such as it was, on the ceiling, with his feet pressed against the tile. Cicatrice was pressing, lightly it appeared, on his shoulder, keeping him in place in defiance of gravity. The immortal's own feet seemed to stand upside-down by their own volition.

And Price dangled from Cicatrice's other hand. With only his pinky and thumb, Cicatrice was grasping Price's Achilles tendon, and, despite Price's wild flailings, didn't seem to have any trouble holding him steady.

Cicatrice peered deeply into Nico's eyes. Somehow his functional eye was even scarier than his red, ruined one. The sensation was uncanny, as though worms were crawling through his bloodstream. But Price had said vampires didn't have any special mental powers. The man's will was simply haunting.

"Is your family paying him to 'train' you? Has he told you what you're worth to him? Freeze-dried noodles and bottom shelf gin?"

"Bourbon actually," Price grunted, his face turning pink with exertion.

"I...I just met this guy," Nico said lamely.

Cicatrice leaned in until their noses were touching.

"You should ask him how his other apprentices are doing."

Nico felt a sickening sensation as Cicatrice released his shoulder and the floor rushed up to meet him.

FIFTEEN

The Red Scare…

Topan sat silently in the absolute darkness. Even the neon light which Valais had found to be barely there was too bright for Topan's tastes. He was a creature of darkness.

Anyone without his senses would have heard nothing. As it was, he only just barely heard the sound of his patriarch dropping to the ground behind him. Cicatrice gripped his shoulder.

"I took a terrible risk trusting your judgment. The hearing has just concluded."

Topan reached upwards and placed his own hand atop his sire's. He turned his face upward and smiled wanly.

"You've always indulged me, Father Cicatrice. How many mistakes have I made?"

"Too many to count."

"You always keep count."

"Yes, I do. Too many to bring up without embarrassing you. And myself."

Topan hung his head.

"I'm sorry. I was certain it would work."

Cicatrice sat down opposite his get.

"You didn't let me finish. The hearing just concluded. Valais said not a word. Nothing about immortals. Nothing about the Inquisition. McCarthy and his junkyard dogs tried every line of questioning. He played dumb about the whole thing."

Topan pressed two of his fingers to his temple and his thumb to his cheek.

"That's good. That's…that's one thing."

"My network of spiders has begun reporting in as well. What you did to Valais is spreading far and wide. Word is out: House Cicatrice is off-limits to Inquisitors. They've already begun shifting resources and rearranging their strategies to focus on the remaining twelve Houses."

Topan leaned forward and dug his fingers so hard into the stainless steel table he left imprints.

"Do you think it'll keep?"

"Topan, I've long told you about the power of legend. There's power in a good story to dictate generations of behavior. It seems I finally got through to you. You've created your own legend. And with that, I think it's time to present you with a gift."

Cicatrice raised his hand and gestured at the two-way mirror. A light inside the observation room turned on. Lee, the trusted head of Cicatrice's circle stood there. Her neck and arms were criss-crossed with razor blade scars. Cicatrice had been draining life force since before Topan had ever met him, but Topan had often made use of the disciples for their blood. He had often remarked, half-jokingly, that Lee's blood was his favorite flavor of them all. Each scar had been from one of his feedings.

Topan rose to his feet.

"Is this what I think it is?"

Cicatrice put his arm around his get's shoulders.

"An old tradition states that the night a get starts his own circle, his mentorship ends. Here's your first disciple, Topan. I hope she serves you as well as she's served me."

Topan's long-dead tear ducts screamed at him as though they wanted to pour forth their salty fruit. But the time for that was long past.

"A hundred years..." Topan whispered.

"A long mentorship, yes. With many good times and bad. But now you're your own man, your own immortal. And my true heir."

A blue and white car rolled up next to Idi Han and puttered along at about her walking pace. She tried not to look over, keeping her head locked on the sidewalk, but the window rolled down.

"Excuse me, miss."

She turned and flashed a smile at the police official.

"Yes, officer? Good evening."

"Good evening. Would you mind stopping please?"

Idi Han came to a halt and turned to face the car. She kept her hands conspicuously apparent. The officer stepped out of his car. He had a baton and a gun on his belt. She had rarely had run-ins with the authorities back home and could only guess what they were like in America. She wondered briefly if she had enough money on her to bribe the man if that became necessary. Cicatrice had only given her a little.

The policeman looked her up and down.

"Ma'am, are you from around here?"

She smiled. Perhaps there was an opening.

"I am from China," she said, perhaps more deliberately than was necessary.

The policeman pushed his cap back on his head and tucked his thumbs into his belt loops instead of keeping one hand on his weapon as he had before. Obviously he considered her no threat.

"Oh, China. Welcome to the U.S. of A. How are you liking it?"

"Thank you. I like it here very much."

"Are you aware there is a curfew in effect for this city?"

Her eyes widened and her mouth gaped.

"Oh, no! No, I was not aware. I will go to my hotel immediately."

She turned to hurry down the road, hoping that would be the end of it, but in a split-second the police officer had drawn his pistol and leveled it at her.

"Stop! Stop right there!"

Idi Han turned to face the officer. He was shaking like he had seen a ghost.

Am I so mortifying?

Slowly she raised her hands, wondering how long she should play this game, whether she would feel bad about ripping his throat out, whether this was one of the men on Cicatrice's payroll and just dropping her patriarch's name would be enough. She opened her mouth to speak but the cop was already shouting.

"Get down on the ground!"

He shoved her to the concrete but then he immediately

became like a balloon caught in an updraft. The police officer flew through the air like he weighed nothing, and came down on the sidewalk across the street, all of his bones shattering, blood leaking from his face. There was no way he could have survived.

"Good evening, miss," a cruel, heavy voice said.

She realized that the police officer had been pointing his weapon not at her but at someone behind her.

Stupid. Amateur. They got the drop on you.

She turned and looked up at her new adversaries. A man who looked like Scav but stood about thirty centimeters taller and broader in the shoulders loomed over her, a sledgehammer in his hands.

"You must be Scav's friends."

"I wouldn't say that," the big man said. "He is my worthless brother, though. Benito Scavatelli. You must be Idi Han."

She didn't take his proferred hand but deliberately rose under her own power. Neither Benito nor any of the thugs he had brought with him moved to stop her. Either they were sizing her up or...

They think I'm no threat at all. But what about my legendary "smell?"

Suddenly she remembered the garland of garlic Cicatrice had insisted upon her wearing. Thoughtlessly, her hand went to it. A smile split Benito's face in two.

"There are only two reasons an immortal wears garlic. Either they're particularly weak and they want to hide it..."

"Or they're particularly strong and they want to hide it?" she filled in the blank.

Benito tapped his nose. He had five thugs with him, and they had fanned out around her, all staying just out of her arms' length. The one man who was bigger than Benito, with black hair that reached down past his shoulders, was carrying a rather excessive length of chain. The other four carried clubs, axe handles, and bricks. All bludgeoning weapons. Nothing that would kill an immortal.

The big man held the chain as though he meant to use it like a whip or a medieval flail, but the point was clear: they meant to subdue her, not kill her. She decided Mr. Chains was the second-in-command.

"I suppose now you're going to make me an offer to come with you quietly and things will go easily?" she asked.

Benito smiled.

"Actually..."

The sledgehammer sliced an arc through the air. Had it connected, it would've collapsed the side of her head.

Well aimed.

She reached up and with her thumb and index finger snatched the hammerhead out of the air, arresting the blow so suddenly that it took Benito off his feet. With a flick of her wrist she swung the handle back around her, sending Benito flying into one of his thugs, and knocking the feet out from under the other three with the hammer.

That left Mr. Chains. Even with her nose full of the garlic she was wearing, she had easily pegged him as the most dangerous of the entire gang, on sight. Unperturbed by his gaggle of friends being taken off their feet, he swung a loop of chain at her, shattering her left shoulder. The follow-up blow cracked her hip.

"Sven!" Benito cried out, "Don't kill her!"

Mr. Chains—or Sven as it seemed his real name was—reached back and cracked a length of chain into her face, pulverizing her eye.

Easy enough.

As Sven tried to pull the chain back, she reached out and grabbed it, allowing him to fling her back over his shoulder along with the length of chain.

"Huh?" the giant grunted, suddenly losing sight of the target which had just been in front of him.

Idi Han caught his left shoulder with her feet, and threw herself forward, wrapping the chain around his neck twice as she passed and dropped to the ground in front of him. Her eye and the side of her skull were still healing, but she already felt her hip popping back into place and her shoulder seemed fully mended.

She turned and saw that Benito and the others were back on their feet.

"I noticed you all brought chains and clubs. Non-lethal weapons."

"The plan was to bring you back alive," Benito growled.

"I don't think you understand who I am."

Idi Han yanked on the length of chain she still held in her hand. The loops of heavy chain around Sven's neck tightened and to the evident shock of the rest of the gang, his head popped off like an overripe pimple.

She reached up and pulled the garland of garlic from her neck, tossing it into the pile that had become of Sven's corpse. The alarm in the faces of the gangsters turned to panic. For the first time they could smell her power—and, more importantly, for the first time she could feel it herself.

"Boys with toys. No idea how to deal with a real woman."

"Hold...hold on!" Benito said, holding out his hand and slowly lowering his sledgehammer to the ground. "Listen, we were wrong to attack you and I'm sorry for that. And I never apologize. Just ask anyone."

Benito gestured around at his other goons who began nodding copiously. Suddenly, the smallest one, a particularly ugly beak-nosed little man with terrible skin, broke and ran.

"Hofstra!" Benito shouted angrily.

Idi Han took the length of heavy chain, newly freed from Sven's body, and slung it forward with a vicious crack. It came down on the soft spot of Hofstra's head and didn't stop until it passed through his crotch, severing the man in two down the middle. The two halves fell to opposite sides of the macadam. Grotesquely, both halves of the split man tried to pull themselves across the asphalt back towards each other, presumably to begin healing.

"Carson," Benito grunted brusquely while snapping his fingers, "put him out of his misery." He looked up, suddenly noticing the look in Idi Han's face. "Is it all right?"

She nodded. They watched as the other gangster, Carson walked over to Hofstra's body. Both of Hofstra's arms reached towards his erstwhile comrade in supplication, the two halves of his tongue trying to say something pleading. Carson glanced back, ostensibly at Benito, who nodded, but his gaze lingered on

Idi Han, who hoped her face was remaining implacable.

He bent over and fished Hofstra's heart out of one of the halves of his bifurcated body. He broke a splinter off his axe handle and impaled Hofstra's heart on it. Hofstra instantly stopped moving. He glanced back. At that moment, Carson was farther away than any of the gang members. If there was a time for him to run, it was now.

Reluctantly, he returned to his place in the semi-circle that had become of the diminished gang.

"Listen, Miss Han," Benito said, "We'll walk. You'll never see us again. I'll give you…whatever you want. Let's just not…split any more heads."

"How did you find me?"

Benito reluctantly pointed at her dress.

"There's a transponder on you. It'll feel like just a tiny…"

Before he finished his sentence she had fished the miniscule microchip out of her right shoulder and crushed it between her fingers.

"Who sent you?"

Benito's mouth opened, he paused, and then finally admitted, "Otto Signari."

"Otto Signari cares whether I live or die?"

Benito exchanged a sidelong glance with the remaining members of his gang.

"Topan said not to touch you, but…"

"But you got it in your heads that I'd make a valuable hostage."

Benito nodded.

"So there probably aren't others coming after me?"

"No."

"But they'll be coming after Father Cicatrice?"

"Yes. A lot."

"All right," she said, "You've told me what I want to know."

Benito pointed tentatively off into the distance.

"We can go, then?"

"Oh, no. You're all going to die. I'm just tired of talking to you."

She cut through the rest of them like butter.

SIXTEEN

Nico's jaws clapped together, pinching the tip of his tongue and drawing blood. His heart was clattering like a locomotive speeding off the tracks. It took a moment for the signals to reach his brain that his legs had not been shattered in the fall. Price sat on the ground, clutching at his shin, but otherwise seemingly unharmed.

Cicatrice was already on the other side of the room, his hands folded behind him, his back towards them. His voice wafted over his shoulder towards them.

"You've had your fun, Price. You can tell your drinking buddies you saw me face-to-face and lived to tell about it. Now get out."

Nico held out a hand to help Price up. Surprisingly, he took it and pulled himself to his feet.

"Boy, you don't rattle easy, kid," he whispered in Nico's face.

Nico opened his mouth to reply, but all of his cool points leaked out with a mouthful of bloody saliva. He pressed his tongue to the roof of his mouth, hoping to staunch the bleeding.

"Trust me, Scar, I take no pleasure in being here. But you and I have a common interest."

Cicatrice turned so that his profile was visible, but not to fully face them.

"And that would be?"

"*Le chasseur du mort.*"

Nico was surprised to hear the French words pour out of Price's mouth like a fine vintage. For some reason (many reasons, in fact) Price struck him as the ugly American type.

"Ridiculous. The Hunter of the Dead hasn't been seen since

I last encountered him. Seven hundred years ago."

Price shook his head and turned to leave.

"Fine, play your games, Cicatrice. Come on, kid."

They stepped out the door, and Price grabbed Nico and put his finger to his lips, expectantly.

"Price. Wait."

Price winked at his charge and together they walked back into the conference room, feigning reluctance.

"Are we going to talk?"

"I'll talk. I promise nothing beyond that."

Price nodded.

"All right, that's something. If you're willing to admit..."

Cicatrice held up a hand.

"Your catamite will have to wait outside."

Price glanced at Nico.

"I guess he means you."

Nico kicked the stainless steel wall and immediately regretted it.

I hope I didn't chip a bone.

The pain didn't make the anger go away. Price had sent him out of the room like a child. A child!

He glanced around. Unwholesome, dead-eyed stares greeted him in every direction. The renfields seemed to carry about their work unflaggingly, while still managing to stare at him.

"Fuck it," he muttered under his breath, "I'm going to play some blackjack."

Technically, he was too young to even be in the casino, but what the hell, he had already gotten past security. Price could come find him. Heaven knew Cicatrice had enough cameras to find him.

He passed by row upon row of creepy *Birds*-like renfields staring at him until he exited the mini-pyramid. He stopped mid-stride upon spotting a lone figure at the foot of the pyra-mid. Under ordinary circumstances he would have thought the girl was extremely attractive, but right now she looked like a drowned rat. Someone had ripped her clothes to shreds.

"Hello," he said, stepping carefully down the pyramid one step at a time.

The girl looked up at him, betraying a look that combined fierce determination and infinite sadness.

"You're an Inquisitor?"

Nico's hand drifted to the bat hanging from his belt.

"You want to find out?"

"I wouldn't try it," she said quietly.

"Is that a threat?"

"It's just a piece of advice."

He looked her up and down.

"I take it that makes you a…"

He trailed off.

"Immortal," she said.

"Immortal, sure." He clambered down to take a seat next to her. "You look like a bomb went off."

"Close," the girl said, running her hand down what scraps remained of what he couldn't tell whether had been a fine dress or a rag.

"So you, um, you work for this Cicatrice guy?"

"No, I don't work for him," she snapped. "I'm his…" she paused, seeming to consider her situation before finally deciding on a word, "friend."

"You're his friend. I didn't know vampires had friends."

"*Goeng-si?*"

"What?"

The girl suddenly rose to her feet and stumbled forward, nearly tripping. Nico jumped up to catch her, but she had only lost her footing for a second. She wandered off.

"Hey! Where are you going?"

He followed her as she hurried to the nearest row of slot machines. The young girl approached a bluehair dumping quarters into a slot machine.

"Excuse me, ma'am," the girl said, "do you have a mirror I could use? Just for a moment."

Without taking her right hand off the lever, the old woman reached into her purse and handed the young girl her compact.

Nico walked up behind her and glanced into the compact. He could see her face like normal. She spotted him over her shoulder in the glass and snapped it closed.

So much for that old canard.

"Thank you," she said, returning the compact.

"Any time, sweetheart."

Somewhat dazed she returned to the foot of the pyramid.

"What was that all about?" he asked.

"You really think I'm a monster?" she asked, "A vampire?"

He shrugged.

"I don't know. I don't even know you."

"My name is…" she looked up into his eyes, "I was about to lie to you."

"Okay."

"My name is Idi Han."

"Nico. Salazar."

He put out his hand. She took it, clasping his fingers tightly for a moment rather than shaking.

"Heh. I think I might practice Idi Han."

"What does that mean?"

"Oh. My…friend. The other Inquisitor. When we broke in here…I shouldn't be telling you this, should I?"

She laughed.

"No, it's fine. Go on, please."

"Well, he said I was this great martial artist. Ho Tan Fow. Do you know what it means?"

She shrugged.

"It doesn't mean anything."

"Yeah, I thought not."

"What'd you do?"

"Um…I hit a lady in the head with a baseball bat."

Idi Han giggled, covering her hand.

"Not Hedrox?"

"Yes. That was her name. Something Something Hedrox. What does Idi Han mean?"

"Oh. That. That's a long story."

"Oh. Yeah. No time for long stories now, I guess."

He glanced back up the steps of the pyramid, wondering how

long the grown-ups would be, and then internally chastising himself for not counting himself among their number. Idi Han wrapped her arms around her legs and pulled her knees into her chest.

"I don't want to tell you what my name means. It's embarrassing. And I've had a bunch of people who keep telling me that I'm this special, magical savior treasure person. It's very annoying."

"You don't want to be a special magic savior whatever?"

"No."

"Well what do you want to be?"

She looked into his eyes for the first time. There was a spark of mischief there.

"You really want to know?" she asked.

He couldn't help the grin that was tugging at the side of his face.

"Yeah, I do."

She blushed.

"It's silly."

"We're two people in extraordinarily silly positions. Who happened to come across each other. Trust me, I won't judge."

She thought for a moment.

"Well, all right. I want to be the person who proves them all wrong. Who proves there's no such thing as destiny or even potential. That I don't have to do anything. That the whole world can just burn for all I care. That's the person I want to be."

Nico opened his mouth to reply but a clatter from above signaled that the great détente between Cicatrice and Price was complete and their apprentices were desired once again.

SEVENTEEN

The Wild West…

Topan hurried down into the mine, his spurs clinking as he ran. After a few months of traveling with his sire he had only just begun to grasp the importance of his new role. He was, if anything, perhaps too over-eager.

He nearly bowled over the Egyptian as he stumbled into the cross-cut where the other Cicatrice houselings had gathered.

"Pardon me, Elder Rahim!"

Rahim nodded and patted Topan's shoulder absently.

"The mortal disciples are all gathered outside, Father Cicatrice!" Topan announced loudly.

Cicatrice nodded and beckoned for Topan to join him at the head of the throng.

"Thank you, my boy. And thank you all for coming. Welcome to Virginia City. I know you've all come a long way and you may be wondering why you're here at all, so I won't waste any more of your time. Some of you older immortals will recall the legend of El Dorado. I've located it not far from here. And no, it is no empire of gold. Rather it is the last Aztec temple: resting place of The Damned."

In a rare moment of indulgence, Cicatrice allowed the elders and the upstanding immortals in the gathering chatter among themselves. He raised a small piece of coal on the toe of his boot and tossed it down the shaft. Topan never heard it strike bottom.

Cicatrice adjusted his Stetson and cleared his throat, regaining the crowd.

"I've decided to move my seat from Paris to El Dorado—what the locals call The Meadows. The only problem is there's nothing there.

It's going to take some time and some doing before a decent-sized city takes root there. It would be interesting though, I think, to help build a city from the ground up. A city designed by immortals for immortals. A city of night."

"A New Necropolis?" Topan ventured.

The mine became very, very quiet. Topan worried he had spoken out of turn.

"Some of you have not yet met my get, Topan. He will need to be built from the ground up as well."

"Forgive me, Father Cicatrice," a woman with her face tattooed as a skull said, "but the boy doesn't exactly smell of impressive power. Certainly not like..."

She trailed off. Topan bit his lower lip. He was feeling picked upon, but didn't want to betray weakness.

"No," Cicatrice agreed, "He does not match the raw natural talent of...others I have chosen. For a long time I believed if I lived in this world long enough I would meet a perfect heir. Someone who, after being granted the Long Gift, would be worthy within a few days. But now I think it must be a slow burn. And as I build my new city, so too will I build my new heir. Until he is ready."

Cicatrice paused, glancing down into the shaft which seemed to stretch blackly into infinity.

"That being said," Cicatrice continued, "Disrespecting my get—and my decisionmaking—with a question like that...let's just say if it happens a second time from any of you, being an elder in my House will not save you from my wrath. Which indeed brings us to our next order of business."

Cicatrice gestured and Rahim quickly pushed a minecart up in front of Cicatrice like an altar. Topan felt like a child sneaking a peek inside a red birthday envelope. From within the minecart a woman stared up at him defiantly. She was wrapped in heavy lengths of chain that looked better suited to anchoring a naval vessel than restraining a person but was otherwise naked. A metal plate had been placed over her mouth and bolted into her jawbones to keep her quiet.

It was the first time Topan had seen a woman in the nude but he felt (perhaps appropriately) more pity than lust.

"Surely even chains such as those can't subdue one of our kind?" Topan whispered breathlessly in Cicatrice's ear.

"*Normally not. But she has been starved. Remember what I told you? About the blood and the earth?*"

"*The blood is the power but the earth is the life.*"

Cicatrice squeezed Topan's shoulder. It had been one of their first lessons. Immortality was granted by the native soil they slept in each night. But their ferocious power was granted by draining the blood of others—and, someday, Cicatrice had promised, there was a still more perfect way of draining power without cutting a vein.

"*Mercy is not a quality I am often accused of possessing,*" *Cicatrice said to a mild titter of laughter,* "*nevertheless it has always been my policy to grant great leeway to my elders. Your affairs are your own inasmuch as they don't reflect poorly on me.*"

Cicatrice glanced down at the chained immortal.

"*Winter was my first and most trusted elder. That makes this difficult for me. Impossible, really. You eleven, step forward.*"

Cicatrice tapped Topan on the back and gestured at a mattock leaning against one of the pylons. Topan went to fetch it as Rahim and the other elders emerged from the crowd, and the lesser immortals receded quietly.

"*I've forgiven Winter and the rest of you many small trespasses. I've never considered it a patriarch's place to enforce the code mindlessly, but rather judiciously. That being said, there are some things I can not forgive.*"

"*The telegrams,*" *Rahim said quietly.*

Cicatrice nodded.

"*Each of you received a message that I would be moving my seat. What you may not know is that each message indicated a different spot—Laredo, San Francisco, and so on. And then when you arrived you received a second message redirecting you here. But my spies in Salt Lake City spotted Otto Signari and a band of fixers arriving just ahead of my dear Winter here.*"

"*Treason!*" *Topan exclaimed, before clapping his hand over his mouth.*

"*Yes, my boy,*" *Cicatrice said, taking the pickaxe from his hand and twirling its handle with a single hand to test its balance,* "*Something I'd refused to believe for some time. Whether for love or money I don't know, but the fact remains your fellow elder has betrayed our House. The undertaking of moving my seat to The Meadows is too important to withstand such treachery. I suppose I've thrown the Signaris off the* scent for a while, but now I'm left with the odious task of meting out judgment to a loved one."

"Kill her, Father Cicatrice, put her down," Topan said.

Cicatrice shook his head.

"No, my boy, the punishment for treason is even greater than death."

"What could be greater than death?"

"Life. Eternal life. I would not do this to an elder without you all being in agreement. Think carefully. For if Winter has fallen this low, then so could each and every one of you."

Cicatrice tossed the mattock to the ground before the feet of the eleven remaining elders. The woman with the skull-face tattoo was the first to pick it up. She looked to Cicatrice.

"I know kings don't kill kings," she said, "but I will ever be loyal to you, Father Cicatrice."

She raised the mattock over her head and swung it down into Winter's heart. Winter grunted and moaned in pain. Rahim approached next and wheedled the mattock out of his former peer's chest. He gestured at the tattooed woman.

"Well said."

Rahim swung and delivered a blow as well. One by one, each of the elders approached. Only the last, a Russian noble by the looks of him, seemed hesitant, but after a moment he too delivered a damning blow. Cicatrice plucked the pickaxe from Winter's chest.

"Then it is almost decided. Rahim, you are now my new senior elder. Topan, you are now my junior."

He pointed the handle towards Topan. Astonished, Topan took it.

"When your training is complete you can take your seat at the table in Rome. Until then I intend not to trade with that reptile, Otto Signari. And your position within my House, should anything happen to me, is now official. And secure."

"But not as your heir."

"Not yet. Now you have a decision to make. For this punishment it must be unanimous."

Unhesitating, Topan drove the mattock into Winter's eye.

"Then it is accomplished. Topan, go fetch Winter's circle. The rest of you leave. We'll meet again tomorrow evening to discuss building up The Meadows."

Topan flew ahead of the crowd out to where the mortals had set up camp on the downslope of the mountain. Most of the mortals were gathered around campfires, but a few armed men were watching over a sad and lonely group of about twenty that had been lashed together and were shivering in the dark.

"Come," Topan said, "Bring the equipment."

Groaning in agony, the mortals rose to follow him. They were all burdened down like mules. When he returned to the crosscut he found it empty except for Cicatrice and Winter.

"Though you are mortal scum," Cicatrice said, "You know our ways, and some of you have proven useful. Other uses could be found for you with other masters. The Long Gift might still be yours one day. But that depends upon your answer to a simple question. You have all been ever-loyal to this woman. Some for decades, some for only a few months. So I understand it may be with varying degrees of difficulty that you answer: who among you will renounce her?"

The mortals looked to each other for answers like beaten curs. The head of the circle was the first to fall to his knees, though, and the others all quickly joined in, cursing Winter's name and begging for forgiveness. Winter screamed all but soundlessly in impotent rage.

"Enough," Cicatrice said finally, "Enough. Set about your work. Dawn is almost upon us."

Cicatrice retreated from the minecart and joined Topan at the entrance to the crosscut. Even in their frigid, exhausted state the mortals scrambled like beavers to carry out Cicatrice's punishment. They assembled the smelting furnace and brought it to a roaring heat—foolhardy work for the interior of a mine indeed. They wrapped sticks of dynamite and barrels of black powder around the crossbeams that held the mine up.

As it became clear what they were doing, Topan said, "Seems a shame to lose all the wealth of the mine."

"You'd think so. It's owned by a Signari, though."

Topan grinned. Finally the mortals came to the conclusion of their tasks. One emptied a sack full of charnel soil over Winter, who sputtered such as she could with her mouth nailed shut. Through her nose she continued to condemn her treacherous circle and Cicatrice and all the world for all Topan could tell.

"The blood is the power..." Cicatrice said.

"…But the earth is the life. She'll live then?"

"For ever and ever. Trapped at the bottom of a mine in a prison of gold."

The mortals finished liquefying a small fortune in gold ore. With some difficulty because of her struggles, they filled the minecart with the scalding metal, sealing Winter away under a bed of native soil. Her struggles and contortions played out for a few moments in the liquid, a hypnotizing dance that Topan couldn't rip his eyes away from. Then the liquid finally cooled and froze Winter in one last pose. The mortals struggled to tip the cart into the long shaft.

"Come," Cicatrice said, pressing Topan's shoulder.

As they left the crosscut, Cicatrice dumped the fuel from a lantern across the entrance to the crosscut, then smashed the lantern in the fuel. A small wall of flame licked up the crossbeams, threatening second by second to tickle the black powder and dynamite. They heard a cheer as presumably the cart finally tipped over, followed by screams as the mortals finally realized what was happening to them. Explosions ripped through the mountain as they emerged from the mine entrance.

"Why did you ask them to renounce Winter if you were going to kill them anyway?" Topan asked as they mounted their horses and joined the snaking line of immortals and their disciples ambling down the mountain.

"I wasn't. I told them their fates depended on the answer to a question. They answered incorrectly."

Topan thought for a moment.

"Loyalty."

"Remember this day, my beloved get. Remember the wages of disloyalty."

Cicatrice folded his hands in front of him. Price remained standing, too wary to sit.

"Shall I order you some tea? A speech therapist, perhaps?"

"The Hunter of the Dead has reappeared. In Las Vegas." They waited in silence for a moment. "You're not going to deny it?"

"I heard a rumor. I'm still trying to determine its accuracy."

Price tossed his cell phone across the conference table. Cicatrice snatched it and glanced at it. The picture depicted a broken lance tip, coated with some supernatural black tar-like or oily substance. Cicatrice tossed the cell phone back onto the conference table.

"You have this…evidence?"

"I don't. But I trust the people who showed it to me."

"And what do you want from me exactly? We are sworn enemies, you and I."

"There is a truce between House Cicatrice and the Inquisition. We don't kill your kind and you don't kill ours."

"This 'truce' as you call it was bought through terror and intimidation. It is the not the foundation for an alliance. It is an understanding between enemies. A cold war, not a friendship."

"It may be all we've got. There was a red telephone between Moscow and Washington during the Cold War. The Soviets and the Americans hated each other's guts, but they figured out a way to stave off nuclear Armageddon together."

"And you think the Hunter of the Dead is the mutually assured destruction that will make us strange bedfellows?"

"Perhaps." Slowly, Price lowered himself into a seat. "Is he real?"

Cicatrice paused.

"Yes.

"Have you really seen him?"

"Yes. I've seen him."

"Do you think he's really back?"

"I think it's possible."

"What's the other possibility?"

"A copycat. Perhaps an oldblood who's gone off the reservation. Dresses up as a knight and starts killing immortals. There's been rumors of a serial immortal killer in the community for some time now. It could all be an elaborate farce."

"What if I told you he killed one of The Damned?"

"Not possible."

"I don't know how you can be certain about that…" Price started to say.

"I am."

Price nodded.

"Well, if you really have access to The Damned and they're

not just some old legend like The Hunter, why don't you go count them? Because I found a dead one last night. And hoofprints leading away from the scene."

"You're certain it was one of The Damned?"

"A lamprey-faced, ghoul-like monster with power that dwarfs even yours? Yeah. I'm pretty fucking sure I saw it. I'm pretty fucking sure I fought it and only got away by blowing up a gas station."

Cicatrice leaned back in his chair.

"The Hunter is back. The Damned are stirring. Strange times we live in."

"Yeah, strange days indeed, Jim. I want to propose that we work together to find The Hunter."

"To what end?"

"To what end? To…stop him. To subdue him. To kill him if possible."

"And why would you want that, Price? Shouldn't you be happy that The Hunter is back? He's doing your job for you. In a few years he'll clear us out of every tomb and hiding hole on the planet."

Price glanced down. A look of shame. Cicatrice leaned forward.

"Cards on the table?" Price asked.

"Naturally."

"He owes allegiance to no one. He killed an Inquisitor, too. I don't know what he wants or what his endgame is, but he's not distinguishing between killing people and killing vampires. Your kind has a code and you have…restraint. This guy doesn't. I think he may be an even bigger menace to mankind than you. If he exists. I'm still not 100% convinced."

Cicatrice placed his elbows on the table and rested his nose on his interlocked fists.

"My intellect tells me there is no chance that The Hunter of the Dead has emerged from centuries of sleep. That he disappeared all those years ago. But my heart screams out that he is back. And if he is, then, yes, mankind and immortals both are in existential danger. He is vicious, soulless, relentless. A killing machine without mercy, without fear. He destroys the undying the same way a man swats a fly. He is indestructible. And he is very, very real."

"I don't believe anything is indestructible. That's what they said about the *Titanic*."

"There might be a way to banish him…to put him back to sleep. You would have to get your hands very dirty. And I don't think you'll like it."

Price bit his lower lip.

"I'm in your office asking for your help. I'm already dirty. I already don't like it."

"Then I will tell you something you don't know. The Hunter of the Dead is drawn to great concentrations of my kind like a moth to a flame. He came to the Necropolis. Then when he scattered us to the four winds, he chased down every large group until finally there were no more groups to chase. And then the code kept us safe: no more than one or two immortals travelling together, no more than a few dozen in any large city."

"I actually know all of this."

"Here's the part you don't. There are nearly five hundred immortals in Las Vegas tonight."

Price's eyes opened as wide as saucers.

"Five *hundred*? How could this happen without anyone noticing?"

"It seems they've congregated in the sewers and tunnels, while the Signaris kept them fed and happy and out of sight."

"In other words your old blood enemies are amassing an army on your doorstep. And you think I should wipe them out for you."

"I told you you wouldn't like it."

Price shook his head in disbelief.

"Five hundred? And you don't care if they're all destroyed?"

"It would be a blow to my kind. We'd be set back many centuries. But it would weaken the other Houses."

"Oh, good. Vampire politics. My favorite discussion topic."

Cicatrice raised his hand.

"More importantly: if The Hunter really is attracted in some way to mass groupings of immortals, it should make him fall back into stasis or go back into hiding or whatever it is that he does."

Price put his thumb against his teeth.

"I don't know, Cicatrice. Even in a daylight attack against five hundred nightcrawlers there would have to be hundreds of renfields. I mean, um…what do you call them?"

Cicatrice shook his head.

"I know what you meant."

"And there's just me and my apprentice. I don't see how we could fight all that. But even if we did manage to stake five hundred vampires in their coffins…it'd take more than a day."

"For two people, perhaps. You would have to call in your short friend and her brownshirts."

"Bonaparte? Why would she help me?"

"For the chance to fully dispatch five hundred of my kind? Sanctioned by me, no less? Wouldn't that be the greatest victory in the history of the Inquisition? Your Bonaparte is motivated by nothing if not hubris."

Price squeezed his eyes shut, as if visibly mulling over the possibilities in his mind.

"This is probably a trick."

"On the contrary. I've laid my cards on the table, as we discussed. My life and the life of my new heir, and perhaps my entire House is in danger. You would alleviate this danger and dispose of The Hunter in one fell stroke. The sacrifice I make is five hundred members of my kind, half the fixers in North America practically. It's a dirty, dirty matter, but Otto Signari brought these circumstances upon us. I did not."

"You'll show me this lair?"

"As soon as my heir returns."

Price glanced at the bank of video monitors behind Cicatrice. He pointed.

"Is that her?"

On the steps leading up to the false pyramid Idi Han sat with Price's protégé. They seemed uncomfortably warm and close. Cicatrice rose and began to walk out to fetch the girl away. Price rose as he passed and placed a hand on his shoulder to stop him. Cicatrice could easily have broken every bone in the man's body, but he had turned out to be a possible solution to all of his problems, unlikely as that seemed.

"Wait. Do we have a deal?"

"We do."

"I'm not sure we do. I need assurances. If I do this, if I pull this all together for you, can you promise me there will be no retaliations? If I do this huge favor for you how do I know two years from now some nightcrawler with an itchy trigger finger won't come looking for me because I killed his cousin or whatever?"

"It's well within my power to promise that."

"Oh, I know it's within your power. But how do I know you'll keep your word?"

"I must trust that you'll keep your word as well. There's a story about a scorpion and a fox…"

"And I'm sure it's a corker. But I want real assurances, not metaphors."

Cicatrice glanced back at the video monitor.

"We each have a new apprentice in our lives and from them will we gain the balance we need. Killing you is a dubious proposition. But I have no doubts about my ability to strike at your young charge, even after my death. As I'm sure your arm could reach from beyond the grave for long enough to strike down my child. So through the children there is a truce. Is that a fair assurance for you?"

Slowly, reluctantly, Price put out his hand and just as tentatively Cicatrice shook it. As they emerged onto the casino floor, Idi Han and the boy were embarrassingly close, nearly nose-to-nose and laughing conspiratorially. They both jumped as soon as the door opened.

"Idi Han," he glanced up and down at his get, whose clothes were shredded near to rags, "What happened?"

"Nothing I couldn't handle, Father Cicatrice."

Price whistled sharply and jerked his thumb, indicating that the boy should join him. Reluctantly, the boy broke away from Idi Han. Cicatrice descended the stairwell and looked into Idi Han's eyes. Already she was able to hide things from him. He would've been proud if it wasn't so infuriating.

"Was the fixer's tale true?" he asked in Cantonese.

She nodded.

"Where was the entrance?"

She told him.

"Very well," he said loudly, "You two will stay here and out of trouble. And away from each other. I'm taking Price on a brief trip. We'll be back shortly."

"Eh, bring the kids along, Scar," Price said, "They need seasoning."

"They're not salads, Price. And I don't want my new charge being influenced by the likes of you."

"All right. Just Nico's coming, then. I want to keep an eye on him. It'll be two against one then."

"Very well, then. Idi Han, you're coming with us as well."

EIGHTEEN

"You and Idi Han seemed to be getting along."

"What's that supposed to mean?"

"What's that supposed to mean?" Price parroted back in a mocking voice.

Nico ran his bat along the macadam, turning it until the blades threw sparks.

"It's not like we ran off to go make deals behind closed doors, you know."

"You'll dull the blade doing that."

Nico lifted the bat and tossed it over his shoulder.

"You know, I could be back in my nice, warm apartment right now with my Xbox and a pound of fucking ganja."

Price gestured elaborately in no particular direction, not knowing where Nico actually lived.

"Well, then why don't you go?"

Nico jabbed the curved top of the bat into Price's chest.

"Because I'm a wanted man. And it just so happens that you lied on your job application and there's no way for the authorities to find that little roach motel you actually live in."

With surprising speed and strength, especially considering his age, Price swatted at the bat, knocking it out of Nico's hands and sending it tumbling away into the street. He took a step forward and suddenly Nico felt how intimidating Price was when he was really mad.

"First of all, I've told you from the start not to follow me around. Second of all, I don't want to hear shit about the way I live my life from anyone who's not paying my bills. And third the fuck of all, if you really want to be an Inquisitor one day—and at the rate you're going, I sincerely doubt that day will ever come—you're going to have to learn to listen to your head and not your cock."

Price rolled his hips around, pointing in various directions as though using his penis as a divining rod. He made a disgusted noise and started to walk away.

Nico could feel his cheeks burning. Glumly, he retrieved his weapon from the sewer grate it had nearly fallen down. He had to run to catch up with Price.

"Carter!"

"What?"

"I'm sorry. It just feels like we've been wandering aimlessly for hours."

Idi Han and Cicatrice had quickly led them to the entrance to the warrens where the Signari fixers had set up shop. Since then he and Price had been back to the funeral parlor Bonaparte called home and found it empty. They'd been wandering the streets ever since.

"I don't like being on my feet any more than you do, kid. But Bonaparte's not at home and she's not answering her phone. We've got to find her and soon if we want to clear out those tunnels."

"Well, maybe we should split up?"

"With an army of angry fixers on the street? I don't think so, kid. Listen, I'll drop you off at the roach motel."

"No, nevermind," Nico said. "I didn't mean to be a dick. I'm guessing this job's not all sex and caviar."

"Not even a little bit. And this wouldn't be the first night I've wasted on a wild goose chase," he added under his breath, perhaps not caring if Nico heard, "or the thousandth."

They plodded along together in silence. Price had talked about all the haunts he and the other Inquisitors spent time wandering—slums, cemeteries, funeral parlors, but most of all just back alleys. The same places where drug dealers and prostitutes and all manner of mortal criminals lingered late at night, as well.

"You know, believe it or not, I know how you feel. Exactly how you feel."

"What do you mean?"

Price sighed.

I wasn't always the asshole I am now, you know. I was young once, too. I was a young vampire hunter. And I believed that they weren't so bad. I fell in love with one once."

"I'm not in love with…anyone."

"Okay, good."

Nico looked at him.

"Well…what happened?"

"Exactly what had to happen. She was beautiful and young and we were in love. And I had to put a stake in her heart. She was a killer. And she would've kept killing. She might not have killed me. But I would have either had to become what she was or destroy her. Can you live like that, Nico? Can you live forever, killing others to live? Trading your soul for a little extra life? Because that's all it is. Everyone dies someday, even the so-called immortals. And in the end, you'll have nothing. If you want to be with her, you'll have to become like her. You make your choice. But if you choose her you'll never see another sunrise."

Nico opened his mouth to protest but a scream pierced the night. It couldn't have come from any farther than a block away. He stopped and turned to look, rubbernecking. When he turned back Price had already made it halfway down the block.

They reached a T-intersection and Price placed his hand on Nico's chest. The older man reached into his bandolier and tossed a stake loudly across the lip of the intersection, deliberately giving it some English so that it would clatter.

The report of three bullets cut through the air and Nico felt the breath knocked out of him as Price slammed him into the wall. When he recovered enough to see what was going on he saw that his back was to the wall, as was Price's, and they were both lined up along the wall perpendicular to the alleyway.

"Just my luck," Price hissed, rolling his eyes and taking his shotgun from his leg holster, "A regular mugging and I have to get involved. Batting a thousand, Price."

"Carter, is that you?"

Nico and Price exchanged a glance.

"Could you say a word to let me know that's you out there, Carter?"

"Why you shooting at me, half-pint?" Price growled.

"Well, I thought you were Blake's backup."

"Blake Turner? The Temuchin fixer?"

"That's the one."

Price whistled appreciatively.

"You caught yourself a whale, Bonaparte."

"Right, I'm coming out."

Bonaparte emerged from the alleyway. She was dressed quite differently from her simple mortuary getup. This time her clothes were decidedly utilitarian, with cargo pockets and an almost World War II-style cut to them. Like Price, she wore a bandolier of wooden stakes.

"Carter. Nico. Good to see you two again."

"Bonaparte," Price grunted.

She rolled her eyes.

"When will you drop that stupid nickname?"

"When you grow a couple feet. And stop telling everybody what to do."

"Wait," Nico said, "What do you prefer to be called?"

Bonaparte bristled.

"I'm an Inquisitor. My name doesn't matter. Only the mission..."

"Oh, for Christ's sake!" Price moaned, "This is why I can't stand your bullshit."

"Well, you're welcome to leave Las Vegas anytime, Carter."

Price's eyes narrowed.

"This is my city. Why don't you and your jackbooted thugs..."

"Carter," Nico whispered.

"Oh, right. I need your help."

Bonaparte chuckled.

"Hardly surprising. You never come to see me for any other reason. Come on, let's talk."

They stepped around the corner and walked down the alleyway. A woman in a tiny little corset of a blue dress lay on the ground. Her head was on the other side of the alley. Price whistled.

"You really got old Blake Turner, huh? I've been wanting a piece of her for years. Looks pretty good for a hundred and fifty, doesn't she, kid?"

Nico felt a bubble of bile burst in his throat. Against his better judgment (or all judgment, really, as his animal instincts kicked in) he puked all over the ground. The two Inquisitors jumped in opposite directions to avoid the splash, but neither's shoe went unoffended.

"Jesus, kid. First body? Better get used to them."

Nico glared at her angrily. He tapped the bat against the ground nervously. Price approached the corpse with almost a bounce in his step.

"This is some good work. Where are your partners in crime?"

Price glanced around the alleyway and up to the rooftops. Bonaparte nodded.

"Actually, I'm on my own tonight."

Price's eyebrows rose.

"Taking a page out of the Book of Price?"

Bonaparte and Nico both rolled their eyes.

"As it happens, the streets are fair crawling with our blood-drinking chums. We're stretched to the breaking point so I ordered the newbies to move in pairs and sent the experienced Inquisitors out on their own."

"I may have a bead on why that is."

"Oh?"

Price and Bonaparte retreated to a corner of the alley to whisper in hushed tones about the army of fixers. Nico didn't mind being left out of the conversation. Now that he had gotten over his initial revulsion, he found himself fixated on Blake Turner's head. He crouched down. It looked just like a ball of hair. A Tribble from *Star Trek*, maybe.

He reached out and poked it. Satisfied that it did not move, he pressed it until her hair shifted and he saw where her severed neck was. Bonaparte had made a clean cut. He glanced back at the petite woman, who was still debating Price. She wore a katana blade on her belt, half as tall as she was.

He pressed on Turner's head until the neck faced downward. Damn, that had been a clean cut. Clinical, almost. He turned the head as best he could using just two fingers, grabbing onto the hair and gently tugging it until the woman's face was pointed towards him. Her eyes were closed, her skin pale. She had a tiny little button of a nose that reminded him of his own mother's.

"*Madre de dios*," he muttered, stifling the urge to cross himself.

Tentatively he reached out with one finger. Aside from Idi Han and Cicatrice (who weren't exactly going to let him poke their faces) this was the closest he had yet been to a real vampire.

He lifted Turner's lip, tentatively out of fear that her eyes would open and she would suddenly bite down. Of course, decapitation worked for everything that lived, even highlanders, so he saw no special reason to be scared. It was just an old hokey superstitious feeling in his gut.

He didn't see the fang. He continued to pull on her lip. Still nothing. He checked the other side. Nothing there either. Forgetting his queasiness, he took both hands and opened the mouth as wide as he could, like the oral hygienist did to him at the dentist's office.

Her teeth were totally normal.

A hand dropped down on his shoulder and he nearly leaped out of his skin.

"What the fuck are you doing, kid?"

Nico swallowed a lump in his throat.

"Can I ask a dumb question?"

"Do you know any other kind?"

"Hey, be nice, Carter," Bonaparte said. "There are no stupid questions."

"Oh, I have heard some stupid questions in my life..."

"Go ahead, Nico."

Nico cleared his throat.

"Well...how come she doesn't have any fangs?"

The two Inquisitors exchanged a worried glance.

"Knock it off, kid," Price said gesturing towards the dumpster, "and toss the watermelon in with the rest of the garbage. When the sun comes up…"

He snapped his fingers, indicating disintegration, no doubt.

"No, no, I'm serious!" Nico said, fighting back the urge to either cry or vomit, he wasn't sure which. Cromit.

"Show me," Bonaparte said, making the itchy palm sign with her hand, "I'm sure you just missed them. I don't kill people."

Nico hastily attempted to grab the head, but was unable to get a good grip on it and seemed to fumble over and over.

"Oh, Jesus Christ," Price said, snatching the head out of Nico's grasp.

Standing in front of Nico, Price examined the head from side to side, looking in first one ear, then the other. He fiddled with her lips, which Nico saw were beginning to go rictus with rigor (if vampires even got rigor.)

"Oh, shit," Price muttered.

Taking the head with both hands on opposite sides, one on the hair, one on the mandible, he prised Blake's jaw open.

"Fuck me. Bonaparte, you fuckup. Take a look at this."

"I swear she's immortal! She's on my list! I have pictures, a file…"

"But where are the fangs?" Price shouted, shaking the normal-toothed head in Bonaparte's direction. "This is just some regular chick you just offed."

Bonaparte seemed near tears.

"You bastard! I swear she had them when she attacked me! She had the strength of ten mortal men!"

"Or maybe you just have the strength of one tenth of a fucking ordinary woman!"

"Price, I swear, you take that back you blackguard, or…I'm sorry, I can't…"

Bonaparte was really crying now, and Price couldn't hold back the laughter any more. Both Inquisitors collapsed into paroxysms of hysterics.

"'Blackguard?'" Price asked, putting his arm around his erstwhile rival as they sat on the asphalt, riddled with laughter, "Where did you dig that up?"

Nico stared on in amazement. His eyes must have been as wide as saucers. Price actually wiped away what must have been an ounce of snot from his nose and tossed it off away into the alley. He proffered Blake's head back to Nico, who took it, and remained frozen, stock-still.

"I'm sorry, kid," Bonaparte said, standing, "I didn't mean to prank you, but my God you are green. Haven't you even given him the textbook yet, Carter?"

"What the fuck is going on?" Nico shouted.

Bonaparte held her hand down and helped Price to his feet. Price shook his head.

"Vampires don't have fangs, kid. You've been watching too many movies."

"Then how do they eat?"

"How do you think they eat?"

"Like through…like…hollow straws in their…"

He pointed up at his own cheek where vampire teeth would have poked out if he had been wearing a novelty pair for Halloween.

"Ain't an animal in the world that sucks blood through hollow teeth. Some snakes have hollow teeth so they can inject you with venom. And if you didn't have long fangs before you died, would you expect to just grow them out afterwards?"

"Where would they even hide them?" Bonaparte asked, "How would they blend in? Just never smile? Or do the tight-lipped thing like…who was that character?"

"Ruthven."

Nico sagged. Blake Turner's head suddenly felt like a 14-lb bowling ball.

"So how *do* they eat, then?"

"Same way as you, kid. At first, anyway. Then they develop a sense for how to draw energy from blood alone. A lot of renfields carry razor blades around their neck for their masters, and some nightcrawlers carry straight razors or knives for the same purpose. Then eventually they reach the point where they can just…"

Bonaparte snapped her fingers.

"Suck the strength right out of you. With a touch of the hand."

"So there's no way to tell if someone you killed is…"

"Here, let me learn you something. Look."

He turned Blake's head towards Nico. Where he expected to see red, the flesh was entirely white.

"She hasn't had blood flowing through her veins in years. A hundred and fifty or so. That's how you can tell she was a vamp when Bonaparte killed her."

"Or I guess you could tell by, you know, checking the fangs," Bonaparte said.

They both started laughing again.

NIGHT THREE

NINETEEN

Earlier that night…

Cicatrice was already standing over her when she awakened.

"You're awakening closer and closer to sundown. I'm impressed. Come quickly. There's little time to waste."

He held out a hand and helped her slough off the dirt of her bed. He removed a leather strap from his neck. On the strap was a massive golden key, marked with Aztec designs and faces. He held the key out towards Idi Han.

"One day this will be your burden. Your responsibility. When I'm gone."

"That won't be for some time, I'm sure, Father Cicatrice."

"Some days I'm not so sure. Follow me."

He led her down into the winding catacombs below the manse. The walls were thick with moss, and steps were carved out of the living rock down into the dank depths below. She followed, looking around in wonder.

"What do you think, seeing this?"

"It's beyond description, Patriarch."

"I agree. It's hard to believe we're still in Las Vegas. But this place existed long before the casinos did. It's why I chose this spot for the Aztec."

The catacombs became tighter the deeper they delved, and what had once seemed built by men gradually gave way to the natural wending caves of ancient, dried-up waterways. Finally they reached a wall of solid rock which blocked their further descent.

"The end?" she asked.

"Look again. Look harder."

Idi Han ran her fingers along the rockface. After a moment, she felt a barely perceptible seam. The rock could be moved, but only be an immensely strong immortal.

"I don't think I can lift this catch, Father."

"Idi Han, after eight hundred long years of life my power is limited only by the laws of physics. In you, I've seen someone achieve that in a matter of days. You are truly my heir. Lift."

Gritting her teeth, she pressed the stone and surprised herself as she managed to lift a few tons of solid rock away.

"Oh, ye of little faith," Cicatrice intoned as he pushed the key into a now-revealed hole.

Turning and pushing, the door opened. Even with the key, only he or she could ever have opened the door, and maybe a handful of others like Otto Signari or the greatest remaining of their kind.

Stepping through the door she found herself on a small outcropping of rock. At the end of the outcropping was an altar, and at its foot was an Aztec headdress. The altar and the floor were slick with red effluvia, and the remains of an infant with its chest ripped open and its heart torn out remained atop the altar. She went to loop around the back of the altar and nearly stepped into a bottomless abyss. The room opened out before her, twinkling like a great sea of darkness, bereft of water.

"What is this place?"

"In the ancient days in my mother tongue they might have called this an oubliette: *a place of forgetting. In the vernacular you might call it…a bottomless pit."*

"There's no such thing," she said, kicking a rock over the side.

She waited, straining, but even with her immensely-enhanced immortal hearing she never heard it hit bottom.

"Normally I would agree with you, but this is a place steeped with dark and mysterious energies. That is one place even I fear to tread. Perhaps it is not really bottomless, but I would not care to be swallowed up by whatever resides down there. Look, up there."

Idi Han looked up and saw spread out in a ring thirteen outcroppings of rock from the ceiling of the cavern. On twelve of them hung a creature upside down, like a bat. They were gruesome, jawless creatures, looking more like lampreys than men. Thin, gaunt, almost skeletal, their skin was gray like a new-borne bruise. And they slept, a fitful, constantly fidgeting sleep, but their eyes were closed and they seemed locked in communion with dark gods.

"The Damned?" she whispered.

"Yes. And one is missing. As Price said."

"How is that possible?"

"It shouldn't be. I make them their daily sacrifice to keep them placated, as you can see."

He gestured at the bloody altar. The dried intestines clinging to the side and the still-clotting baby on its face proved his point.

"Well, Father Cicatrice, shall we take a closer look?"

"What do you mean?"

Idi Han placed her foot on the wall. Taking a deep breath (though physiologically she had no need to) she placed her other foot next to it. She finally understood how to walk up the wall. Cicatrice was no sorcerer. It was a simple parlor trick. Her feet curved hard, clinging to the rock wall. She was simply so strong now that she could clench the wall with her feet.

She began walking upwards, gaining her confidence, until finally she stood on the ceiling as Cicatrice had during their first meal together. As always, he was a cipher, but either wishful thinking or her own immortal senses suggested to her the faintest glimmer of pride in his eyes. He eschewed climbing up the wall altogether, opting to leap so hard he "fell" end over end and hit the ceiling feet first.

"Try that next time."

"Give me a few days, at least, Patriarch."

"You are a precocious student. But clever. Lead the way, my most esteemed heir."

Idi Han took a few steps with confidence, but when she found herself over the yawning chasm, began to worry, and almost to falter. Even Cicatrice feared that hole, and she could see why. It practically called to her, whispering in her ear, saying, "Fall, fall, drop into me, let me swallow you up." It was far more powerful than any vertigo she had ever felt in mortal life. She wondered if there weren't really dark powers at the bottom of the pit.

She felt Cicatrice place an arm on her shoulder, and she began to walk again with confidence, past the sleeping forms of the remaining twelve Damned. They reached what amounted to a tree stump, carved or naturally occurring in the rock, or perhaps the result of a circumcised stalactite. *She leaned down to examine it.*

A few feet away, like a scar in the rock face, a great crack had appeared in the ceiling. She walked over and ran her hands along it. It was massive, easily fat enough for one of the lamprey-like creatures to burrow into and escape.

"He burrowed through solid rock," she said. "It must be hundreds of meters to the surface."

"Easily," Cicatrice agreed. "It's troubling. I'm not pleased that he has been destroyed, in fact I find it a great insult, and a great question. Who could defeat one of The Damned?"

"Do you think that the Inquisitor did it and hides his guilt from you?"

"Carter Price is a child in all but age. He could do this the day Otto Signari kisses me on the lips and calls me his brother again."

"Well, there is much to consider. But if you'll forgive my weak stomach, Father Cicatrice, I am still only a few days old and being here makes me queasy."

"I'm much older than that and I would still prefer the safety of that outcropping. Leave The Damned to this…strange nest."

They made their exeunt far quicker than their entrance. Once back in the safe glow of the dismembered infant, a thought struck Idi Han.

"Is there anything unusual about that particular member of The Damned?"

Cicatrice put his hand to his chin and thought.

"She was called The Seer. She knew things before they happened, supposedly. Was very sensitive to changes in the weather or even in political winds."

"Then she knew things before they happened. Like that The Hunter of the Dead is here?"

"I'm still not certain that would be enough to wake even The Seer. The only thing I can think of that would awaken her would be that if she sensed The Damned were about to be awakened."

Cicatrice clutched the golden key around his chest.

"How could that happen?" she asked.

"Only if something happened to me and I wasn't here to grant them their sacrifice each day."

"Then there may be something to Signari's threats?"

Cicatrice shook his head.

"It's an idle exercise at best to attempt to predict the future. And it's complete masturbation to attempt to stop it. Nevertheless, it's a fool who doesn't take precautions. Why don't you take this?"

He pressed the golden key into her hand. She shook her head and shrunk back.

"No, Father Cicatrice, I am not ready for that responsibility."

He patted her hand in a manner which could have been comforting in any other person.

"As I said, it's not your responsibility. Just a precaution. If anything does happen to me, then The Damned will still not awaken."

And what if something happens to me?

Tap-tap-tap.

Nico moaned lightly and rolled over. Price's floor might not have been the most comfortable place on the planet, but he felt safer there than most places in the city.

Tap-tap-tap.

"¿Qué coño?" he muttered, looking up.

He almost gasped, but stopped himself. Instantly he was awake.

Idi Han was at the window.

He rose, wishing he was wearing more than boxer shorts polka-dotted with red hearts. It was too late, now. She had seen him sleeping in what he was wearing. He snuck over to the window and tried to jimmy it open. It began to creak. He glanced over at Price, but he was stupendously drunk and had passed out in his chair. She reached and helped him raise it from the outside, keeping it absolutely silent.

"What are you doing here?" he whispered.

"Can we talk?"

He glanced down at the street.

"We're on the eighth floor. How are you…?"

Her feet clung to the wall as though she were wearing suction cup shoes. As he considered it, at a certain point strength would seem to defy physics. If you could cling to the side of a speeding train with just your pinky, you would seem to be a magical creature.

"I'm sorry to wake you," she said, "it's just that I have no one to talk to. At least, no one who doesn't want to use me or train me or sell me or..."

He nodded.

"I...I understand. Let me just grab something to wear."

As he pulled on his crunchy, days-old work uniform (with nameplate still attached) he silently cursed himself for not buying some new clothes or at least throwing this set in the wash. He pointed down, indicating the ground floor.

"I'll meet you downstairs," he mouthed.

She opened her arms.

"I could save you the trip," she said.

He eyed her up and down.

"Maybe when we trust each other a little more."

She shrugged and disappeared from the window. He stuck his head out and saw her, already on the ground, pacing, and waiting for him. He eased the window shut and hurried out into the hallway as fast as he could without making any noise. In Price's flophouse the elevator only occasionally reported for duty to the proper floor, and this was not one of those times, so he found himself hurrying down the stairs.

He burst out onto the street and was greeted by a wave of cool, exuberant air. Even in long pants and a hat he was chilly, but Idi Han in her short dress seemed unaffected by the weather. She seemed as pleased to see him as he was to see her.

"So," he said, "what, ah, what's up?"

"Can we take a walk?" she asked.

He glanced up at the roofs and night sky.

"Is Cicatrice here?"

"He doesn't know I'm here," she said. "He said he had some business to attend to alone so I snuck out."

"Quite the rebel!"

"Nico. Please."

"I'm sorry. I know this can't be easy for you. All...this."

He made an expansive, circular gesture. He didn't even really know what he meant by it, but Idi Han apparently did.

"You have no idea how strange it is to be told you're special, you're important, you're the most important person on the planet."

"Wish I had that problem."

"You laugh, but where I come from no one ever tells you that. They tell you how unimportant you are. How you're only as good as what you can do for others. You Americans are used to being told you're the prettiest and the richest and the smartest."

Nico snorted. He gestured for her to take his arm and they started to walk down the street.

"You think I'm an American?"

"Well, aren't you?"

"Sort of. It's complicated."

"What isn't?"

"Yeah. I'm American enough for all the bad things but not American enough for all the good things."

"Stuck between two worlds?"

"Yeah, you could say that."

They walked along in silence for a moment.

"Cicatrice said you two lived up to your end of the bargain."

"Don't I know it. I've been in the sewers since dawn this morning. Bonaparte—there's this lady, Bonaparte. I don't know her real name. Anyway, she has all these gangs of people and it's all like marching in step-like little automatons. Kind of like what you were saying about China. And they dropped all this tear gas and smoke and all these humans, just regular humans came running out of the tunnels."

"Disciples," she said.

"Cultists," he agreed, "Coffin guards. Price calls them 'renfields.' But in the end they're just ordinary people. Sad, but ordinary people. And they all come flooding out and we tell them to surrender and some of them do but…"

He trailed off.

"In war there are casualties," she said.

He shook his head.

"This didn't feel like a war. It felt like a slaughter. My wrists are, ah, chafing." He waggled the wrist of his free hand to show what he meant. "Because I spent all morning pounding stakes into inert bodies. Chopping heads off of…corpses. How many people did I kill?"

"None. We're not people."

He stopped and turned to look at her.

"I don't believe that."

She stared into his eyes.

"I've seen things…done things…you would find unforgiveable."

"You and my sainted grandmother both. Sometimes I wonder if being unforgiveable is the only real human condition."

She placed her hand on his shoulder.

"You really mean that?"

TWENTY

Price's eyes snapped open. Nothing in particular had awakened him. No special noise or sound of the night had disturbed his slumber. He woke often, a dozen times a night sometimes.

Bad dreams.

"Kid?" he whispered.

No response. He heard a click and instantly he was on his feet, machete in hand. A tiny flame illuminated his dump of an apartment. It belonged to a match, which belonged to a hand, which belonged to a person, facing away from him in the lone folding chair which decorated his digs.

The shadow figure brought the match up to an unfiltered cigarette nestled in a bone holder. Then with a casual flick the flame disappeared and the blackened match dropped to the floor. The shadow took a long drag from its cigarette, and then puffed out a cloud to fog up the apartment.

"There was a time," a voice, syrupy with malevolence intoned, "when my kind was not relegated to the shadows. And there will be again."

Price glanced around the room, wondering what to do. He'd never been caught so naked…literally and figuratively…before. He held the blade level and perpendicular with the ground, in Cicatrice's general direction.

"Where's the kid, Cicatrice?"

"The people of this land tell a story. Once upon a time a fox was bathing in a river. In some versions it's a fox, in others it's a frog, the end result is really the same so it doesn't really matter. We'll call it a fox. A scorpion approached the riverbank.

The fox was a wily hunter but even he feared the scorpion's deadly sting, so he started to swim out into the river, knowing scorpions can't swim.

"And the scorpion called out, 'Please don't run from me, Brother Fox. I'm not here to harm you. I just need to get to the other side of the river. Will you take me on your back?'

"Now the fox was intrigued but he wasn't stupid, so he replied, 'If I carry you on my back you will sting me and I will drown.'

"And the scorpion replied, 'That would be foolish. If I sting you we would both drown. There, you see? Our mutual safety is assured and if you aid me, you will have my gratitude, and my gratitude is worth much.'

"The fox thought and thought but he couldn't figure out any trick. If one drowned, both would drown. So, albeit reluctantly, he let the scorpion on his back and started to swim. When they were no more than halfway across the river, *snap*! The scorpion stung the fox.

"As the fox began to drown he said, 'Why did you sting me? Now we will both drown.'

"'I had to,' the scorpion replied, 'I'm a scorpion.'"

Cicatrice turned to look over his shoulder at Price. His face was silhouetted in the moonlight, and looked cold, alien, and whiter than the moon.

"Where's my apprentice?" Price asked, hoping the machete wasn't quivering in his hand.

"No one was here when I arrived. He must've realized the futility of what you do and fled."

Price glanced around the room.

Did he abandon me? Why would Cicatrice lie? If he wants to hurt me, he'd taunt me about having Nico somewhere. Did someone else snatch him up? Bonaparte? The Signaris?

"Get out, Scar. Get out now."

Cicatrice stood, and pressed lightly on the chair, sending it flying backwards towards Price. Price dove out of the way, cursing his nakedness as his balls slapped against either thigh. The chair flew past Price and smashed into a mangled wreck against the wall.

"It's not so easy to exorcise a demon, Price. You invited me into your life. Invited me onto your back. When the fox agreed to help the scorpion they both momentarily forgot who they were."

The point of the story dawned on him.

"But they never stopped being what they were."

Cicatrice grinned. Price was certain he had never seen the immortal smile before, wasn't even certain if he had ever smiled before. The effect was cadaverous, and chilling.

"Now you understand."

Price roared and rushed at Cicatrice, bringing the machete across his front in a long arc aimed at the vampire's neck. Cicatrice easily ducked out of the way and caught the machete between his index finger and thumb, arresting Price's charge completely and making his teeth chatter. Cicatrice snapped the blade out of his hand with a motion that almost shattered Price's wrist and tossed it out a window, sending pulverized glass exploding outward into the night and tinkling down against the backdrop of the full moon almost like fairy dust.

Cicatrice stood between Price and his cache of weapons in the closet. His mind raced. There was only one weapon on this side of the apartment. He scrabbled with his sore wrist at the wall, reaching for the ceremonial stake with his name carved into it. With his fingertips he fumbled with it, forgetting whether it was glued to the plaque or merely hanging there, but before he could even wrap his hand around the wooden shaft, it didn't matter anymore. Cicatrice had grabbed his wrist.

Whipping him around like a ragdoll or an unwilling dance partner, Cicatrice easily held Price a few feet off the ground by only his wrist. Then he let him drop to the floor, where he promptly crumpled into a pile like week-old laundry. Price grimaced, rubbing his forearm, and wishing he hadn't landed on his tailbone. White-hot pain radiated out through him from his coccyx.

"Go on, then," Price grunted, "Kill me. I'm obviously outmatched. At least show me the respect of not toying with me any longer."

"Respect? I have no respect for you. No respect for your

profession. No respect for your person. You're a joke. The Inquisition's always been a joke. I tolerate it because it's no more dangerous than tolerating a Bigfoot society or the Search for Extraterrestrial Intelligence. Who cares if mortals want to waste their time believing they make a difference?

"But you, Carter Price, you in particular I have no respect for. I am an individual who understands his power and understands the power of organizing. But you have always been so certain that you alone could take on the world. Your friends who tried to organize? They were right. They might make a difference someday. Cowboys like you will always end up like this."

"I should've clarified, Scar. Toy with me, torture me, whatever you want, but for the love of Christ, enough with the speechifying. Go ahead. Suck me dry."

Price stuck his neck out as best he could towards the vampire.

"Death? That'd be a mercy. Don't you know, Price, the Inquisitor always becomes the strongest immortal? I was once like you."

Cicatrice rolled up his sleeve and held up his wrist, which was covered by a gauze wrap. He ripped away the gauze and bared his wrist, complete with the mark of the Inquisition. The tattoo bubbled and burned, as though it were constantly torturing him.

"It's burning you. My God, you've got a little faith left in you, Scar."

"It is the constant reminder of my human weakness. I will bear this pain eternally as a constant reminder of what I once was. Of what I despise now. Of you."

"I find it hard to believe you were ever anything like me."

"Believe it. I was the first of your kind. I founded the Inquisition. But then my matriarch taught me what it was to be immortal. Now I will grant you the same gift as punishment. You will learn what it means to be a scorpion."

Cicatrice pressed his fingers to Price's scalp.

TWENTY-ONE

Mesoamerica…

Before the Europeans came to Tenochtitlan, the natives worshipped immortals, whom they revered as gods. They sacrificed the hearts of virgins in elaborate ceremonies designed to keep the sun rising each morning. In reality only the highest caste of priests knew that their sacrifices were really being made to immortals.

Then the conquistadors arrived.

Cortes and his men arrived on the shores of what is now called Mexico. Cortes ordered all of his ships burnt so there could be no retreat. The only hope for his men was to conquer an empire. And with the help of gunpowder, horses, and treacherous native politics, they succeeded.

The Aztec priests were shot, mid-way through their sacrifices to appease the gods. The pyramids where the immortals resided to receive their sacrifices were reconsecrated in the name of a carpenter from Judea, far across the sea.

Fourteen of the most powerful immortals from across the empire managed to escape the wholesale slaughter of Cortes and his men. They went north, far north to a place beyond the reach of the Aztecs, beyond the reach even of men, to a profane, unholy place.

The pyramid there was a reversal of the Aztec ones. It descended down into the ground, and terminated only at a vast abyss. Some believed this was the dark source of the power of the immortals. Others believed they had crawled up out of Hell and this was the spot where they had emerged. Whatever the truth of the tales they told, this was the place where the immortals had decided to sleep, and wait for Cortes's reign of terror to recede. When the Spanish left, they were to be awakened. One among the immortals had the gift of sight, and pre-dicted the Spanish would not leave until civilization was in the throes of a grand apocalypse.

The least of the immortals was tasked to be a caretaker. He would stay awake, watching over the others as they slept, communing in the dark with ancient evils and gathering their strength for a time when they intended to take back these shores. The thirteen slept, and the last waited, sealing up the others with a golden key. Each day the caretaker sacrificed a virgin, stolen from a far-off village (for at that time all villages were far off) to satiate the bloodlust and demand for sacrifice of the others. The key was passed down many times, but the Spanish never left, and in fact men began to encroach even on that dreadful place. The thirteen great ones were referred to collectively as The Damned, and the fourteenth as their steward or caretaker.

After the coming of the European immortals, with their tales of the Necropolis and The Hunter of the Dead, it was decided that The Damned represented too great a threat to the status quo. They were a danger to those who kept their heads down, followed the code, and kept The Hunter at bay. So it was agreed that they would remain sleeping for eternity, or until the age-old dream of an Empire of Immortals was at last realized.

She lay beneath him, nude except for two necklaces around her throat. One was a golden key which looked Mexican in design. The other was a delicate silver (or silver-colored) series of Chinese characters. He wrapped his arm around her waist and pulled her up into him as he thrust. She wasn't reacting like any other girl he'd ever been with. She wasn't a cold fish, but neither did she seem to be enjoying herself.

"Is it all right?"

She replied in Chinese, apparently forgetting herself, then pounded his chest with her fist. She left a throbbing bruise.

"Not right now," she said, apparently repeating herself. "It's about to be. Don't stop. Don't stop."

Her face remained impassive and he felt confused and even a bit worried, but a moment later she wrapped her legs around his waist and began practically kicking him into her. She began to moan loudly and her head went back, her back arching and the top of her head laying nearly perpendicular on the pillow, as though she were presenting her throat to him.

He felt the warm thrill of orgasm, as he had hundreds of times before, but there was something else there, a sense that she was drawing him into herself, needed him, was hungry for him, was draining him.

As he came he shuddered, and felt a ripple of pleasure run through him. Somewhere he had heard that the French called orgasm *"la petit mort"* or "the little death." He'd never really understood that before, but in the instant that his mind seemed to void itself, filled with nothing but the absolute carnal pleasure of Idi Han's body, he understood.

When he came back to himself she was smiling up at him, a devilish little grin. She wasn't breathing hard (naturally—she didn't breathe) but her skin had darkened, and was almost glowing. She put his hand in his hair.

"I'm sorry, Nico," she said, "I think I took a little too much out of you."

A sharp pain tugged at his scalp.

"Ow!" he said, slapping the spot where she had pulled out the single hair.

She held it under his nose. He stared and took it from her fingers, rolling it between his own.

"A gray hair? I didn't think…Jesus, I'm only twenty."

"That was my fault," she said, rubbing his chin. "When you…uh, what's the English word? We never really studied this sort of thing in school."

"Urm," he whispered furtively, "ejaculate?"

She nodded, not repeating it.

"Yes. When you did that, I felt your life essence and I…I may have taken a little too much."

"I thought only really powerful va…uh, immortals could do that?"

She shrugged and smiled again, like a kitten this time. He rolled down off of her and lay on the bed beside her. He reached over, letting his hand slide across her breast, and fingered the golden key.

"What's this?" he asked.

Chuckling, she took the key off her neck and dropped it into the drawer of the nightstand.

"That is not for prying eyes."

"Oh? Some sort of super-secret squirrel vampire business?"

"Yes, precisely."

He nodded. Then he fingered her other necklace.

"Okay. How about this, then?

"No, that's not a secret squirrel."

He chuckled.

"I've been staring at it all night.

"That's what you were staring at?" she asked, raising her hand to cover her breasts demurely, as though she had been snubbed.

He grinned broadly. "Well…you know what I mean. What is it?"

"It was a gift. From my favorite uncle, before he passed away."

"I'm sorry to hear that. How did he die?"

"He was a worker in a metal shop. His arm got caught in one of the machines. He didn't lose it, but gangrene set in. They amputated, but it was too late."

"That's a sad story."

She shrugged.

"You work with dangerous things long enough and they'll hurt you. But in the good old days, when he still had both arms, he made this for me with some scrap. I think I was his favorite niece the same way that he was my favorite uncle. He never said so, but he did make me this."

"Is it your name?"

She looked down at the characters.

"My name? No. At least, not my proper name. It was one of his nicknames for me. I used to pick him poppies sometimes from down by the river. So he called me his little red flower… no…blood flower."

Nico fingered the metal.

"This is Mandarin for blood flower?"

"Cantonese."

"What's the difference?"

She tapped her teeth, thinking.

"Well, you're from Puerto Rico, right?"

"Right."

"What's the difference between that and Cuba?"

He furrowed his brow and sat up.

"Oh, tons of things. I mean, for one thing…oh, I get it."

She smiled. He lay back down and she began to trace invisible pictures across his bare chest.

"Why did you ask to look in that woman's mirror? Does your reflection go away eventually?"

She shook her head.

"I don't think so. I think that's more of a metaphor than anything else."

"How do you mean?"

"Well, you know, a lot of serial killers refuse to look in the mirror. The police go in to raid their lairs and they find all the mirrors smashed, all the pictures ruined. Like they can't bear to look at themselves, or something."

TWENTY-TWO

The door to Price's apartment exploded inward. Stunned, Price threw himself flat to the ground, but grunted in pain as a hundred splinters embedded themselves into his hip, thigh, and leg. Pushing with his right leg and scrabbling with his elbows he pulled himself out of the way.

Looking up, he saw that Cicatrice had been torn to ribbons, chunks of wood sprouting from his eyes, forehead, chest, crotch, and extremities. Cicatrice was stunned only for a moment, and his body began to forcibly eject the splinters and shards of wood as his wounds healed. To aid the regenerative process, he began pulling some of the larger pieces out by hand.

"Cicatrice!"

Price looked towards the missing door. A man he didn't know stood there, eyes blazing. He was kitted out in what Price instantly recognized as one of Bonaparte's uniforms. A layer of chainmail, covered over with a (theoretically) impregnable SWAT team uniform. The chain was made of rosary pieces, and the pads were covered with religious iconography, making all the armor theoretically hateful to a bloodsucker. Like all of Bonaparte's men he wore iconic rings on every finger, and carried a sword on his hip and an automatic shotgun with heavy stopping power in his hands.

The man had his visor up so that Cicatrice could see his face.

"You look at me, Cicatrice! You look at the man who's going to kill you. You recognize me?"

"Oh, Patrick," Cicatrice said calmly, the last of the wood shards popping out of his body and tumbling to the floor, "Finally realized little Francis was missing, did you?"

Patrick bit his lower lip and raised his shotgun at Cicatrice, obviously wanting to taunt the vampire but clearly so roiling with fury that he couldn't think of anything to say.

"You tell me what you did with him! I've got the money. You can give him back if he's still alive. I'll let you walk away."

"The money? What are you a child, Patrick? Who did you think you were dealing with? What did you think would happen when I said your firstborn was down payment?"

Tears were streaming down Patrick's face.

"I...I...I..."

"Uh uh uh, what? You thought it was a metaphor? A joke? A reference to the *Merchant of Venice*? Yes, lots of shylocks deal in literary references. Your boy's been dead for days. He died the day you defaulted to me. He made a meal for my daughter. She didn't speak of it, but I suspect he was delicious. Well, not that it mattered. She was voracious at the time."

Screaming, Patrick rushed at Cicatrice.

"No, you moron!" Price cried out, reaching out, but it was too late. Cicatrice had taunted him into forgetting all his weapons and fancy gear.

With expert aim, Cicatrice knocked the helmet off Patrick's head, sending it flying until it embedded itself into the mortarboard of Price's apartment wall. Cicatrice cupped Patrick's head with his hand and began digging his fingernails into his skull.

"You ruined my life," Patrick shrieked.

"Then allow me to relieve you of it," Cicatrice whispered.

Cicatrice pressed until Patrick's head exploded like a raw egg. Brains, chunks of skull, nose parts, and various effluvia rained down on Price and his floor.

"All right, we gave the father his chance!" a familiar voice shouted. "Move, move move!"

Cicatrice bared his teeth like a feral predator. The game was afoot. Bonaparte's men began rappelling in through the windows, and a squad poured in through the door Patrick had blasted open. Metal began to fly through the air, as shotguns discharged from every side and Cicatrice was caught in a 360° crossfire. His body was reduced to a ragged pulp and splattered to the ground.

With their visors down, Price found it impossible to identify any of the Inquisitors. One of them cried out, "Go, go, go! Move in for the kill!"

The Inquisitors began holstering their firearms and drawing cutting implements and religious icons. The wretched mess of gristle and muscle which had been Cicatrice pulsated on the floor. The first man on the scene charged forward with an axe, and brought it swinging down in an arc at what had formerly been Cicatrice's head.

A pseudopod which had gradually reordered itself into a flayed human hand snatched the axe head out of the air, stopping it in mid-collision and snapping both of the axe-wielding Inquisitor's arms with the impact in a sickening series of crunches. Cicatrice roared, flipping the axe over and swinging it one-handed so that he easily cut through plate, chain, and ankles alike, severing both feet in one motion and sending the unlucky axe-wielder tumbling to the ground.

"He's recovering!" Bonaparte shouted, "Don't let up the pressure!"

Within just that space of time Cicatrice had recovered to the point that he had the appearance of a skinless man, a gruesome illustration out of *Gray's Anatomy* but instead of lying blandly on the page, he was raging out like a furious bull.

Chastened by their comrade's double amputation, the rest of the Inquisitors maintained their distance. Several had crucifixes attached to the ends of long poles. One of the Inquisitors reached out and pressed the crucifix at the end of his pole to Cicatrice's chest, where his ribcage was still trying to reform.

The open flesh of the vampire's chest sizzled where the silver icon touched it, and ceased to mend. With a hand which still had bone fingers poking through raggedly flowing meat, Cicatrice grabbed the crucifix, which caused his still-ruined hand to sizzle, and flung it towards the missing door.

The force of Cicatrice's yank took the Inquisitor who had been holding the crucifix off his feet. He stumbled and fell right into Cicatrice's armpit. As though he were cracking a nut with a nutcracker, Cicatrice squeezed with his armpit and shattered the Inquisitor's helmet, which flaked away like the shell off a hard-boiled egg.

Cicatrice wrapped his bloody, mending arm around the Inquisitor's neck and caught him in a chokehold. The man's face turned purple and he slapped uselessly at the monster's arm, as though tapping out of a for-fun wrestling match.

Cicatrice's eyeless skull, dancing with muscle and sinew like a dot matrix printer gradually laying down words, leaned in towards his captured prey. The grotesque visage opened its mouth, its stump of a tongue just coming back together enough to say, "You picked the wrong fucker to fuck with!"

Suddenly the captured Inquisitor's hair began to gray and his skin began to wrinkle. Skin began to re-cover Cicatrice's body as his healing process went into overdrive.

"No, you idiots!" Price grunted, scrabbling across the floor and snatching a pistol out of the holster of an Inquisitor who wasn't paying attention. "Don't let him feed!"

Price leveled the pistol at the captured Inquisitor's head. The world was still swimming from pain and revulsion, but Price had held guns level in far bleaker situations. Price didn't recognize the kid, but he vaguely reminded him of Jerry Govarti, an Inquisitor he had run with back in the '70s.

"Sorry, Jerry."

Price put one in the back of the kid's head. Cicatrice roared with frustration, his meal suddenly spoiled and twitching from nerve impulses.

The air stank of blood, offal, and the spilled bowels and bladders of the dead. It had been a long time since Price had been caught in quite such an abbatoir, and he took the opportunity to turn and retch up whatever little was left of his supper from that evening.

"Give him another whiff of grapeshot," Bonaparte ordered.

The Inquisitors poured metal into Cicatrice like there was no tomorrow. Several came down to clicking their empty shotguns. Price dragged himself into a corner and propped himself up to get a better look at the action.

He had never particularly liked Cicatrice, per se, but he had always had a certain respect for him, and like any reasonable individual, an intense and implacable fear. As such, he didn't like seeing the mighty man reduced to a ruined lump of protoplasm. The Inquisitors didn't let up until they had practically pureed him.

This time, the mass that had been the vampire patriarch was very slow to reform into anything resembling a human form. The gelatin-like mess quivered and raged in one or two directions, but its regeneration lacked the urgency it had shown last time. Even a vampire House patriarch was subject to the laws of physics, and Price had deprived him of his meal. He would fast be running out of energy, arcane or otherwise.

Bonaparte took off her helmet and knelt down at Price's side.

"How are you doing?"

"I'm great. Fuck Folgers. This is how I like to start every day."

Bonaparte put a hand on his shoulder and she even seemed to smile.

"Do you need anything?"

"I could use a juicebox. Maybe one of those, what do you call those things that you use to watch a play better? Opera glasses."

She squeezed his shoulder.

"We'll get some paramedics out here to see to your leg shortly. We just have to finish up first."

Price nodded. She rose and turned back to her men.

"Icons! Put one on each limb and at least one more on the center of gravity."

Eight Inquisitors stepped forward tentatively with crosses on poles like the poor, unlucky Jerry Govarti-looking fellow. One held down each of his feet and hands and a fifth placed his on Cicatrice's side. Where the crosses touched Cicatrice's bare, exposed flesh sizzled and burned and the area around it ceased to heal.

Bonaparte strode across the room like a Roman conqueror at his own parade. She stepped gingerly over the bodies of her fallen comrades and came to a stop over Cicatrice's body. He had seemed to stop fighting, finally accepting that he was pinned. His face had recovered to the extent that he could speak and turned to look up at Bonaparte balefully with his Martian eye.

"Why did you let that buffoon lead your charge?" he croaked out.

She examined her fingernails.

"He came to me. I promised a chance to put you down. I let him take it. He did not do so well."

Cicatrice glanced around the room as visors went up and helmets came off.

"I recognize some faces."

"All of us have sworn revenge on you for one reason or another. This was an all-volunteer raid."

Cicatrice cackled, a mirthless sound that chilled Price to the bone. The man was normally so perversely incapable of showing emotion, even now, at the end, it seemed completely alien for him to do so even mockingly.

"If every man who's ever sworn revenge on me had taken it, I'd've been put down a hundred thousand times by now."

"Just once will satisfy me." Bonaparte nudged Cicatrice's right wrist with her boot. "I see you were an Inquisitor once. I've always considered it a special duty to put down former Inquisitors who have been turned. The same way I put down my own father, who taught me everything I know. It's a matter of respect for the office."

"Kings don't kill kings," Cicatrice whispered.

Bonaparte nodded. She pulled open the Velcro of her riot gear and reached into her blouse to draw out a beautifully carved wooden stake. She held it over Cicatrice's good eye so he could get a good look.

"Remember this?"

He nodded.

"It was the closest I ever came to being killed."

Bonaparte tapped her glass eye with the point of the stake.

"Me, too. I refuse to use this on any other nightcrawler. This stake's reserved for you."

Cicatrice nodded. Then, with an unholy roar he arched his back and brought his spine back down on the floor with an earthshattering crack, ripping a massive hole in the floor. As Cicatrice's body disappeared, the five Inquisitors who had been holding him down stumbled.

One tripped over her own feet and nearly tumbled into the hole in the floor, but managed to grab onto the edge with both hands just in time. She managed to pull herself up so that almost her entire torso was above floor level, but then her arms were locked and she was having trouble getting her legs up.

"Help," entreated the Inquisitor who had nearly fallen into the hole, a 30-something woman with a short mop of black hair, "Give me a hand, I need to…"

The raven-haired woman's expression changed to one of alarm. Bonaparte and another Inquisitor rushed to grab her shoulders and a sickening rip split the air, followed by a prolonged splat. Bonaparte and the other helper were suddenly caught flat-footed as the black-haired Inquisitor suddenly came rocketing up out of her precarious position as though she had suddenly become fifty pounds lighter.

As they fumbled inelegantly with the body, Price saw that her body had been ripped in half at the navel, and her intestines and lower GI tract had unspooled down into the apartment below. Lengths of viscera still hung from the half-woman, trailing down into what was no doubt a gruesome scene in the lower apartment.

Bonaparte blinked the blood out of her eyes, but that was about the extent of her confusion.

"Go, go, go!" she shouted, pointing around the room. "He's on the next floor down! If you have a rig set up rappel down! Everybody else take the stairs!"

The Inquisitors who had come in through the windows began jumping out of them, and the others scrambled through the missing door. All except Bonaparte, who remained standing there, a grim look on her face.

"Don't do it," Price said.

"He'll be gone otherwise."

"You'll break both your damn legs."

She shrugged.

"I never planned to walk away from this, anyway."

Grimacing, Bonaparte dropped into the hole. Price watched as only her fingers were visible to him, grabbing onto the edge. Then she grunted and let go. He lay back, for the first time realizing how fast his heart was racing and how much pain he was in, from his leg. Every nerve in his lower body was screaming at him, and probably had been the whole time, but he'd either been so full of adrenaline or so distracted by the histrionics he hadn't noticed.

He glanced around the blood-spattered room. The walls were painted with effluvia, and broken bodies lay in every horrific position imaginable.

"Jesus," Price muttered, looking around at the wreckage and eviscera strewn about his apartment, "I'm never getting the security deposit back on this place."

With considerable effort, Price pulled himself forward on his elbows, nearly slipping several times on the bloody surface of his floor.

"Fucker," he muttered as he skinned one elbow, but it wasn't nearly as long as he had expected until he was over the lip of the hole in his floor and able to look down.

Cicatrice was at the window, but an Inquisitor in a rappelling rig appeared, and though he seemed startled, leveled his shotgun at the vampire and pulled the trigger. Cicatrice jumped out of the way, though he still caught a good shoulderful of buckshot.

The vampire was still naked, the only vestiges of his clothes a few tattered strings and the all-but-ruined plate of armor he wore over his heart and upper ribcage. His skin was almost all gone and in places bone showed where his flesh was still mending. It was impossible to miss that after his second round of being blown to bits, he was healing much slower.

Bonaparte was on the floor, her shotgun leveled at him. She was limping ever-so-slightly. Perhaps she had turned her ankle in the drop, but she had certainly not shattered both legs as Price had expected. A door to Cicatrice's left opened and Bonaparte took her eyes off him for a split-second.

"Shit, look out!" Price shouted, reaching out as though he could affect the course of events just through willpower alone.

But instead of going for the heavily-armed and armored Inquisitor, Cicatrice snapped up the five-year-old girl in her pajamas, with a stuffed rabbit in her hands, who had emerged from the bathroom.

"Santa?"

Price slapped his hand to his forehead.

"I live above fucking Cindy Lou Who."

"Scar! Don't touch her, Scar!" Bonaparte growled, holding out her hand as though trying to Force-choke him.

But it was too late. The little girl dangled in Cicatrice's hands the same way the bunny rabbit dangled in her's.

"Would you look at these awful people," Cicatrice said, his voice distended into a rasp by his missing lips and half-wrecked voicebox, "all trying to hurt dear old Saint Nick."

He leered at the little girl, his face an eyeless sodden mask of gurgling meat. The girl shrieked at the horrific visage, and from the room opposite her parents emerged. The father had a baseball bat in his hands, but seeing the scene of a walking museum display surrounded by highly armed SWAT teams, they hung back.

"Scar," Bonaparte warned, not lowering her weapon.

"What?" Cicatrice rasped wetly, "I should have a heart? I should fret over the innocents? I'm aflame with hunger. And I have no time for your hypocrisy." He dangled the girl in-between himself and Bonaparte like a human shield. "You wouldn't hesitate for a second to open fire on me."

"What?" the mother cried out in anguish. "You're cops! You can't..."

The father put his arm around her waist and pulled her in tightly. Suddenly it couldn't have been more obvious that the strange people in their home were not police.

"Don't do it, Bonaparte," Price whispered. If their roles were reversed he'd call the whole thing off, even if his life were forfeit, so long as Cicatrice let the girl walk away.

His nerves screamed at him, wondering how long it was going to take the rest of the Inquisitors to trample down the stairs to the lower apartment.

"You're right," Bonaparte agreed, "I won't hesitate. The question is, if this is your last stand, if they tell stories of this after you're gone, do you want them to say the last thing the most powerful vampire of all time did was drain a little girl when he was surrounded by armed Inquisitors?"

Cicatrice peered down into the petrified girl's eyes, who now resembled a real rabbit more than her own stuffed one.

"Perhaps you're right. I'll take what I want from you. She can just die."

Cicatrice ran the razor-sharp edge of his pinky nail across the little girl's throat, slitting her from her ear to ear. He tossed the limp form towards the shrieking parents and with a roar and one last brutish effort rushed at Bonaparte to rip her head off. Bonaparte braced, getting off only one round with her automatic shotgun before dropping it to the floor and raising her fists, rosaries wrapped around them like brass knuckles.

The Inquisitors who had come in through the window hesitated to shoot with their boss in the line of fire. As if on cue, the door burst open. A ginger-haired Inquisitor with a massive unruly beard stood at the head of the squad, his boot raised as he had just kicked the door down. As he flew through the door he stepped right into the line of Cicatrice's charge. Cicatrice reached forward, pushed his hand into the bearded man's throat, wrapped his fingers around his trachea, and ripped it out wholesale.

"Sorry, Jimmy," Bonaparte whispered as a hellstorm of weapons consumed and dropped Cicatrice for the third and final time.

The men with their crosses moved in and subdued him with far greater ease.

"Do it quickly!" Price cried out, from overhead. "Don't waste any more time. Don't lose any more men."

Bonaparte looked up at him and he noticed that her glass eye had rolled backwards in her head in the scuffle, so that it looked like she was looking up at him with one normal eye and one pure white orb.

"They knew the risks when they signed up," she replied.

This is why we'll never get along. People are nothing to you but pawns in your chess game.

Whatever power animated Cicatrice seemed to have all but ebbed anyway. It was all over but the shouting. Bonaparte loomed over him.

"I haven't seen a sunrise in eight hundred years," he

whispered. "I always thought I wouldn't see one for another thousand. My life has been a dream. And I don't want to wake up."

Bonaparte's voice was tender, even wistful as she reverently placed the stake over his heart.

"Did you really think you'd live forever?"

She kicked away what little remained of the metal armor, revealing the mark of Cicatrice over his heart. With an overhand arc she drove the special stake into the scar, where it embedded a few inches into his skin. Cicatrice grunted and coughed. Bonaparte stood, and with a finality of thought and action raised her boot over the stake and stomped down.

TWENTY-THREE

The Dark Ages...

Cicatrice stood there, the steaming red ichor dripping from his sword. He stared down at his opponent, whose vestments were now glowering with a spreading stain. Lily walked up to him, her feet wobbling underneath her. She placed a hand on his cheek.

"Ever my defender. Ever my strong right arm."

Cicatrice bowed deeply.

"It is my inexpressible pleasure to serve you, Matriarch."

"When the time comes, my love, my crown...is yours."

He nodded and watched as she retreated into the burgeoning dawn. The field was slick with carnage. At Lily's order, the warriors who remained were turning the dead and the dying. Many of them would be reduced to the diminished state the Moors called ghul, *but a few would make for mighty warriors. And more importantly the Crusader army was cracked, crushed, defeated.*

No thanks to Signari. He was to have brought reinforcements and instead he has fled. I shall never forgive him for this.

A light groan emanated from the broken body at his feet. He knelt down, and at his touch the White Bishop cringed. For a man who had just been run through, Cicatrice was astonished to see him still breathing. A wicked thought entered Cicatrice's mind, a thought he could not exorcise. Finally he gave in to it.

"Such a mighty opponent," he whispered, "and now what? Reduced to nothing. You are nothing. You can do nothing to stop us. And now you will join us."

Cicatrice reached out and pressed his fingers to the bishop's head. He had yet to learn the fine art of siring, but he was certain that the feeling he felt was wrong. As he poured his essence into the dying man, he felt his own being polluted. A disgusting taste touched all the senses except his main five, as though drinking water tainted by brackish swamp muck.

Cicatrice removed his hand and shook his head, clearing it.

"No. No, your faith is a poison but you can not wield it against the likes of me. I am the scion of the Necropolis, heir to Lily the Only. You will be my first conquest."

With a violent gesture, he reached out and grabbed the bishop's head with both hands. The man tried to wrench away, but Cicatrice held him fast. Closing his eyes, he pressed his forehead against his foe's.

What he had taken at first to be his own weakness, he now recognized as a battle of wills. The disgusting force flowing into his own essence was the dying man's faith, but he was aware enough to wield it like a weapon. Cicatrice pressed through the muck and imagined himself plunging his sword into the man's back again. He focused his energy like the point of a blade and drove it, like a light cutting through the darkness of his belief in God. Lily had done much the same to him, and having been through the process once on the receiving end, he felt more secure this time being the deliverer.

"Take it. Take it all."

Suddenly the man began to quiver and quake, Cicatrice's desired effect achieved at last. As the arcane energy that animated Cicatrice's corpse took root in the bishop, what little blood had not spilled out of the through-and-through hole in his chest and back began to pour from his eyes, his nose, his ears, his asshole and the tip of his member. And then he flopped over, dead like a fish thrown onto dry land.

Cicatrice tumbled backwards onto his ass. The fight had taken everything from him. Cursing blackly, he saw that he had failed. His first attempt at siring had produced a stillborn get. Not even a ghul. And the sun was beginning to rise in the sky. He forced himself along, on three limbs at first, and gradually pulling himself to his feet, to return to the Necropolis. He joined the slow trickle of new warriors off the battlefield and into the sacred burial chambers and mausoleums that housed the immortals during the day in the Necropolis.

Agony blossomed in Idi Han's chest. She gasped like a fish out of water, clutching at the blankets and surging up from the bed.

Nico scrambled out of bed and stared at her writhing form, panic in his eyes.

"What is it? What's wrong?"

Her nerves drowned out her ability to speak. Once she had fallen from a mule and had the wind knocked out of her. It had been horrifying, being simultaneously unable to breathe, unable to take a breath, and unable to fathom what was happening. It had been a few seconds of sheer madness, and now she felt that same way again, except…she didn't have to breathe, didn't have to do anything, and she had barely felt even pain in a muted, theoretical sense since she had been brought across.

"Idi Han? Idi Han? What is it?"

He was running his hands through her hair, but she still had no idea what was going on.

"I don't know," she replied in Cantonese, and though it took her a moment to realize he hadn't understood, he didn't ask her to repeat herself. His lips were a thin line.

"Look," he said after a moment, pointing at her right breast.

The sheets were still over her, blossoming red. Delicately, he pulled the sheet down. She stared down, expecting the worst. Her scar, the mark of Cicatrice, was bleeding. She reached down and touched it, wincing from the white-hot pain that shot through her body where the finger touched. She stared at the blood, baffled. She sniffed it, tasted it.

"I thought vampires didn't bleed," Nico said.

She stared at him. The initial flush and surprise of pain had receded to a dull, aching throb.

"I thought so, too," she agreed, "Is it real?"

He delicately placed the tip of his pinky against her wound. She winced and bared her teeth.

"Sorry," he muttered. He sniffed at his finger and let his tongue dart over it briefly like a lizard's. "I think it's real."

She jumped to her feet, and was astonished to find herself shaking. All the physical reactions which had seemed so *de rigeuer* in her old life had gradually faded until she had stopped missing them. And now that they were back, and in a shocking degree, it was far more terrifying than if they'd never left.

"I have to go," she said, and rummaged in the nightstand for the golden key.

"I'll come with you," he said, reaching for his shirt and hat which were hanging over a chair.

"No," she said, pressing his chest with what she thought was nominal pressure but was actually so forceful it forced him to sit, "it's best you don't come with me. Just wait. I'll be back in a bit."

He sighed. She stamped her foot, again forgetting her own strength and putting a small crack in the linoleum beneath her feet.

"Please don't be a child, Nico."

"I'm not," he said. "Actually I'm feeling rather mature just this second. But that still doesn't mean you're coming back."

She cast her eyes downward. It was probably true. She sat down on the edge of the bed.

"I…want to see you again."

He shrugged.

"Me, too. But I guess it's not in the cards. Dogs and cats, you know."

She slipped the golden key around her neck. As she did so her hand brushed against her blood flower charm. She slipped it off.

"Take this," she said.

He shook his head.

"I can't."

She grabbed him by the wrist and pressed the charm into his hand.

"A promise. I want it back. So we'll have to see each other again."

He looked down at the strap of leather dangling out of his closed fist.

"Maybe. But in what capacity, I wonder?"

After a stumbling, fumbling run through the city, certain there were Signari partisans around every corner, Idi Han reached the Aztec. She looked around, in every corner of the casino, but business proceeded as usual. Grandmothers pulled at the arms of slot machines. Wealthy young bucks and older angrier players worked on their tables.

Where's the chaos? Where's the tumult?

A security guard stared at her.

"Are you all right, ma'am?" he asked.

"Where's Mr. Cicatrice?"

"Uh, I couldn't say, ma'am. I just work here. But are you all right?"

He pointed at her chest. A blossom of red was staining her dress over her scar.

"Yes, I just need…"

"Maybe I could call you an ambulance. Or at least set you up with some help."

He reached under his booth and pulled out a first aid kit.

"No, no, I'm fine," she said, "I just need…"

She spotted a stand selling pizza nearby and snatched a handful of napkins from a dispenser. She packed the napkins under her shirt. The security guard stepped in front of her.

"Ma'am, are you twenty-one?"

Little pissant piece of shit do you have any idea who I am?

"Oh, of course," she muttered, reaching into her bag and pulling out a business card which was decidedly not her passport or identification card. She reached out to hand it to him but just as it grazed his fingers she dropped it to the floor.

"Oh, my goodness," she said, "I'm so clumsy."

"It's quite all right, ma'am," he said with a smile, bending over to pick up the business card.

She placed her hand on the back of his head and bounced his skull against the floor like a basketball. He was immediately completely laid out.

"Walk it off," she muttered and two-stepped toward the plastic pyramid in the center of the casino. She climbed over the velvet ropes and slipped into the door marked CASINO PERSONNEL ONLY.

When she entered the control room absolute silence dropped over the brethren. They all looked up and seemed aggrieved not to see Cicatrice. Hedrox approached her. She dropped to her knees and knuckled the ground before her.

"You have a telephone call, Matriarch."

"Stand," she said. "Show me."

Hedrox led her into the conference room that served Cicatrice as an office. All eyes followed her as she moved.

"I'll have that security guard let go."

"No," she said, "it's fine. He was doing his job."

"Nevertheless…"

"I think I made myself clear, Hedrox."

"Of course. My apologies, Matriarch."

She winced at hearing Hedrox use that term again. She had hoped the first time was a mistake. She didn't want to ruminate too long on what using it twice meant. Hedrox opened the door for her and she stepped inside. Hedrox walked over to the telephone sitting on the far end of the conference table and lifted the receiver off the hook. She stopped, her hand quivering, and looked at Idi Han.

"What is it?"

"It's not my place…"

"Spit it out, woman."

She stared at her like a child who had broken her favorite toy.

"Do you know where the patriarch is?"

She shook her head. Hedrox nodded. She pressed a button and put the receiver to her head.

"Matriarch Idi Han is here. Yes, Elder. Just a moment."

Hedrox walked past her toward the door.

"I'll leave you in peace, Matriarch. And I'll have a clean dress brought."

"Oh."

She glanced down at the ruined *cheongsam*.

"Anything in particular?"

"No. I trust your judgment."

"There is something…yes, I'll bring you something."

Hedrox nodded and left. Slowly Idi Han walked around the table. She stared at Cicatrice's chair for a moment, but couldn't bear to sit in it. It seemed somehow too symbolic. Standing off to the side, she placed the phone to her ear.

"Hello?"

"Is this Idi Han?" the voice on the other side of the line asked.

"Yes."

"My name is Abdul Rahim. I am the elder of House Cicatrice in Cairo. Perhaps the patriarch has mentioned me?"

No. Never.

"Yes, of course, Rahim. He speaks of you often."

"I am gratified. Have you…felt the patriarch's passing?"

She gasped.

"So it is true? That's what the bleeding scar means?"

"Yes, Matriarch. I have spoken with all of the House elders, from London to Tokyo. There can be no other explanation."

She touched her bleeding chest reverently. Certain she was crying, but she pressed her hand to her cheeks and there were no tears there.

"I have felt it. Will…will the bleeding stop?"

"I do not know. This is unprecedented, Matriarch. We should not be capable of bleeding."

"I understand."

"I do not wish to bore you with bureaucratic details, but some explanation is necessary. I do not know how far the patriarch has educated you. But just as there are thirteen Great Houses, each house has thirteen elders. Or, more accurately, I should say, twelve elders and the patriarch. The patriarch obviously rules his own seat—Las Vegas. And we represent his interests in the seats of the other Great Houses. Every House patriarch can convene a council in his own seat of himself and the twelve elders from the other Houses, acting as ambassadors and speaking for their patriarchs or on his behalf. I am senior amongst the elders both in age and in station. You're familiar with this system?"

"I've caught bits and pieces of it, yes."

"In a time of interregnum—that is, after a patriarch's death—sometimes there are power struggles. I won't pretend we aren't a fractious people. Sometimes no heir has been appointed, in which case the elders must make a decision about which of their number to elevate."

"I understand," she said, "You've been chosen as the new House patriarch. It only makes sense. You're the senior elder. I will bow to you in all your wishes."

The other end of the line was silent for a moment.

"I don't wish to be the cause of a power struggle. Our kind has suffered too great a loss already. There will be no recovering from the death of Cicatrice.

"I think you misunderstand me, Idi Han. I have known Father Cicatrice…knew him, I should say…for many centuries and I have never known him to make an idle decision. Nor, with the exception of choosing Topan as his get, have I known him to make a false step. But now I think I understand even that mistake. Topan was brought across because one day he would bring you across. And you are our new matriarch."

"I can't. I'm only a few days old. I can't handle that responsibility. That's madness."

"Father Cicatrice told us all much of you in just these past few days. He asserted with great certainty that you were to be his heir. He made no question of it, and he made me not question it, either. I have conferred with all of the other elders, and even a few of our stronger lesser members. All are in agreement. All are in harmony. You were heir, undispusted, and now you are matriarch, undisputed. House Cicatrice is now yours."

TWENTY-FOUR

Price lit a cigarette and glanced over at Bonaparte, who was still discussing matters with the parents of the dead girl. Almost every Inquisitor had at least one leechified corpse in their family. Bonaparte was probably giving them her best recruiting speech. Probably identical to the one she had given him years ago. Probably identical to the one she had given that poor shmuck Patrick a few days ago. He was no lip reader but he watched her mouth flap, wondering if the words were the same.

"I know you're hurting. I know you're not just hurting from the loss of someone close to you, you're feeling like the entire world is burning down around you. Everything you thought you knew, everything you were so certain of, out the window. So you know the truth. Some people are of the opinion that knowing the truth, even if you do nothing about it, doesn't change your life at all, just knowing is good enough.

"I'm of a different outlook. I wish to god I had never slipped down the rabbithole. Wish I could go back to the way I was. They say ignorance is bliss and damned if that isn't true. But now that I'm not ignorant anymore, I can't go back to living with my head stuck in the sand. When I was a child I thought as a child, I spoke as a child, I acted as a child…well, you know the rest.

"So you have a choice. Plan A is to leave. Lie about what you saw, about what happened to your loved one. Don't tell another soul because the people that don't believe you will think you're crazy and the people that do will want to hurt you for knowing. You pull up stakes, you move across the country, maybe to a different country, you try to start again. Hire a bunch of shrinks, try to get a good job to pay for them all. Try to forget what happened. Spend all your money on booze and pills and talk therapy and just try to make it all go away.

"And it probably will. It'll probably all go away and never brush up against your life again. It's like getting struck by lightning, being exposed to a vampire. It rarely happens twice. Unless you run around with a foil hat on. And eventually you'll convince yourselves that it wasn't really a vampire, it was just a bad man, and you'll finally at some point even stop having the bad dreams and just let it all slip through your fingers like sand through an hourglass.

"Or there's Plan B. You can fight. You can do good. You can avenge her. You saw what we did in there? We were too slow to help her. But you become a vampire hunter like us and you'll be able to save other people's loved ones from other vampires. You'll slowly make a difference. Every time you kill one of those bloodsucking freaks, a little bit of your conscience will be alleviated. You won't forget. You'll remember. And you'll make a difference. That's Plan B. The choice is yours."

Yeah, maybe some of the specifics had changed, but it was the same general come-on. With a gung-ho kid like Nico, it would've worked in a heartbeat. With a middle-aged couple, though, there was always the illusion of starting again. Always the dream of another child, another city, rebuilding together. Sometimes couples came on board, but in a way both tended to tether the other to the temporal life. Widows and widowers were always an easier sell.

They weren't buying it. The man was trying to reason with Bonaparte and the mother was just shaking her head. Bonaparte nodded, handing them a fat wad of cash and warning them, presumably, not to tell the cops. It was an especially good warning in this town, where every cop, whether he knew it or not, was on the take. Everyone in Vegas either reported directly to Cicatrice or reported to someone who reported to...

Damn. He's gone.

What was going to happen now? There'd be a power struggle. That was all but written. Idi Han was a smart girl, but with movers and shakers like Otto Signari and Cicatrice's old heir on the scene, she wouldn't stand a chance. If House Cicatrice existed tomorrow, it would either stand as a puppet to another house, a shadow of its former self, or it would be carved up by the other Houses and devoured piecemeal. Either way, there was going to be a power vacuum, and nature abhors a vacuum. Price worried if it would mean an expanded war, and what that would mean for the Inquisition.

Bonaparte walked up to him.

"You all right?"

"I'm walking," he said.

He lifted the leg of his new pair of pants, wincing as he did so. His entire right leg was basically bandaged up like a mummy, but he could still flex it with more or less his regular control. The medics in Bonaparte's band had cut his nice pants off.

"How much morphine have they got you on?"

"Enough."

"Got a present for you."

"A present? For me?"

"Well…more of a burden, really."

"A chore, you mean?"

"A chore, yeah."

"How did I know?"

Bonaparte rubbed her hand up and down her opposite wrist.

She's nervous. That's not good.

"Listen, Carter. You've run the numbers same as I have. The Houses are at war. The Hunter's around. I've got a feeling tonight's going to be a late goddamned night. I can't really spare any men. But we can't just let this go undealt with, either."

Price nodded.

"I wouldn't let you take it anyway."

He leaned over and grabbed a burlap sack from the ground and tossed it over his shoulder.

"Oh, one other thing."

Bonaparte reached into her pocket and held out something balled up in her fist. Price held out his palm and she let it drop.

It was a ring, black, made of volcanic glass and inscribed with tiny, horrific images. He had seen Cicatrice wearing it.

"The ring of a House patriarch. Don't you want it as a souvenir?"

Bonaparte scratched the back of her neck and shook her head.

"No. Doesn't seem right taking it somehow. Besides, maybe the Cicatrices will kill to get it back. In which case, better you than me."

Price rolled his eyes and dropped the ring into his pocket. "Thanks."

TWENTY-FIVE

A knock came at the conference room door. Idi Han looked up from her brooding, her head still nestled on her fist.

"Enter."

Hedrox stepped inside. She was carrying a suit bag. In her other hand was a clipboard with a pen dangling from it. She hung the suit bag on the coat rack.

"Elder Rahim advised me what happened. I...weep for your loss, Matriarch."

She looked up at the cultist, as though noticing her for the first time.

"Isn't it a loss for you as well, Hedrox?"

She bowed deeply.

"An immeasurable loss. Words cannot convey how I feel today."

"Tell me what happened."

"Inquisitors, Matriarch."

"That's a single word, Hedrox. I said tell me what happened."

She nodded.

"Of course. My apologies. I didn't know how...explicit you wanted me to get."

"As explicit as you are aware or capable of being."

Hedrox folded her hands, along with the clipboard behind her back.

"Father Cicatrice left at approximately 01:05. He didn't tell us where he was going, but that is his wont. Our network of cameras and spies revealed the rest. He arrived at Carter Price's apartment at approximately 01:30."

The same time I was with Nico.

"Price's apartment? What was he doing there?"

"I wasn't privy to the patriarch's…"

"I mean take an educated guess, Hedrox."

"Oh. Yes. Well, I noticed he and the patriarch had been working together on some sort of project recently. I would assume it was to do with that. You would probably know more on the matter than I, Matriarch."

"What happened? Price killed him?"

Hedrox laughed, caught herself, then stopped.

"Oh. Um. No, Matriarch. A single Inquisitor fighting the patriarch would be like a…an ant attacking a full grown man."

"I see. But swarms of ants have been known to take down lions."

"Just so, Matriarch. You understand precisely."

"So Price and his goons turned on Cicatrice."

Idi Han brought her fist down so hard on the arm of her chair that it shattered.

"Son of a bitch. To think I trusted him."

Damn you, Nico.

"It's best not to place your trust in Inquisitors, Matriarch."

"Cicatrice often warned me not to place my trust in mortals at all. What's on that paper you've got?"

Hedrox nodded and hurriedly placed the clipboard before her.

"Ah, yes, well, the patriarch, that is to say, the former patriarch, he never anticipated his own death, I mean none of us did but…"

"Stop. Jabbering."

"Yes. I'm sorry, Matriarch. He did ensure that we were prepared for any contingency. This is a list of his most important priorities. He did not explain the first entry on the list, but I believe it may make more sense to you."

She looked at the clipboard. Most of it was bureaucratic nonsense. Immortals requesting permission to bring across a favored mortal as a get, appointments to attend, bribes to make, and quite a bit of the usual business of running a casino and an entire town. Mostly he wrote in English. But the number one entry on the list was written in a few Cantonese characters, obviously for Idi Han's benefit.

"Virgin sacrifice. Daily. You must never forget or fail to do it."

The Damned.

"Did you provide the patriarch with a child or an infant every day?"

"Ah, yes. The patriarch said he preferred a virgin for his morning snack. He said he didn't care the age, but, you know, the only way to be sure most times, especially in Las Vegas, was to choose someone too young to be otherwise."

She nodded.

"Is that my new dress?"

Her head bobbing, Hedrox hurried over and unzipped the garment bag. She drew out a magnificent *cheongsam*, pure white like the *tangzhuang* Cicatrice had worn, and with the same red hourglass embroidered on the back.

"Pure spider silk," she said, "Made to your exact measurements. Uh, they'll never change now, now that you're an immortal. I don't know if you knew that."

Idi Han rose and held out her hand. Hedrox hurried it over to let her feel the fabric between her fingers.

"This must have cost a fortune."

"Oh, very much so. Father Cicatrice ordered it made the moment you arrived. I had not hoped to give it to you so soon, however."

She smiled fondly as she ran her hand across it. A gift. A posthumous gift from her beloved mentor.

"It's magnificent," she said, "There's just one problem with it."

Hedrox blinked.

"Problem? I checked it over myself, I had a dozen of the best tailors look at it."

Hedrox looked the dress up and down, trying to spot the hidden imperfection which had escaped her notice. Idi Han chuckled.

"It's not an imperfection with the tailoring, Hedrox. The problem is it's white. House Cicatrice is the House of Death. All our symbols are of passing."

"Oh. Father Cicatrice told me that in China white is the symbol of death, not black like here. He wore one just like it."

She nodded.

"I know I'm just a farm girl, Hedrox, but I'm not stupid. I know what color is the color of mourning both in America and back home. What I mean is I think I'd prefer it in red."

She swiped out at the cultist with a preternatural speed and sliced a gash on her nose. A splotch of red blood dropped onto the *cheongsam*, staining it terribly. Hedrox gasped, and tried to wipe the blood away.

"Let me ask you a question. How stupid do you really think I am?"

"I…I don't, Matriarch. I'm sorry, I'll have the dress taken back. Whatever color you like, I'll have it for you within the hour."

"That's really the problem, isn't it, Hedrox? You think Cicatrice's gifts are in any way your domain. You've despised me since the minute I arrived here. Isn't that right? Tell the truth, damn it."

The cunicular look in Hedrox's eyes disappeared as though it had never been there. She placed the dress and the garment bag down on the conference table. For the first time she had the look of a serious woman instead of a pawing sycophant.

"Yes, I despised you. He granted you the Long Gift. Who the hell are you? Some shit farmer from halfway around the world? I've served him for twenty years. As head of his circle for ten. If anyone's earned the Long Gift, it's me. I don't give two goddamns for all your immortal politics and posturing. I just care about what I was promised."

Idi Han felt a tickle at the back of her throat. She put her hand demurely to her lips to try to hide the giggle. It didn't help. A moment later she was laughing, full-throated, wide-eyed, guffawing at the ridiculous woman before her. As though she had had a fit, it gradually passed.

"You buffoon. Idiot. Have you ever seen a disciple granted the Long Gift? It doesn't happen. You're useful idiots. If you were of any value as an immortal, you'd've been made one. Immortals don't bring others across because of years of servitude. They bring them across because of inherent power. An inherent power I possess. I can smell it, we all can. Yours is so weak, I don't even think you'd survive the turning process. You'd be reduced to one of those kitchen midden ghouls."

Hedrox's eyes narrowed.

"Then it is true."

She nodded.

"But you already knew it was true. You knew it was true when you had the Signaris jump me. And you damn sure knew it was true when you tipped off the Inquisition that Father Cicatrice would be alone in Price's apartment."

She smiled.

"Still think I'd be such a weak immortal now? I have the killer instinct. And I don't suffer slights lightly."

Idi Han reached down and fingered a broken splinter from the chair. She ripped a chunk of wood out of it, a dangerous, jagged chunk. "Too bad you'll never find out."

"Now!" Hedrox shouted. "Now!"

Hedrox turned to look at the closet. Idi Han looked, too. They both waited patiently for a moment, but nothing happened. Idi Han walked over to the closet.

"When you said, 'now,' was this door supposed to open?"

She opened the door. The sickening vision of grue within made Hedrox immediately drop to her knees and vacate her stomach on the carpet.

"Ohhh…well, now I'm going to have to make you lick that up. But I suppose when you shouted this door was supposed to open and these two assassins of yours were supposed to jump out?"

Hedrox nodded, tears streaming down her face. Idi Han stepped into the closet and emerged with the industrial-strength paper shredder Cicatrice had kept in one corner of the room. The blades were still sticky with blood and chunks of intestine.

"You see, this first one here, I fed him piece by piece into the paper shredder."

She shook the basket. It groaned wetly with a full bag. She popped the mechanism out of the top and kicked it over. A thick, bright red, porridgy sludge like ground beef that had been run through a food processor and pureed spilled out on the floor. Chunks of shattered bone sparkled throughout the mess of liquified assassin.

"But then the mechanism jammed. I mean, it was a strong motor, but there's only so much bone and ligament it can chew, you know? So the second one, well, he had to go slower. I guess that was more fun, anyway. I always wondered what would happen if you just pulled a man's bones out, one at a time."

She reached into the closet and pulled out a floppy, almost shapeless semi-human form on a coat hanger. The boneless man had been heavily bound and gagged with packing tape. She laid him over her arm like a waiter with a serving napkin. She kicked a pile of what seemed to be a full human skeleton of bones out of the closet and scattered it amongst the flesh porridge.

"Old Floppy here survived almost until I pulled out his skull. I could hardly believe it when I plucked out each of his vertebrae one by one."

She made a wet sucking noise as she replicated pulling out the man's backbones on his sagging carcass.

"And I really couldn't believe it when I got each of his ribs out. I mean his heart and lungs are probably...down here now."

She gestured at the flaccid man's boneless pelvis, which was fat with sagging organs.

"It was the skull, though, nothing to be done. I tried a couple of different ways but there was no way to get it out without getting the brain out, too. But don't worry, I put it back."

She raised the head and showed where she had jammed the brain back into the toothless mouth, filling it up, as though the assassin had been gagging on his own thought organ.

"I just always wanted to see what someone without any backbone looked like. I guess I could've just waited a few minutes until you came in."

"Please, God," Hedrox was muttering.

She knelt down behind her, wrapped her arm around her neck, and jabbed the splinter of wood into her ear.

"No, no, no," she said, "None of your asinine, empty praying. Cicatrice has been your only god up until now. And now I am. And I am a vengeful goddess. You're going to suffer far worse than either of these two clowns. I didn't even care about them. They were just marionettes, dancing on strings. You were the puppeteer. And frankly, an attempt on my own life, that only makes me so mad. Not exactly not mad, but I expect that sort of thing. You, though, you killed a man more important than a father to me. So you're going to suffer in ways you've never dreamt were possible. But first things, first. You're still my loyal servant, for the next however long I let you live. You're going to clean up this whole mess. Starting with that pile of sick you just vomited up. Then we'll move on to the rest. You always wanted to know what it was like to be an immortal. And I told you you'd never be better than a ghoul. So time to find out."

She shoved Hedrox's face to the floor into the pile of putrid, still-warm throwup.

TWENTY-SIX

Nico stepped through the door and very nearly retched. Reaching into his pocket he grabbed a handkerchief and held it over his face. He looked around the room. Every surface was coated in gore. Body parts hung in places both expected and bizarre, like a child casting laundry on every surface. And in the center of the tempest of grue, Idi Han sat in a broken chair at the end of a long table, looking blank.

"Idi Han!"

He jumped forward, slipped on a puddle of blood, and skittered to regain his footing. With a little more care he hurried over to the other side of the table.

She was wearing a dress a little bit different from the one she normally wore. For one thing it was red, a dark red. He touched the fabric and realized with a sinking feeling that it was still wet. The dress wasn't red; it was soaked in blood.

He grabbed her hand and pressed it.

"Idi Han! Idi Han!"

Slowly, as though it were a creaky old puppet in a midnight '50s horror movie, her head turned toward him. She blinked, but the blank look did not abate.

"Are you all right? Are you okay?"

A thin smile cracked her lips.

"Of course, Nico. Why wouldn't I be?"

He gestured at the nightmarescape all around.

"This place looks like a war zone."

"Does it? I thought it looked like a slaughterhouse."

Nico pressed his hand to her cheek and her forehead. Both felt cold as ice and he suddenly felt foolish for checking. Something was wrong with her, though.

"Well, either, way," he said, patting her hand, "What happened here?"

"There were some mortals who made some unwise decisions."

Nico sank to his knees. He felt as though someone had just punched him in the gut.

"You did this?"

She nodded.

"It looks like you…tortured them."

"I did."

He took his hands off of hers. She didn't respond. He rose to his feet and stumbled backwards. He nearly tripped over a chair, but grabbed it to steady himself.

"How could you? This is a horror scene. Don't you have any remorse? Don't you have any feelings left?"

Idi Han puckered her lips and dismissed his concerns with a wave.

"Oh, come on, Nico, they were only mortals."

"I'm a mortal," he whispered.

"You know what I meant."

"What am I, special to you? Like a pet? A concentration camp commandant's favorite Jew?"

"How perfectly banal. How beautifully bourgeois of you. You eat meat, Nico, I've seen it."

"These aren't animals. Animals don't feel. Animals don't think."

"We're all animals, Nico."

She rose from her seat. He backed away from her, until his spine struck the door. In an eyeblink she was on top of him, her hand against his cheek.

"I want to be with you, Nico. Don't you want to be with me? Don't lie. What's the point in lying?"

His throat was so parched he had trouble speaking.

"Of course I want to be with you. But you'd have to change. Swear off this kind of…evil."

She turned her head, like a cat examining a mouse before delivering the *coup de grâce*. She took his hand and pressed it to her heart.

"I think you're wrong about who has to change. You feel that?"

"I don't feel anything."

"Exactly. The pain and the suffering of the world slip away when you're like me. All the weakness of guilt and fear, all those useless feelings, worrying about other people...they just get numb. And then they go away. I could grant you this gift. I'm already strong enough to do it."

She began to drain just a drop of the energy away from his hands to prove her point. He snatched them away.

"I can't," he said.

"It's glorious, Nico. You have no idea."

"You talk about guilt and fear fading. What about love and passion? What makes you think those will stand the test of time? What you're feeling for me right now, how do I know it's not a vestigial piece of your real self. The real you. What was your name before?"

"It doesn't matter. It's not who I am anymore. That girl died and I don't care if I never hear about her again. I'm Idi Han now. Queen of the Night. And you could be my king."

"I'd rather die a person than live forever as a thing."

Her eyes narrowed.

"A thing? You think I'm nothing but a thing?"

He had no words, but gestured at the depravity of the blood-speckled room.

"Get out now. For what we had together, I'll allow you to leave."

Nico scrabbled at the doorknob, not taking his eyes off of her. After a moment, he realized how silly he was being, and just turned his back to her to open it. If she meant to do him harm, it didn't matter whether he could see her or not. Before leaving, he turned back one last time.

"You know; I would've been your mirror."

TWENTY-SEVEN

"There was a time," a syrupy, cruel voice intoned, "when our kind was not relegated to the shadows."

"And there will be again," she whispered under her breath.

"Aren't you forgetting something?"

Startled, she looked up, nearly jumping to her feet. Cicatrice stood before her, his hands folded customarily in front of him.

"I thought you were a memory."

"If I am, then I'm here to remind you of something."

He pointed at her chest. She clutched the golden key she wore there. She drew it out and stared at it.

"This is a dream."

"Our kind do not dream."

She waved the key towards him.

"You always have quite a lot to say about our kind, don't you? What we should do, how we should we act, what we should feel, what we are."

"It is the code."

"The code you wrote, isn't that right? The code you came up with. To protect us from The Hunter of the Dead. And now he's here anyway."

"You're wasting time. You must feed The Damned, Idi Han. If you don't…"

She cast the key away with such force that it smashed through the two-way mirror which looked out over the casino. The key sailed through the air and landed behind a bank of slot machines up against the wall. One day one of the janitors would have a very lucky pay day if he did his job well.

"You're supposed to be a ghost, then? A shade? An echo?"

Cicatrice looked at the floor.

"No, don't look away, look at me!" she shouted. "I have something to tell you. I'm glad you're here. You and Topan and Signari and everyone always talk about how powerful I am, how strong I am. I never felt strong, even standing toe-to-toe with another immortal. But, now, for the first time, I understand what you all mean.

"It's not that I'm strong. It's that you were weak. For seven hundred years you lived in fear. You pretend to be a mighty man and others quaked in your shadow. But the truth is you've been a scared little boy, terrified ever since that day you first saw The Hunter of the Dead. And this, all of this, your code, your Houses, your patriarchs and your elders, and your endless apprenticeships, and your carefully chosen gets and all of it…it's all a ruse. Whistling past the graveyard. Keeping our numbers low so that you never have to face the terrifying Hunter again. Isn't that right?"

He looked at her, but said nothing.

"You were weak. Too weak to let The Damned roam free. Too terrified of the consequences. Terrified The Hunter would return, terrified the mortals would learn of our existence. And now I know why you all call me strong. Because I'm not scared of any of those things. And I'm happy to watch everything burn."

She turned to look out at the casino. It was far from peaceful, buzzing as it was with humanity, blinking lights, smoke, the whirring of machines, the cadence calls of dealers, and all manner of hustle and bustle. But it was ordinary. It was normal. Pedestrian. After tomorrow she would never be able to see this scene again.

"Aren't you proud of me, Father…?"

She turned to look at him, but there was no one there. Grimly, she pressed a button on her telephone.

"Yes, Matriarch?"

"Bring me two pots of makeup. One white, one black. Contact Otto Signari by whatever means we have at our disposal. Tell him I want to talk. That I'm ready to negotiate the surrender of House Cicatrice."

TWENTY-EIGHT

With a burlap sack over one shoulder and a shovel over the other, Price strode into the cemetery. A ghoul clambered up on top of one of the headstones, silhouetted in eerie light against the moon. Eyes gleaming yellow, it stared at Price. Price threw the sack to the ground.

"Guess I haven't been keeping up with my regular extermination work with all that's been going on the past few days."

The ghoul hissed, its eyes darting back and forth. It went both ways with feral ghouls sometimes. Sometimes they ran, sometimes they attacked. This one attacked. Price waited until the ghoul was in perfect range and swung the shovel in a perfect arc through the air. It connected with the ghoul's chin and severed the top of his head from the rest of him. The cap of his head tumbled to the ground. Its yellow eyes blinked, roved, and fell still.

Price raised both arms to the air and made the imitation of a hissing audience.

"And the crowd goes *wild*! Yeah! Carter! Carter! Carter!"

Price paused and scrunched his face. His little baseball charade had reminded him of Nico. He sighed and tossed the burlap sack over his shoulder then struggled to grab the ghoul and drag it by its heel while simultaneously kicking the top of its head like a puck across the blacktop. He came to a rest with his burdens at a grave marked AOIFE PRICE.

"Hey, ma," he whispered, running his finger along the engraved name.

He sloughed the sack atop the grave, and kicked the ghoul's

body and head top until it was in the same spot. He jammed the head of the spade rigidly into the earth and slouched down against the burlap sack. Reaching into his pocket, he drew out his flask, unscrewed the top, and took a sip.

"*Slainté*," he muttered

He tippled a few drops onto his fingers and ran it across his mother's name. As he tipped his head back to take another sip, out of the corner of his eye he spotted a white-clad figure busying itself at a nearby grave. Price leapt to his feet; hand on the shotgun on his side.

"Relax," a dark, heavy voice intoned.

Cicatrice rose from the grave, a handful of white orchids in his hand. He walked up and proffered them forth. Price reached out and slowly grasped the handle of stems.

"For your mother."

"Did you just steal these?"

"Well, Price, I would've called and had my florist send some around but considering I'm dead and in that sack right there, my options are limited."

Price thought about it, shrugged, and placed the flowers at the base of his mother's stone. He lay back down against Cicatrice's body. Cicatrice walked around to the other side of the grave and lay down opposite him.

"Are you real?"

"What is reality? What is a dream?"

Price grunted.

"That's very poetic but it's hardly an answer."

"I wonder what kind of an answer someone like me could give. 'Yes, I am real' or 'No, I'm not.' Either way seems somehow disingenuous."

"Are you a ghost?"

"I couldn't say."

"A hallucination, then?"

"Probably. I suppose that's what science would say. But then science would also say there's no such thing as vampires."

"And the real Cicatrice wouldn't call himself a vampire."

"And a hallucination couldn't pick up a bouquet. So. Here we are."

Price took another drink. He looked upward. The stars were bright and he felt like he could see them all. The moon practically eclipsed the rest of the sky. It had been so damn long since he had just sat and looked at them. It made him wistful for another time. Back when he had been Nico's age, maybe. Although who knew if a kid like Nico even looked at the stars anymore. Kids never seemed to look up from their smart phones. Nico was a good kid, though. A good boss, come to think of it.

"How's your leg?"

Price nodded.

"Interesting that you ask. I'm…on quite a lot of morphine. But once they got all of the wood out and made a little, you know, Tinker Toy log cabin out of it, basically the damage was all nominal. Not like I was going to walk around with a cord of lumber in my leg, but basically I'm all patched up."

"That's good to hear."

"Do you really give a shit?"

"Not in the slightest."

"Then why are you here?"

"Oh, I'd say the most likely explanation is that I'm here to convince you to give my body back to Idi Han for proper burial."

Price laughed and shook his head.

"I knew it. I fucking knew it."

"Knew what? That there's still a dignity and an honor in death that even the voices in your head would like you to acknowledge?"

"No," Price said, elongating the short word, "not that. I knew even in death you'd try to get out of this. You're like a weed that can't be pulled out, even by the root. I'm not stupid, you know. I know that staking or beheading isn't the end. It just incapacitates you. A night in your native soil and you'd be back on your feet."

"Ah," Cicatrice said, "then you think I'm trying to trick you. So be it. Bury my body in some fake grave you've bought just for the chance. While you're at it, why not jumble up my parts with some dead feral ghoul's? That's the dignity befitting the end of the greatest immortal of his age."

"It's not fake."

Price ran his hands through the soil of his mother's plot, which had overgrown with grass. He pulled out a chunk and let it sift through his hands, disposing of the clod of grass.

"Well, I know your mother's not buried here. Not really. She was one of our kind at the end."

"I know."

He rose. Feeling the shift in the sack that contained his mortal remains, the shade (or whatever) of Cicatrice rose as well. With the spade, Price scratched a small trench around the gravesite.

"She's ash now. I burned her right here on this very spot. I know this is just a monument to her memory. I know she wasn't herself at the end. I don't know what it is about your kind. Idi Han's not the Idi Han she was before she died. I doubt you're the same as you were either."

"I'm not. That's why Cicatrices choose an immortal name."

"What was your mortal name?"

"If I am a hallucination, then that's something I couldn't possibly know."

"And if you're not?"

"If I'm not then it's something I would never tell."

Price tapped the spade over and over again into the groove he had just dug. It was an affectation more than anything else.

"My mother—my real mother, I mean, not the thing your kind turned her into—would be proud that I ended your legacy in her name."

Price flicked his Zippo open and on with a single move.

"Don't," Cicatrice said.

Price tossed the lighter onto the burlap sack and watched as the remains of the greatest vampire of his age and some anonymous degenerate ghoul burned up together. He turned to say something witty, but the shade of Cicatrice was gone.

NIGHT FOUR

TWENTY-NINE

Deep in the bowels of the Earth, The Executioner's eyes fluttered.

Food.

She waited. Her gut twisted; an unfamiliar feeling.

Caretaker. I hunger.

She wrapped her head back in her hands and waited. A bony hand, chilly as a frozen lake, wrapped around her shoulder.

Executioner.

She opened her eyes. A deranged creature stood before her, his jaw missing, his skin sallow and nearly sloughing off the bone. He looked like a horror out of time, but there was something familiar about his features, the low cut of his brow, the way his nose turned to the left. Her mind raced across five centuries of slumber, trying to recall the creature's name. He had once been a bloody jaguar warrior of Tenochtitlan, but his name had fled her entirely.

The Seer is gone.

The Warrior pointed across the way to the Seer's spot. She was indeed missing. How irritating. How noisome. She was tired. All she wanted to do was slumber, slumber for a thousand years. But now she was hungry, her guts ached, and The Seer was missing.

She shook her head trying to form a picture of The Seer in her mind. She had been a beautiful maiden…hadn't she? A sorceress who had looked to the entrails and chicken bones to tell what would come. A panic settled in The Executioner's heart.

She couldn't recall her own name. She had meted out justice

for the Emperor. "His own hand," he had called her. A tall man, a fat man. What had his name been? Frustrated she moved to bury her head in her hands and was shocked to see that they had turned to bony claws. In horror she reached up to feel her face and found that she, too, had the aspect of a jawless lamprey.

She turned, seething, and spun, as the other eleven approached her from their stations. She recognized each in turn, The Hermit, The Scholar, The Priest, without being able to recall a single name. They all had a single thought on their minds.

Where is The Caretaker?

Has he taken ill?

Perhaps he's been detained.

We should give him twenty-four hours.

Yes, it is early to panic.

Perhaps we should seek him out.

What if he's been killed?

What is the world like? Are we free to roam?

I fear the worst.

If the worst has come to pass, we must be prepared to take action.

Their thoughts filled her head, jumbling, jangling, and straining against one another. She felt pulled in eleven different directions, as every strain of thought fought for prominence. Some were more panicked than others, but as they bickered and debated all began to grow agitated.

Silence!

The thousand competing thoughts receded away, and the others sat quietly, waiting for her words.

If The Seer were here, she might tell us what has come to pass. But she is not. If The Caretaker were here, he might tell us what has kept him. But he is not. So we must act as though we have been left to our own devices. Which we have. So I wonder if the apocalypse The Seer foresaw has at last come to pass.

And if it hasn't?

Then we shall bring it. Besides, I hunger. Let us feast.

THIRTY

The night air was chilly and full of mysteries. The wind battered her hair, turning it into a manta ray fluttering on the jetstream. She had never been higher than the top floor of the Aztec before. Now, standing atop the very peak of the Stratosphere Tower, she felt like a god.

The ball of her right foot was balanced precariously on the spike that terminated the dizzying height of the tower. Her left foot was in free fall. At first she had held her arms out for balance, but that had been a weakness, a mortal conceit. The muscles in the center of her foot were easily strong enough to maintain her balance, even if she were struck by something heavy. And the wind was making its best effort to topple her. It was exhilarating.

"Ahoy, there!"

She looked down. A few rungs below, on a tiny catwalk that seemed more designed for a suicide than a maintenance man, Otto Signari in his resplendent armor stood next to Topan.

"Might I have word with the new matriarch of House Cicatrice?"

She nodded. She raised her arms above her head in imitation of all the times she used to dive into the river back home. With only her foot to push off of a tiny spike, she flung herself up into the air, did three somersaults, and came down with a clang next to Signari.

Upon seeing her countenance, Signari took a step back, nearly knocking into Topan, who stood on his other side. The catwalk was so narrow they couldn't stand abreast.

"Lily," he gasped.

"You like it?" she asked, having to remind herself not to finger the facepaint for fear of smudging it. With black paint she had cut out the lower right quadrant of her face, and then replaced the teeth and skullbones with white.

"It's…quite striking."

"She's trying to psych you out. Typical Cicatrice bullshit," Topan muttered.

He wore a black armband embroidered with the red mark of Cicatrice, identical to her own. She wanted nothing more than to reach out and rip it off, along with the rest of his arm.

"Psych me out? Come now, Topan, there are no opponents here to psych out. We're just adults having a conversation about the future. Idi Han, I'd be lying if I said I truly mourned the loss of Cicatrice, the way you obviously do. We were often at odds. But I never failed to respect the man, and he was the greatest of us."

"I suppose that makes you the greatest of us left."

He nodded.

"Your words, not mine. Nevertheless, you have my sincere condolences. Certainly he could have gone better than to a pack of Inquisition dogs. Better at my sword, at least." He patted the pommel of his weapon. "There would have been honor in that. And you have my word House Signari will hunt down every one of those Inquisitors. It's just a small matter, a gesture of goodwill, if you will."

Idi Han bowed her head.

"Thank you. For your condolences. And your gesture."

"This is a magnificent meeting place you've chosen. It really is quite a view."

"You'll forgive the impetuousness of inexperience, I hope, and as you said, I am in mourning, but I am in no special mood for pleasantries. If you don't mind, we have some rather important business to discuss."

"Of course, of course. Would you prefer Cantonese?" he asked, switching over to her native tongue.

She shook her head.

"I'm in the New World now. In so many, many ways. Best I get used to it."

He nodded.

"Well, there's no arguing with that. Your disciples told me you were ready to surrender. So I take that to mean you understand where the council stands on the matter of Cicatrice's rightful heir."

Signari reached out and clapped his gauntleted hand on Topan's shoulder.

"The boy here studied at the feet of the master for longer than most immortals living today have been alive. He has our full support. Now I understand this may be a bit…tricky, as Cicatrice had some harsh words for him in the end. But we're not here to worry about old grudges. If I was here to worry about old grudges, there are five hundred corpses I could lay at your feet. No, we're here to do what's best for our kind. That means having a safe, secure House Cicatrice. And that means putting Topan back in charge."

Idi Han folded her arms and nodded. The wind caught hold of her hair and made it billow behind her like a veil.

"And where would that leave me?"

"Well, you are Topan's get. There's the issue of your illegitimacy. I've spoken to the council at length, and it took some doing, but considering how well-documented it was and witnessed by multiple immortals that Cicatrice accepted you as his own, we're willing to consider you a full member in good standing of House Cicatrice. And after a probationary period of, let's say, fifty years, we'll restore your position as Topan's full heir. It's not good to have an illegitimate heir, but memories tend to fade and in half a century or so you'll have your own reputation and it won't matter so much."

"That's very generous of you. So all I have to do is give up House Cicatrice and I get to go back to being Topan's sex slave."

"Sex slave? You flatter yourself."

"Topan," Signari said sharply, "Idi Han, let's not bullshit one another, agreed? I'm well aware of your differences. Topan tries to downplay them. But I know him and I've got a good feel for you. So here's what else I've got in mind for you. I personally am without a get at this particular juncture in history. There were a few good potential mortals I had been watching, but none had really jumped out at me.

"So, knowing the gulf between you and your sire, I volunteered before the council to take on your training. That's an offer only a House patriarch can make, and I made it for you. Fifty years, it's a nice round number. I don't like to keep my gets around for a century or two, that was more Cicatrice's thing. Out of the nest and fly on your own as fast as possible, that's my philosophy. I already know you're a fast learner.

"I think in ten years, maybe twenty-five, I could give you my blessing. You could found your own circle, come fifty years from now the probation ends, you become an elder for your house in my seat in Rome and two, three hundred years from now I think you'll be an even better House matriarch than either your sire or your grandsire was. I genuinely believe that."

She paused, and put her fist to her chin.

"An interesting proposal. Topan gets the House and I don't have to go back to him?"

Topan growled.

"Quiet," Signari said, striking him in the chest, "Yes, that's right. It'll all be legal."

"But the thing is I'm already matriarch of House Cicatrice. The elders even recognize me. Cicatrice's will was quite explicit."

"Is it really a responsibility you want to take on? You haven't even learned to drink blood yet. Two, three hundred years, absolutely, I see a great future for you as one of the greatest House matriarchs of all time. But right now? You still have to learn how to be an immortal, girl. Don't put that level of stress on yourself."

"Perhaps you're right. I get confused sometimes just dealing with Cicatrice's circle."

Signari held out his hands palm upward and shrugged, a ridiculous gesture from a man so armored, accompanied by an equally ridiculous duck-faced expression.

"There, you see. Circles are tricky to manage. Damn tricky. All you need is time and experience."

Idi Han smiled, and feeling the paint on her face, wondered how it was distending with her grin.

"For instance, would you believe a coup was possible from within your own circle?"

"It's been known to happen."

"They just tried to kill me, my disciples. Well, Cicatrice's. Well…really, Topan was the head of circle for a while."

Signari's smiling, overly avuncular expression disappeared. Without his teeth showing, the very vicious look behind his eyes was obvious.

"That's a terrible thing to hear. Under my tutelage, I would teach you how to spot rebellious disciples before they ever became a problem."

"And would you teach me how to spot betrayal from my own heir? My own senior elder, my own most beloved get? I know you're not dumb, Signari, and I know you've been at odds with Cicatrice since before the concept of Great Houses had been invented. And I also know that since the day Topan orchestrated a ceasefire with the Inquisitors, House Cicatrice has stood head, shoulders, and belly over all twelve of the other Houses combined. House Signari likes to act like it's Pepsi to Cicatrice's Coke, but the truth is it's more like RC Cola."

"Maybe you can just stop beating around the bush and tell me what you're getting at," Signari said, placing his hand surreptitiously on the pommel of his blade.

"You decided to go toe-to-toe with House Cicatrice all of a sudden? When you've been terrified to for seventy years? Most people would ask why, but most people would already know. No, I'm afraid I won't turn my House over to Topan, because Topan is more Signari than Cicatrice. He's your lapdog, your clown, your puppet, your Manchukuo. You decided you could take on House Cicatrice because you had a mole. I talked to Hedrox, Topan. I tortured every last bit of the plan out of her. You were behind it all. Sending Cicatrice to his doom. At the hands of Inquisitors. As long as you were planning it, you could have let Signari here wet his blade, like he so gravely desires."

"Watch it, little girl. I am patriarch of a Great House."

"As am I, Signari, and I know now why Cicatrice held you in such contempt. You are beneath contempt. You act as though you're a warrior, but you wouldn't know what to do in a straight fight. You're a conniver, a sneak, a thief."

Signari wrapped his hand around the pommel of his sword

and secured his scabbard with his offhand.

"Otto," Topan said, "don't lose your temper. Remember how important she is to me. I mean, to our plans."

Signari slammed his elbow backwards into Topan's gut, shattering the other man's spine and doubling him over.

"Shut up, you sniveling Cicatrice dog. I've had to hold my nose and treat with you, but I'll be goddamned if I'll let you take liberties with me. And as for you, you tiny bitch…"

Idi Han held up her hands, as if surrendering.

"Patriarch, you're overreacting. I'm just proposing a slight alteration in terms."

Signari narrowed his eyes warily but didn't take his hands off his weapon. Slowly Topan rose and stalked off as far as he could possibly get from them on the narrow catwalk, sulking like a beaten cur.

"What sort of alterations?"

"What if, instead of all that stuff you said, I just released The Damned and let them have their way with this city?"

A low chuckle grumbled in Signari's throat before erupting as a full-throating bellow.

"The Damned. First The Hunter of the Dead and now The Damned. It's like I'm finally getting to meet every immortal legend all on the same night."

"You don't think they're real?"

"I know for a fact they're not. The same way Scar always passed around that story about his mysterious death-dealing foe. To keep us in line. Yes, he developed the nuclear option five hundred years before mankind split the atom. The Damned. I'll believe it when I…"

Suddenly, out of the corner of his eye, Signari spotted the shadow figures on the ground. From up here the people looked like ants. But amongst them, twelve spiders leapt and crawled and slashed and slaughtered their prey. Signari hurried to the railing of the catwalk and stared down in horror.

"They can't be real. What am I seeing?"

"The last full measure of devotion. My final tribute to Cicatrice. I did what he could never do. Released the monsters of a bygone era onto the modern world."

Topan joined him and stared down. With both their backs to her, Idi Han slammed the back of her fist into Signari's lower back. She felt his spine shatter and the solid metal railing distend and finally break as Signari fell through it, tumbling from the tower. She turned on Topan.

"Sire," she said, with a curtsey.

Topan smiled.

"Come now, little one…"

"Don't call me that."

He held up his hands as though surrendering.

"Idi Han. I'm sorry. It's a good name, an excellent choice. Powerful. Seductive. Just like you."

She dropped to a crouch, pawing at the catwalk with her feet, preparing to leap and destroy him in a single stroke.

"You're going to suffer a fate worse than death, Topan."

"Now, now, be reasonable, Idi Han. With Cicatrice out of the way, we have a chance to pave our own futures."

"I'm not going to punish you because of what you did to Cicatrice."

"No?"

She shook her head.

"That was between you two. I'm going to punish you because of what you did to me."

A piercing roar cut through the air and Idi Han whirled around to see a flash of metal and fur arcing in a parabola from the ground. Signari, his armor dented and smashed from his collision with the ground, his sword flashing in the moonlight and twinkling in the starlight, brought it swinging towards her neck.

Signari was fast, and if he had remained silent perhaps she would have missed his return leap and been decapitated. But his battlecry had afforded her just barely enough time to leap out of her crouch. The sword passed through her midsection, severing her spine, heart, and the top of her ribcage from the bottom. A powerful blow, by any measure.

She felt her bones and ligaments rebonding even as he raised the sword for a backswing. She watched, her senses so acute that the world seemed to move at a snail's pace. Signari's mouth was frothing with foam, his eyes glimmering with anger, and he was shouting some unholy cry. The metal of the catwalk was dented from the impact of his sabatons.

In a strange sense, despite her urgency, time seemed to move interminably slow as he returned his sword across the same arc that had passed through her, this time aiming slightly higher for her neck. It would strike. There was no avoiding that now. She had only one chance.

She reached out and grabbed his wrist with both hands, but didn't arrest his swing. She could feel her shoulders and head dangerously shifting on her torso. Her body would need only a few seconds to repair itself, but until then the outcome was uncertain. She didn't want to be left without a torso and legs, desperately scrabbling to defeat the Signari House patriarch.

She gritted her teeth, rubbing them against each other like sandpaper as they pulverized top and bottom to powder. There was no more waiting. She could tell his swing had reached its point of no return. It was either move now or be decapitated.

Feeling as though her shoulder and head were about to pop off from the strain, she threw off his swing with a sickening wrench. Signari's sword arm ripped out of the socket and went flying off into the night from the exertion. As she had feared, her freshly cloven body slipped apart from the effort. She found her head and shoulders facing right, while her torso and legs below her still pointed forward, the two parts at nearly perpendicular odds.

"Tiny bitch," Signari murmured, wondering at his missing arm.

He stepped forward, slightly off balance, apparently trying to swipe her top half from the tower. Arms akimbo, she grabbed her belly and back and straightened herself out. The flesh was almost smarter than she was, and though she had righted herself slightly off, as it healed, her two halves pulled themselves into alignment.

"I've had that sword for eight hundred years. If it's lost, there will be consequences."

"Your entire arm is missing and all you're worried about is

your big swinging dick…I mean sword? You really are the Otto Signari Cicatrice told me about."

He chuckled, his affected mirth back on display for just an instant.

"And you really are a Cicatrice. All talk. No action. All bravado. No substance. You know, a lot of people think that living forever is the greatest thing that could possibly ever happen to them. Something they rarely dwell on is that living forever means you can be tortured forever. I have all kinds of places set up just for punishing upstart immortals like you. Do you have any idea what the punishment for laying hands on a House Patriarch is?"

Idi Han cocked her head.

"I don't know. Is it any worse than the punishment for killing one?"

"Kill me? That's a joke. Topan!"

Idi Han whirled around, bracing for Topan's attack. She cursed herself instantly as she saw her sire had disappeared, long since fleeing the battle. But now, of course, she had her back to her adversary. He punched through her back, his fist passing through her ribcage both in the back and in the front, and plucking her heart from out of her chest. He held it out, unbeating, before her, as he lifted her off her feet, impaled on his forearm.

"Now, there's a stroke of luck," he said, pointing at a sledgehammer which a construction worker had left on the catwalk. "If I had my other arm I'd just rip your head off. But now we've got to do it the hard way. Shh, shh. Relax, darling. Sometimes the hard way is more fun."

She struggled, kicking, trying to extricate herself from the arm penetrating her, but there was little she could do. The sledgehammer lay on the floor, heavy enough not to be blown away by even the strongest wind.

"Oof. That handle looks a little dull. Not much of a stake, is it? Well, we'll make it work. Enough force and you can push a square peg through a round hole. That's pretty much what you've been trying to do your whole life anyway, isn't it?"

She relaxed and let Signari take her away. There wasn't really any pain anyway, just a weird feeling of fullness and violation. He stepped on the head of the sledgehammer, turning the head and bringing the wooden handle up into the air. He pressed her expurgated heart to the top of the wooden handle.

"You could've had it all. Been my adopted get. Even Matriarch of House Cicatrice one day."

"As your lapdog!" she spat out.

"Yep. As my lapdog. That was happening either way. That was in the cards since the day Topan approached me. Now, though? You crossed the line. I'm going to get you staked and when you wake up it'll be in one of my torture chambers and that'll be eternity for you. Good night, tiny bitch."

Signari raised his arm and her whole body with it to slam her heart down on the wooden handle. As soon as her legs were high enough, she wrapped her legs around the sledgehammer handle and brought it swinging backwards. Signari toppled as the hammerhead slipped out from under his foot, and the entire weight of the tool swung up between his legs, pulverizing his testicles to pulp and shattering his pelvis.

He dropped to his knees. Now with her feet planted back firmly on the catwalk, Idi Han had the leverage she needed. She grabbed the railing with one hand and wrenched herself counterclockwise, yanking Signari's other arm out of the socket with a loud, gutwrenching pop.

She turned to face him, literally disarmed, as he rose, his hips and balls mending. His severed arm was still planted through her midsection like a flag at the North Pole. She reached out and took hold of her heart with one hand. With the other, she folded down his thumb, index and ring fingers, and pinky, until only his middle finger was out, pointing at him.

He growled and lowered his head to charge her with a headbutt. She tried to yank the severed arm through her chest, but found it was so dangly with bits of armor and thickened up towards the bicep that it was easier to push it back out and cause less damage to herself. She returned her heart to its rightful home and pirouetted out of the way of Signari's charge. He tumbled to the floor of the catwalk, initially finding it difficult to raise himself back to his feet without his arms.

With a surge of immortal strength he bent his legs and popped himself upright.

"You know what's going to happen now, tiny bitch?" he growled.

"Yeah," she replied, "I'm going to beat you to death with your own arm."

Raising Signari's arm over her shoulder the way Nico wielded his baseball bat, she proceeded to do just that, smashing Signari's face to pulp. He staggered against the railing and nearly toppled over, but she grabbed him, flung him to the floor, and began pulverizing his bones with his own arm.

When she finally finished, Signari had been beaten to a bloody mess, his fancy armor all dented and smashed in so that it barely resembled its original gleaming look. The only part that was even remotely still holding together was his breastplate. She wrenched it off his chest and ran her finger along the edge.

"Oof. That seam looks a little dull. Not much of a blade, is it? Well, we'll make it work. Enough force and you can push a square peg through a round hole."

Signari grinned wide at her, most of his teeth missing and struggling to regrow from the jaw.

"Cicatrice is dead. I still hurt you first," he managed to form through his devastated jaw and tongue.

"It doesn't matter who strikes first. It only matters who strikes last."

She brought the dull piece of armor down and severed Signari's head from his body. She lay down, breathing hard, and feeling an incredible hunger rumbling in her body. But there was no time to rest yet. Topan was still on the wing, and The Damned were making mincemeat of the city.

She rose and tossed Signari's head, arm, and body to the wind, in three different directions. The morning sun would dispose of him permanently.

"Tiny bitch," she muttered, spitting into the wind after him.

THIRTY-ONE

Renee leaned over and whispered in her husband's ear, "Jesus Christ, Jon, I thought you said Vegas was a place you could take your kids."

Jon Pickup shrugged and made googly eyes, as if displacing all guilt. All up and down the strip men continued to catcall and click stacks of prostitute—sorry, "call girl"—flyers together. The whole place was like a din of clicking, buzzing insects. Even though her daughter, Ava, seemed to be delighted just by all the lights, noise, sound, and action, Renee quietly hoped this was about as unsavory as Sin City got.

"Well, what do I know?" he replied, his British accent unmistakable though tempered by a decade in the USMC. "I'm not even from here. You should know these things."

"That 'I'm not even from here excuse' was hoary about the time Ava was born."

"Whorey?"

"You know what I mean."

"Well, you still love me."

She planted a peck on his cheek, glorying in leaving behind a purple smudge of lipstick.

"You're lucky you're pretty."

And he was. Rugged, tall (well, taller than her, anyway) with a Marine Corps-chiseled body and a chin to die for. (Although she suspected he would've taken care of his body whatever his day job was.)

Ava reached out to grab one of the hooker fliers. The man snapping them shrugged, seeming to feel that his job was more to blanket the city with fliers than check to see whether a six-year-old had the wherewithal or resources to hire a prostitute. Before Ava could put her grubby little mitts on the thing, Renee snatched her daughter up off the ground, swinging her through the air as though it had been deliberate.

"Wooh," she said, "you're flying!"

"I'm flying, Mommy!" the precocious six-year-old cried out, putting her arms out as though she were Superman, "I'm Superman!"

"You sure are. Jon, can we please find something kid-friendly to do?"

"Oh, well, sure. There's shows…"

"I'm not sure a six-year-old is going to want to sit through David Copperfield."

"Well, what about Wayne Newton?"

"Wayne Newton is dead."

"No. Is he? No. Well, they've loosened the curfew. We can head down to the Hoover Dam."

"Damn!" Ava announced proudly, "Damn damn damn damn!"

A concrete overhead walkway connected two casinos. A gaggle of half-assed Batmen, mangy-looking Elmos, a few non-descript knockoff characters that resembled no cartoons in pop culture Renee was aware of, and what was either SpongeBob or a bar of walking soap hung out at the street level entrance to the walkway. Children Ava's age and younger were gleefully running up to their favorite characters (as played by drunken street hoods) and begging for free iPhone pictures that ranged in price anywhere from $5 to a punch in the mouth for not paying your $5.

Renee blew a puff of air out of the corner of her mouth, lifting up a dangling lock of her bright orange hair. Sometimes she wore it in a Mohawk, and sometimes down like today, but usually in fun colors that she and Ava would pick out together. Ava was a perfect little blonde, which came from God only knew which side of the family.

"Ava, do you want to get a picture with Elmo?"

Ava's eyes opened wide as she looked out at the

barely-dancing, barely-capering, mostly-leering costumed characters. Ava shook her head furiously and buried her head in Renee's neck. Renee shot daggers at Jon.

"Why does she hate Elmo?"

Jon's cheeks reddened.

"Oh, yeah. That's my fault."

"Explain now."

"You remember when that Elmo impersonator got arrested in Times Square for, you know...?" Jon made a "snort snort" motion with the side of his nose.

"Vaguely..."

"Well, I didn't want to have to explain what D-R-U-G-S are to the poor kid, so I told her that, ah, Elmo and the Count had been eating the other muppets."

"Eating?"

Ava nodded in her mother's nape.

"Yeah. Killing the other muppets and eating them. I mean, he's a vampire."

"Elmo's a vampire?"

"No, the other one. The 'ah ah ah' guy."

Ava wrapped her arms tightly around her mother's neck.

"No Elmo!"

Renee jabbed Jon in his armpit.

"We are going to discuss this later. Although it sounds like a pretty awesome conversation."

"It was!"

With some difficulty, she prised the child from around her neck and placed Ava on the ground, then crouched down to her level.

"Look, Elmo's not eating anyone. See?"

She pointed over at the barely-capering, barely-waving, generally coked-out characters. None were making any motions towards eating the children within their grasp. Mostly they were making Cassius's itching palm sign towards the touristy parents. Nevertheless, Ava shook her head.

"Oh, well, maybe you just can't see right. Would wearing mommy's glasses help?"

Ava pondered it for a minute, but there was no arguing with

the acute desire to be like her mom. After a period of deliberation deemed appropriate by a six-year-old, she nodded. Renee took off her bitchin' clear purple frames and stuck them on Ava's head. Ava made a big show of adjusting them like binoculars, and looking over at the assembled characters.

"Ooh, mommy, who's that?"

Renee squinted to see without her glasses on. A new crowd of "performers" was approaching. She wondered if they worked in shifts. More likely, she reflected, they probably worked by having turf wars. The new gaggle seemed to be dressed the same as one another, but she couldn't tell for the life of her what they were supposed to be, not without her glasses on.

"Who's that, Daddy?"

She punched Jon lightly.

"Oh, um…actually I don't know. Teletubbies?"

"You're no help whatsoever. Here, honey, let me have my glasses for just a second and then you can borrow them again later."

"Okay, Mommy."

Renee took the now-greasy lenses back from her daughter, rubbed them against her Rosie Killjoy scarf, and took a second look. Her lips immediately pursed in wonder. Twelve horrific, sallow-skinned mutants were loping onto the scene in a Flying-V with all the speed and balletic movement of Alex's gang of droogs from *A Clockwork Orange*. Only bowlers and eyeshadow would've completed the look.

She had to admit, though, bowlers would've ruined the effect. These were no cheap, store-bought costumes. They looked like professional Hollywood makeup artists had done them up. How they had achieved the missing lower jaw effect was beyond her. And their long, Neanderthal-like arms and pinched, gaunt, sallow limbs were works of art.

"Ooh, monsters," Renee said, her eyes sparkling. "Must be some kind of special thing for Halloween. What do you think, Ava, you want a picture with a gruesome, grisly, creepy crawly?"

Ava clapped her hands excitedly. Renee and Jon had been horror aficionados for years, and though they weren't eager to show their daughter *Cannibal Holocaust* or *Nekromantik*, they had been gradually introducing her to the fandom, mostly through '30s Universal monster movies and fun things like making spider cupcakes and that sort of thing. Elmo, a mere muppet trying to teach her ABCs was banal, but a horrific ur-vampire thing? That was exciting.

"All right, relax, honey," Renee laughed as Ava practically pulled her along to the street corner. "They'll still be there in a minute."

A wide ring had formed around the twelve newcomers. They seemed really committed to their role, hissing and lunging and dangling their fingers towards the crowd. The SpongeBobs and other clowns had backed off, giving them a wide berth, and the other parents were seemingly confused, while loose kids were hiding, running up, running back, and giggling, as though it were a scare game.

Renee finally released Ava's hand when they were a few feet away and she skipped up to the head of the formation, apparently the leader of the pack. Ava grabbed at the poor woman's hips and tugged on her skin as though she were wearing a skirt, as she had done to Renee many times before.

"Oh, no no no, honey," Renee said, running up and pulling her daughter away, "don't touch. You could mess up her makeup. Remember how hard it is to get your makeup just so?"

Ava nodded.

"Okay, just be nice." She grinned up at the jawless woman. "Sorry about that. Really, you look amazing. Are you supposed to be anything in particular?"

The monster cocked her head inquisitively, a splendidly alien and/or animal gesture. Such commitment!

"Sorry! Monsters. Got it."

Renee scurried back to Jon's side.

"Uh, Renee…"

"Hang on, I just want to get a picture."

"Are you sure this is just a street performance?"

Sighing, Renee planted her hands on her hips and turned to look at her husband.

"They really do make you take your brain out and put it in a jar, don't they?"

"Hey! You were a jarhead, too!"

"I am a jarhead, honey. Once a jarhead, always a jarhead. Now our daughter is having fun for the first time since we got here, so please…you know what, I don't want to turn into that nagging mom. I just want a picture of Ava. You ready, honey?"

Much to both Renee and apparently Ava's surprise, the monster woman reached down and grabbed Ava by the scruff of her neck and lifted her up bodily off the ground. Renee had a sudden impulse to hurry over and help, but Ava was giggling, and the woman really was doing her best to make this a fun time. Ava was laughing so hard she had to cover her face to hold back the explosion of laughter.

"Perfect. Perfect! Thank you. Hold that for just a…"

Renee raised her iPhone and started to open her picture app when suddenly the monster woman reached over and grabbed Ava's hair, snatching the scalp from her head in one swift motion.

"Is…is that…" Jon muttered, sounding dazed.

The monster woman lifted Ava to her nose and sniffed at her now exposed skull. Ava was screaming bloody murder. Apparently not liking what it smelled, the leader tossed Renee's daughter over her shoulder and the other eleven creatures in the Flying-V scrambled to snatch Ava to pieces.

Renee's phone dropped to the ground, shattering into a thousand component parts, all scattering to Hell and gone. Before she even knew what was happening, her arms and legs were pumping and she was charging full tilt at the monster woman, an unholy war cry on her lips.

The monster snatched her out of the air and held her up, squeezing her head like a ripe lemon. Jon was running too, and then he was in the monster's other hand.

"I'll kill you! What did you do to my daughter?"

The creature held Renee up to its face and as its hot, angry breath struck her full in the mouth, she realized that the missing jaw and the sallow skin was no makeup. This was a real monster. Then she felt the strength ebbing from her, a coldness spreading through her body. In its other hand, Jon was convulsing, frothing at the lips, and an instant later blood began spewing from his mouth, ears, and eyes.

Renee opened her mouth to scream some other obscenity, but her own mouth was sticky with blood, too. She felt the blood rushing out of her every orifice. The warm, flowing redness in her veins was replaced with an aching cold. She shuddered, shook, and finally a moment later was flopping. Blackness descended on her.

When she awoke the world was violet and she was throbbing with hunger.

THIRTY-TWO

Aknock came at the doorjam. It registered somewhere in Price's groggy state but not sufficiently for him to actually rise from his mattress.

"Price!"

"Go away," he muttered into his pillow.

"Price, this is ridiculous. I'm coming in."

He turned his head just enough to the side so that his words might register to whoever was on the other side of the tarp which he had used to cover the missing door.

"Oozit?" he slurred.

Professor Kasprzak stepped through the tarp and planted her hands on her hips.

"Where's the boy?"

"What boy?" Price muttered, finally rolling over onto his back.

She stomped in and stopped in surprise, just short of the huge hole in the floor.

"Are you allowed to live in here like this?"

"Probably not."

"This place should be condemned."

"I should be condemned," he said, pulling the pillow over his face, "Condemned to Hell. Go away, Holly Ann."

She snatched the pillow away from his face and grabbed him bodily, surprising him with her strength. She shoved his head under the kitchen sink and turned the water on. He struggled to get away, but she held his head under.

"How are you this strong?" he groaned.

"I've wrestled snakes more impressive than you. Now are you going to wake up?"

"Yes, yes, I surrender!"

He held up his arms as best he could, sputtering under the water. She let him go. He looked up, blinking at her.

"Where is Nico Salazar?" she repeated. "Your apprentice."

He shrugged.

"Hopefully on a plane back to Puerto Rico."

"You don't know where he is?"

Price slumped into his chair. He scrabbled at the ground, trying to find a bottle that might have some hair of the dog left in it, but they were all empty and his flask was in his jacket, half a world away on the other side of the room.

"He left me, Holly Ann. Probably the smartest thing the kid ever did. Hung around me much longer he would've died, just like my last apprentice. Tired of getting kids killed."

"So you have no idea where he is?"

Price screwed up his eyes.

"Why are you so interested all of a sudden?"

Kasprzak leaned against the kitchen counter.

"You know both you and the vampires come to me for information."

"Yeah…"

"Well, the word on the street is that Nico Salazar alive is worth his weight in gold right now."

"The kid? What the fuck for?"

"I was hoping you might tell me."

Price scowled.

"If I had to guess…I'd think it has something to do with Cicatrice's new…"

Price paused.

"What?"

"…Heir. He's dead, Holly Ann."

"Well, that's the rumor, but…"

"It's no rumor," he stated flatly. "Which means she's the matriarch now."

Kasprzak looked as if she was about to lay an egg. But before she could say anything else, a breathless Nico came hurtling into the apartment. He very nearly tumbled into the hole, but Price jumped up and grabbed him.

"What happened to the door? What happened to the floor?" Price shook him.

"Where you have been? Why'd you leave without telling me?"

Nico stared down at the floor and shuffled his feet.

"Remember how you told me not to be fooled? That vampires aren't people no matter how much they look like us?"

"Ah," Kasprzak said, "so the lad's got a case of coffin fever."

"You son of a bitch!"

Price slammed Nico in the stomach with the butt of his shotgun. He doubled over in pain and dropped a water bottle he had been carrying to the floor.

"That's for not listening to me."

He held out his hand and helped Nico to his feet.

"Jesus Christ," Nico muttered when he got his wind back, "you could've just said, 'Told you so.' What's the professor doing here?"

"She was worried about you, as it happens. Apparently you're the new toast of the underworld. Jesus, I need a drink."

Price grabbed the water bottle Nico had been carrying and unscrewed the cap. He put it to his lips.

"Don't drink that!"

"Why not?"

"It's holy water."

"Holy water? What the hell would you get holy water for, kid?"

Price replaced the cap and tossed it back to Nico.

"For…for fighting. Don't you two know what's going on?"

Kasprzak and Price exchanged a glance.

"What do you mean?"

"I mean…the city's on fire. They need us, Carter. They need us now. This…this is what the Inquisition is here for, isn't it?"

"If Cicatrice is dead, it would mean utter chaos in the vampire community," Kasprzak said, "I would recommend we all head down to the Aztec, *tout suite*. If anyone can put this genie back in the bottle, it'll be Cicatrice's new heir. Who…if I'm following everything correctly…you have a rather good relationship with, Nico?"

"Uh…that day has kind of passed."

"Well, sorry, kid, nobody likes talking to their ex, especially when they're a goddamned vampire matriarch, but the world's at stake, so you'd better swallow your pride." He hissed as he took a few steps. His leg was still bothering him. "I'm in no mood to walk. We'll take the Caddie."

"Let's just hope she hasn't done something stupid," Kasprzak said.

Price, Nico, and Kasprzak entered the Aztec. No guards stood to bar the way as they had before.

"What's going on here?" Kasprzak asked.

"I thought the guards had standing orders not to let Inquisitors through."

"Well, where the hell are they?" Price asked.

Price glanced at the booth where the guards normally stood. A telephone sat there, every single one of its dozen or so incoming call lights blinking an urgent red. He exchanged a glance with Nico.

"What? What is it?"

"I think your girlfriend did something stupid."

"Oh my," Kasprzak said, tugging on Price's jacket, "'stupid' doesn't begin to describe it."

The professor pointed at the cage in the center of the casino where chips and slips were turned into bills and coins. A hulking gray Damned vampire approached the cage.

"Shit!" Price said, pushing Kasprzak and Nico behind him as he drew his machete.

The coin-changing clerk had obviously been working in Vegas a long time. He took a glance at the strange gray monster and without batting an eye, said, "How many chips would you like, sir?"

The Damned reached between the bars of the cage and took hold of the clerk. He pulled him through, though his hips got caught where his head hadn't, and in spite of his screaming, ripped the clerk in half. The Damned held the torso of the poor clerk, even as the end of his spinal cord dangled, and granted him the Long Gift. Like a dead frog kicking its legs while being electrified, the half-clerk twitched and jerked in The Damned's embrace until finally the jagged bottom of his torso opened up like a floodgate and a wave of blood poured out. The Damned dropped the newly-minted half-vampire to the floor, where he pulled himself along furiously, afflicted by the hunger of all newly turned nightcrawlers.

"There's not just one," Kasprzak said, pointing.

Price glanced around the casino. No wonder all the guards had been called away. He counted no less than five Damned, stalking through the badly lit, loudly beeping place. The bings and pings of the hypnotizing machines and games which served in normal times to keep players focused on the games instead of the world outside were keeping them equally distracted from the encroaching carnage.

A tourist couple in Aloha shirts walked by the stunned Inquisitors.

"What's going on here, Bertie?" the man asked loudly.

"Must be some kind of a floorshow."

Price watched with terror as one of The Damned swooped down from the ceiling and snatched up the couple, one in each distended hand, and poured its dark power into them.

"We need to…we need to protect the people!" Nico cried out.

"The hell with that!" the professor exclaimed. "We need to protect ourselves. Let's get out of here!"

"Both of you, relax," Price said, trying to keep his breathing even.

The Damned were distracted by a smorgasbord of easy targets. Bluehairs lined up at the slot machines pulled away at levers, blissfully unaware of their disappearing neighbors as they traded their Social Security checks for paltry returns. They refused to even look up as their neighbors screamed their heads off. "There's only one safe place in this city right now. And we're only a few hundred feet from it."

He pointed at the gaudy plastic pyramid in the center of the Aztec. The distance between them and it was slick with blood and littered with bodily excretions and other effluvia.

Freshly-minted vampires and ghouls prowled the floor, the ghouls licking at the blood and gnawing the entrails, the vampires disinterested. All started to turn towards the three breathing heroes. It seemed they were surrounded.

"Only a football field," Kasprzak muttered, "but what a football field."

Nico swallowed a lump in his throat and hefted his bladed baseball bat.

"We have an advantage," Price said, "They're brand new which means they're weak. The lust for warm flesh is still on them so they'll lash out foolishly. We can make it."

"In any case we have no choice," Kasprzak said sourly.

Nico brandished his bat and pulled out the bottle of holy water and pressed it toward her.

"Do you need a weapon, Professor?"

"You may as well not even bother, son. Holy water is about the worst choice in vampire-fighting equipment."

"What…what do you mean?"

"Kid," Price said, "for a holy icon to work it has to be in contact with a person of faith. As soon as you toss that, it becomes nothing but regular water."

"Shit," he muttered under his breath, stuffing the bottle back into his pocket.

"Not to worry. I didn't come unprepared."

She unfurled the satchel from her shoulder and placed it on the ground. She busied herself for a moment constructing something. A moment later she rose with a device that resembled a long wand, with three rotating buzzsaw blades arranged vertically along its length. The handle was designed for two-handed use, to keep it steady and horizontal. Leave it to the curly-headed professor to be full of surprises.

"Gentlemen," she said, "if this is to be my last stand, I am proud to be making it with you."

"Likewise," Price said, nodding at his friend and his apprentice.

"Jesus," Nico shouted, "you two talk like we're dead already. I'm way too young and beautiful to die."

Price clapped Nico on the shoulder.

"Come on, pretty boy."

The three heroes plunged boldly forward, swinging and slashing their weapons. Price picked off a few ghouls with his shotgun, which sent the others scattering. The vampire who had been Bertie jumped at Nico, emboldened with fleshlust, and managed to duck a devastating swing from his bat. Once she was within his guard, his feet betrayed him and he slipped on a pool of blood, tumbling to the ground, his bat rolling away from him.

The vampiric tourist ripped at him like a dog with its favorite toy. Price hissed in empathy as she ripped four long chunks out of his face with her scrabbling fingers. He kicked her hard in the ribs, but even a brand-new vampire was not so susceptible to physical force. He hesitated to bring his machete down, worried that any swing that would take her head off would end up lodged in Nico's chest.

Luckily, Kasprzak felt no such compunction. With clinical precision she brought her whirring blades down gently on Bertie's neck and watched as the vampire's throat pulverized below her. When the vampire stopped moving, she lifted the buzzsaw away. Nico shook off his burden like a dog shaking off the rain and rose to his feet, grabbing Price's hand for help.

Nico turned and nearly instantly returned the favor, smashing his bat into the face of a ghoul loping towards Kasprzak's back, arms outstretched like a mummy. The ghoul toppled to the ground, dead.

"Hey, these gray things are a bit easier than the regular vamps," Nico said.

"No shortage of those either."

The monsters began to scatter as they realized their easy meal was more porcupine than bunny. Nico nearly took the first step of the plastic pyramid on the chin, but Price grabbed him and helped to prop him up. The three humans stumbled up the steps and plunged inside. Cicatrice's inner sanctum, which had been previously buzzing with activity, was eerily quiet. A few emergency lights glowed, and there were signs of struggle and leftover body parts hinting at the fate of his renfields, but the room was otherwise empty.

Nico ran his hand across his head, presumably to wipe away sweat, but it came away bloody.

"Wow, that was easy."

"Fuck," Price said, angrily throwing his machete to the ground with a clang.

"Fuck, indeed," Kasprzak agreed, nodding.

"What? What am I missing? We made it. Didn't we?"

"You're missing the big picture, kid," Price said. "We made it, yes. But those things are loose in the city now. The Damned are dangerous but if they're turning people then now the city's going to start getting clogged with newly-turned vampires and ghouls. And they'll all be afflicted by the hunger."

"Usually a vampire chooses his get—his offspring—with great care and watches over them carefully," Kasprzak explicated, "but these vampires haven't learned the code. They'll go wild and feast on every person in sight. With The Damned loose we could be looking at the vampire population to approach near-epidemic levels. And with the newborns left unchecked the slaughter will be historic."

"Then the city is..." Nico started.

"Fucked."

THIRTY-THREE

A thump came at Damiana's door.

"Go away," Sephera said loudly, "we're not to be disturbed."

The second thump smashed the massive doors to splinters, like an icicle shattering. Damiana rose from her seat at the head of the table, her hand tucked reflexively into her chest like a chicken wing. Sephera dropped to her knees behind the table, one of the ridiculous ray guns the Teslans always seemed to be working on in her hands and leveled at the intruder.

"It's best that you see me now."

As the smoke and debris cleared, a diminutive figure resolved in the doorway. Damiana didn't recognize her, but had a suspicion whom she was.

"Dramatics like this aren't necessary, Matriarch," Damiana said.

"Funny," Idi Han said as she stepped over the threshold, "It wasn't more than a few days ago that your patriarch and that woman there pointing a weapon at me did much the same to intrude on my manse. Unbidden. Unwanted."

"Sephera," Damiana said quietly, "would you kindly lower whatever that thing is?"

Sighing, the Teslan rose from her defensive stance and lowered the ray gun, but didn't toss it away.

"Mother Idi Han," Damiana said, "I think you'll find that I am not my old patriarch."

The tiny woman stepped more ambitiously into the dining room. She ran her finger along the back of a chair and examined the mechanism for moving meals around the table. Finally she settled on lowering her hands in a clump at the small of her back.

"No, I guess you're not. I assume you're the one everyone calls 'the lepress.' May I ask your real name?"

"Damiana."

"Is that your birth name or one you acquired after being brought across?"

"It is a false name. We Signaris can choose whether to keep our old names or not."

"I was never given such a choice. But I think I understand now why."

"Yes. It's a tradition in your House. There is much to recommend tradition. And the code."

Idi Han smiled. It was a cold, mirthless smile.

"I suppose you're referring to the old canard 'immortals do not kill immortals?'" Idi Han put her hands on the back of a chair and squeezed, splintering the wood into forms shaped like her hands. "You have nothing to fear on that front from me, Damiana."

"I wish you would have extended that same courtesy to my patriarch."

Damiana limped over to a shelf on the wall and retrieved Father Otto's sword. She tossed it forcefully onto the table.

"Kings don't kill kings, isn't that right?" Idi Han said. "And yet your patriarch arranged to kill mine."

"We can hardly be held responsible for the actions of the mortal Inquisitors," Sephera grunted.

"Nevertheless, I consider it a score settled, not a dangling thread."

"And what about the five hundred immortals from every House that Cicatrice ordered killed?" Sephera grumbled, "Are those a settled score as well?"

"I can hardly be held responsible for the actions of the mortal Inquisitors."

"Cute. Very cute."

"Enough, Sephera," Damiana said. "What does bring you to my manse this evening, Mother Idi Han?"

"Well, Mother Damiana..." Idi Han waited to see if she

would protest the title. Damiana simply raised her hand, where she had managed to jam the obsidian ring of stewardship onto her deformed thumb. "…as you've probably guessed my business is not exactly settled this evening."

"The city is in flames," Sephera said, "and the Damned are on the wing. There'll be no cover-up this time. Not even Cicatrice at the height of his power could've covered this up. An entire mortal city destroyed. And you're worried about what exactly? Settling old scores?"

"Topan," Damiana said.

"Yes," Idi Han agreed.

Damiana struggled into a seat and folded her arms as best she could.

"If we were still doing business in the old way I'd make a bunch of protestations about why you came to me looking for your old sire and what he's worth to you and so on and so forth and we would probably dance about for the rest of the night. But I was never as partial to humiliating repartee as Father Otto was. The truth is we all know Topan is here, hiding, a lost princeling who thinks the Signaris are going to crown him as a puppet patriarch. So let's say we dispense with all of that."

"Fine with me," Idi Han agreed.

"The question is, how do you go forward? As Sephera pointed out, the old way of doing things is over. We can't hide in the shadows any more. You've seen to that, haven't you?"

"Has it occurred to you that perhaps that's for the best?"

Damiana reached out and placed her hand on the pommel of Father Otto's sword.

"Father Otto and Cicatrice hated each other as no two men in history ever have. And yet they saw eye-to-eye on this: the code, the vast web of misdirection, secrecy, hiding. Now our whole way of life is endangered. People will be looking for us. Not just the Inquisition. Everyone now."

"Perhaps we should have revealed ourselves long ago."

"Madness," Sephera said.

"I agree the world is ours to inherit," Damiana said, "but caution and prudence have served us for almost a thousand years."

Idi Han took a seat.

"I feel like I'm being lectured. And I know that's probably not what's going on here. Because if we were trading lectures, I would probably say that the twelve Houses that turned against us upended seven hundred years of tradition and…what was it? Caution and prudence? All scrabbling for short-term gain. That you all tested the resolve of House Cicatrice and found it not wanting. That you all brought a plague down upon yourselves. So I know that we're not going to lecture each other. I think we're just going to come to a new way of moving forward."

Damiana raised Father Otto's sword so that the blade was before her nose.

"I swear by the Sword of Signari whatever hostilities, whatever mistrust once existed between our Houses…is at a conclusion."

They both looked to Sephera. She nodded.

"The rest of the council will not pursue war without House Signari on our side."

"Then it seems we have peace…if you wish it."

"I do wish it. In exchange for one small indulgence."

"Topan?"

"Yes."

"You would've been better off asking for something else. I have no love for that piece of shit. He's hiding in his guest chambers. Down the hall, past Father Otto's. You'll recognize Father Otto's."

Idi Han rose.

"Good evening."

Idi Han twisted the door handle to the patriarch's opulent visiting quarters, easily breaking the lock. She stepped inside and saw Topan was already crouching in the open windowframe.

"Idi Han," he whispered.

"Were you planning to leave?"

He glanced out the window at Las Vegas below. Damiana's manse was actually the top three floors of the Hotel Citroën, billed as luxury suites booked for years in advance to the public.

"I suppose if you're here—unmolested, as it seems—my hostess has grown tired of me."

"You could put it that way."

He sighed.

"Not a lot of places left for me to run, then, are there?"

She held out her hand.

"Come inside, Topan."

He glanced out the window again.

"If you run, I'll find a way to make it worse."

He looked at her.

"I'm not so sure there's anything worse than what you're going to do to me."

"I'd find a way."

He stepped back in and sat down on the edge of the bed.

"Where will it be?"

"There's a pit beneath the Aztec. I'll probably drop you in there."

"Ah, yes. El Dorado. The Aztec temple. You know, he never let me see it. He said one day when I was ready it would be mine."

"But you were never ready."

He smashed his fist into his other hand.

"Do you have any idea what that's like? Pure mediocrity? To be held back by your own lack of potential? Nothing I could ever do would ever make me special like you. Not even finding you."

"There comes a time when you either excel or you don't."

"I thought I had excelled once. I brokered the truce between us and the Inquisition. That led to half a century of House Cicatrice expanding without any meaningful opposition. You would think that would be enough for him to trust me. But then twenty years ago he called me back in and said I was to go back to being his apprentice. Demoted. And then ten years ago he released me again and said he didn't care what I did."

He looked up at her, his eyes shining with the look of a broken dog or a child that had never been praised. She sat down and put her hand in his hair, and gently lowered his head to her lap.

"I know what you want, Topan. I know what you need. I understand the closure you're looking for."

"You do?" he whispered.

She nodded, though he couldn't see that. She stroked his hair like a pet's.

"You want me to say that I understand all that you did. That in the end, I forgive you, even if Cicatrice never could. That he never forgave you for being mediocre, that he saw in you all of his own worst impulses and that that wasn't fair and that that wasn't you and that you deserve to be judged on your own merits. And that you understand the punishment you're about to receive, but that this is the closure you need first."

He nodded. She patted his head one last time then wrapped her fingers around his throat. She crushed every vertebra in his neck with a single sharp snap and pressed his protesting face into her lap, like a deranged mother smothering her child.

"Well I'm not going to give any of that to you. I grant you nothing. Not peace of mind. Not absolution. Not even forgiveness. You were a failure. You were judged a failure by a man who never showed you anything but leniency. And worse than that, you were a traitor."

Topan struggled, slapping at her as best he could with his arms, but she ignored the blows as though they were mosquito stings.

"I don't forgive you for what you did to me. You were not special for discovering me. You were like a conquistador, claiming a land of plenty for his own as though he had conjured it out of thin air. I was always there. I was always me. You? You aren't special because of me.

"And you are going to suffer the worst fate there is. I'm going to crucify you on a pair of I-beams and bronze you in liquid metal. And then I'm going to toss your still-living body into a bottomless pit to be forgotten and to suffer forever. And here above you'll be erased from the history books. Your name will be scratched out of all records. All anyone will know is that Cicatrice was succeeded by Idi Han, and no one stood between them. All of that and you won't even have the solace of being told I forgive you or that Cicatrice never stopped loving you.

Because I don't. And he did."

Finally she let him up. He looked into her face, his mind racing and fevered.

"I'm sorry," he whispered.

"Yes," she agreed, "You are sorry."

THIRTY-FOUR

Price pushed open the door to Cicatrice's conference room.

"Idi Han," he said in a sing-song voice, leading the way into the room with his shotgun instead of his face.

He peeked around the door. The room was a nightmarescape of inside-out people but the one he was looking for was missing.

"Damn," he said, turning back, "We should decide whether we're going to hunker down in here or…"

Price stopped dead in his tracks. Nico was on his knees. Behind him, Kasprzak held two pistols, one leveled at Price and one jammed in the back of Nico's head.

"Your blade, Carter."

Price looked down at his machete. Briefly, he considered whether tossing it would manage to connect with the professor, but that was all theatrics and he'd never been any good at that sort of thing. He let it slip out of his fingers and clatter to the ground.

"My blade but not my gun?"

Kasprzak grunted out something akin to a laugh.

"Use it if you want."

There was not much chance of Nico not getting caught in the blast. And anyway, Price suddenly had a nagging suspicion that the weapon wouldn't do much good against his old friend anyway. He dropped it into his leg holster.

"You're one of them."

Kasprzak nodded. She reached up and opened her blouse to reveal a plate of armor lying flat across her breast. She lifted it to show her mark of Cicatrice.

"Have been for a long time."

"How long?"

"A long time. You know Cicatrice liked to know things. And that was always the impossibility about you damned Inquisitors. Can't be bribed, can't be bought. So damned idealistic. You're easy to play, though. And now the whole house of cards is coming tumbling down."

"What's that supposed to mean?"

She smiled wickedly.

"I've got files back in my office on just about every Inquisitor in the country. It's taken nearly a century. But for what it's worth, you were right, Carter. If you'd stuck to the cell system, you would've been nearly impossible to hunt down. Bonaparte's aggression made for a string I can pull until the whole sweater unfurls. Now that The Damned are loose, the Inquisition is the last thing standing between us and total global dominance. Time for us to step out of the shadows."

"I worked with you. I trusted you. I thought you were my friend."

Kasprzak shrugged.

"Maybe you knew deep in your heart. But maybe you also knew what I knew when I was just a mortal scholar. In the end, the immortals win this war. So I want to be on the winning side. I'll never die now. But you will. Why fight a futile battle, Carter?"

"Because there are still things worth dying for."

Kasprzak tapped Nico's head.

"Cute. The matriarch wants this one alive. Not sure if as a lover or a get. Maybe both. Come on, boy."

Nico rose in spite of the gun to his head. He turned and faced Kasprzak.

"Fuck you. I'll stand with Price. I'd rather die an Inquisitor."

"Well, the matriarch was pretty clear on this point."

Kasprzak cold-cocked Nico with the gun and as he passed out, she tossed him over her shoulder like he weighed nothing. She stared at Price.

"Not going to protest?"

"No," he whispered, "I want the boy to live, too."

"Good enough. But as for you...The Damned would like a word."

From the infinite inky blackness behind Kasprzak, a hulking gray vampire with sagging, desiccated breasts emerged and gripped Kasprzak's shoulder. In her wake, ten other creatures of similar appearance emerged. Kasprzak gripped her temples as though in the throes of a migraine. She turned to the female leader of The Damned.

"Yes, mistress, this is the one."

Kasprzak was struck by another sudden headache, and belatedly Price realized they were communicating with her telepathically or something. She turned to Price.

"I told them that you had something to do with the death of one of their own. It was rather important to them to settle this account personally." She shrugged. "Good luck, Carter. I always did enjoy our conversations. You're not bad for a mortal, but, sadly, that's all you'll ever be. My lords and ladies."

With a bow, Kasprzak disappeared. Price turned his attention to the encroaching monsters. There was no question of reaching for his fallen blade or even for the firearm rather more comfortably hanging at his side. The fight was absolutely hopeless. He had faced a single Damned and barely been able to escape with his life, let alone defeat it. Eleven may as well have been an army.

He set his teeth, balled his fists, and to his surprise, smiled.

"I'd love to hear a little disco. But either way…let's dance."

Price came out swinging but didn't even land a blow. In a split-second, The Damned were on top of him, their snatching hands restraining his limbs and forcing him to the ground. Who knew what gruesome punishments they felt fitting recompense for the loss of one of their own?

"I hope you choke on me, you bastards!"

THIRTY-FIVE

Nico awoke with a start, heart racing arhythmically. He had been draped like a piece of laundry over a pair of metal trash cans in a dank alley. He glanced around, his eyes not yet accustomed to the darkness, but he didn't like what he could hear.

Voices, a million voices, were hissing in the darkness all around him. The world seemed to swirl in circles around him. Eyes glowed, red, yellow, and white as a mob of vampires pressed in towards him. He climbed up onto one of the trash cans and snatched the lid off the other to wield as a shield.

Kasprzak emerged from the crowd, beating back at the newborn vampires with Nico's baseball bat.

"Out of the way! Out of the way! Back, you bastards!"

She led a ghoul, glistening with what seemed like a fresh coat of slime and wearing the uniform of a police officer. She had wrapped the ghoul-cop's belt around his neck to use as a leash.

She gave Nico a toothy smile.

"What's going on?" Nico asked.

"Vampirism is like a virus, Nico. It spreads and it spreads and it spreads. Up until now certain factors have kept us in check—natural immunity, you might say. But those days are over. Why don't you come down from that silly spot and join me?"

She held out her hand.

"Go to Hell."

Kasprzak chuckled.

"Oh, I don't have to. It won't be long now till Hell comes to

Earth. Look how long it took to turn the whole city. Hours. In a month the world will be ours. I've been expecting this for years. I had just been waiting for Cicatrice to let loose The Damned. I admit I'm surprised it turned out to be that bitch get of his."

Nico nearly lunged off his perch, but the vampires all surged forward at the idea, and he retreated.

"Ah! So you do care about her. I could let them rip you to shreds, Nico. But the matriarch doesn't want that. She wants to spend eternity with you. You've been fast-tracked to be granted The Long Gift."

"By you?"

Kasprzak chuckled. She reached down and stroked the ghoul-cop under its chin.

"No, not by me. I'm still a bit too green to be much skilled at turning others. In all the chaos tonight I thought I may as well practice a bit, but unfortunately old Kolchak here was the best I could do. Mother Idi Han doesn't want you to turn out like this. She'll either do it herself or have one of her most trusted oldbloods do it. You'll be fine, Nico."

"'Fine.' You call being a bloodsucking fiend 'fine?'"

Kasprzak's expression darkened.

"You're as stubborn as I was at your age. But wait until you're just a little bit older. Bit by bit death becomes a reality instead of a far-off nightmare. There'll come a time when you won't hesitate to sacrifice others to keep yourself alive. Even if it means sacrificing every other person in the world."

"Sounds like a real jolly philosophy. Look around you, prof. This isn't sustainable. Slaughter everyone? How are you even going to feed yourselves?"

"Oh, there are ways, Nico. The Necropolis had a booming system of agriculture. Humans can be farmed. And just think about the advances we'll make. Just like industrial farming today. Chickens don't need beaks. They just peck each other. Veal cows don't need to stand. Imagine humanity downgraded from masters of the earth to livestock. What do you need arms or legs or a cock for? They're just extremities siphoning off precious blood. That's the future. But that doesn't have to be your future, Nico. The matriarch wants you by her side. You won't get another chance like this. Most people never do."

Nico pursed his lips.

"Maybe you're right."

"Of course I'm right."

Nico took her hand, and like Baryshnikov she lifted him bodily and set him on the ground. Nico let the pin clatter to the ground and dropped the garlic grenade.

"But I don't want to live in that world."

As white smoke that smelled like an Italian bistro filled the alley, Nico pushed and shoved his way through the scrum. It seemed he had chosen his moment wisely. The newborns were particularly confused to suddenly be unable to "smell" their prey.

"Idiots!" he heard Kasprzak shouting as he managed to shove his way out into the street, "It's just garlic! Grab him! Don't let him escape! The matriarch will have my ass."

The city was on fire. Gunfights raged in the distance, smoke rose from half the buildings. Screams and madness filled the air. Thinking fast, Nico wrenched a manhole up off the ground and slithered down into the sewer.

Nico had spent the better part of the day before in the sewers and hoped that he might come across some landmarks to help him figure a way out of this scrape. He pounded down the corridor as fast as he could.

Where should I go? They've probably cordoned off the city. If I can prove I'm still human, that might be the best way to find help.

Kasprzak's voice echoed through the underground.

"Where are you going to run to, Nico? Give up now and make it easy on yourself. You could be one of the greats, you know! You know why we turn Inquisitors? Because they make the best vampires!"

Nico felt his resolve harden. He spotted an overturned coffin he thought might have belonged to a gang of Druids.

No. I'm not going to run. Price is back at the Aztec. He needs my help if he's not already dead. And if he is, he may need it even more.

He didn't relish the thought of putting down his friend, but it was no doubt something that occurred to every Inquisitor at some point. Suddenly he hit a dead-end. A crosspipe with a crank faucet blocked the entire passageway. Nico turned around to go back the way he had come, but it was already too late.

Shadows flickered in the depths. A host of vampires turned a corner, Kasprzak in the lead, with her pet ghoul Kolchak on a string. Nico was confronted with a wall of vampires in front of him and a wall of pipe behind him. Above his head, a faucet dripped, as though ticking off his last remaining seconds on this earth.

THIRTY-SIX

Price pinched his eyes shut and ground his teeth together.

This is it. I won't give them the satisfaction of screaming. At least I'll go out like a man.

A loud clomp suddenly cut through the hisses of The Damned. The claws clutching at him stilled. He ventured to open his eyes. To a one, each of The Damned had turned their heads 90 degrees towards the front of the conference room. Price turned, too, just as a second clomp cut through the stillness.

Outside the entrance to the room, astride a massive charger with one foot raised to slap down a third time, sat The Hunter of the Dead. The breath caught in Price's throat as he thought to himself that there was no way this could be a faker or a pretender. The man—the thing—was like an inkblot smudged on the surface of reality.

The Damned rose, almost releasing their grips on Price's clothes as an afterthought. He was forgotten. One of The Damned reached out, grabbed the conference table which was bolted to the floor, and flung it through the bulletproof glass windows. It smashed to splinters in the chaotic confusion of the casino below.

The Hunter tucked his spur into his horse's flank and it pressed forward, smashing a horse-and-rider shaped hole in the wall like something out of a Bugs Bunny cartoon. With this larger-than-life figure in it and twelve grotesque monstrosities the conference room suddenly seemed dreadfully small.

Price glanced around, wondering if there was somewhere to hide, wondering, in fact, if hiding would even matter. If the window frame wasn't still lined with jagged glass that would have cut his hands to ribbons, he would've considered sneaking out that way.

Then again, how often do you get to witness a grudge match like this?

The Damned who had tossed the conference table so heedlessly growled and leapt across the room, covering the whole distance in a single bound. As bulky and unwieldy as a suit of armor made him, The Hunter seemed to have no trouble snatching The Damned out of the air, impaling it on his lance. The Damned's own momentum drove it the rest of the way down the lance, until it and The Hunter were practically face-to-face.

The impaled Damned hissed, its tongue writhing lasciviously in the air, even catching The Hunter's helm and licking some of the oily goo from it. The Hunter sliced its head off. The rest of The Damned backed up, forming a semi-circle, and Price suddenly realized that he was in the keystone position, directly across from The Hunter.

Oh shit.

The Hunter dropped his lance and drew his sword across the gauntlet of his opposite hand, raising a shower of sparks. One of the sparks caught the oily substance coating the sword, causing it to erupt into flames. The Damned shrank back from the fiery apparition, and Price watched as the two nearest the broken window dove out for safety.

The black knight charged down the center of the room, straight towards him. Price dove out of the way, rolling towards one corner as best he could. The Hunter pulled his horse to the right, and swept in an arc, hacking and slashing at each of The Damned as he came. The fire spread with each step, consuming the knight's armor and finally igniting the horse.

Each of The Damned screeched as they struck out futilely at their attacker, their normally devastating blows reduced to a child's tantrum. Blade cut through flesh and fire caught their sallow hides. The Hunter was transformed into an avenging demon, inferno made flesh. Price had never heard a horse scream, and in a way, the death cries of the Hunter's mount as it was consumed by fire were even more horrific than the unholy roars of The Damned.

The Hunter cut the Damned down one by one, even as his horse collapsed and died underneath him. When he fell, only one of The Damned remained, and it watched, transfixed, as the tar-like substance was used up, and The Hunter was reduced to a smoldering pile of metal covered by a mound of horseflesh.

Price felt his heart racing a mile a minute, and didn't know if he would be able to bring a word to his lips even if he wanted to. The Damned were monstrosities but the devastation he had just witnessed raised something akin to pity even for them in his heart. The last of The Damned tentatively approached the smoking pile that a moment before had been an avatar of fury, striking down its brothers and sisters in wrath.

The Hunter flipped the ton of charred horsemeat off of him as though kicking off a twisted blanket. The Damned didn't even have time to shriek as he shoved his sword up through its missing jaw and into its brainpan. He rose, lifting The Damned off the ground as though he had skewered a shish kebab.

The last of The Damned struggled in agony, trying to pull itself off the sword which had been thrust through its brain, but when The Hunter raised it off its feet, it no longer had the purchase it required. He reached out with his free hands and pulled its arms off as though plucking the wings off a fly.

He punched through The Damned's stomach and pulled out a handful of intestines and let them spill to the floor, where more and more of its guts piled out afterward. The thing practically seemed to be sobbing before he finally reached out and with a pinch of his gauntlet separated its head from its torso.

Then The Hunter spotted Price.

THIRTY-SEVEN

Kasprzak swung right and left with Nico's bat, bashing heads in and knocking teeth out. The angry mob of vampires and ghouls was hard to hold back, but they obviously respected strength, and Kasprzak was a powerful vampire. She turned to look at him.

"This is foolishness, Nico. Surely it's better to give in. At this point do you have a choice?"

Nico shook his head and sighed loudly.

"How could you, Professor? Knowing what you know? Knowing what these things are? How could you willfully join them?"

Kasprzak shook her head.

"Knowing what I know? You have no idea what I know, little boy. Let me tell you something: did you know that every choice you make results in the creation of another universe where you made the opposite choice? Everything you could have ever possibly done somewhere out there you did.

"And that's not some new age bullshit, either. That's science. Rock hard fact. Quantum physicists can't explain the way sub-atomic particles function unless this is true. Every choice you make is a coin flip and every coin flip creates another reality where heads was tails or tails was heads.

"When you're young, when you're a teenager or in your twenties, the world's your oyster. Everything's ahead of you. Stretched out before you are an infinite number of possibilities. You could be the president or you could be a massage therapist."

"Or a tenured professor?"

Her eyes gleamed and she smiled falsely.

"Or a professor! Yes! But then you know what happens when you start making those choices? You start closing off all those other realities. And then you find yourself in your thirties or your forties and you realize that all those choices you made when you were a goddamned teenager ended up being your path. And there's no straying from the path. You can rage against it, you can have a mid-life crisis and buy a sports car or fuck a cute TA, but there's no leaving the path. And you realize that all those millions of opportunities you used to have are now just weights around your neck. Because there's just this.

"And maybe you didn't pick the right path. Maybe you didn't pick the one true path. Maybe destiny is real and maybe you were supposed to end up a deli manager, Nico. But you were young enough to choose to be a vampire hunter instead. And becoming old and realizing that you'll never become all those things you could've become? It's a fate worse than death."

Kasprzak lowered the baseball bat to the ground. The newborns and the ghouls seemed oddly focused on her, like animals craving the attention of their master. In a lower voice she continued.

"Then imagine someone comes along and says you can have a new life. And they're not a huckster and they're not a Bible thumper or a self-help book writer just after your dollars for a pretty lie. They're offering you a new life. A genuine chance to become something you never were before. Not just that, but another lifetime. Another lifetime to reinvent yourself and another lifetime after that, and another and another and another. You think you know so much about the world, Nico? You're twenty. Come back to me when you've lived in it a little while."

"Yeah. I might be ignorant like you said. And I'm sure not old and depressed yet. And I get it. Everyone gets old and depressed and regrets their youth. And there're some people like you who'd trade their soul to the devil to change things. But I know somebody else like that."

"You mean Carter Price? The man-child who wishes it was still the '70s? Who's never had a real job in his life?"

"You're goddamn right. He fucked up his youth just as bad

as you. Worse, by the looks of it. But the difference between you two is, no matter how shitty his life got, he never stopped trying to live it. And I'd rather go out like Price. In any reality."

Kasprzak laughed.

"Well, the matriarch can't say I didn't try. There's no miracle that'll save you now, Nico."

"Yeah, well, God helps those who help themselves."

Nico turned and yanked on the red crank wheel behind him. A light spray opened up from the sewer pipe blocking his path, and as he yanked it harder the blast turned into a punishing wall of water, striking Kasprzak and the solid center of her minions and pushing them back.

Nico stood to one side as the torrent flooded the passageway. In a few seconds the water rose and dampened his pants. The flood rose almost to his knee before the water ran dry, diverted from whatever mysterious path of sewery architecture it had been stolen from. The swarm of monsters before him were drenched and waterlogged, and many of the ones in the path of the pipe had been knocked over.

Kasprzak clambered to her feet.

"Impotent," she growled. "Petty. You're a poster boy for the whole Inquisition. Rip him apart!"

She pointed in his direction, as if releasing a pack of war hounds.

"Oh, woops," he said, "Forgot the most important ingredient."

He unscrewed the cap of his bottle of holy water and let it drop into the floodwater below. Like electricity passing through a current, his faith was channeled through the holy icon...which had become a flood, drenching every vampire and ghoul in the assembled mob.

The newborns shrieked, pulling at their wet clothes, trying to get them off. Their legs, sunk ankle-deep in holy water, burned, causing them to drop to their hands and knees, which burned them further.

Nico watched in wonder as every drop of water that touched the skin of every one of the vampires burned, sizzling and smoking. In fact, the passageway was filling with acrid smoke.

Much as he wanted to stay, he was pretty confident that the holy water wouldn't kill the monsters outright, and that its potency was likely to fade as it dispersed. It was best to be gone before that happened.

He snatched his bat up from where Kasprzak had dropped it and hurried over to a metal ladder leading up to the surface. Suddenly he felt a hand around his ankle. He looked down to see Kasprzak, her body looking like a skinless burn victim's. She had been soaked from head to toe in the initial torrent.

"You mortal scum," she screeched through her dissolving face.

"Sorry, Professor," he said, "I'd meant to spare you this."

He brought the bat down and lopped her hand off at the wrist.

"But I hear those ghouls don't much care what they eat. Maybe you could've been a million things, but turns out you're just carrion."

He swung the bat again like a golf club and severed her head.

As soon as Nico's body left the water entirely, it was like flipping a switch. The newborns and the ghouls, though not instantly healed, were no longer burning like in acid. And as Nico had suspected, a number of ghouls, including the cop-ghoul Kolchak, immediately spotted the chunky mess that had become of their erstwhile mistress. As he mounted the ladder, he heard the sound of the ghouls tearing away at Kasprzak's severed hand, head, and the remnants of her body.

THIRTY-EIGHT

Smoke still wafted out from between the plates of The Hunter's armor. Behind the scorched faceplate his face was inscrutable. Price felt a twitch in his hand.

You're getting old, mate.

"Fuck it," he spat out.

He reached into his deerskin jacket and pulled out his flask. He poured what was left into his mouth and, as if by a miracle, the twitch disappeared.

"You want to tangle, old timer? Why not? You wouldn't be the first mythical beast to try to fuck with me today."

Price grabbed his machete and unsheathed it. Almost as soon as it was clear he felt a sharp pain and could've sworn his hand had been cut clean off, but when he looked down he saw that the machete had been simply knocked away so fast his wrist had nearly shattered. The machete flew out the missing window and planted itself in the middle of a roulette wheel, flopping from side to side.

The Hunter reached out and wrapped his gauntleted hand around Price's throat. Price scrabbled at the armored forearms of the giant, but could not find any purchase. With his windpipe squeezed shut yellow cigarette burns began to appear in the air, quickly followed by great black splotches.

As if it was happening to somebody else, he felt the Hunter drag him over to the missing window and push him out, holding him up in the air over the casino. Price pounded desperately against the armored menace, but to no avail. As The Hunter squeezed, preparing to snap his neck, one final thought occurred to him.

Show him your ink.

Price raised his arm up into the air, fist balled, hoping that his tasseled sleeves would fall away far enough to reveal his Inquisition tattoo.

Come on, you son of a bitch. We're on the same side. Why do you kill Inquisitors, too?

The world seesawed around him and if the sight of the green cross made any impression on The Hunter, he didn't let it show. Suddenly the blood came whooshing back into his ears and the air surged into his lungs as The Hunter released his grip. Unfortunately, that also meant that the floor was coming rushing up towards Price at a violent speed.

Price's leg caught on the last step of the plastic pyramid, but the rest of him splashed down into the artificial moat below. In movies, water always seemed to make for a miraculously soft landing for heroes, but Price felt the wind knocked out of him as the surface of the water slammed into his back. It was softer than the floor, perhaps, but not particularly soft.

Why didn't he kill me?

The answer came as he surfaced, gasping for air and looking back up at the pyramid from which he had just fallen. Ghouls and newborn vampires were scaling the steps of the pyramid, eager for flesh and viscera. They either smelled the remains of Cicatrice's dismembered circle or else thought The Hunter was a new target. Whatever the reason, they were pouring into the conference room, hanging off The Hunter's arms and legs, trying to bite through his charred armor.

Sucks for them. A lucky break for me, I guess.

Groaning from the fall which had reminded him of how fucked up his leg had been, he splashed out of the moat and onto the casino floor.

Two sets of yellow eyes immediately appeared before him.

"It's just one thing after the other with you fucking people, isn't it? If you two want to throw down now, I'm going to need a drink."

Price pushed between the two remaining Damned and limped over to the nearest table where a serving girl (her face had been pulled clean off her skull) had collapsed with a tray of drinks. He grabbed the nearest one and downed it.

"Yech," he said, making a face, "Mai tai."

He turned back to see The Damned, no longer confused by his impertinence, advancing on him. Behind them, staying tentatively back from their masters probably more out of fear than respect, a small army of ghouls and newborns was gathering. Overhead, The Hunter was ripping through their ranks like tissue paper, sending the tide of bodies that had been climbing the pyramid right back down in fear, and straight towards Price.

"Better stay back," he said, plucking the cocktail umbrella out of his last drink and jabbing the pointy end in their direction, "I *will* use this."

Judging by her shriveled grey breasts, The Damned on Price's left had once been a woman. It lunged at him and he immediately dropped to the ground and rolled, hoping that it had gotten a mouthful of felt and wood. He popped back up on the other side, forcing himself to remain spry despite the pain zigzagging through his leg. He was exactly where he wanted to be.

Well, not exactly. Exactly where I want to be is a beach in Tahiti. Then again, those bastards might be serving mai tais.

To his delight, the female Damned did indeed headbutt the gaming table to his front. She looked up angrily, her tongue lolling disgustingly out of her throat.

"On second thought, maybe I'll use this."

Price grabbed the handle of his machete from the table behind him and recovered it with a snap of his wrist, which sent the roulette wheel flying into the crowd of baby nightcrawlers and also reminded Price of the sprain or strain or whatever that The Hunter had just given him.

God damn I'm getting old. Well, probably won't get much older at this point.

The female Damned tentatively began to crawl over the table with the de-faced waitress. Her partner, a bit less adventurous, slowly followed her lead. The ghouls and the newborns began to encircle him, some crawling under the tables and others flowing down the spaces between the tables like deadly lava floes.

Hissing at the pain in his leg and his wrist, Price clambered up onto the roulette table. It was no good having his legs taken out from under him while he was concentrating on The Damned. Besides, how many Inquisitors got to make a crazy last stand on top of a roulette table?

"I'll tell you what. You want me?"

Price let his deerskin jacket drop to the table. Not wanting to pull it over his head and blind himself for even a split-second, he sliced through his undershirt with the machete and let that fall away, too. Hisses of pain came in unison from all sides.

The green cross of the Inquisition was the least of Price's tattoos. His entire back, chest, one sleeve, and one half-sleeve were covered with liturgical tattoos. Crosses, saints, scenes from the Bible, depictions of Christ and the destruction of evil by the will of God. Price's entire body was a holy symbol and all the vampires backed away from the glorious vision in fear.

"Come and get me."

The lesser vampires cowered in fear and pain. He slashed and slashed down into them, lopping off heads left and right, trying his damnedest not to let his machete get caught in one of their skulls. Finally the female Damned leapt up on the roulette table. Price tried to take a swipe at it in the air but missed.

My wrist is really killing me.

In retaliation, The Damned brought its arm slashing down sideways and gouged four jagged stripes out of Price's face. Grunting, Price slashed again and again with his machete, but The Damned parried each blow with its forearm. Each time the machete struck the thing's wrists, the wound immediately began to heal.

Emboldened ghouls and newborns scrabbled at his feet, trying to trip him up. The blood from his wounds began to pour into his eyes, coloring everything red.

Fuck. This is it, I guess.

The leering visage of the female Damned hovered into view as he tried to blink the blood out of his eyes. He lost almost all sense of direction and perspective. Suddenly he felt a blast of warm, fetid air in his face. The Damned's hands clamped down on his shoulders. The blood disappeared from his eyes for an instant as he felt an icy slug of a tongue lick the blood away.

The female Damned pressed its forehead to his.

You're going to suffer for what you did to The Seer.

Who are you?

I had a name once. Now I'm just an Executioner.

You're in my head.

Yes. I'm going to tear your mind apart like tissue paper. And then all these lesser rabble can have your body.

If you're in my head, can you see what I see?

A psychic shriek filled Price's ears (brain?) as their mind-link broke. The Hunter of the Dead had wrapped his gauntleted fingers around The Executioner's head and peeled her away from Price. The Damned struggled, shrieking in his grip. Price didn't hesitate. He thrust the machete into her throat, cut left, then swiped back right, severing the ligaments that bound her head to her body even as they healed.

Price dropped down on the other side of the roulette table, making sure that it was between him and The Hunter. He glanced around to see the ghouls and newborns scrambling away from The Hunter's wrath, like cockroaches when the kitchen light comes on. The last of The Damned was scampering away with them, scaling the walls like Spider-Man and disappearing through a skylight that had not been a part of the building's original design.

Price watched as the roulette table rose up in the air as though possessed. It seemed to hover there for a moment, before it came crashing down. The Hunter held only a jagged wooden table leg from the table he had just smashed to matchsticks. Price scrambled backwards, crabwalking until he ran into another table leg.

"These things are bolted down," he muttered.

Then he felt the table leg jab into his ribcage. He reached out and grabbed it, trying to push it away from his heart. Had The Hunter mistaken him for a vampire? Could he no longer tell the difference? Is that why he killed humans and vampires indiscriminately?

Price stopped struggling when he realized that The Hunter had pressed the flat edge of the table leg into his chest. Price was breathing heavily, his body glistening with sweat. He looked up into The Hunter's inexpressive mask.

The Hunter peeled off his chestplate, revealing a scorched and seared chest which quickly healed and turned to the ordinary pallor of vampiric skin as soon as the metal was gone. He removed his helmet, his face a ghastly charred skeleton. As the seconds passed, the seared flesh flaked off, eyes, tongue, and ears regrew, and the Hunter's face slowly materialized. Though pale and vampiric, he clearly resembled the caricature of the White Bishop from Kasprzak's book.

"What are you…what do you want?"

The Hunter made no response. Instead he pressed the jagged edge of the wooden beam Price was now bracing into his breast and collapsed.

"God damn it!" Price howled as the massive weight of the armored man came down against him, all concentrated on his bruised and now cracking ribs.

Price struggled as the Hunter, now dead, continued to sink down, centimeter by centimeter on the wooden stake. Price groaned in pain, sweat dripping from his brow and blood continuing to flow into his eyes from his wounds. The Hunter's corpse had nearly reached him. When it came the full way down the stake he would be pinned and unable to move at best, and would have his intestines crushed at worst.

Price began laughing. Partly it was the pain, but partly it was the madness of it all.

I can't believe I survived all that and now I'm going to die from being crushed to death by this fat fuck.

THIRTY-NINE

Nico climbed out of the sewer, panting, and heaved himself onto the street. He wanted to just lay there and sleep but the sounds of slavering ghouls below made him grab the manhole cover and replace it. He struggled to his feet. The Aztec wasn't far off.

He cracked his bat on the ground, pleased at the jolt it gave him.

"Still alive, motherfuckers! Still alive."

He hurried towards the entrance to the Aztec, his weapon poised over his shoulder. A mob of salivating ghouls and newborn vampires were fleeing in all directions from the place. He even thought he spotted the sallow grey flesh of one of the monsters that had attacked the Fill-Up.

"Batter up!" Nico roared, swinging away at what had formerly been a tourist in a zoot suit.

The man's head flew away in an arc that would've made Babe Ruth proud. Nico swung again and again and connected a few more times but to his surprise the beasties were hardly paying him any attention. He stopped and stood still in a tide of vampires as though he were a rock in the middle of a creek. None of them stopped to attack him.

They're scared shitless.

He glanced at the entrance to the Aztec.

Maybe I should be, too.

Nico had to smash the glass to get through the entrance doors. Only emergency lighting kept the casino aglow. The place had been torn to shreds. Holes gaped in the ceiling, tables and slot machines were overturned, gory blood and viscera coated every surface. And yet the place was so silent he could've heard a mouse break wind.

In the false pyramid in the center of the casino, he saw the remains of the Hunter's handiwork. By his count, eleven Damned. Plus the one that had attacked the Fill-Up made twelve. That left only one unaccounted for. Maybe he had seen one running away after all.

Instantly, his attention was wrenched away from his back-napkin arithmetic by a gurgling cry of pain from his mentor, broken and dying.

"Price!"

Nico hurried over, sliding to Carter's side. The Hunter of the Dead, his helmet and breastplate missing, was lying, impaled on a solid stick of wood, and crushing Price's legs and hips.

"Carter! Carter!"

Nico didn't want to believe it but he felt the tears flowing from his eyes.

"Fuck! *Fuck!*"

Nico swung around in a circle and threw his bat as far as he could.

"Jesus, kid," Price said, awakening with a cough, "did your puppy get cancer?"

Nico tried to swipe away the tears from his face as best he could and dropped down to Price's side.

"Carter! What the fuck happened here?"

Price glanced around at the blasted battlefield.

"Ah, not much. I seem to recall challenging The Hunter of the Dead to a game of backgammon, but he wasn't really up for it."

Nico put his shoulder into The Hunter, trying to dislodge him from Price's body. Price slapped him in the ear.

"Ah, quit it, kid. My hips have been pinched clean through. That body is the only thing keeping me alive. As soon as you lift it my guts are going to come pouring out."

"Don't say that, Carter, you'll be fine as soon as..."

"As soon as they find a cure for being sliced in half? Look, kid, it's a medical curiosity I'm alive. Or. You know."

"A miracle?"

"Yeah. Something like that. Reach in my jacket over there and grab my phone."

Nico grabbed a tassel on the deerskin jacket and pulled it over. He fished out Price's cell phone.

"Call Bonaparte. Tell her you're here."

Nico flipped open the phone. He prepared to scroll through the "B" section of Price's address book, but there was no need. He only had one number on the whole phone. Nico pressed it.

"What is it, Price?" a man's voice answered.

"Uh, this is Nico Salazar. I'm inside the Aztec."

"Understood. Wait where you are. We'll send you a pickup. Does this mean Price is not coming?"

"He's…no, I don't think so."

Nico snapped the phone closed and stuck it in his pocket.

"There's something else for you. Check the inside pocket. It's not, you know, done, but…well, I guess it's time."

Nico reached into the inside pocket and pulled out a small wooden stake, one of the ones from Price's bandolier. Price had started to carve something into it. Four letters. N-E-K-O.

"That's not how you spell my name."

Price glanced at the stake, then at the nametag Nico still wore.

"Ah, shit. Well, you get the point."

Nico laughed and cried at the same time. It was a strange sensation. He put his hand on Price's stubbly cheek.

"Carter, I just want to say…"

"Forget it. Really. Just…kill some fucking nightcrawlers. And don't turn into Bonaparte."

Nico reached down and took his mentor's hand.

"I'll keep the Price dream alive and well."

The whir of a helicopter approaching sounded overhead. Nico glanced up through one of the holes that had recently been busted in the ceiling by fleeing monsters and saw the Inquisition helicopter. A light shone down and spotted him, followed by a rope ladder. Nico looked back down at Price but the older man's hand had already gone limp. Nico grabbed the ladder and started to climb.

The helicopter took off towards the outskirts of the city.

There seemed to be a running battle on every block between newborn vampires and police, National Guardsmen, and Inquisitors. From up high all the people looked like...well, not ants, just like small people. Finally they reached the edge of the city which Nico saw was being quarantined with bales of concertina wire and military checkpoints.

The helicopter set down and the pilot pointed toward a tent marked with the symbol of the Inquisition. Nico took off, ducking to stay below the still whirring blades as the helicopter took off again. He entered the tent to see a map affixed to a standing corkboard and whiteboards recording various statistics: The Battle of Las Vegas playing out in real time. Bonaparte stood there with a military commander and what was probably the chief of police for Las Vegas.

"Crossbows have proven more effective than we initially thought," the police chief was saying.

"Of course," Bonaparte agreed. "We're dealing with newborns. They won't have had time to cover their hearts."

"I just wish we had more."

"My people will get you more. We stockpile crossbows but we rarely use them."

She snapped her fingers at a nearby Inquisitor who nodded and hurried off.

"Are you going to need some on the barriers, General Harris?"

The Guardsman shook his head.

"It's not exactly 'one shot, one kill,' but we've got enough firepower to take them on. The men have been improvising Molotov cocktails and other explosives to destroy them. But even our small arms have enough stopping power to slow them down and turn them back from the barriers."

Bonaparte folded her arms.

"So the city's bottled up tight?"

"None of those bastards are getting through."

Bonaparte nodded.

"Soon it will be sunrise and then things will go much easier for our hunter units. We'll have to go down into the tunnels and the sewers, and conduct door-to-door searches."

"That'll be a cakewalk after tonight," the policeman said. "My real concern is the source of the outbreak, these super-vampires."

The policeman knocked on a blurry picture of one of The Damned which had been Scotch taped to one of the whiteboards.

"How many of these are left?"

"One," Nico said.

All three heads turned towards him.

"Who are you?" Harris asked.

"He's one of mine," Bonaparte said.

He glared at her.

"No, I'm not. I saw remains of eleven of The Damned. And I think I saw one of them escaping."

The police officer turned to Bonaparte.

"You said there were twelve to start with?"

"Thirteen originally, but, yes, as of today, twelve."

"Well, that's good," Harris said, "Eleven down, one to go. Almost there."

"That needs to be our top priority," the police chief said. "One of those plague vectors escapes and this could start all over again in another city. Excuse me, ladies and gentlemen if there isn't anything else, I have to get back to my command center."

"I'd better run before I turn into a pumpkin, too," Harris agreed.

After the appropriate nods and handshakes, the two officials left the tent. Nico stared after them.

"Didn't you have trouble convincing those starched suits that vampires were real?"

Bonaparte shook her head and gestured for him to sit in a folding chair across from her.

"Not really. They worked for one for long enough. My biggest worry was that the corruption was deep, but when it came down to brass tacks they just liked Cicatrice's money."

"So they stepped up when their citizens were endangered?"

"Yes. Well, endangered publicly anyway. Can't forget that tolerating Cicatrice led to years of missing persons cases dismissed with a handwave."

"But I suppose none of us exactly have clean hands."

Bonaparte gave him a sidelong glance while she opened a bottle of cognac and poured two glasses.

"You're referring to…?"

"You must've known this would happen if you put Cicatrice down. He was the caretaker for The Damned."

"I knew it was a possibility."

"That's why you spent your life building this army."

"Partly that. And partly because I do believe this is the way to beat them. Can I assume Carter is not going to be joining us?"

"He's gone. The Hunter, too."

Bonaparte seemed surprised.

"I'd been wondering if we'd flush him out. Well, all's well that ends…well, you know what I mean, kid."

"You were wrong, you know."

"In which capacity?"

"You know Professor Kasprzak?"

"Yes."

"She was one of them. Before I put her down she said she knew the name of every Inquisitor in America. Because of your system. If we'd done it Price's way, they'd all still be safe."

Bonaparte was silent for a moment.

"Well, good thing you put her down then, kid."

She clinked her glass against his. Neither of them stated the obvious. Whatever Kasprzak had put together had certainly not died with her. There would be files, that likely would already be in the hands of the vampires. And their long secret war was no longer a secret.

An Inquisitor came hurrying in, holding a laptop. He had rabbity little beady eyes.

"Ma'am! Ma'am! You're not going to believe this!"

"What?"

"There's been a rash of attacks in New Orleans."

Bonaparte ran her hands down her face. She corked the cognac.

"It never rains but it pours. Are they confirmed vampires?"

Rabbit Eyes shook his head.

"Werewolves," he whispered.

"Well, shit. It's been a while since I've had a good wolf hunt. Most everybody will have to remain here for the cleanup tomorrow, but we'll have to at least send some scouts. Don't want the trail to get cold. You know how cagey werewolves can be."

"Yes, ma'am."

"Gather up five or six volunteers and put them on a chopper." She eyed Nico up and down. "I don't suppose you'll be joining us for either effort?"

"I'm not really a joiner," Nico replied.

A thin-lipped smile quirked her face.

"How did I guess you'd say that? Too bad. You would've made a hell of an Inquisitor."

"I am an Inquisitor."

He held out his ceremonial stake towards her. She tapped the spelling mistake and grunted a laugh.

"Typical Carter. Well, congrats, kid. I can give you the name of a good tattooist in New Orleans."

"Thanks, but I think I have some business left in Vegas."

Bonaparte nodded.

"Good luck, kid. There should never be ill will between Inquisitors."

She stuck out her hand. Nico took it.

"Um…one last question…if you don't mind. Do you know what happened to Idi Han?"

"None of my men have captured or killed her. I can let you know if they do."

"Oh. Thanks."

She gave him a sidelong glance.

"I take it you'd rather deal with her?"

"Yeah. I think maybe I owe her that."

Bonaparte shrugged and clapped him on the back.

"All right. She's your problem now, kid."

Nico reached into his shirt and drew out a small metal necklace bearing her nickname: Blood Flower. He ran his finger over it.

FORTY

Earlier that night...

Suddenly The Hunter froze in mid-air.

"Hello?" Price whispered.

"Hello, Price."

"Idi Han?"

He felt her delicate fingers run through his hair. Her other hand, disproportionately tiny, was holding up the hundreds of pounds of muscle and metal.

"Are you going to let me up? Or...is this a revenge thing?"

"Did you kill Cicatrice?"

"No."

"Who did?"

Price wheezed. Too much pain.

"Bonaparte. Her gang."

"How did he go?"

He turned his head as best he could to look into her eyes, which were gleaming with something like earnestness. He struggled to reach into his pocket and handed her the obsidian ring.

"It was like watching a pack of jackals take down a lion."

She didn't smile, but he could tell she wanted to. She was learning to hide her emotions like her master had.

"I released The Damned. I wanted to change everything."

He coughed. He didn't like the look of the blood spatter his hacking was leaving on the floor.

"I think you've succeeded then."

"I can grant you death. Or..."

She trailed off. Price looked up at the arrested figure of the armored giant. He seemed, if anything, at peace. In an instant, everything became clear to Price.

He saw her in the shadows. He saw in me a successor. She has no idea about any of it.

"You can grant me the Long Gift."

She cocked her head.

"Is that what you want?"

He smiled.

"You know…I think it was Cicatrice's last wish that I join you."

"But is it yours?"

A lifetime unfurled before his eyes. A dozen lifetimes. Chasing down nightcrawlers into the deepest, darkest corners of the earth. Becoming a boogeyman beyond all reason to the most powerful beings in existence. A lonely, solitary, maddening existence. But one where he could finally do some good. And prove that smarmy Bonaparte wrong once and for all.

"Do it."

He felt her open his shirt and carve something over his heart. Then he felt an icy finger of darkness drive into his chest from her fingers.

Eyes closed, Price listened for the sound of the helicopter blades to fade. When they were gone, he flipped the half ton of man and metal off of him like it was nothing. He pulled himself to his feet. Rather than being split in half as he had told Nico, he was feeling unusually spry. His leg and wrist ached with a dull pain from the night's events, but he felt them growing stronger already.

The clawmarks across his face he knew would never heal. Neither would the mark of Cicatrice on his chest. Technically, his wrist and leg never would either, and he would always carry the vampire equivalent of a limp, but as time passed he would become so powerful only he would ever notice it.

The pain that would never fade, though, was from the tattoos that still covered his body. He still carried his faith and his body was a holy symbol. He would carry this excruciating pain every day of his new eternal life, just as Cicatrice had carried his Inquisition tattoo.

Price snatched up his deerskin jacket and wrapped himself

in it to cover the smoking tattoos. He grabbed The Hunter's discarded helmet and stared at it.

"Why?" he whispered.

"I had to," a syrupy, malevolent voice whispered in his ear, "I'm a scorpion."

Price looked up but the casino was eerily, painfully empty. *Just my imagination.*

Becoming one with his pain, he headed outside and stumbled into the parking lot. He fished into his pocket for his keys and dropped them under the car. His vision was becoming blurry. Perhaps it wasn't so strange that he was hallucinating.

"You need to feed."

He turned his head. This time the voice had been Idi Han's. Was she following him, watching over him?

Or have I simply gone 'round the bend?

Stories told of what happened to vampires who didn't feed, especially on their first night, when the hunger was uncontrollable. They turned to ghouls and madmen, walking skeletons, deranged, crazed, uncontrollable…

No.

He pushed the worries, along with his hunger, deep down into his mind. He focused on the pain of his searing flesh. It became like a candle in the night, then a lighthouse: a beacon. He finally understood what had driven The Hunter of the Dead: a hunger that could never be sated, a pain that could never be salved, and a boundless thirst for revenge.

He turned the key and sat down in the driver's seat. Idi Han was sitting next to him. Or perhaps not.

"You people always say the blood is the power," he said, "but it's not, is it? It's the hunger that's the power."

"I don't know about that," she replied, "But I do know one thing."

"Oh? What's that?"

She leaned in and whispered in his ear, her breath hot on his face, "There was a time when our kind was not relegated to the shadows. And there will be again."

AUTHOR'S NOTE

Thank you for reading HUNTER OF THE DEAD. Whether you liked it or not I hope you'll take a moment to leave a review on Amazon or your favorite book review site. Reviews are vitally important to me as an author both to help me market my book and to improve my writing in the future. Thank you!

-Stephen Kozeniewski

ACKNOWLEDGMENTS

This book would not exist without John Waxler's insistence (and financial investment.) He has been a tireless champion of Cicatrice, Idi Han, Price, Nico, and the whole crew. That it exists now is more a testament to his boundless faith, persistence, and support regarding this work than my own.

My eternal gratitude goes out to Sharon Stevenson for helping MacVicar sound less like a crappy American author's idea of what a Scot sounds like.

Thank you to Renee Pickup (and her whole family), Holly Ann Kasprzak, Lily Luchesi, Nikki Howard, Alessia Giacomi, the Light Brothers, Stevie Kopas, Brian Keene, and everyone else who lent their names to the usually terribly fated characters in this book.

Thanks to Claire Ashby, who believed that I could write a vampire novel that didn't suck (ha!)

Thanks to Elizabeth Corrigan (who won the contest to name Cashley) and Mary Fan for their unflagging, sometimes daily support.

I'd like to thank Matt Worthington and the Sinister Grin Press crew for releasing the first version of this novel and Paul Goblirsch and everyone at Thunderstorm Books for making the limited edition a reality. And finally, David Niall Wilson and the Crossroad Press crew for bringing this latest version to life.

Finally, my thanks go to my best friend and partner, Amy Lower for making my life what it is.

ABOUT THE AUTHOR

Stephen Kozeniewski (pronounced "causin' ooze key") is a two-time winner of the World Horror Grossout Contest. His published work includes the Splatterpunk Award-nominated THE HEMATOPHAGES and its Indie Horror Book Award-nominated prequel SKINWRAPPER. He lives in Pennsylvania, the birthplace of the modern zombie, with his girlfriend and their two cats.

BIBLIOGRAPHY

Billy and the Cloneasaurus
Braineater Jones
Clickers Never Die
Every Kingdom Divided
Hunter of the Dead
Skinwrapper
Slashvivor!
The Ghoul Archipelago
The Hematophages

Curious about other Crossroad Press books?
Stop by our site:
http://store.crossroadpress.com
We offer quality writing
in digital, audio, and print formats.